THE CRY OF CTHULHU

By

Byron Craft

The CRY of CTHULHU

(Formerly The Alchemist's Notebook)

www.ByronCraftBooks.com

ISBN: 1523479760
ISBN 13: 9781523479764:

DEDICATION

To my wife Marcia, who never stopped believing in me.

WARNING

The statute of limitations has run out. What I stole from Miskatonic University, they still want back. They want to hide the truth.

The theft of what the news media called the "Alchemist's Papers" was made public in January of 1984 but the cover-up that followed, and the failed attempt to retrieve them, left the story only half told. The truth is a fold in the soft and otherwise smooth surface of time. It is a harbinger of evil so destructive that the current state of the world, plagued by terrorism and economic chaos, would only be a footnote in history by comparison.

The tabloids had a heyday with the story, claiming apocalyptic doom, while the mainstream media labeled it as another crackpot interpretation of the "Book of Revelations." Neither were accurate. Miskatonic University of Arkham, Massachusetts had done an effective job of discrediting the papers and me, and until now, no one would publish them.

The one piece of information that they were unable to keep from the public was the existence of a covert organization within the university itself. We were a group of select scholars that investigated what appeared to be supernatural occurrences all over the world. It was alleged that during some of these investigations the group had acted like vigilantes, taking the law into their own hands, passing out judgment where they saw fit.

My name is Thomas Ironwood. I was a resident professor at

Miskatonic and head of the Physics Department. I was a member of the group, known then, to only a few, as the "Mythos Department." My confessions to the press were not out of remorse for any wrongdoing, rather as a revolt against my colleagues who were becoming dangerously lax in their retaliatory measures.

I believed then, and believe even more today, that the individual stories of Faren and Janet Church, and Faren's great Uncle Heinrich Todesfall, constitute a warning to an already endangered world and should not be suppressed. The rampant ignorance in the world has left me no alternative but to come out of hiding and go public with the documents.

The plausibility of our planet being threatened by an ageless horror may automatically arouse suspicion to the authenticity of the following chronicles and possibly create a backlash from the more serious elites in the media. How Miskatonic acquired the papers may be questioned. Why hide them if they are only a hoax?

The chronicles are authentic. They required some editing to clarify the timelines. The accounts original forms were as a journal, a diary and a series of tape recordings. They have been edited into separate narratives subsequently breaking the work down into four parts.

With the help of my publisher, we have struck out redundancies which often occur in personal journals and eliminated digressions which the elderly Todesfall was guilty of doing when his mind would stray from the story and wander unchecked into the intervening years. Faren Church's was the least polished of the narratives because his was a hasty account left on tape and required more extensive editing.

For the remainder, we have left well enough alone. The chronicles accurately tell the whole story without additional enhancement.

***

It lives and breathes not only in the depths of N'Kai,

but in the deepest regions of our nightmares.

Found amongst the papers and tapes stolen

from Miskatonic University.

Author unknown.

PART I

THE SCHLOSS

From Janet Church's Diary

I am almost out of Valium, only one more pill left. The stress is beginning to get the best of me. The tranquilizer is the only thing that has made life bearable for me these last few days. I wonder now what will happen next, if they will come for me after the drug runs out, or if I will be allowed to numb my last few minutes.

They won't come close to the schloss now. I have the lights burning in every room. I even have the oil lamp I found going, and every candle I could lay my hands on are lit.

They won't come this minute. They won't come until the mist hides the stars and the moon.

Dear God! I am not even sure who they are!

***

This evening, the mist rolled up from the hollow and engulfed the schloss and beyond. It moved across the road, lingering in low spots and ditches until the entire countryside was covered by the milky vapor. It spreads throughout the thick woods for miles, and on humid nights, such as this, it has often reached as far as Valsbach.

The countryside surrounding the house, even on the brightest days, is desolate and foreboding. Now, at dusk, the twilight lends the field behind our house a strangeness that sets it apart from the rest of the area. It suggests a watchful malevolence to the ancient trees, to the descending marshes with their thousands of chirping insects and the incessant croaking of frogs, to the time-worn and vine-covered stone walls pressing in upon the perimeter of the old estate, closing in on our home as if intent upon holding me fast.

Thick vapors from the hollow swirl and eddy about the schloss and the room in which I sit fills with moisture. The fog ascends in spirals from beneath the door, and its long, wet fingers creep across the carpet with caressing strokes.

Crowning a grassy summit, whose sides are wooded near its base with gnarled trees of the black forest, stands the old home of my husband's ancestors. For centuries, its lofty tiled roofs and tower have looked down upon the rugged countryside. The exact age of the house is not known. Its roots, I guess, must go back centuries, before the beginnings of the Church family line. I know very little about the family lineage not being a Church by blood, only by marriage.

The villagers say the ancient house has always been here. They tend to be superstitious and sometimes given to fanciful tales. One teller of these stories is a homeless old woman who makes her living sifting through the back alleys and dumpsters in town. Her name is Ilsedore Hulse, and she is probably the oldest living resident of Valsbach.

Once when I was able to get her alone and ask about my husband's ancestry, she confided in me that the house had a blackened past and that, "evil still prevailed there as sure as the trees of the Black Forest have leaves and the creatures that dwell there have eyes." She summed up our meeting by informing me in a dramatically lowered voice that the old house was there even when her great-great-grandmother was a child.

Superstition plays an important role with these people, and their fears can be justified living in an isolated area far from anywhere you, and I would consider the mainstream. I can excuse their actions; their attitude towards us, however, is less than tolerable. It did not take me long to accept the shunned indifference by the shopkeepers and townspeople.

What I did consider strange is the lack of visitors to the surrounding area of the schloss. Travelers seldom enter the woods that border our property, and none come within walking distance of the old house.

I have never seen any wild animals on our property. The woodland creatures, if there are any, are probably wise, because the overall aspect of the region would give anyone the impression of leering death. The ancient lightning-scarred trees seem unnaturally large and twisted, and the other vegetation abnormally thick and feverish; while curious mounds and hummocks in the weedy, pitted field behind our house, remind me of snakes and burial plots.

The strain is critical now, by tonight, I am afraid that if my husband does not return home . . . I will be murdered.

The woods appear to close in tighter about this lonely house.

***

Damn it, where is Faren? He better get here soon.

I have to remain calm. I won't end up screaming into the night. I'll start at the beginning. The record must be complete. I'll tell you about my husband. I'll tell you about Boston, Chicago, and New York before receiving the telegram, and I'll tell you about this place.

I met Faren while still living with my parents in Ipswich, that's in Essex County, Massachusetts. At the time, I was in the midst of making what I thought were two very important decisions. One, should I keep pursuing a major in art history and, two, how to clear up my complexion, when an old Dodge van lumbered down the street and died in front of our house. "Bring our boys home" and "Impeach Johnson" was painted on its side in day-glow colors.

The sound of the ancient motor in its final death throes was followed by the slamming of the driver's door. A moment later the hood was violently flung up and amidst the fury of clanking tools and sharp cursing, a full head of tightly curled hair shot out.

"Have you got a piece of wire?" he shouted. Then he added impatiently, "A bobby pin, a shoelace, anything? Don't just stand there; I have to strap this distributor cap down, I've got to be in Chicago tomorrow."

I wore my hair down and with a headband in those days, and

although I knew I didn't look like I had just come from a hardware store, I felt embarrassed that I hadn't and blurted, "I'm wearing sandals."

His blue eyes looked right inside of me, and then he cracked a smile on one side of his face and said, "Hey, what's your name?"

I was back in junior high again being asked to go steady for the first time in my life. The sensation shot through me; I became flushed, I am sure he picked up on it because he relaxed some, and with a broader smile stepped forward, wiping his hands on an oil-stained rag.

"I'm Faren. Faren Church. You still haven't told me yours."

It didn't take us long to get acquainted. I was able to get the required length of wire from my dad's garage, and in the time it took him to make the repairs on the van, he was off, and I went with him.

Now, don't misunderstand. I wasn't that kind of girl. That was years ago, another era, and people were a lot different then. I know it sounds lame with the "new morality" that's around these days but it's the truth. Times were so uncertain then, the war was on, and life just didn't seem as permanent as it should have been.

Besides, there was something about him that first day. He was so sure of himself. He had his whole life planned out and knew where he was going. That was an unusual trait for a young man in those days, with the war in Vietnam in full swing and not knowing if he would be attending college in the fall term or taking cover in a rice paddy.

Faren had a passion for photography then, which although has dimmed some, still prevails. His van was cluttered with telephoto lenses, tripods, light meters and other assorted technical paraphernalia. Faren loved life in the truest sense. He seemed to live just to capture its beauty; while on the other hand, his aversion for cruelty and brutality inspired him to exploit it in hopes of revealing its vulgarity.

Faren hated the war. For many months we traveled together to different colleges in the Midwest, joining in demonstrations and rallies. Faren felt that we were making a difference and, besides, if we kept moving around, the draft board wouldn't catch up with him.

Our days were long and happy. We would normally have breakfast and if we could afford it, lunch while on the road. When we came to a university, Faren would always find an off-campus student house or a commune that would put us up for the night normally with dinner as an added measure.

We never seemed to quite run out of money. Faren was very resourceful. I remember once when all we had was five dollars between us and the van broke down (it was always doing that) outside of Goshen. Goshen is a little town in Indiana where the entire economy is based on the manufacture of recreational vehicles. There were a half a dozen service stations, restaurants, more churches than the Texas Bible-Belt, and a city hall. I must say they had a lovely town hall. In fact, it was the pride and joy of Goshen, and Faren found a way to make it pay off.

We hitched a ride into town leaving the van at a service station. Faren took several photographs of the new city hall, being careful to get the most dramatic angles. It had rained earlier that day making the building and surrounding parking lot glisten in the afternoon sun. Next, he and I went to the local high school, and Faren paid a photography student our last five dollars to develop the film, under his supervision, of course. After a short drying of the negatives, he selected one and blew it up into an 8x10 print. Next, we liberated the frame from around a diploma belonging to a chemistry professor in an empty adjoining classroom and framed the masterpiece.

For Faren, it was a simple matter to walk over to the town hall and straight into the township supervisor's office and solicit his work. You can imagine my surprise when less than half an hour later, out strutted Faren with a hundred bucks in hand. After all, no one had thought of taking a favorable picture of the building to hang in its lobby. The Mayor of Goshen was pleased, and we had wheels under our feet once more.

Chicago ended our trek. The aftermath of the riots that occurred during the Democratic convention still lay in rubble when we arrived, and I found myself picketing outside a police precinct with a group of strangers chanting "Free Tom Hayden." We had been there outside of twenty minutes when a young man ahead of me, holding a sign that read "Students for a Democratic Society" turned, raised his voice above the crowd and asked, "Who in the hell is Tom Hayden?"

Before I could answer the young man, the chanting was disrupted by several helmeted policemen garbed in riot gear and wielding clubs. They herded our group into an arrest wagon. They drove us around the back where they moved us to a small windowless room. We were booked for creating a disturbance and demonstrating without a permit. That means we were photographed, fingerprinted and forced to spend the night in jail. Most of us were released the next day after paying a small fine, except for Faren. The police had run a check on his selective service status. He was classified 1A, draft eligible, and they took him away from me.

We were at least fortunate enough to have two weeks together before he was sent to boot camp and in the following three days Faren and I were married. We never left each other's side during those fourteen short but wonderful days. Every night we talked for hours late into the evening about the draft, the war, our future and a solution out of the mess.

A prison sentence was out of the question so we couldn't just escape in the van. We weren't far from Canada, but Faren would not go. He loved America far too much to exile himself from it forever. Faren wasn't like the majority of the anti-war radicals. He was against the war, of course, but not for pacifist reasons. He thought that restricting our military with "no-fly zones" and "demilitarized zones" became a no-win scenario littered with unnecessary casualties. He believed that we should make it an all-out war and get it over with or get out. Nevertheless, the only alternative seemed for him to go where the military sent him and stick it out for the next two years. It was my job to wait.

Because of our youthful naïveté, we felt that there was a strong likelihood that Faren could stay clear of any action. Faren was certain he could talk to someone in charge and make them aware of his photography skills. He would probably end up stateside for two years taking group photos of all the generals and their families.

For a while, it seemed that our little fantasy had come true. After the completion of basic training, Faren was sent to Sheppard Air Force Base in Texas, which was to be his duty station for the next twelve months. I followed and took a part-time job cashiering at K-Mart in nearby Wichita Falls. I also signed up for some afternoon classes in typing and shorthand at a local business college. Working checkout was not my idea of a career, and I wanted something more lucrative to do for the next couple of years. Then, when Faren's term in the Service was up, we would work on having a family.

The following year Faren got a month's leave and surprised me with a trip to New York City. Neither of us had ever been there, and it was tops on our list of places to see. There were several art museums I wanted to visit, many plays on and off Broadway to see, an unlimited array of ethnic restaurants to sample and, of course, the usual tourist haunts. My parents had given us some money for an anniversary gift, so we rented a small furnished two-room apartment in an old brownstone and settled in for the next thirty days.

It was our second to the last day in New York City when Faren told me he was being shipped out to Vietnam.

The fighting was quite heavy in South Vietnam, and I was afraid that Faren would end up in the middle of it. I still look back at it now with a large degree of apprehension, because even today, Faren refuses to talk about it.

When we first met, his blue eyes were clear as crystal and seemed to gleam with determination. These days, their brilliance has dimmed considerably. On occasion, he will have his quiet moments lasting for several hours; on others, he will lapse into a depression.

Faren can be his old self at times. Days will go by without us ever realizing there was a war and that our lives were painfully interrupted but then it will creep up on him and he gets lost in himself. It is ironic that Faren, a man who abhorred violence, was forced to participate in one of the most senseless and futile of all wars. While here I am in the present writing down what may be my last words in a house which overlook a place where one of the largest bloodbaths in history took place.

Our separation was sudden and painful. At once I found myself alone and in a great city. I decided to stay in the small apartment we had taken for the month. There was no reason to return to Wichita Falls, and I had always preferred the East Coast. Somehow I imagined that if I gave up that apartment, I might not see Faren again. It was kind of a superstition I had about that place. I was determined to live there until the day came that my husband and I would be reunited.

Childish as it seems now, that old run down brownstone took on a certain charm for me. It became an asylum, a hiding place. My first week alone I main stayed myself by keeping Faren alive and well in my mind and pretending to be a good little housewife, cleaning, and scrubbing and fixing up the apartment while my husband was away at work photographing the mayor of New York City or some make-believe visiting foreign diplomat.

I would have gone crazy if it had not been for the intervention of Emma, who lived down the hall. Emma had three children ages four through eight, and a husband employed as a hardware representative for a small wholesaler who spent more time on the road than he did at home. Loneliness made the perfect basis for our friendship, and it wasn't long before we found ourselves spending all of our free time together. Emma had a part-time job at Macy's where she would go after packing her two eldest children off to school and the youngest to daycare. I found a position as a stenographer with a large shipping and transport company and every afternoon at twelve thirty sharp we met at Brennan's Cafe for lunch.

Life became a little more bearable by then, and I was beginning to enjoy myself. After a few weeks, Faren's letters began to arrive, and my spirits were once again lifted by the knowledge of his safety. It wasn't long before I detected emptiness in his letters. They were written with a good attempt at being cheerful, but he never made mention of what he was doing let alone where he was. There was an air of secrecy about his correspondences. It was evident that I was being spared, but from what, I never knew.

Emma would encourage me from time to time, and if it hadn't been for her friendly intrusions, I probably would have slid back into self-pity and remorse.

Strength became my key and Emma showed me the way. I wish she were with me now. We would laugh during our most troubled moments and decide to cry only on the silliest of occasions, such as the separation of Lucy and Earl on "Days of Our Lives" or a broken heel on a favorite pair of shoes.

Maybe it was reverse logic that kept us going, but it helped to make the days and weeks pass quickly. After all, time was our worst enemy, and we fought it with every weapon we could lay our hands on.

We would spend weeks rating the different meat markets and grocers in the neighborhood. More out of boredom than economics, we made a study of all the local retailers. Who had the lowest prices on dairy products, the freshest vegetables, the best buys on laundry detergents and God be praised if it happened to be double coupon day! Along with our tabulated results and massive coupon clippings, we would spend an entire day to do our week load of shopping. Starting uptown, we would swoop down upon the unsuspecting merchants with canvas shopping bags in tow, carefully selecting our buys from store to store, with each stop calculated to bring us closer to home concluding at the local deli for coffee and Danish.

***

We fought the battle and won the war. My battle on the home front, that is, was victorious, although the fighting in South Vietnam was winding down to a costly stalemate. I was ecstatic as many wives were at that time with the news of the return of their consorts. On a summer afternoon one year after our parting, Faren came home.

We cried when we first met. I bawled like a baby and Faren had to hold on to me through the baggage check and customs at the airport and for most of the cab ride home.

We locked ourselves in the apartment and didn't come out for days. Emma at times would slip little notes under our door to see if we were still alive and on one occasion, she and Harry left a care package on our doorstep containing assorted fruits, cheeses and a bottle of wine.

The days of our secluded bliss helped erase the many long months of loneliness and despair I had felt a longing for Faren's return. After a while, I flung open the door and greeted the world with newly awakened anticipation.

Life had never been happier for me as then; and right now, I wish we could return to those days.

It took Faren quite a while to find a decent job. The economy made it hard enough to find work back then, but Faren wasn't motivated into doing anything special. That's when I became aware of the change in him. When he should have been out job hunting, he was content to stay at home and watch television all day. That wasn't like him.

Although Faren wasn't wounded in Vietnam, he did spend a month in a military hospital in Germany before being sent home. I have never been able to find out why he was there and Faren has remained tight-lipped about it to this day. What happened to my love to make him moody and listless?

When he did manage to land a job he was usually discharged within the first couple of months. He became unemployable. In the years that followed he was let go from at least a dozen different companies.

Faren seemed to be on the road to recovery when he took a job with a small factory on the east side that made fasteners. Faren worked there for almost a year before he was fired. I became frustrated when it happened. I was at my wit's end. I had thought that this time it was going to be different. Faren would not talk to me about it. I wanted him to get help, but he would not open up. He just sat there and stared off into space like he always did whenever I tried to pull it out of him. He retreated from me frequently. He appeared to be in a trance when he was in these moods. He looked preoccupied. As strange as it may sound, he looked like someone who was waiting for something to happen. Like the people, you see sitting around bus terminals occasionally glancing at their watches.

I still held on to my secretarial position. I had to. There were times that my salary was the only money coming in for months on end. Any thoughts I had about having children were put aside in lieu of obtaining a weekly paycheck.

The next day I visited the factory on my lunch hour. Al Durbano, the owner, and manager of the small stamping plant was a warm and friendly man in his early sixties. I was surprised when Mr. Durbano told me that he and his wife were very fond of Faren. The Durbanos were a childless couple; they found qualities in Faren they would like to have seen in their own son if they had been so blessed. His feelings for my husband were genuine. I could tell that it was difficult for him to say anything negative about Faren. Mr. Durbano apologized for having to let Faren go but said that it became unavoidable. Faren, he said, was habitually late almost every morning and sometimes wouldn't report for work at all. On other occasions, he would leave for lunch and not return until the next day. When he did show up his work performance was superior to everyone else and he had an excellent ability for learning different facets of the business quickly. Due to his poor attendance, many times different projects that were dependent upon him suffered. "It got to the point," said Mr. Durbano, "that we couldn't depend on him anymore. Never phoning in when he was going to be late or not come in, never explaining when he returned."

By the beginning of his third year home Faren started drinking heavier than usual. It started in the evening with several drinks during and then after dinner. Then as time wore on, I would come home to find empty beer cans in the kitchen. Faren never became mean when he got drunk. His character was far from violent. Instead, he withdrew more and more into himself becoming almost lethargic, as the years went by we gradually grew apart.

***

In 1979 the position Faren obtained with the Emmerson and Prynne Company put our lives back on track again. Faren was reduced to doing odd jobs around the neighborhood and for our landlord by then. Faren came across an ad in the classifieds. They wanted someone with a background in photography, and it said they preferred veterans. Even though Faren had not picked up a camera in several years, the ad appeared to be written with him in mind. It took some encouragement, but I got him to go and apply for the position. Faren rummaged through some of our things for early photos and dusted off his old portfolio.

The day after his interview we received the good news. He got the job! The position was as head of the photographic department, and it paid extremely well. Like a piece of elastic that has been stretched out of shape, and then released, Faren snapped back. He became enthusiastic for the first time since the days of the war.

Faren's daytime drinking stopped altogether, and we started making plans again for the future. We were even able to put some money away and have the apartment re-decorated.

Emmerson-Pryne apparently was a large corporation that had several holdings. Faren worked for the public relations division, and the main office was just a few miles from our apartment. Things couldn't have been better. Faren was happy with his job, helping promote everything from the New Coke to Geraldine Ferraro. The close proximity of his job left us a lot of free time to spend together. After a while, I quit my job and threw away my diaphragm.

Harry and Faren had become good friends through the years. Faren was able to get Harry a job with one of his firm's local accounts. The new job kept Harry off the road and at home at nights and on the weekends. Emma's dream come true.

Every Friday evening, the four of us would take in a movie around the corner and then head for Lim Gardens to fill up on shrimp, fried rice, and Sake. We would then take our good cheer with us by way of a long stroll back home. The scars of Vietnam had disappeared from both our lives.

When home, Faren and I would follow those delightful outings on the town with passionate lovemaking. Many an evening I would sit up in bed, long after he had fallen fast asleep, listening to the faint bleating of someone's car horn, while watching the bar across the street through our bedroom window turn off its neon sign signaling the last call for drinks. I remember how I felt during those moments. Secure and at peace with my world, my continued vigil for existence fulfilled a desire that, at a time when Faren was not well, had been rendered hollow and empty. The city had once again become a beautiful place to live. Time Square, Central Park, all of New York was no longer a lonely giant but the great carnival of colorful lights and endless amazement I had once known. The days always held some new adventure for me but the evenings took on a personal nature meant only for me to interpret.

***

The nights were peaceful then, not like they are now. Now terror lurks at every turn. If only I had some insight, some omen to warn me of this nightmare if only I could have prevented that day when the telegram came, and our lives radically changed. If only I could transform this moorland view from my window to the scene, I used to observe through the narrow casement in our little apartment.

At the time the news arrived, that signaled our departure, Emma and I were planning another shopping spree (one of our little pleasures that never ceased with Faren's homecoming). The telegram came addressed to my husband, and I signed for it. Faren would not have been home for hours, and curiosity got the better of me. I tore it open while Emma peered over my shoulder with eager curiosity. I had to read it over several times before the full meaning of its contents became clear to me. The return address was from a Campbell, Pickman, Lumbly and Ward, Attorneys at Law. It read:

> MR. FAREN CHURCH: YOUR GREAT UNCLE HEINRICH TODESFALL OF VALSBACH, WEST GERMANY HAS PASSED AWAY STOP YOU ARE THE ONLY HEIR TO HIS ESTATE STOP PLEASE CONTACT OUR FIRM AS SOON AS POSSIBLE. D. WARD

It was like in the movies. I couldn't believe my eyes and Faren was even more astonished when he read the message. He arrived home unexpectedly that morning. He was so surprised by it that he was almost speechless. We were both dumbfounded to learn that Faren had any relatives in Europe. The discovery of an unknown relative didn't seem to make much of an impact on him though. In what appeared to be a stupor of bewilderment he kept muttering about an unbelievable coincidence.

The irony that baffled Faren wasn't revealed to me at first. I still can't help from wondering now if coincidence had anything to do with the situation that developed. Was it also a coincidence that brought Faren home early that morning?

His company had chosen him to head up a new International Project in Southern Germany, in the same area as his inherited estate. Faren and a group of employees from the Emmerson-Pryne Corporation were selected as technical advisers to the Army Corps of Engineers and the American and German Armed Forces for the aerial photography and mapping of an area in the West German Black Forest...a short distance from the village of Valsbach.

As Emma and Harry saw us off at the airport, we promised to

write often and to return someday and pick up where we left off. All of our belongings were crated up in a large steel container where they were shipped by freighter, at the expense of Emmerson-Pryne, to a coastal town in Germany called Bremerhaven. From there, they would be transported by rail to Stuttgart and then by truck to our schloss just outside the village of Valsbach. Our route would take us first to London to refuel and then one more stop at Munich (or Munchen as the natives call it). The company had arranged to have a rental car waiting at the airport in Munich when we arrived, and we spent the next ten days leisurely touring the countryside that ended up at our new home in time to meet the delivery of our furnishings.

That was a radical change in our lifestyles. It took a lot of talking on Faren's part to convince me even to make the move in the first place. Faren was very persuasive, though, and the amount of money they offered was ridiculously huge. The excitement of travel was very tempting. "It would be the honeymoon we never had," he said.

Faren's assignment was a one-year employment contract. His income in that period would be three times what he was currently making in New York. The money helped Faren realize a means to an old dream. To be the owner and operator of his studio and to work freelance developing his client base. The name "Church Photographic" rolled pleasingly off his tongue. Faren was more like his old self than ever. The idea took him. Excited by the adventure, I didn't want to disappoint him.

It took less than a month to get organized for the trip and surprisingly less to cut through the legal red tape of our attorneys in Providence and the overseas inheritance laws.

Faren made a journey to Providence to confer with Mr. Ward, the lawyer handling Heinrich Todesfall's estate. Before coming home, he made a side trip to Massachusetts. It was a good one hundred twenty mile round trip out of his way to pick up the deed to the schloss (our estate in Germany) which was being held for safekeeping in a bank in Arkham. Faren stayed over before returning the next day.

It was during that trip of his that I became aware of a change, this time, within myself. I discovered that inside of me grew the seed of our first child. We had been trying unsuccessfully, for quite awhile, to have a baby. The pregnancy made me hesitant to leave New York. Faren was very persuasive though but not without consideration on my part. In fact, he became overprotective to the point of becoming a pest. His concern for my goodwill reached a culmination of over-regard when one afternoon after we had reached Stuttgart (about sixty miles from our destination); he turned up with a black Labrador retriever in tow. This eighty-pound hunk of animal was to be left alone with me while Faren traveled back and forth between Valsbach and Fort Blish. This was my guard dog!

***

Thirty days after the receipt of the telegram, we arrived at the old schloss. Before I knew what was happening, we found ourselves in a country so primitive that it seemed remote from human contact. We drove along a little-used road past a few tumbled down shacks where people had once lived and which had long since been taken back by the encroaching forest. It wasn't a desolate country by any means but was instead an area thick with the growth of twisted and gnarled shrubbery.

The road we traveled on made an abrupt turn to the right, and we found ourselves motoring up a steep incline. High up, crowning the top of a large hill, whose sides were layered with more of the same tangled shrubbery, stood the timeworn house of Faren's ancestors, Schloss Todesfall. I was immediately taken back by the castle size and proportions of the house. A large tower centrally fixed in the structure spiraled up taller than any of the century-old trees that brooded around it. It looked more like a battlement than any conventional widow's walk you might see along the eastern seaboard of the United States.

As we came closer to the house, we could see that lingering seasons had taken its toll on the ancient architecture. Stones had fallen from its foundation, and sections of wood framing were badly in need of paint. Vegetation threatened to strangle the steps, and front porch and all the walks were crumbling and ill kept.

The gravel road that became the driveway to the old schloss was long and curved around towards the back. As we made the turn toward the rear of the structure, my eyes became fixed on the lead-paned and pediment head window located on the south wall of the tower. An instant before I thought I had detected a movement from one of the curtains. At that moment I lunged violently forward, slamming my right shoulder against the dashboard.

Startled, more than hurt, I looked at Faren trying to understand why he had stopped suddenly. A wave of fear passed over Faren's face and quickly gave way to anger. He stared straight ahead. If the car had been an open convertible, I would have left it at that moment startled and traveling straight up.

Standing in front of our car not two feet from the front bumper was an old man. He was tall, several inches over six feet and his frame was thick, slightly overweight, harkening to past days of a powerful youth. His face was masked by a mustache and full beard. The beard was a shockingly bright shade of silver, several inches in length terminating to a point. The man wore a vested tweed suit which was open at the waist and exposed a gold watch chain strung through the buttonhole. His appearance might have been comical, dressed as if he had stepped out of an old British film, but his lack of any expression sent cold slivers of ice down my back. His complexion was pasty gray and his eyes, although set back behind a pair of wire-rimmed spectacles glared at me. The elderly gentleman's stare remained transfixed, not wavering for an instant while I felt his eyes weighing heavily upon some dark part of my soul, pinning me to the back of the car seat in fear.

The slam of the car door snapped me back to reality in time to observe Faren rounding the front fender, obviously not affected by the man's stare. He questioned the old man harshly, demanding an explanation as to his presence.

Faren's mirror lenses aviator sunglasses glistened in the hot afternoon sun making him appear menacing. He was always in the habit of wearing those damn glasses that glare back at you with your reflection. I remember shortly after he came back from Nam, I asked him about them. I said that they were very intimidating and he replied: "I know, that's why I wear them." Faren's glasses didn't seem to help at first, nor did his raised voice and harsh language get the old man's attention. He simply kept glaring at me. Even Vesta, the name I had bestowed on our Labrador, seemed to cower in fear from his stare. Her head was draped across the rear of the car seat, and she emitted a low growl.

Faren's sunglasses did help in the outcome. The sun was high above the horizon and undisturbed by the absence of any clouds. The sun's rays reflected off of his lenses and played a beam of light across the old man's eyelids. As if released from a trance, he stepped backward eying Faren up and down before he spoke. His voice low and accented sounded more British than German. Making a statement rather than a question, he said, "You are Faren Church."

By this time, Faren was unnerved, and I sat quivering head to toe. Our untimely welcome to the neighborhood left us both a bit dumbfounded. All Faren was able to do was mutter a few feeble introductions.

It was at this time that I realized that the three of us were not alone. A fourth stood back towards the rear of the house. Another elderly man, much older than the first, stood watching us. He was wearing coveralls, holding a shovel in one hand and a ring of keys in the other.

We soon learned that our welcoming committee was Dr. VonTassel, a close friend of my husband's great uncle. The other man was Rudolph Hausman, the caretaker of the ancient schloss. Mr. Hausman, we were told, would occasionally drop in on the late Heinrich Todesfall to see if there was anything he needed and at times affect small repairs about the schloss for a modest fee.

The Doctor's demeanor softened after a while, but the old

caretaker kept his distance and occasionally during our conversation, would shoot us a long sidewards glance that made me believe that he disapproved of us.

VonTassell eventually made several attempts at being congenial and suggested that we dine together some evening in the future. I could not suppress the sense of distrust that I felt towards the Doctor and his companion. Somehow I sensed that his presence there to welcome our arrival was only a pretense, covering up some other motive. What that motive was, I did not know, but I was relieved when Faren dismissed them all with a few cordialities. He informed Mr. Hausman that his services were no longer needed and that we were capable of taking care of the house ourselves.

The old caretaker was reluctant to give up the keys and wouldn't part with them until Faren promised not to go into the summer house, an old run down shack at the rear of our property that had been boarded up. The old man had most of his tools stored there and wanted to keep them locked up until they could be moved. Faren agreed, and we bid them goodbye.

We walked around the schloss several times before trying the back door. The old house was terribly run down, as I have said, but even under its neglected state, it seemed to bear a certain amount of grace and charm. It must have been a grand house in its day and possibly with a lot of work it could be once again. I began to take a fancy to the old framework with its ornately carved trim. The wood framed portions of the house were old but older still was the central structure which was built from blocks of stone. The tower, entirely comprised of stone, except for its conventional casements, appeared to be the oldest. I was beginning to like the house, and quite possibly I was learning to accept the fact that this was to be our home for the next year. I decided to make the best of it.

When we had first learned of our inheritance, we had imagined a stately manor luxuriously decorated and in good condition. The employ of Mr. Hausman by Faren's Great Uncle was a good indicator that the interior of the old schloss had been under continual upkeep. No such luck. We were very disappointed when we entered the house for the first time. Such filth in one place I have never seen in my life and hope never to see again.

A leak in the roof ruined the carpets and rugs, and the entire house reeked of mildew. The kitchen was comprised of a large walk-in pantry and a long hardwood sink board which was covered with a thick layer of dirt and grease.

There were six large bedrooms upstairs, the largest of which must have been used once as a nursery. At one end of the room was a king-size four poster bed and in a corner stood a dusty old baby crib. The walls of the bedroom were covered in a light blue wallpaper adorned with prints of small children happily cavorting through a meadow bearing baskets of flowers. The paper was faded badly except in spots where there must have been framed paintings. In fact, these silhouetted areas left un-faded by the sun's rays peculiarly circled the room. All around the chamber on every wall, the outlines of where the pictures had once hung the same distance apart. The outlines consisted of only two sizes and shapes alternating with one another; one long rectangle, and then one oval configuration of equal length, then another rectangle and so on, encircling the room.

The nature of the paintings and where they are now can only be guessed. Although Faren's great uncle left no money to speak of, he did leave nothing owing on the house with the taxes paid several years in advance. Faren and I theorized that if there were any paintings at all, they were probably sold by his uncle to pay taxes and debts.

The room must have been used by the old man because all the other bedrooms had been sealed off years before and were void of any furnishings. He must have sold their contents as well to pay his bills.

We accepted this rationalization for the lack of a better one and decided to convert it to the master bedroom. Its large terrace afforded a nice view of the summer house and the surrounding grounds with one of the smaller bedrooms doing nicely in the future as a nursery.

I did wonder why the largest room upstairs had been used as a nursery, and I couldn't help thinking it a bit weird that someone would adorn the walls of a child's room with so many paintings. They may have been of Nursery Rhyme characters popular in the period when the old man was a child. Possibly he had been spoiled as a child, lavished with expensive surroundings, given the largest bedroom, maybe the crib was a nostalgic reminder to him of days long gone.

Besides the sleeping quarters, there were two other rooms upstairs. One was the bathroom made evident by a crude set of plumbing, the other a locked door leading probably to the tower above. We went through the ring of keys given to us by the caretaker but found none that would fit the lock. Faren suggested that the key might be lost and when he had the time he'd remove the hinges, and we would have a look at what was up there.

The cellar of the house was cold and damp. It was an appalling hodgepodge of old lumber, broken glass, and strewn pottery. Heinrich Todesfall must have used it as a workshop because in a corner there was a rough oak bench littered with many pieces of glass, bits of wire and several badly worn tools. At one end of a large stone wall stood about a dozen wine casks, the wooden sides of which were all caved in from centuries of rot exposing their bare interiors. While at the other end, adjacent to the work areas, was a massive five-sided archway that had been bricked up. The basement must have been larger at one time and later probably sealed off some of the older, more dangerous parts of the antique foundation. Running straight across the room, the full length of the cellar floor and disappearing behind the sealed arch was a narrow crack in the stone floor, in all probability the cause of the extreme dampness.

I found very little use for the musty cellar considering the spacious house above, besides, to all appearances; it was probably a harboring place for rats. Faren, however, thought it could be put to good service someday with plans in mind to make it into a workshop for himself.

When Faren started to clean the cellar a few days later, he discovered a ledger. It appeared to be his great uncle's journal. It was in the old man's hand and to our surprise, written in English. Faren and I only glanced through the pages and put it aside making a point to read it at a later date when time prevailed, and we weren't rushed getting the house in shape. When it did come time to read it, the journal was nowhere to be found; it had disappeared.

Our work was definitely cut out for us. Faren got busy that afternoon and patched the hole in the roof, while I took a chisel and a scouring pad to the sink board in the kitchen and scraped away years of neglect. In the days that followed, before Faren had to start his new job, we tore out all the old carpets and drapes downstairs, scrubbed everything in sight, patched plaster and painted the kitchen, parlor and dining room, not to mention all the floors we repaired and varnished. I kept Faren busy traveling back and forth to town picking up supplies while I made curtains with the aid of an old treadle-operated sewing machine I found in the hall closet.

Besides our tremendous tasks of cleaning and remodeling, the house was antiquated when it came to modern conveniences. Much to my disappointment, the house was almost void of any electricity except for a single line that had an outlet in the parlor and our bedroom. To the former, Faren hooked up our television, but not without some difficulty; something about converting the set from AC to DC or DC to AC or some such thing.

Our stereo was useless, and the refrigerator was powered by a heavy duty extension cord that ran from the parlor to the kitchen. Every time I ran the vacuum downstairs I was forced to unplug the fridge, connect the vacuum cord and alternate the procedure when done.

All the water was piped in from a well by something that was called a gravity pump, and at times it would back up flooding the kitchen floor. The furnace burned coal, but luckily it was in operating condition, and coal was still in plentiful supply in the region.

The cast iron cooking stove in the kitchen was my biggest challenge. Although converted to kerosene at one time, the old gentleman still used it to burn wood, leaving all the burners fused shut and useless. Faren spent a good deal of his time repairing and replacing the copper tubing and valves. The stove must have held a raging fire within its cast-iron shell because most of the original kerosene conversion parts were reduced to a molten pool by a steady and hot log fire. The replacement of the stove was virtually impossible. No gas or oil was piped out this far from Valsback, and our single small source of electrical current was too weak to carry the heavy load of an electric range. We had to stay with the kerosene method which meant storing the fuel in several five-gallon containers on the back porch, which in turn had to be carted into town from time to time for refilling. It took Faren a week to get the old relic in working order and about the same amount of time for me to grow accustomed to its cooking surface.

Our furnishings didn't arrive until the second day. The delivery men worked incredibly fast as if they could spare no time in getting our belongings unloaded and themselves back on the road. We had to spend our first night in the sleeping bags we brought until they came. I wasn't about to sleep in the old man's bed. Besides our bedroom set, we didn't need much of our old furniture. The house, except for the five out of the six bedrooms upstairs was furnished with several antiques many of which would fetch a good price back in the states.

Most of the furniture I guessed was made by hand and probably from the Black Forest region. Carved from the great oaks and walnuts that are plentiful in this area, some of these pieces must have dated back a couple hundred years.

My fascination for the craftsmanship was overcome by the eerie feeling I had when we first removed the dust covers that protected them. The workmanship was surprisingly fine in detail, and the subject matter was by far, unlike anything I had ever seen in art appreciation class that I had in college.

There were demon headed armrests and snake-like spindle work that reminded me of certain books I had seen picturing gargoyles and serpentine figures chiseled in the stone walls of many cathedrals from around the world but there the similarity ended. Everything else in the carvings was alien to any art form I had studied. Strange angles, the unusual curvilinear structure to all the backs of the chairs and the fantastic animated-like appearance of the designs that gave the illusion of movement when stared at for long periods of time. Hauntingly, some of the pieces reminded me of the snake-shaped roots of the trees on our property.

I was captivated by the carvings displayed within every piece. There was another reason for my attraction to the works though, but it's as elusive to me as the identity of the unknown artisan. It is a gnawing feeling that tugs at me. As if the intricate patterns chiseled into the hardwood had mesmerized me into submission, much like the Doctor's eyes that had an unsettling effect on me.

One piece, in particular, was a high back chair upholstered in crushed velvet. It looked like a throne. Its back reached a good six feet in height while the arms of the great thing were immense in proportion compared to the rest of the furnishings in the room. The armrests terminated in two large talon shaped hands with its claws curled downward.

The portion of the chair that was the most frightful was the head. A serpentine sculpture in appearance at first, but upon closer examination, it took on an octopod form with bat-shaped wings and a collection of eyes. An assemblage of biological parts perched like a crown over the head of anyone who sat in the great chair. The hard slick black walnut surface shone with signs of excellent care which was counter to anything else in the house. Faren's great uncle must have used it constantly because its good condition was marred by the appearance of the heavily worn velvet in the seat. The chair when we found it was facing the fireplace with many of Heinrich Todesfall's books and papers piled high around it.

The old man's chair above all else aroused a sense of curiosity in me. The carvings, although repulsive, conveyed a hidden meaning. The answer to which at that moment was unknown. I was determined to know more.

Later, I made a special trip into town with Faren to locate information on the carvings in hopes of learning more about their history and subsequent development as an art form. Although the local library was abundant with information on the subject, very little of it was in English. Nevertheless, I left the library with an armload of books on early German Wood Carvings with intentions of making a bilingual acquaintance either through some of the local townspeople or by way of Faren's co-workers.

It was at this time that I met Ilsedore Hulse and first came face to face with what I called a shunned indifference by everyone I met in Valsbach. As soon as the town's people found out that my husband and I lived at Schloss Todesfall or that our last name was Church, they would avoid us like the plague. Ilsedore Hulse, on the other hand, used to relish our little meetings. I perceived in her a psychological attitude akin to a pleasure sometimes derived by people who enjoy a hazardous brush with danger. Maybe she was a little unbalanced. The old gal was an unsavory sort, but she was the only one in Valsbach that would talk to me.

It was around about then that I first noticed a prevalent and almost compulsive mispronunciation of my married name by the locals. My legal name is Church but the body of the villagers no matter how many times I complained would invariably say "Kirch." Even Ilsedore appeared to gain an apparent gratification from pronouncing the family name incorrectly.

Ultimately I learned that "kirch" was the German translation of the English word "church." I couldn't make a direct correlation between the two, however, because I wasn't pronouncing it with a hard German "K" sound, rather the conventional "ch" of the English version and the spellings were dissimilar.

I wondered if the Todesfall's had for some reason fallen into disfavor with the people of Valsbach and that possibly some of the family members in hopes of disassociating themselves changed their last name to "Kirch," obviously symbolic to a religious reverence. Then quite possibly the name could have been Americanized when that branch of the family migrated to the United States. It seemed plausible because either name did not meet with approval. The disapproval by the residents of Valsbach was painfully clear, and my visits into town became short and infrequent.

In two more days, we had the old schloss habitable, overcoming many obstacles that give me a feeling of pride when I reflect back on how well we handled them.

So, by the time Faren embarked on the first day of his new assignment our household was well in order.

Faren's daily leaving again marked a change in my life. I was the one staying home now. New York was a million miles away, and I missed the companionship of Emma. I had grown accustomed to the hustle and bustle of city life, and I didn't know if I could get used to a straight diet of isolation and housework. It was scary, but the change became far more dramatic and frightening than I imagined it would be. Faren had left me in the old house alone before, but it was only for an hour or two when he ran to Valsbach for supplies.

The only occasion we had been separated longer since we came to the countryside, was an evening shortly after we had noticed the disappearance of the Todesfall's manuscript. Faren drove into Stuttgart to meet with Dr. VonTassell, a round trip that should have lasted nearly two and a half hours but was more than five. When returned, he announced that he had made arrangements for VonTassell to make regular visits to our home. We had a whopping fight. I was furious that he would make arrangements like that without consulting me first. Faren argued that a local physician would be safer for me than to risk a long drive to the Stuttgart Hospital months from now. I told him I didn't like the Doctor, but he dismissed it as being childish. He said that Dr. VonTassell's practice brought him into Valsbach three days a week and that he was the only medical man in the region.

I made sure we made up quickly though. Because what I didn't tell Faren was that it made me uneasy to be left alone for that long in the old house, more so than a visit from Dr. VonTassell.

When the renovations kept me busy, I didn't have time for much of anything else. Then, however, things were a little different. Besides my usual housework, there wasn't much to do, and at times I felt that my imagination ran wild.

After the bulk of the work was behind us, spring finally arrived. I considered growing vegetables to occupy my time. I remembered the caretaker, Rudolph Hausman, on that remarkable first-day mention with a weird chuckle that a garden of Faren's uncle existed somewhere to the rear of the house towards the field out back.

I told Faren of it that morning as I walked him out to the car. He was overly cautious of me doing any physical work to the point of not wanting me walking around on my own. I brushed it off in good humor and accused him of being a mother hen. I was only into my fifth month and just beginning to show. My cheeks were rosy, and my energy level was high, and besides, I wasn't about to let him interfere with my pastime. After all, Faren's job would keep him away until after sunset every weekday leaving me a period to while away the plotting of the garden and to leaf through seed catalogs. And, if I grew tired of that, there was always letter writing to Emma, which I did a lot of, or studying the books on woodcarvings. The art of the local carvings had still, with increasing degree, captured my curiosity to the point of preoccupying most of my evenings until Faren's return.

So that morning I kissed Faren goodbye, and after waiting until his car was a good distance down the road, and out of sight, I headed straight for the vacant parcel of land in search of Heinrich Todesfall's garden.

It was while turning towards the rear of the property that I detected a slight movement from above in one of the tower windows and for an instant, I imagined the faintest suggestion of a shape behind the lace curtains. My first impulse was to go up there and examine the tower and its interior for myself but ruled it out when I remembered that the door was still bolted fast from the inside and there was no key. I decided to make Faren dismantle the door that evening and thus end the mystery of the locked room. I am not given to fright easily, and the unknown would just have to remain that way until later. I had better things to do.

Our backyard is separated from an enormous field by tall grass and a tangle of shrubbery. The undergrowth is deep and goes back several hundred yards until it blends with the tall oaks and pines of the Black Forest. I felt uneasy when I first noticed a definite line of separation in color and makeup between the appearance of the backyard and that of the field beyond. The grass was tall, whitish-green and strangely brittle. So brittle, in fact, that underfoot it would become crushed into a fine white powder. I tried to find a clearing that could was used as a garden or a trail into the woods, but on this occasion could not stand the sight of those morbidly large boles, or those vast serpent roots that grew in abundance and twisted malevolently before they sank back into the earth. Several yards in, I was up to my waist in the tall grass, and I began to feel weak and nauseated.

I was mad at myself. I have had these attacks before, of course, but my timing was lousy. I had been looking forward to this exploration all week, just waiting until Faren was out of the way only to be held back by morning sickness.

It's difficult for me to recall what followed. I was overcome by a dizzy spell and must have staggered back to the house and fallen asleep on the sofa in the parlor because later that is where I woke after an unsettling dream.

The dream was unusual. I usually do not have fantasies or nightmares. I seemed to be in a maze of shrubbery with no way out. The earth shifted and moved under my feet making it difficult to stand. The ground violently erupted, hurling huge chunks of earth in all directions. From beneath the soil, a large black surging horror came. It was neither liquid nor solid; a frightful mass floundered momentarily then poured straight up from below spewing an array of long tentacles. The earth tilted, and I lost my footing, tumbling backward. The tentacles lashed out with lightning speed grabbing me by the legs and dragged me through burr patches and shrubbery towards the blackness. Two of the appendages hauled me by the ankles while a third came upon me dripping wet with a dark inky substance running the tip of its appendage along my leg and quickly up my skirt. Its cold, slimy flesh explored my undergarments and fondled me. I tried to scream several times, but no sound came out of my mouth. No matter how hard I tried, my cries always fell mute. An invisible blanket of silence muffled any sounds from coming out.

It was dragging me closer to itself. I couldn't have been more than fifteen feet away from the thing. It was more than a creature, more like a being; a being that acts and grows and shapes itself by other laws than those of our nature.

The entire scene changed abruptly. Out of nowhere appearing to float on a thin layer of mist was the stocky, silver-gray Dr. VonTassell.

He was waving his arms awkwardly over his head and at the same time throwing handfuls of a gray powder into the air. The old Doctor began to call out words, words too difficult to understand. I mean to say they were words but not like any I had ever heard before, it was foreign. The words or sounds became a guttural sing-song.

"YGNAIIH . . . YGNAIIH . . . THFLTHKH'NGHA . . . YOG SOTHOTH " rang his cries.

I recall the slimy arms retracting from my body and the ground beginning to close in. I remember trying to stand with little success, and a hand from out of the nothingness grabbed me.

I awoke with a start to see Faren standing over me with his hand on my shoulder. I was laying full length on the sofa in the parlor. Only momentarily befuddled I regained my senses recognizing reality from fantasy.

I felt like a child. I had slept the entire day away with the breakfast dishes still in the sink. Faren understood though and chalked my dilemma up to morning sickness and "the queer little things that women do when they're pregnant." Then he proceeded to clean up the kitchen and cook dinner on my behalf.

I was still a little dizzy when I sat up but regained my composure in a matter of moments. I wasn't about to let Faren do all the work. I had to prove that I wasn't physically handicapped. Determined to give him a hand, I started to rise but briefly halted when I noticed something strange. The hem of my skirt was badly soiled, my nylon stockings were run, and my ankles were covered with burrs. What immediately caught my eye above all the rest and struck out blaring like a painted sign in six foot high letters was the small thin markings that started above my feet and went up past my thighs. The markings were of the appearance and consistency of black ink.

***

A nice hot bath, a glass of wine and a short while later I was feeling my old self again. After dinner and with a little coaxing on my part, Faren obtained some tools from the cellar, and we proceeded to dismantle the door that barred our entrance to the ancient tower. A good fifteen minutes passed before we had the door down and off its hinges. A cast iron circular stairway was revealed to us. Very similar in design to the iron steps I have seen inside the old lighthouses that line the eastern seaboard from Maine to Massachusetts. With one exception. This staircase was of a hazardous construction. As if someone hurriedly threw it together for a crude but simple access to the floor above. It was poorly formed with many of the steps installed in a crooked manner and the absence of any railing to hold on to made the climb upward precarious. For obvious safety reasons, it wasn't at all surprising that the tower door had been locked shut.

The metal staircase spiraled up to only one floor which was at the upper-most level of the steeple. We climbed the stairs one at a time fearing that it might not withstand our combined weight. Eventually, we gained access to the room that was cloaked in mystery ever since our arrival.

You can imagine our disappointment when we discovered the room to be empty. The interior, except for some cheap lace curtains on the windows, was void of any furnishings or wall hangings. Although from the outside the cupola structure was cylindrical, on the inside, oddly enough, was comprised of five plastered walls. Pentagonal in configuration with small wood framed windows set in each wall about three feet above floor level.

It was apparent that the small five-sided chamber hadn't been occupied for a long time, perhaps years, because of the heavily dust-laden walls and floors. The air in the room was stifling caused by the tightly closed windows.

At the east end of the room was a window seat and above it the casement overlooking the rear of our property. A glimpse through the dusty pane of glass afforded us a view of the entire horizon. The evening sky and all its constellations I mused would be a splendid sight from up there. I made a mental note to come up there some starlit night and enjoy the scene. It was still light out, and the entire landscape to the rear of the house was below, and I could easily survey the area in detail from the height, first regarding the driveway, the summer house, then recognizing the color separation in the greenery, and finally to my delight a clearing. It was a small clearing, but a patch that somehow had been cleared within the center of the abundant vegetation. Could this be the garden?

Faren wasn't pleased with my find, although he still complained that I was taking on too much, he did agree to let me have my way providing, "I take it easy."

Just as we were about to leave the tower room, I noticed something so peculiar that for an instant my blood ran cold. The top of the window seat like everything else enclosed within the five walls should have been covered with dust, but it was not. The varnished wood lid, except in one corner, had been wiped clean. The clean finish was in no way as startling as the dust-laden corner. The corner of the seat exhibited a small impression so clearly on its surface that it makes me shudder even now when I think about it.

The marking would be considered familiar or commonplace under any normal situation, but under the prevailing circumstances; a room, sealed for months, perhaps years, with no other visible exit, it took on a meaning that was both curious and appalling. I thought my eyes had deceived me, because there before us tracked into the years of dust was a small doll-sized imprint of a human hand and just below the latched casement deposited upon the sill was the missing key.

The key was indeed the one we had looked for, and it fit the dismantled lock to the tower. How it came to be inside that lofty chamber, I am not sure, and whether it was the only one, and not a copy, that was left behind, I still can't say. I do know that the events of that afternoon and the coming nightfall left me chilled far beyond anything the night air could produce.

Faren and I spent a good deal of time studying the print until the coming darkness rendered it invisible. We speculated as to its cause for quite a while. Although Faren thought that it could be made by a raccoon or an opossum, I found it difficult to form any opinion at all.

I am not a light sleeper and normally have little trouble falling to sleep, but that evening I was caught up in thought over the baby-like handprint, the key and the speculation as to their origin. I probably would have laid there until dawn or until mental fatigue would have eventually taken its toll if it hadn't been for a mild earth tremor that shook the bed slightly. At first, I attributed it to thunder in the hills, but unlike most thunder that's preceded by lightning, there was none. No electrical flash lit up the night, and the sky from our south bedroom window was black as coal.

Faren still rested undisturbed. I got up and crossed to the veranda which faced out over the field and summer house. The evening sky provided no light whatsoever. My eyes slowly adjusted to the gloom. Gradually I could make out parts of the field in great detail. The earth appeared to glow with a faint green iridescence coming from the north end of the turf. Fog rolled in gradually obscuring the landscape, and the angle of view from the bedroom terrace was insufficient for me to discover the source of the light.

Being, I know now, foolhardy, and moving quietly on my tip toes so as not to upset Faren, I decided to climb the tower steps for a better look.

The green luminescence filled the five-sided chamber and cast an eerie veil across the walls leaving all the corners dark. From the rear casement, I could perceive the moonless and starless heavens. Far below I beheld the mysterious aurora radiating past the outermost edge of the tall grassland; its beams scintillating against the leaves and branches of the great oaks until they were swallowed up and digested by the vastness of the Black Forest.

As if in answer to the phosphorescence a thick mist came out of the forest flowing between and around the mighty tree trunks pouring over the field and mingling in a glimmering splendor with the green light. The clearing I had spotted earlier that day was an emerald haze. I thought I detected a brief movement in that direction, but my attention was averted when I felt a cold breeze on the back of my neck.

For an instant, I became paralyzed with fear recalling the stuffiness of the afternoon air caused by the tightly closed windows. I overcame the paralysis and slowly turned to face the open casement. The sun-faded lace curtains stirred in the night air. The bottom sash was ajar. In the corresponding moment, I detected the odor of decaying flesh. It was so vile that I became dizzy at the smell. To the right of the open window and peering directly up at me from out of a darkened corner, no more than two feet above floor level were a pair of glaring red eyes.

***

The events of that evening seemed like a bad dream in the cold light of day. I had fled the tower that night in a panic, leaping several steps at a time, eventually losing my balance and slid down the last few treads on my backside.

It took all the strength I could muster to lift the tower access door and put it back on its hinge plates and slip the pins back into place. The lock was dismantled when the door was removed, but the latch was still operable, and I secured it with a chair wedged tightly under the knob.

I scared the hell out of Faren with the racket I made. He came stumbling down the hall half-awake wielding a flashlight like a club. After mumbling that a creature had gotten into the tower somehow, he lifted the door back off its hinges and marched up the iron steps.

The rest is anti-climactic. There was nothing up there. The small room was empty. The only evidence to support my red-eyed phantom was the open window.

I put any notions of talking about it with Faren out of my head the next morning. I felt a little foolish believing that I had overreacted to something that wasn't as unusual as it had seemed under the circumstances. After all, my little creature of the night might have been a small animal like Faren had suggested, and the window may well have been unlatched all the time leaving it easy for a raccoon to open. I felt much braver before noon. In spite of it, I still didn't feel bold enough to inspect the tower again and decided to put it off for another day.

I had gotten Faren off to work without a hitch, and after the breakfast dishes were done, I headed straight for the field. This time I knew the location of the clearing and walked in that direction. I hesitated briefly just short of the area where the tall grass begins. The north end of the field where I saw the strange glowing light the night before presented a view on a higher plain or level than on my last trip into the tall weeds. I could have been mistaken, but the ground looked slightly higher, more elevated in that area than it had been. It formed a low hill that spread out for about a hundred yards disturbing the shrubbery. Narrow cracks in the earth fanned out from its center. The rise was puzzling, but it was the clearing that I sought in the southern and opposite direction.

It was very windy that day as I walked towards the open field. The constant draft of air from ahead practically roared through the trees. I was well on my way when I sensed a gradual change in the quality of sound. The noise of my footsteps remained constant, as did the muffled roar of the wind beyond but now there was something else, something that filled the intervals between the wind and my footfalls. It was the sound of movement, not from where I stood, but from within the tall grass.

I paused, peering forward. A narrow clearing in the overgrowth forming a corridor stretched ahead. I could see nothing moving there, but as the rushing of the wind subsided, the silence was again broken by the other, fainter noise. What did it remind me of, it frightened me?

Something cried out, a whimper in the distance but it came from behind me. I turned abruptly in that direction. Besides the low weeping voice, the only thing that reached my ears was the crunch of my footsteps amid the dry, brittle grass and the sound of my heavy breathing.

Focusing my attention on an area deeper in the woods, I came upon a tall clump of weeds. There was a low sobbing coming from the other side, parting the lank greenery, I looked in. A little girl about ten years of age was lying on her back in a circular clearing. She was startled and wild-eyed as if in pain. Fearful of my approach, she recoiled and drew back with a start. I tried to comfort her, calling gently to her inquiring if she was hurt. Her breathing became even more labored. The girl cringed away from me and kicked at the ground with her feet. Again I asked what was troubling her but obtained no response, only more hysterics. I stooped down in an attempt to console her, and she shrank from my touch.

"I won't hurt you," I said in vain, trying to gain her confidence. Instead, she quickly got up, screamed painfully, staggered out of my reach and fled the clearing disappearing into the wood.

I was still squatting on the ground when she was out of sight. I was stunned. I didn't know what to do next. I shouted for her to come back but to no avail and gave it up after a couple more attempts. I thought about running after her, but I dismissed the idea. The child wasn't interested in talking to me, and my knowledge of the surrounding woods was too limited to permit a chase. She most likely didn't speak English, and a foreigner running after her yelling unintelligible words would probably increase her panic.

Strewn across a mound of dirt were her school books. Hoping to glean some information as to her identity from their contents, I bent over and started to stack them into a pile.

As I reached to pick up the last book, something in the grass caught my eye. A rusted metal Nazi swastika, about the size of a poker chip, lay on the top of the mound. I examined it for several seconds, and because of its badly rusted condition and the deep impression it had left on the earth, I decided that it couldn't have belonged to the young girl and must have been laying in that spot for many years. I tossed it aside, picked up the last book and started back in what I thought was the direction home.

I heard a light, regular metallic clanking somewhere in the distance. It was the same noise I had heard earlier before being distracted by the frightened child. For some reason, I don't know why the rhythmic sound of metal being struck generated feelings of alarm and dread within me. I quickened my pace and covered a good deal of ground before realizing that the path I chose was the wrong one, and in fact, I had been traveling deeper into the woods past a thicket of dead and twisted trees into areas increasingly overgrown and wild.

The clanking increased in volume, growing louder and louder by the minute until the magnification became so great that it resembled the peal of a blacksmith's hammer striking an anvil. Looking back now I can't say for certain if that increase in sound level was real or imagined, it could have been my imagination although it was real enough at the time to be deafening. It was so loud that if it hadn't been for the armload of books I was carrying, I would have cupped my hands over my ears to block out the clamor.

The banging became the explosions of cannon fire. I thought I was in the middle of an artillery range. For a moment the air filled with the smell of burnt gunpowder.

I stepped up my pace and started to run. Blinded by fear, I nearly collided with a tree but managed to side-step it at the last second. I didn't run much longer; only moments later, stopping dead in my tracks, when hit with the realization that I was standing in the center of a clearing. The clearing, the very reason I came here in the first place. It was no longer as important to me as it had been before. There was a difference between that morning's journey and the one of the previous day. Then I had merely been curious about exploring the woods and what I would find. Now I was terrified.

The opening in the brushwood was much larger than I had estimated. At least a good hundred yards in length and width, with only a few large oak trees scattered across its plain. The ground wasn't as level as I had expected and there were no signs of a vegetable garden or once cultivated soil. The earth in the area had been disturbed and heavily dotted with a series of mounds. Some of these were boles of compacted clay no more than six feet in length. Many of these mounds bore the evidence of recent digging.

The explosions stopped the moment I entered the clearing, but the light metallic clanking persisted. Towards the center of the glade, just off a little to one side, standing upright from out of the earth and located at the head of one of the boles was a short wooden pole. Atop the pole was a helmet, of a type, the Germans wore in those old war movies. The metal headpiece was clanking in the breeze.

The graveyard setting of the glade made me tremble. I don't know what I expected to happen. The tranquility of the setting, combined with the eerie atmosphere, put me on edge. I walked a full circle around the old army helmet and started back towards the woods. The second my back was turned, the explosions started up again. Without hesitation, I spun around and stared down at it as if expecting the post and helmet to be the source of the noise. I was frightened by the coincidence, for at the very instant I laid my eyes on the helmet the explosions subsided, and the clanging once again resumed. I stared long and hard at the rusty headgear as it rocked in the light afternoon breeze, the brim lightly tapped against the wood.

Slowly, not believing my powers of perception, I turned my back again on the site. Within the same breath, the explosive sounds burst forth. I made a mad dash for the wood at an insane rate of speed that amazes me even to this day. I hadn't covered much ground before losing my footing. I tripped on one of those damn serpent-shaped roots that grow over the land in morbid proportions. I fell face forward onto a pile of dirt and laid there gasping for breath.

The books were sprawled out in front of me. The detonations had stopped. Even the metallic clanging stopped. My ears had been blessed with silence only to be interrupted by the scratching of pine needles amongst the breeze. I was dazed and distraught, and oddly enough, the first thing that greeted my eyes was a clock. Yes, I know it sounds crazy, but here I was in the middle of nowhere, out of breath, mentally and physically exhausted and of all things I had come face to face with was a timepiece that shouldn't be! A glass cover shielded the clockworks, and the body was embedded in a thick block of black granite. It was much like any contemporary clock except it only bore the single hour hand, which pointed directly at twelve.

My eyes traveled up the chunk of black stonework. It was a monolith and must have stood eight feet tall but from my angle, lying on the ground, it appeared much taller. The great black stone was surrounded on three sides by underbrush, which accounted for its subsequent concealment until then. Its surface had been engraved with designs of writhing figures only half visible in the shadows of the surrounding trees. Crowning the top was an array of tentacle shaped sculptures, the lower half of which en-wrapped a devil-eyed figure. The repulsive design of the snake-like appendages reminded me of the creature, that dark thing that had squirmed its way out of a crack in the earth and into my dream, or was it a dream?

Paralyzed with fear I stared at it for several seconds. My eyes eventually drifted back down the monolith to its strange clock-works. Below, etched into the night-black masonry, was an inscription. Engraved characters I found easy enough to read even in the shadows. It was short and brief. It was so powerful that I jumped to my feet with ice traveling up my spine and fled the scene. It read:

Heinrich Todesfall
1901-1983

I ran and ran. I ran as if hell itself were at my heels. I am not sure of the direction I took, but I did travel in circles for awhile. By some means, I managed to obtain the correct headings and ended up back at the schloss.

If I live through this, I will never forget what happened within the remaining next few moments. A mental disorder overcame me. It must have been a series of delusions brought on by my encounters in the glade. I felt like a child lost and frightened, afraid of my own shadow coming home to find my parents not in. I raced to the security of my bed. I wanted to pull the covers over my head and shut out the world around me.

I sprinted upstairs, scarcely taking notice of the opened door to the tower, and flung myself full length upon the bed clawing at the sheets and blankets. Almost at once, I was between the heavy spread and the mattress. It was when I was attempting to pull the bedclothes over my head that it happened. My pillow had several small spots of dirt across the clean white surface. It didn't seem that unusual at first. Except for the even interlacement of the soiled tracking upon the linen, it didn't impress me as anything more than a troublesome stain. Not until I noticed that the spots weren't just specks of dirt, but soiled hand prints identical in size and shape to those we had discovered the day before in the tower tracked into the dust on the window seat.

***

Nightfall and the distant chirping of crickets were my next recollection. A star-filled sky was in plain view from my bedroom window. A soft yellow light filtered through the open door to the hallway.

I was half sitting up in bed sipping a cup of tea which Faren held for me. His face was in profile, silhouetted against the light of the lamp atop the bed table. His brow was furrowed, and the rest of his face beneath the pale light displayed soft lines of concern.

A thick wool blanket covered my legs, and I had been tucked in snugly about the waist. It was a while before I could speak in complete sentences but Faren was patient with me only prodding me gently from time to time with questions about my well-being.

I told him about my walk in the woods, about the little girl I met there, and the discovery of his great uncle's grave. I felt uncomfortable in relating anything more. I wasn't interested in sparing Faren the rest of the details, but after noticing that the soiled pillowcase had been removed and replaced with a clean one, I became reluctant to disclose anymore. When I asked about it, Faren answered in an evasive manner saying that he had spilled tea on it while I was unconscious and he took it to the cellar to be washed. There was no teapot in the room, and my cup was full. I was about to press him further about it when he mentioned that he had telephoned for the Doctor.

I felt uneasy around VonTassell, and although I couldn't quite put my finger on the reason, I knew he could not be trusted. I told Faren as much, but my protests fell on deaf ears and shortly, the aged physician was on our doorstep.

Dr. VonTassell believed my condition was, "The results of getting the old house in order, brought on by overwork, nervous tension, and an overactive imagination," he said. Of course, my pregnancy was the main contributor.

He prescribed a sedative, Valium, and a good nights rest. I wasn't sure that it was a proper prescription for a pregnant woman, but I welcomed the thought of a tranquilizer. When the Doctor went downstairs to get his bag, Faren went with him. In a short while, I could hear the two of them arguing in the parlor. I couldn't make out everything they said, but I gathered that they were discussing the Doctor's diagnosis. Faren shouted, "I'll prove she's not hallucinating" and VonTassell asked him to keep his voice low. I was about to yell out to ask what all the commotion was about but stifled the cry when I heard my husband leave the room and the screen door off the kitchen slam shut.

I didn't like being alone in the house with the Doctor. His touch reminded me of a corpse; it was cold and clammy. I found it easier to swallow the pill quickly he offered so he would leave me alone.

It wasn't long before I heard Faren enter the house again and through the haze of my Valium stupor, I managed to listen in on pieces of their conversation.

They were more civil towards one another again, and I heard Faren offer VonTassell a drink. They must have talked for quite a while because I kept nodding off and waking up to their muddled conversation. At one point in their talk, the Doctor raised his voice slightly and some of what he said, although partly muffled, became audible. It was only the fragments of a sentence, the first part of I am sure of but the last word was foreign to me, and I will have to spell it here phonetically. He said, "The coming of Thoo-Loo."

The last thing I remember before dozing off for the rest of the evening was hearing the footsteps of Faren and the Doctor on the cellar staircase. It was too far away to perceive much of anything else, and besides, there was thunder coming from the hills again. It was much louder than it had been before, making it increasingly difficult to hear. I do recall one sound other than the thunder. Unrelated as it may be, I am curious about what I heard or thought I heard that evening. It was a little later. It came from the cellar, I think. It was a low dull scraping. It sounded as if something heavy was dragged across concrete.

I awoke late the next morning to find Faren having coffee in the kitchen. He seemed distant in thought, and a bit unnerved. He was holding something in his hand and jumped with a start when I entered the kitchen, dropping it to the floor. He tried to conceal the object from me. His movements in retrieving it were not fast enough to stop me from getting a good look. It was a dagger, very old looking, and an antique I guessed, and oddly enough, it bore the same grotesque serpentine design carved into the face of Heinrich Todesfall's tombstone. The figure haunted a vague recess in my memory.

Fumbling to retrieve the knife and giving the impression of one caught off guard, he explained that after VonTassell had left the night before, he had gone down into the cellar and discovered the dagger wedged between a large crevasse in the masonry.

Again, I caught Faren in what I believed to be a lie. Even though I was in a drugged state that evening, I know what I heard. It was the sound of two people going down the old rickety staircase, not one. Besides, didn't I hear VonTassell utter those strange words just before he descended the cellar stairs? Why was he so evasive? What was he trying to conceal from me? I was about to ask those very questions when the telephone rang. Grateful for the interruption, Faren left the room for the parlor and to the phone.

I was preparing breakfast when he returned. He was relaxed and more at ease with himself. The telephone conversation seemed to have had a soothing effect on him. Faren told me about an acquaintance he had made. He was an American serviceman by the name of Jim Ruttick. Thrown together by Faren's job at the air base the two didn't have much in common besides the English language, but in these parts, the disposition of the language barrier was good grounds for any friendship.

I couldn't help sympathizing with him. I knew what it was like not to have anyone to talk to during the day. Not being able to communicate with anyone in town, let alone the indifference I had encountered there. I missed my good friend Emma and the delightful afternoons we spent together. For the first time since I came to this isolated place, I stopped feeling sorry for myself and realized that Faren must have been suffering as well.

The tears welled up in my eyes, and I fell easily into his embrace. He spoke gently and in conciliatory tones. He told me of the argument he had with VonTassell that evening. The Doctor had questioned the credibility of my story and Faren went into the glade to locate the proof. Faren's search was not in vain because it produced the young girls' school books and the grave of his great-uncle. He had even discovered the girl's address printed on an inside cover and had made arrangements to return the books the next day. Faren didn't say anymore, nor did he mention if the Doctor had done me any further disservice, but I didn't care. Faren's belief in me was all the comfort I needed.

I felt relieved. I felt I could trust Faren once more even if there were a few things left unsaid by him. Hindsight now tells me this was a mistake. I wanted more than anything to confide in him, to open up. So, I told him of that first afternoon that I entered the field and of my strange dream. I vividly described the twisted tentacles that wriggled up from beneath the earth resembling the roots and undergrowth in the area, and of my odd, but timely rescue by Dr. VonTassell.

My story was painful, yet it served as a release for my pent-up frustrations. The tears flowed in streams down my cheeks. Faren begged me to stop but the telling of what had happened during those past few days outweighed the grief, and I continued my account from the reverie of that first afternoon to my dream state of the previous evening carefully going over each event leaving nothing untold. All the while Faren held me in his arms attempting to comfort me the best he could.

When I was done telling my story, he wiped my cheeks dry and held me close. It had been a while since I had experienced the softer, gentler side of Faren's nature. I had almost forgotten those times.

Naturally, he had always displayed signs of concern, but in the past few weeks, the physical contact was removed until that moment. We had both been too caught up with our remodeling chores that we had devoted little time to each other. Faren had also become more distant in the bygone weeks than usual.

I am sure he believed most of what I told him...except for the dream, of course. Doing a humorous, but a poor imitation of W.C. Fields he declared it the probable result of something I ate disagreed with my digestive system. He lightheartedly quoted Dickens' "A Christmas Carol" in the same voice, "An undigested bit of beef, a blot of mustard, a crumb of cheese, a fragment of an underdone potato." We laughed together realizing how ridiculous everything seemed under careful scrutiny and I somehow became more willing to forget my husband's indiscretions.

***

That was Sunday and Faren, and I spent the day at home together. We spent the rest of the morning and most of the afternoon in one another's arms. I'd close my eyes and imagine that we were back once again in our cozy little brownstone and Faren seemed willing to play along lavishing me with long slow caresses suspended by intervals of passionate love-making.

Our day together was more in accord with our life in America than it had been since our arrival. Our bliss remained undisturbed until around three in the afternoon when Jim Ruttick showed up to join us for a late lunch.

Jim was all right, I guess, but I thought he was a little crude. A real character, but he was an American, and it was very refreshing to meet a native countryman. Sergeant James Ruttick was about six feet two inches tall and must have tipped the scales at the least, two hundred and twenty pounds. He was about thirty years of age; he had blue eyes, thin sandy brown hair and was in the habit of carrying around a baseball cap in his back pocket. His stature claimed a definite fondness for beer, clearly displayed by a bulge that hung over his belt buckle.

To my delight, I learned that he was a New Yorker, from Brooklyn no less, and although he spent most of his life there, it had been a good while since he'd been to the Empire State and we were still able to exchange several pieces of related big city info.

My husband's friend was a compulsive gum chewer and talked out of the side of his mouth in the delightful nasal tones of Brooklyn. Sergeant Ruttick was very comical, and he lent a lightheartedness to a day that so badly needed uplifting.

The afternoon passed quickly. Jim ate and drank like six commandos just returning from a long survival mission. Faren and I enjoyed every minute of his company. Jim, on the other hand, acted like he was back in the states, feeling obligated to return the favor of a free home-cooked meal. Faren had mentioned in passing that he had to take Vesta to the veterinarian for her shots. The sergeant, becoming very attached to our black Lab, insisted upon taking her there himself and bringing her back as well the following evening, in time for dinner, of course.

It didn't go well though when Faren presented Jim with that vulgar looking knife that he found. The Sergeant had prided himself in being a weapons expert of sorts and was said (as told by the Sergeant) to have a formidable collection of both modern and antique weapons. Whether he was truthful in his claim or it was an over exaggeration due to all the beer, I can't say, but the knife dumbfounded him to the point of nearly becoming embarrassed when he couldn't identify it; only speculating with wild theories as to its origin. Faren didn't venture further with any inquiries of his own. I think he was concerned with troubling me, so he let the matter drop.

What did seem a bit unsettling was later, after the lunch dishes were soaking, and we were having coffee in the parlor. Jim had recently bought one of those new Polaroid cameras and brought it with him in hopes of acquiring a few pointers from Faren on photography.

No sooner did he announce his new purchase than Faren and I found ourselves hustled together at one end of the parlor so Jim could take our picture. I protested that my hair was a mess and to please give me a chance to change out of the old house dress I was wearing but the sergeant from Brooklyn wanted to remember us just the way we were, and no pleading on my part would change his mind.

The bulb flashed, the picture was taken, and I headed straight for the kitchen before he decided to take another.

A couple of minutes later, while I was putting the dishes into soapy water, I detected disappointment in Jim's voice. There was something wrong with the photograph. I heard him ask Faren if any outside light could have gotten into the camera to spoil the shot. Faren didn't think so.

I came up behind Jim and peered around his shoulder. The picture was in focus, the color was good, and you could see Faren and me clearly, however off to the right, appearing to hover in space over one of our end tables were two faint spheres of light that were blurred indicating movement. The spheres, or balls of light, were situated one atop the other with the bottom one about twice the size as the top. With the stretch of the imagination, I thought I saw a face on the smaller, uppermost sphere. Three darkened areas located where a mouth and eyes might be. I studied it closer and imagined two faint streaks of translucence, shaped like arms, reaching down. It was legless and supported itself on two spindly limbs. It looked up at the camera. At once, I thought of the baby handprint that had been tracked onto the dusty window seat and across my pillow. I shuddered and returned the photo to Jim.

The rest of the day was pretty much uneventful. Jim and Faren attributed the image to a spot on the film. To eliminate all doubts, Faren set up his Nikon on his tripod and took several time exposures, promising to develop them the next day at his lab. Whatever happened to those pictures I don't know? To this day Faren has never mentioned them.

Jim on the other hand, managed to get us to pose for another photo in the same spot as before. That one developed without a blemish.

Our new found friend left before dark with Vesta in tow. Faren and I retired early that evening. It had been a good day. The two of us had gotten a lot of our problems out in the open, we had a tender afternoon together, and Jim Ruttick had brought a little sunshine into our lives.

I slept most of the evening soundly. Not even the thunder in the hills kept me from my slumber, even on one occasion, just before I dropped off, a thunderous crack sounded like the earth splitting open. I was undaunted. It was the first time in a long while that I felt happy and I fell quickly to sleep.

I probably would have remained that way until well past daybreak if it hadn't been for Faren. I awoke a little before sunrise to the sound of his screams. I arose with a start and fumbled with the lamp on the bed table, illuminating the room. The splinters of light played havoc on my eyes for a few seconds. Squinting, I saw Faren recovering, no doubt, from a bad dream. He had broken out in a cold sweat and was shivering from head to toe. He recovered momentarily, however, and regained his composure. I hadn't known him to have nightmares; still, I have heard that war can play a cruel trick on a person that may not manifest until years later. I don't know what frightened him and Faren refused to discuss it telling me to go back to sleep.

Before turning out the lamp, I noticed something odd though. The bottoms of Faren's feet were filthy as if he had been walking in the mud without shoes and socks. Even the sheets on his side of the bed were soiled.

***

I made what will probably be my last trip into town today. Jim gave Faren a lift into work leaving me the car to do some shopping.

Faren looked tired and older; a bit of graying around the temples and his eyes displayed pain. I don't believe he wanted to leave this morning. There was a pleading expression on his face as he went to the door, he kept hesitating to look for one excuse after another not to leave and get in Jim's car until the very last minute. As he walked out, he mumbled something about us maybe not having to stay in Germany as long as we had intended.

I made the short trip into town arriving there at ten only to be slighted by some people on the street. I have always been greeted with a lukewarm reception, however, this time I was unable to communicate with any of the shopkeepers. Everyone I encountered evaded me, or simply refused to speak to me.

I noticed an abnormally large crowd of people mingling about the local newsstand and went up to investigate. My fluency in German is still weak, perhaps a little better than the typical tourist, but I was able to glean enough from their conversation and the boldly printed headlines splashed across the daily paper. It appeared that a murder had been committed during the night and the victim was a young girl. The child had been gruesomely slain. Something about the girl's head and arms. The only other word I could make out was "vicious." On the same stand, to the left was the American serviceman's edition printed in English. That paper's byline mentioned the murder was similar to a series of killings that had occurred just a year before.

I was shocked when I picked out the name "Kritchner." The same last name as that of the young girl I met in the woods two days ago. I attempted to buy a copy of the newspaper, but the peddler just ignored me. I was mad, tired of being overlooked. Shouting at the man to sell me a paper, I shoved a handful of coins in his face. Tears of anger rolled down my cheeks. In spite of my emotional display, they all just stared at me, the peddler refusing to sell. All I had managed to do was draw more attention to myself. I thought the crowd was going to turn on me. One man shook his copy of the local Gazette at me screaming unintelligibly. Another shouted "bosheit" and "zauberer," while the others just glared. I threw a handful of pfennigs and Deutsche Marks at the rack of papers, one of the bronze coins narrowly missing the head of the stubborn man behind the counter. I snatched a copy and fled.

I ran back to the car and sat there for a while with the doors locked and the engine running. When I unfolded the newspaper, I realized that in the excitement I had grabbed the German edition. Disgusted with myself I threw it on the back seat. If I hadn't known any better, I could have sworn that I was accused of the poor child's death.

For some reason, I couldn't find it in my heart to cry. I suspect that anger had taken hold of me and I wasn't about to give in to their abuse. I had come into town to buy groceries and other supplies for our home like any citizen would, yet the body politic of the village had elected to ignore me. The reasons for which, I was not quite sure. The only other locality within the region was Stuttgart, and that was an hour's drive one way. I hated this borough of ignorance and alienation. I hated Germany and most of all; I despised our way of life.

While wrapped up in remorse and self-pity I spotted Ilsedore Hulse behind me in the rearview mirror rummaging through one of the cobblestone back alleys.

Ilsedore was the only one who had talked to me in the past. I approached her with money and a shopping list in hopes that she would pick-up the few things that I needed. Ilsedore did my bidding while I waited in the alley trying to be inconspicuous. The old woman after surprisingly little coaxing, but still with her usual unsavory gusto, hurried off and returned, after what seemed to be an ungodly length of time, carrying two sacks of groceries and my list filled. Although she only gave back half of the change that was due me, I found it very easy to overlook when the groceries were in the back seat, and I was driving home.

***

Logic blossoms in the light of day, but when night comes, it withers quickly at the shadow's touch.

Holy Jesus, how could I have been so blind? Was this the real answer? All that has happened to me was not a product of my paranoia. How much of what I remember from the past few days had actually taken place, all of it? Not that I can fault myself. Most of us try to avoid any reality that is unpleasant. I know now that what I saw and experienced in the glade, in the tower, even in my bedroom and quite possibly my dreams, was real. All the same, I don't want to face it.

Moreover, the implications of the past week linked with what I now have read are nothing less than the book of revelations. It weighed heavily on my mind. Could it all be? The proof or at least some written verification of it now lay in my hands!

I had found the notebook of Faren's great uncle, the old manuscript that mysteriously disappeared shortly after its discovery. Faren had it all the time! He kept the knowledge of it from me all these weeks. He knew the history of the old house. He even knew what had gone on here before his uncles' death. Good, God! There never was a garden. It was a garden of the dead. A graveyard, unmarked for those who fought so long ago and died, with no family left to claim their remains.

I came upon the manuscript after returning home. While parking the car, I noticed the corner of one of the rolled up yellow pages protruding from beneath the front seat. I brought it into the house along with my packages and spent the rest of the afternoon wrestling through pages of stylized script written in a crabbed hand.

PART II
THE ALCHEMIST'S NOTEBOOK

The Journal of Heinrich Todesfall

If I am successful, I shall survive while my home will be reduced to a pile of rubble. I say if, lest I grow overconfident, for while the forces I aid are truly formidable, blind circumstances and the ill health that accompanies old age may yet work my undoing. There are other forces as well, obscure and invisible, implacable in their opposition to those I serve, who may not look upon my activities with disinterest. Should they become aroused or alert, I may not survive to complete my task.

Thus I set this down on paper so that what I have learned will not be lost should the worst come to pass. They may still be freed, and even after death, those servants, such as me, who have been faithful and unswerving in their loyalty to them may be resurrected from the earth to reign as princes to the kings over this world.

As much as I would like to leave this for my only friend, Peter, who from time to time has successfully come to my aid, I am afraid the effort would be useless. He is not a relation and cannot be part of the Todesfall destiny.

I have come to suspect over the years that there is a special quality in the blood of the Todesfall's. Given more time as an adolescent, before the proposed Thousand Year Reich had begun its journey, I feel with an intuitive certainty that my solitary studies would have eventually confirmed it. There are no living relatives of mine in the fatherland, but some were rumored to have traveled to America after a bitter separation that severed all ties and left our family numbers in Deutschland severely crippled, dwindling now to one.

I have contracted a group of solicitors in America that will locate any surviving heirs in the event of my death. That is why I have chosen to write this in English. If after reading this brief account of my life and the examination of the volumes of material I have amassed over the years, then maybe my work will continue, by the hand of a relative I never knew.

And so, cousin, nephew, relative, let me begin by saying that like our fathers before us, and except for a few intervening periods, of which I shall speak later, I have lived here at the schloss all my life, watching through the years this once proud estate dwindle, degenerate, to a group of tottering buildings and plots of weed-choked ground.

I came here shortly after my birth. I never knew my parents. My mother died giving birth to me, and my father died mysteriously just three days after I was born. The exact cause and particulars leading up to his death to this day remain a mystery to me. When I asked my uncle (my guardian) about those events, he answered in a quiet voice that there were some things that I was not meant to know.

A solemn, even melancholy environment, you may say; and indeed this is so, but an environment well suited to my disposition which was to be a sedate scholar and a visionary. My childhood was spent pouring over the ancient tomes that filled the schloss' grand library. In that beloved place, separated from the mainstream of society and its distractions, I learned to develop a keen eye for the truth; a clear perception which would allow me to accept what I knew must be in the years to come.

But I had another place, a special place like that which every boy has to retreat from companions and the world, a dark, wooded hollow, a short distance from Schloss Todesfall. This hollow was unlike any in the Schwarzwald, where my estate stands, calm and quiet, isolated, so devoid of life that even the chatter of squirrels and birds were unknown. It was an ideal place for me to read and meditate, shielded from the harsher sunlight by brooding pines. It was not surprising, then, that it was this place, more than anything else, the schloss or my other non-significant holdings on this estate, that would years later draw me back home.

I knew little of the outside world, let alone the social and political conventions of my time and consequently, I was bewildered when I first heard my uncle, with whom I lived, mention the word "depression." I didn't take much notice when the supply of oil for our lamps and stoves became scarce, eventually dwindling to nothing, nor did I take particular heed when my uncle finally relieved the servants of their duties. In retrospect, with the carelessness of childhood, I took little heed of anything until one afternoon when my uncle's voice echoed out, rousing me from the hollow.

I ran to the schloss, a thick book in hand, and met my uncle at the entrance in a somewhat agitated state, for it was rare for my uncle to call me at that time of day. Although he hid it well, I could sense that he was disturbed. I was about to ask if something was wrong when I heard voices from inside our home. With a brusque gesture, my uncle motioned me to follow him into the study.

Two men, almost invisible in their black uniforms save for their pale hands and grim faces in the dark study, stood solemnly. One of them quickly moved to me and shook my hand, smiling with a rictus that even one as young and naive as I instantly recognized as a pretense.

"Young master, greetings," said the uniformed man as he continued to pump my hand in camaraderie enthusiastically. "I am Lieutenant Erich Clausen, and this is Sergeant Kessler." He released my hand and looked at my uncle expectantly.

"You must tell him," said my uncle. "I cannot."

"Your attitude will be remembered, Herr Todesfall," said the second man, stepping forward. He was about to continue when Clausen motioned him back.

"Well, then, Master Todesfall." He paused, looking down on me.

"We have spoken to your uncle at some length about your future, and he has decided..."

My uncle then broke his stoic silence, a wave of rage engulfing his face. "You would have him believe..."

Sergeant Kessler growled, "I would suggest silence, Herr Todesfall." My uncle stopped and placed his hands on my shoulders. "Heinrich, my son," he had never addressed me as such before, "remember and know in the years to come, that I did all I could." He stepped back and left the room, turning at the door once to stare at the two intruders with a gaze of withering hate. The door was closed, leaving me alone with the two men.

The sergeant said to Clausen, "Why do we play games with this one, Lieutenant? We waste time."

"This boy is not like the others. He has lived in seclusion here all his life he is unaware of the events going on in the land. I merely attempt to ease his transition, and you are hindering me."

I could see that the lieutenant did not like his companion. He turned to me again.

"This is a great day for you, young master, for today begins your initiation into manhood."

"I want my uncle," is all I could think to say.

"You must learn that you cannot be a burden to your uncle forever. Look about you! Can you not see that this place is falling apart, that your uncle is an old man who cannot properly afford to raise a kinder. It is time for you to assume your duties to Deutschland, to your Fuhrer."

His voice became less stern, almost gentle. "You will learn to be a man where we are taking you, to be a soldier of Deutschland but you will also have the companionship of other young men like yourself. You would like that, wouldn't you? You cannot really like living here alone with an old man too busy to concern himself with an energetic lad like yourself, without friends and companions your age. With all these dusty books," he added after a pause, surveying the study.

"I like my home," I stuttered.

"And in time, you may return here...after you have completed your duties to your country. There is a great rebirth in the land, and we need red-blooded men like you to help usher in our new age. The whole world is watching us, waiting for us to rescue it from its disease. This is a sacred duty, which only we of Aryan blood, that blood which flowed through Vikings, can accomplish and it requires unstinting dedication from all of us, even our sons."

The study door opened again, and my uncle entered, carrying a satchel. The one called Kessler took up the bag as Lieutenant Clausen took hold of my shoulder, guiding me out of the Schloss. Blinded by tears, I looked over my shoulder to see my uncle weeping silently. It was the last time that I saw him. Thus I entered the youth camps of the National Socialist Party.

The physical world can be cruel, but the indifferent cruelty of nature cannot begin to compare to the viciousness of those I encountered during my indoctrination at the youth camp. It was among the many lessons I learned while becoming an officer of Deutschland, and learned very quickly; quickly ascending the military ranks at a pace far beyond my peers. Because of this, and because of my naiveté of social mores and standards, I became the object of constant harassment by my fellow students. I learned to endure it. Those who tormented me too often, however, soon learned that I was not one who could be toyed with. Of those occasions, I prefer to say nothing.

On the other hand, I came to love the system the National Socialist Party had to offer. It was a well-oiled machine made efficient by the supreme race that maintained it. It was a system that would make all the other countries of the world march to the step of the New Order or be crushed under its boot.

Upon reaching adulthood, my enthusiasm for the party had awarded me the title of lieutenant, and I graduated from the youth corps with honors, for I was the youngest lieutenant in my camp. From there it was a simple matter to rise even higher in the Wehrmacht, eventually being promoted to colonel.

The elevation of my status was very important to me at this stage of my life, for rank gave me the power I was taught to desire above all else. Rank also brought to me something that I discovered I did not want . . . responsibility. I still sought solitude from others, but it became impossible to attain as I shouldered the burden of more and greater duties. My first major command came at age nineteen when the first Blitzkrieg was executed against Poland; the Third Reich had begun its glorious march that unfortunately lasted only some fifteen hundred days from the first sound of gunfire.

Fighting in the Polish Territory was my first battle towards expanding Deutschland's borders, but the last battle for me was fought almost seven years later on that tract of land in the Schwarzwald which was once my home. I say once, for shortly after I left Schloss Todesfall, my uncle had died and the estate had been expropriated to pay for back taxes.

It was black April. It was 1945. In every major town, air-raid sirens wailed incessantly. The armies of the Third Reich were collapsing on all fronts by then. Berlin would soon fall, a city of raging fires and death everywhere and I had been assigned to establish a field command in our old family Schloss, which, despite the fact that it was owned now by the state, remained empty, a neglected skeleton of its former self. The library, to my disappointment, was in ruin, the shelves were almost bare of books, and the roof had acquired a small hole which allowed the rain to pour in, ruining the fine thick carpeting and the hardwood floor. Reluctantly we made the schloss our base of operations with small hopes of preparing a counter defense against the approaching Allied Forces. A recrimination born in Hell, for we were undermanned, underfed and ill-equipped.

Bloodlust is a phrase that has become shop soiled. It wasn't visible on the tired, hungry faces of my men to begin with but sitting, waiting in the long hours for something to happen changes a man. Your closest friend is a gun barrel, warm in the sun of the afternoon and icy cold by night. The thoughts of self-preservation, kill or be killed, became dominant. Even human compassion flies away with the wind, as I learned the first evening of my return to the schloss.

My officers and I were examining a map of the hollow by

candlelight inside the moldy study. So impoverished were we at this final stage of the war that we had not even the luxury of a portable generator to provide electric lights to prepare our battle plans when we heard a scream from outside. I drew my sidearm and ran out to find a half a dozen of my men arrayed in a circle. In their midst with clothing disheveled and torn, was a middle-aged woman pushed about and fondled roughly. I fired my Luger into the air.

The men's laughing and jeering stopped.

"How dare you," I roared, feeling the muscles of my face contorting in knots of rage, "are you soldiers or beasts?"

"She's just a Jew, Colonel," said one of the woman's tormentors. "And, probably a thief as well. We found her on the estate grounds."

"There's nothing here to steal," I snapped, "and I seriously doubt if there are any free Jews walking Deutschland now. And even if she is, she is still a woman, to be treated with respect."

There was some barely audible grumbling, the beasts were being thwarted from enjoying their prey, literally having it snatched from their jaws, and I wondered for a moment if they were considering turning on their commanding officer. One of my officers whispered in my ear. "It's been a long war, Colonel, the men are demoralized, tired and hungry, and we cannot afford even a single desertion."

I looked at the terrorized woman, who gazed at me for mercy. "We are already as good as beaten," I said in a low voice. "Take her then, but away from here, we have plans to make, and I don't wish to be interrupted."

I re-entered the schloss, hating myself as the woman's cries receded into the woods.

"Be sure they are ready by 0600 hours," I said tersely to a lieutenant as we returned to study the map.

That night was the eve of days of battle to come, days of attack and counter-attack that began with a sweeping to and fro across my beloved hollow that now had become an insane chessboard littered with the battered bodies and machinery of both German and Allied forces. By the end of the week, the Allies overran us. What was left of my regiment had fled or surrendered.

A few of my officers and I avoided capture, hiding in the sub-cellar beneath the schloss while the Allies moved on.

A day later, we stole from our hiding place and left the estate. My hollow had been scarred by artillery fire and stained with the blood of both armies, their bodies scattered across the ground like so much refuse. We slowly made our way through the forest to a field hospital outside of Stuttgart that had once been a schoolhouse. Later, I learned that I had been in a state of shock and the march had taken us over two weeks to complete, hiding at times in the woods from Allied troop movements. The trek had seemed like no more than a few days, and I remember little. It was May 2nd, 1945. Tired of the years of fighting by then, I was no less surprised and pleased to learn that the war had ended.

In the bed next to mine was an infantryman who had lost both arms at the shoulders from a mortar bombardment. Incredibly, this man was ecstatically happy. When queried, he replied, "I just received the news. Hitler has killed himself, and the Devil has departed with him! Germany is free of the evil at last!"

I didn't have the heart to disillusion the poor deceived soul. Many of us who labored in the rarefied circles of the military knew the truth. We were betrayed by the treachery of morally bankrupt leaders. The Jews would now succeed. Everything that our beloved Deutschland stood for would change, forever. That truly was the evil!

Ever since my stay in the hospital outside Stuttgart, I have been possessed with a drive to explore that truth. As I lay there, recovering, the words of the infantryman kept ringing in my mind. I saw the horrors around me in the tiny hospital, men dying and mutilated from the war, and I kept wondering if this had to be. Why didn't we have control over our fate? I couldn't bring myself to believe that men were created to serve unseen gods and grovel like slaves their entire lives in our world? We were the master race. We should have been the masters of our destiny, not the despoilers of it.

In my depressed state, I reflected upon my childhood years. The Todesfall family had its own belief, a sort of religion. My uncle had alluded to it several times as the truth of truths. He called it the Tanistry, and I was to learn of its ways when reaching manhood. That catechism never came to pass, because I was taken from him at an early age. I have always been resentful toward those two Nazi officers that took me to the youth camp for that loss.

And there was something else, a passage I had read in my youth that kept flowing in and out of my thoughts. It was something I had read, a long time ago, in my uncle's library. The words tempered my spirit and gave me a strength and realization of a new purpose to my life. The words began to become clearer, and they seemed to almost spell out in my mind:

IN HIS HOUSE IN R'LYEH
DEAD CTHULHU WAITS DREAMING.

It was virtually meaningless at the time, but the words had a comforting effect on me. I believed it to be a fragment of a much longer work out of something I had once read, possibly from a poem wherein the next line stood on the clouded edge of obscurity from my memory.

"If only I could remember the other words," I kept thinking, "there would be an answer."

Although my purpose, perhaps I should say, my fate remained obscure; my soul was reborn in the knowledge that I had to examine the old books and the scrolls that once graced my uncle's library or at least ones like them. That driving curiosity eventually became a quest which took me to countless libraries across Europe.

Fearing the tribunal in Nuremberg, I assumed a new identity and Heinrich Todesfall slipped into obscurity for a while. It was not until much later that I realized that I was not on their wanted list. I knew Goering; I knew Canaris, Heydrich, even Eichmann. I knew them all. All of them either committed suicide or were tracked down one by one and executed but not me. I had not spent my time in service eliminating the Jews so that after the war I would be tracked down like a criminal. No one wanted me. I was not, as the Americans say, "newsworthy."

Only a few months after leaving the army I left Deutschland under secrecy and journeyed to London where I secured quarters on Great Russell Street. There I stayed, shunning all human contact, while I examined the arcane documents housed in the British Museum. Later, I made several trips to Paris seeking further material in the Bibliotheque Nationale.

I spent a short time in Prague under the disguise of a Russian geology student then carried the investigation to Klausenburg in Romania where, after three months, I returned to the fatherland, residing in Neustadt for six months until moving on to Austria. My studies awarded me a professorship at a university in Austria which served to supplement my dwindling monetary reserves and allowed me to amass enough money to buy back my ancestral home. The longing for the return to my childhood years of solitude and security had little bearing on the reasons for the purchase of the property. Rather, I was both elated and overcome by the paradox of the situation I found myself in at the time. It took several years to acquire the money to buy back the schloss, and within that time I made one of the three important discoveries I was destined to make in my life. While in Austria I came upon a rare find, a handwritten, Latin translation of the Necronomicon. The ancient book was sent to me by a fellow researcher from America who had recently taken a teaching position at the University of Heidelberg. I do not know how he came upon this book, but it was sent with a hand-scrawled note proclaiming that I should be very interested in its contents.

I remembered such a book as a child in my uncle's possession. I spent all my free time pouring over the text, and it was one evening in my small study at the university that I stumbled upon the location of the gateway. My translation was unmistakable and the more involved I became in my investigations, the more it verified my conclusions.

It was this place and the mysterious forces of its long, continuous history which had brought me into being and which has now drawn me back to it. It must have been the secret, the "great truth" my uncle would have revealed to me if time had permitted. It was the place of our God, the true God of our fathers. In a way, it was the holy ground, and I was the heir to its secrets like all the Todesfall's before me. I was the Tanist.

Many so-called antiquarians had theorized about the gateway's location, some believing it to be in Malaysia, while one resident professor at the Miskatonic University in America had gone so far as to place it exactly in a group of nineteen islands off the Malabar Coast. A laughable Japanese investigator said it was in Burma, on the Plateau of Leng, guarded for ages by the tcho-tcho people. Another Asian scholar speculated that it was near Africa, just fourteen miles off the Skeleton Coast. But they are all wrong. I alone know the true location of the great dimensional prison where the Old One has been forced to dwell, and I have located that dimensional gateway known to some as the realm of N'Kai. It is outside of Stuttgart in my beloved mountainous Schwarzwald.

***

Upon acquiring the finances necessary and not wanting much for physical comforts, I retired from the teaching profession and took up residence in the once august estate. The old house was a painful sight to my eyes. The ancient tower of the library had been torn and opened to the winds, and the central framing of the house was crumbling under the slow yet might pressure of time.

I boarded up all the openings but one which I left for an entrance and exit. I had need of little money, for the house was paid for, and the forests yielded an endless supply of firewood and game. The surrounding vegetation provided many roots and herbs to help sustain me.

It has been twenty-five years since I regained Schloss Todesfall and in that time I have left my estate only on three occasions. The first was only a week after I settled in at the manor when I made a brief journey to Austria to make arrangements for the transportation of my many books and research notes, as well as the other articles needed to sustain me on my lifelong pursuit.

My second excursion from my house didn't come until after five years when I made a long journey by train to the coastal town of Bremerhaven. The trip almost exhausted my savings, but the outcome was so important that it outweighed the cost.

In Bremerhaven, I was to meet with a sailor who hailed from the New England port town of Innsmouth in America. I met the man outside his dingy hotel on the waterfront. He was a strange person, and from the way that he stood and carried himself, I thought he must be deformed. He couldn't have been too much over five feet in height when standing erect, but of this, I cannot be certain because he always stood slightly bent over and stooped shouldered. He spoke to me with a jerking, blubbering voice. Although I found him to be revolting, I pressed on in my objective.

I had, by that time, corresponded heavily with the Esoteric Order of Dagon, an organization in America that conducted research similar to my own. Through one of these correspondences, I was assured that this man possessed one of the five missing Dead Sea Scrolls and this particularly rare find could be the key to unlocking the gateway.

We went inside a bar next to the hotel to negotiate over some schnapps. The establishment was dark and full of assorted groups of sinister-looking figures. Many of their features were lost to me in the dim light and smoke. The noise of laughing and shouting was grating on my nerves. After five years of solitude in the Schwarzwald, a crowded barroom was like visiting hell to me, and if my quest had been of any minor significance, I surely would have stood up and left the premises.

Two prostitutes found their way to our table and began to solicit our favors, but I shook them off. They sneered at me and turned their attention to my companion. One of the girls looked down at him, and he turned his head so she could make out his features.

"Do you not want my patronage?" he said with a devilish grin, "I am sure you would find me unlike any other you have known."

She gave a little shudder and then told her friend to find other customers quickly.

The whore had been correct in finding my associate's features to be disturbing. His bulging eyes would almost glow in the dim light of the bar, and at one particularly heated point in our conversation, I thought that they would fly from their sockets. His lips were thin, and his face was a very pale gray colour, and his skin was loose and flabby.

I had little money, and so I tried to appeal to his sense of humanity and ended making a false plea for science and humanity. I explained to the strange gentleman that my purpose in obtaining the scroll was to enlighten the world with the knowledge that could be acquired from it. The only response I received from him was a swilling of his liquor, a process that was nauseating because when he drank, his lips curved in and became a slash across his face, giving the impression that he was without lips. After the final drink, which emptied the contents of his glass, he glared straight at me and said, "Man, I want the stone."

I had in my possession what I considered to be nothing more than a good luck piece; a small star-shaped stone which was used traditionally by my family giving the possessor imaginary protection from evil. My uncle had told me the legends of this relic which he called the Stone of Mnar. It was said to have been very old and was handed down through countless generations of my family. It was for that reason I didn't care to use it as a bargaining tool.

How he knew I was in possession of the stone I never learned. It was obviously the only item of exchange that the seafarer from Innsmouth cared for, so I was finally obliged to offer it to him. To my amazement, the creature knocked the stone from my grasp with a nervous jerk of his left hand. My astonishment increased when for the brief moment our hands touched, I noticed the fine webbing of skin between each of his fingers, and the cold and clammy feel of his skin made me draw my hand away in revulsion.

The American merchant sailor scooped the stone up from the table with a pocket handkerchief never touching it with his bare hands. I watched this person from Innsmouth tremble holding the star-shaped object between the folds of the handkerchief and stare with bulging eyes intently at the rough textured surface. Then, before I knew what was happening, he slapped down a long metal tube, and after bounding from the table and upsetting his chair, he ran from the bar with the stone still clutched in the handkerchief.

My first impulse was to grab the tube and open it on the spot, but common sense and the knowledge of the pirates and criminals being all around me in the closed setting overcame my eagerness, and I stood and walked calmly from the dark establishment. Upon arriving back at my room, I wasted no time in uncapping both ends of the metal tube. From within I imagined the odor of sea air and dead oceans. Rolled up in the tube was a thick yellowed piece of parchment, which would have to be removed carefully.

To my surprise when I turned the tube on end, about a dozen metal strips fell out and scattered across the floor. They were copper, and there was writing on them. Getting down on my hands and knees, I started to fit the pieces together. It was a scroll. Not one of thick parchment or leather that I had expected, but a copper one.

Copper scrolls were not unheard of to me. I had read about them. They did not fall within the scope of the other Dead Sea Scrolls. One, in particular, was a non-religious document, but it had stimulated more curiosity and speculation than the other scrolls. It was found by archaeologists in a cave near Jericho during the excavations of 1952, but the metal had become badly oxidized during the centuries, so much so that the scroll could not be unfolded. It was, therefore, carefully divided into longitudinal strips so it could be read the same as the one I found myself the possessor.

This was not the famous Copper Scroll. That one was a treasure map. It listed over sixty hiding places where gold, silver, aromatics and other scrolls are said to be deposited. Although the treasures were never found, the precious metals were supposed to add up to almost one hundred tons. It was not a treasure map because, after a quick scrutiny of the ancient copper fragments, I knew my search had ended. Even more, for this valuable document wasn't only a vague prospect for the key to the gateway, it was the key in every sense of the word. In lieu of a better term, this copper scroll was a plan and diagram for the construction of a most incredible device. Horizontal and vertical bands of hieroglyphics boarded the metal on all four sides, and at the center, in perfect clarity was a detailed engraving of a machine.

My enthusiasm would have been overwhelming if not for a strange feeling I was harboring at the moment. The reaction of the man, in the bar, had been very strange, indeed, and I could not help but feel that I was the pawn in a much greater turn of events that I could realize. I pondered over the loss of the Stone of Mnar that had been with me ever since childhood and could not help wondering as well which one of us got the better part of the bargain.

***

As I stated before, there was a third and final excursion from my ancestral home. A trip that was the longest by far, taking me a great distance from Deutschland and lasting over two weeks.

The machine or device was the link to unlocking the doorway between our world and the other, but there were words needed to call forth the forces from across the dimensional void. Of this, I was convinced because my years of research always indicated the usage of a formula uttered in conjunction with certain astronomical phenomena and the machine.

The exact knowledge of these words I did not possess at the time. All my translations from the Necronomicon and other ancient writings turned up several inconsistencies. The construction of the device from the diagrams in the scroll would take a long time, perhaps years but the outcome would be useless without the proper formula.

It was in 1955 that I decided to break from my self-imposed secrecy and wrote of my problem in a long letter to the Esoteric Order of Dagon in Innsmouth, Massachusetts. The fraternal brotherhood in America and its council of the unknown nine was the only body of knowledge that might have been willing to send assistance.

Their reply was quick and generous beyond my belief. I had written explaining the condition of my exhausted finances and was surprised to find in an envelope that had arrived along with plans to temporarily smuggle me out of the country and into America, a bank draft for five thousand Deutsche Marks.

It unfolded that another copy of the Necronomicon existed. An English translation had been kept under lock and key at the Library of Miskatonic University in Arkham Massachusetts ever since 1928 when it first came into the possession of the college. Although it was on display at the University Library, any studies or copying of the book were forbidden by the administration.

It was proposed by the Order of Dagon that if obtained the collation of the two texts might produce the answer to my problem. Their reason for their generosity was reported to me as purely academic, a small price to pay for the knowledge that may be derived. I did not waste time questioning my good fortune rather I took quick and decisive action.

I left the following week, cabling ahead in code to Innsmouth of my impending arrival. I traversed the southern border of my country by rail, through the western tip of Austria, then after changing trains across northern Italy to the port of Genoa.

As prearranged, I took passage on a freighter bound for the West Indies that I assumed must have been paid handsomely to make such a wide detour to set me down illegally in American waters.

The war had been over for ten years by then. Even though I was not wanted for any war crimes, the United States of America, in those days, did not look kindly on ex-officers of the Third Reich who tried to immigrate to their country, even for short periods of time. Visas were almost impossible to obtain for someone with my background.

The captain of the freighter was a suspicious swarthy looking Italian that never spoke to me, nor in fact, did any of his crew. Consequently, I spent most of my time below in my quarters.

The journey took almost a week, and one night, under cover of darkness, I was lowered overboard into a small sloop within sight of the eastern seaboard of Massachusetts.

According to plan, I had a compass and small flashlight with me and following the instructions in the letter carefully used the light sparingly so as not to be spotted. Our rendezvous was to be an old lighthouse on Ogre's Tongue Cape, a point of land extending out from Innsmouth into the sea. I was very fortunate there was no moon, but the sky was clear and filled with stars that marked my way. Even though we had encountered much fog during our voyage, there was none that night and about fifteen minutes after being lowered into the water; I sighted the silo-shaped outline of the stone building.

An hour of rowing brought me up to the shore of the cape and the base of the lighthouse. The foundation of the old structure on one side had been exposed to the ocean through the continual eroding of land by the sea.

I hung on to the stones steadying the small craft in the current confident that I had made the journey unseen. It was very unlikely that I was sighted from shore. The freighter had moved on noiselessly at quarter speed with all her lights off the moment I was safely overboard, and I presented a very difficult target to spot. The sloop had been painted a dark color with all its shiny parts blacked out and I was clad in an old pair of black naval officer's leathers I had purchased before leaving home.

I was to wait at the base of the lighthouse for them to come. I did not know if they were to come from the bank above me or by water, but I waited, searching the darkness around me for their arrival.

I shifted my position in the sloop, and my left hand ran across the slippery masonry. I felt several indented marks in the stone and seconds later with both hands exploring I discovered that they traveled in a straight horizontal band across the face of several stones. It felt like lettering. Risking discovery, I lit the surface of the rocks with my flashlight. Carved into the stone, in English were the words; "Here Do Sirens Beguile Mariners." A cold chill swept through me. I quickly unzipped my jacket and removed my Luger that I had brought. It had been my officer's pistol during the war, and I was glad at the moment that I had it with me. I cocked the breach putting a bullet into the chamber, feeling comforted that the gun was primed and easily within my grasp. I slipped it back into my jacket and was about to read the inscription for a second time when I heard the sound of oars slicing the waters.

I spotted their light first. Two wooden boats approached. Each with three men on board; two rowing, while the others sat on the bows carefully shielding their lamps from the shore. The man ahead in the lead boat shouted in a heavy guttural accent for me to put out my light. I did as instructed and eventually followed behind them to a section of badly decayed fish docks. When on shore, one of the boats remained taking the sloop from the freighter in tow and back to deep water where it was sunk.

They escorted me passed a row of equally decaying buildings. The harbor was dotted with a few decrepit cabins, moored dories, and scattered lobster pots. Turning to look back on the sea I could make out here and there the ruins of wharves jutting out from the shore to end in crumbling neglect, those farthest south the most decayed. And far out to sea, despite the increasing tide, I glimpsed for the first time a long black line scarcely rising above the water made visible to me then by the lights from the coast. It was a reef, and as I looked, I noticed that the line appeared unbroken all the way to the tip of Ogre's Tongue. I realized that the two boats must have guided me through an invisible but navigable passage.

The man from the lead boat's name was Marsh and he, obviously in charge, led us again, this time on foot, to the north end of the town. The rest were dark, unkempt men of sullen visage that walked clumsily in a silent almost evasive way.

There were few street lights, but when finally passing beneath one on a corner I saw the face of the man called Marsh for the first time. My feelings were mixed with surprise and disgust of his features. He was almost bald, and his skin was a particularly dark shade, and it appeared shiny, excessively oily. I was surprised not so much by his unusual appearance but how much his features were like those of the sailor I met in Bremer Haven a couple of years before. He was from Innsmouth as well. Could they have been brothers?

Soon cross streets and junctions began to appear; those on the right leading to the shoreward realms of unpaved squalor and decay, while those on the left showed signs of departed grandeur in the way of boarded up large square Georgian style houses, many with hipped roofs, cupolas and railed widow's walks. So far, I had seen no other people in town, besides our small group. After a while though, there came signs of sparse habitation, curtained windows here and there, and an occasional battered automobile at the curb.

At one point, I spied a group of dirty, simian-looking children playing around a weed-grown doorstep. Somehow they were more disquieting than the dismal buildings, for almost every one of them had peculiarities of face and motions which I instinctively disliked and was becoming uncomfortably aware was also shared by the men from the boats. They were not of Aryan stock.

So this was Innsmouth.

I longed for my rundown schloss that in my mind seemed palatial by comparison and in a naive moment, I wondered if this seaboard town was indicative of American life.

I must have been a comical contrast to my six dark and shabby companions, but the few people that we did pass did not seem to take any particular notice. Most of the men from the boats were dressed in tattered overalls and wool coats. I don't think any of them stood more than five and a half feet tall, but this was hard to tell because like the sailor I had met in Bremer Haven, the manner of their carriage was round-shouldered and sloppy. While I, on the other hand walking amongst them, towering three inches above six feet, my white hair cropped just above the ears wearing black leather slacks and matching jacket should have produced stares.

We met no one on the street after that, and presently we began to pass more deserted houses in varying stages of ruin. After a while, we changed direction to a narrow side street, and I saw the white belfry of a fairly well-preserved brick structure which I took for a small factory. The group stepped up their gates, and we ran at a light pace across two stretches of brick sidewalks and a cobblestone pavement to a large pillared doorway. While Marsh fumbled with a ring of keys, I noticed under a dim street lamp that the structure's once white paint was gray and peeling and the black and gold sign on the pediment was faded, and I could only, with difficulty, make out the words "Esoteric Order of Dagon."

I was ushered into a long dark hall and quickly down a set of cellar steps. A door closed behind me, and I was relieved when the darkness was finally interrupted by a bare light bulb hanging from a cord in the ceiling. My relief was short lived. The light, being disturbed by the tug on a pull chain, swung back and forth. Under the intermittent electric glare, I made out my six guides. We stood in a small storage room, a fruit cellar and Marsh who sat on a barrel of apples bid me to eat something saying that I might not have another chance for quite some time. It had been several hours since my last meal, but I declined all the same for thoughts of hunger were pushed from my mind by the revulsion I felt for these people.

They all looked alike with only slight variations. Perhaps they were all related, or maybe they were the results of inter-marrying. Besides their thin, stooped shouldered appearance and uncommon complexions, they all shared the same afflictions and deformities. Dull, expressionless faces with receding foreheads and chins, bulging blue eyes, noses flattened against the face and small ears. Two of them, although having the same coarse-pored, grayish cheeks as the others, displayed thin yellow hairs that straggled and curled in irregular patches to below the chin giving the impression of diseased flesh.

Their hands were large and heavily veined and had a very unusual grayish-blue tinge. One of the blond bearded pairs had the last three fingers of his left hand joined by the webbing of skin, and after a casual inventory of the others, I discovered that they all had their digits joined, in the same manner, some to a lesser or greater degree.

What I found to be the most revolting about them was the shriveling of flesh on their necks. The skin puckered and sagged into loose sickening folds and creases. Marsh who appeared to be the oldest of the six had the most pronounced wrinkling, and it gave the impression of deep slits in the sides of his neck.

When we came out of the cold night air and into the close quarters of the small room, I immediately became aware of a fishy scent, and in a matter of minutes, the smell increased to the nauseating odor of dead sea life.

I recalled the words inscribed into the stone foundation of the lighthouse and remembered tales in romantic literature from my homeland about the Lorelei. About dangerously fascinating amphibian creatures, that lured boatmen to shipwreck by their singing. Could there have been any truth to these legends? If so could some distant relatives of that antediluvian marine culture exist today, thousands of miles from the Rheine River in a decaying New England seaboard community? My research over the past years had uncovered many strange things but never anything to substantiate my wild fantasy.

I shook loose from the strange thoughts and clung to the revulsion and hatred that I was beginning to harbor for their kind. If it were not for the task that was before me, the success of which depended upon my close association with these mongrels of human life, I would have exterminated them all with the gun in my coat.

I laid my racial disgust aside for the moment and listened to the plan that unfolded from the thin-lipped mouth of the man called Marsh.

In an hour we were to journey to Arkham, a neighboring town. The Innsmouth bus that only operated by day and normally picked up and deposited its passengers at the Gilman House Hotel on State Street would make an unscheduled evening stop at the church, the cellar of which we at the time occupied.

Except for the driver, I was to make the trip alone. They gave me a map of Arkham and a floor plan of the library which showed in careful detail where the book was kept. The driver had instructions to wait for me for no more than fifteen minutes. After that, I would be on my own. If successful, we would return to Innsmouth an hour before dawn. They also had a room prepared for me at the Gilman House Hotel where I would stay until later when I would be fetched once again under cover of darkness and smuggled out of this decaying country.

When the hour had come, and before stepping onto the bus, Marsh extended a hand and something glittered.

"Here, you'll need this," he said. It was a key on a small gold chain.

"It's the key to the front door of the Library of Miskatonic University."

I did not ask how he came upon it but wondered why if it was going to be this easy that he and his men had not attempted the theft long before. I took the chain from him. I was wearing gloves. I put them on shortly after entering the fruit cellar as a precaution against any possible contact between their flesh and mine. Marsh's eyes fell upon my gloved hand and then back up at me. His expression was of boredom as if he was used to that kind of treatment. We said nothing more to one another, and I boarded the bus.

In a few minutes, the small motor coach of extremely poor condition and the color of dirt rattled up State Street and out of town. We passed a number of crumbling, and probably empty houses along a country road and then finally emerging into a long, monotonous stretch of open shore country.

As I looked ahead, I watched the driver's bent rigid back and greasy head become more and more hateful to me. The back of his head, almost hairless had a few straggling yellow strands upon his gray scabby skin.

Resting on the dashboard was a narrow faded pasteboard sign that normally would have faced the windshield but was turned inward. The half legible lettering read; ARKHAM-INNSMOUTH-NEWB'PORT. The windows of the bus were heavily soiled and combined with the evening darkness; it was difficult to make out much of the landscape. For a moment I glimpsed the sandy line of an island as the road drew near the beach and later when our backs were to the sea and as the narrow road veered off from the main highway, I caught sight of dead stumps and a long line of cliffs that made me homesick for the Schwarzwald.

After what seemed to be an eternity, we came upon the lights of a city, Arkham. I was surprised when we drove into that town. It, like Innsmouth, was of remarkable antiquity, but unlike that old fishing village, it was in a high state of preservation. Beautifully kept Georgian and Victorian buildings and houses intricately trimmed and laced with delicate ginger breading all taunted me with their beauty. It was like a painting. A lot like pictures I had seen in books on early American history. Unfortunately, I had to divert my attention from the sightseeing and keep my eyes on the street signs and the direction the driver was taking. I had spent most of the trip studying the map of Arkham, memorizing the major cross streets and thoroughfares that surrounded the University.

We pulled to a stop in front of a drug store on Market Square. The driver without uttering a word caused the rear side door of the bus to slide open, and I stepped out onto the empty street. It was a little after three in the morning, and there was no one in sight. All the shops and businesses were closed for the evening while Arkham slept.

I knew where I was; in the center of the business district, less than a quarter of a mile from the University. I checked the map once more to be doubly sure of my position then hurried across Market Square, past the Providence Hotel, then around the corner and up Sentinel Avenue to the lights of Federal Walk and College Hill which led me to the campus grounds and eventually to the front steps of the library. A burglar alarm hung on the wall to the right of the fluted stone casing that surrounded the doorway. I was surprised at its simplicity. I had to fight down my amazement and keep from laughing out loud at the stupidity that had gone into designing the thing. The alarm, large and probably loud enough to wake up half of Arkham was within arms reach, and it was a simple matter to remove the base of the housing and disconnect the two wires that activated the bell mechanism.

Simpler still was the ease that I opened the door. The key that Marsh had given me fit perfectly and the lock gave no resistance. I stepped confidently across the marble vestibule and into the general area of the library. The floor plan had been accurate, and I was able to find my way through the biology and reference sections to the anthropology section with only the occasional use of my flashlight.

As I crossed the hall to the small genealogical reading room where the book was kept, I heard the savage barking of a dog behind me. The great watchdog flashed around the corner of some aisle shelves. I squeezed off a round, and the dog fell on its side softly whimpering, coughing blood with a large tear in its chest made by my automatic.

I had to move even faster after that, afraid that the gunshot would have attracted attention from the outside. Light from another building on College Hill streaked through an uncurtained window illuminating the body of the dog. I ran across the intervening darkness to the small reading room on the other side. I moved quickly, drew the shade on the one window in the room and turned on my flashlight. The beam leaped across the dark space and fell on a glass cabinet in the center of a table. The case was only a couple of feet across and resting on a pedestal inside was an old leather-bound book. The frame of the case was bolted to the table top and glittering at its base was a brass plaque which read:

NECRONOMICON
ENGLISH TRANSLATION
By
FRANCIS DEE M.D.
ACQUIRED FROM THE WHATELY ESTATE

The top had been hinged to form a lid that was locked. The butt of my automatic broke through the glass with one stroke, and seconds later I had the book in my hands. A tingle of excitement ran through me when I touched the binding. It was not as thick as my Latin translation of the work. The pages although yellowed and brittle with age were of a thicker and newer stock than my copy, but still, it was nowhere near its length. It had been condensed or abridged, in some way, or pages were missing. I hoped and prayed to the Old Ones that those pages did not include passages that were part of my search.

Engrossed with my treasure and exhilarated by the power it would bring me; I carefully turned the first few leaves of written words forgetting for the moment where I was. My engrossed enthusiasm kept me from hearing the tottering footsteps that must have come down the hall. I did not realize that there was someone else in the library until the lights came on.

I jumped dropping the book into the glass case. I had been discovered. A man stood at the threshold of the reading room. He was alone and unarmed. He was elderly, in his seventies, I guessed, possibly older. He wore a tweed vested suit with shirt collar opened and a tie hung loosely around his neck. He must have been in another area of the library all the time. The old caretaker's mouth continuously bobbed open and closed, but I never heard his words. I was oblivious to his inquiries. He was the only thing that stood in my way of leaving. I had little more than a worthless contempt for him. My movements were quick, reflexive, I squeezed off a round from my Luger, and a black dot appeared on his forehead. His head jerked, and he fell backward to the carpet.

With the Necronomicon in hand again, and the flashlight tucked in my jacket pocket, I ran from the scene overturning a stack of books in the biology section as I fled. Briefly stopping at the front door, I peeked outside and found the way clear I stretched my legs into a wide, fierce gate and soon left the grounds of Miskatonic behind me.

I had made the entire trip of a few blocks and back unseen, and within the fifteen minutes, they allotted to me. The driver sat behind the wheel of the bus staring ahead, never turning to look when I approached. Inside the bus, I shouted for him to drive off. His movements in getting the engine started and on our way were languid, and I felt deliberate. Perhaps he was unaware of my mission. I paced up and down the aisle between the seats. Forgetting myself, I shouted orders in German to be quick, but his actions remained the same as we crept away from the curb. Not until I pressed the barrel of my gun against his revolting face and screamed in his tiny ear did he increase the speed of the motor coach.

I did not relax until we were in the countryside once again with the lights of Arkham out of sight. Not until I felt we were at a safe distance did I let the driver ease back on the accelerator and I sunk into a seat down the aisle from him. I did not like being close to one that had the "Innsmouth look." The thought of being around these disgusting people for another day was unsettling. I was suspicious of them and their purpose. Was I just a pawn? I was still unsure if I was being used to fetch the book for them or if the motives they presented were genuine. What stopped them from obtaining the Necronomicon themselves? Maybe, I thought, they feared the people of Arkham. The "Innsmouth look" would surely cause them problems anywhere. Then there was that foul odor that preceded all of them and that guard dog. The smell could easily instill savage excitement in any dumb beast.

Another thing baffled me. If the people of Innsmouth were using me, then why the elaborate plan to bring me into the country if they were not sincere? They could have easily hired someone locally to do the job, or could they have? Quite possibly the reputation of their kind was widespread, and it might have been necessary for them to import an outsider.

Things were moving too quickly, and my mind raced. The course of my thoughts ran that way, and parts of it still puzzle me today. Sitting in the bus, I gave up wondering, but not my hatred for them. If I was allowed to return home with the book, then they were truly my benefactors, but I could not suppress my racial disgust. My nerves were on edge, and after the incident at Miskatonic and my run-in with the driver, I would have gladly murdered them all in their beds.

At the Gilman House, a sullen looking night clerk let me have room 428 and after climbing three flights of stairs, exhausted with no sleep in over twenty-four hours, I threw myself on the cheap, iron-framed bed. I lay there, tired and hungry, wishing I had taken Marsh's advice and eaten something when I had the chance.

The room was a dismal rear unit with two windows and bare cheap furnishings. The door to my room did not have a lock on it, but there was a small bolt fitted to it, as there was with the two lateral doors to the connecting rooms. Relieved to be alone but still suspicious of my benefactors, I inspected the bolts and with all three found that the jambs were cracked in the area around them and nailed back together again as if they had been broken in at one time then repaired.

Even if a man is hunted day and night, eventually he needs a place to sleep that is secure. I had known this before leaving home and recalling a trick taught to me by a friend in the Gestapo years ago, I had brought with me a dozen wood wedges about six inches long. After checking that all the bolts were drawn tightly, I drove the wedges with the heel of my boot between the cracks at the bottoms and tops of the doors, securing them against entry.

As dawn brightened, I felt safer but did not undress. I laid down reading Dee's copy of the Necronomicon until overcome by exhaustion; I fell asleep.

I had a dark shadowy dream of dim mists clogged with fitful screaming. I was elevated somewhat as if standing on a hill and below me, men and women cried out in agony. Then from out of the mists came monstrous black, rubbery things with wings and no face that snatched me up by the stomach and carried me off through infinite leagues of black air over towers of dead and horrible cities. Finally getting me into a gray void where I saw the needle-like pinnacles of enormous mountains miles below, they let me drop.

I awoke to darkness and the sound of pounding at my door. I had slept over twelve hours, and Marsh had sent two men around to fetch me. My departure was taking place as planned.

Later and after walking over some of the same deserted streets I had the night before, we came to a wharf that had a small boat moored to it. Marsh and two others accompanied me as we rowed out to meet a fishing trawler bound for Spain. It, like the freighter, had been hired to take me as a passenger. I was impressed once again by the ingenuity of these Innsmouth people and wondered what connections in black marketing or smuggling they must have possessed to carry out my transportation so efficiently.

I kept on guard all the way to the trawler, my hand never leaving my gun but there was never any indication of foul play amongst them. When climbing the ladder to board the trawler, I stopped and looked down at Marsh who was at the bow of the rowboat attempting to give me a hand up. I drew my Luger and pointed it at the bridge of his almost non-existent nose. For an instant, I imagined his gray face splattered all over the small boat below, then feeling generous for all the good they had done me I smiled, holstered the weapon, and clamored up the side of the ship.

***

In the years that followed, I lived apart from the outside world, but I did not dwell alone. In that now singularly evil looking wooded hollow that had at one time held for me the memories of a happy childhood, rested hundreds of unmarked graves bearing the last remaining vestiges of my regiment. If a human being lacks the fellowship of the living, he inevitably draws upon the companionship of things that are not.

For a while, I went about naming them, and when weather permitted, I would sit amongst them as I did years before at my lectern in Austria and discuss any current research problems I was experiencing at the time. Through the years we all became very close, they the classmates and I their instructor, so it was because of this friendship that I didn't feel the least bit uncomfortable in asking them to give up the only valued possession remaining to them. You see, it was about this time that I was experiencing one of my most difficult problems. I was attempting the construction of the machine which primarily consisted of gold, silver, and several small mirrors.

The mirrors were no problem for the walls of the schloss were practically adorned with them, and I had years to fashion tools and learn to cut them to the exact specifications of the plan. Silver did not present a problem either for only a small quantity was needed, and I owned an old silver teapot which provided more than enough of the precious metal.

The gold presented the problem. The entire machine was predominantly gold in its construction, and there was none to be found anywhere on my estate. The thought of obtaining work of any kind to acquire the money needed to purchase the gold was distasteful to me. My solitude had become very dear through the years and any contact with the outside world, no matter how temporary, was an unbearable thought.

It was in this moment of despair that I turned to my old regiment for help. I put the question to them, and being as close as we were, I did not consider it rude to take something for which they had no further use. It took several months to extract all the gold from their teeth that I needed. Finally, I removed the gold bridgework from the right side of my mouth, both as an act of good faith to my friends from the grave and to acquire the last amount necessary to complete the task.

Three years elapsed in the construction of the device. I cut and shaped hundreds of pieces of mirror glass to obtain the five pieces I finally used on the machine. My uncle's kitchen stove would glow red hot, at times being used from sunup to sundown. I fashioned a small kiln within the oven and melted the silver and gold to construct the various components and many times I had to melt the articles down a second, third and even a fourth time until the proper molds were achieved to perfection. Time meant very little as long as there was enough to complete the project because I knew the result would make me immortal.

When the machine was completed, a wave of depression came over me, unlike anything I had felt since the end of the war. Although my recreation of the ancient device was perfect, it still lacked two very important parts, the likes of which I could not decipher from the plans. I again turned to the Esoteric Order of Dagon for guidance. I had made an exact copy of the scroll containing the plan, and I mailed it to my correspondents for advice.

As the weeks passed, I began to question the wisdom of my actions. Any doubts I harbored about the act were soon alleviated when one morning, less than two months later, there came a knock on my door and I was greeted by Peter, my friend and confidant through years of letter writing, carrying a carved, wooden box under his arm. The carvings on the box were similar to those of ancient Hyperborean hieroglyphics I had seen in the Book of Eibon, but the total combination of symbols was unfamiliar to me. You can imagine the wonder and utter amazement I felt when, after the brief conversation with him and a quick scrutiny of the contents of the box, I found that he had produced the missing components that were lacking in the completion of the mechanism.

I broke out an old bottle of brandy I had been saving since the war. After a few hours and several drinks I brought him up to date on my research, and he informed me of his activities since our last correspondence the year before.

Peter, his full name I have withheld for obvious reasons of secrecy, was the head of the council of the Unknown Nine, the governing body of the Order of Dagon. Although we never met when I was in Innsmouth, I was happy to see him, noticing with relief that he was physically normal, not like the others I had met there.

It unfolded that he left the Esoteric Order of Dagon after a dispute over the course of his studies. I was flattered to learn that his studies followed a similar path as mine and that since he had seen the copy of the machine diagram I had sent, he spent the next few weeks plotting to steal the two articles he knew would be impossible for me to fabricate. They had been kept as religious artifacts by the people of Innsmouth, kept in the very same church I had been in on that insane night in 1955. His office on the council gave him certain liberties that made the theft simple and his escape from the eastern seaboard all the more easy. Since the council had a copy of the diagram in their possession thanks to me and the two necessary parts, they had decided to build the machine and attempt the crossing themselves. Except Peter disagreed with the place of the coming and that is when he decided to come to my aid instead.

As the evening passed, I became careless with my emotions, so long had I been starved for human companionship that our relationship grew in one evening of drunken stupor. Soon I eagerly agreed to a part-time association with him. We even went so far as to make a pact on paper decreeing our determination to resolve the mysteries of the universe. In the midst of our alcoholic stupor and enthusiasm, we carried the jest a little too far. Before parting for the evening Peter and I drew up a document in which we swore allegiance to the great and mighty Cthulhu and signed it in our blood.

I would have been better off that evening if I had retired and gone to bed after wishing Peter a good night rather than behaving like a foolhardy drunk. I could not wait until morning, with a more sensible head, to see if the two pieces would fit the machine properly. I had to know if I had followed the specifications correctly in building the device. Did the pieces indeed fit?

I staggered down the cellar stairs, across the stone floor and eventually into the vault. It is my bastion below the earth. The combination that unlocks its door is only special to me.

It took me a few moments to master the lighting of a candle. In my state, I had difficulty in lighting a match. After managing to get a candle burning, I had no difficulty making the pieces fit. In fact, it surprised me that they fit so remarkably well. I was very proud of my workmanship.

I stared at my finished masterpiece for several minutes without moving. I am not sure how to explain my actions next. Perhaps it was the excitement of the achievement, the years of work culminating into a silent accomplishment…curiosity? I don't know what ran through my head at that moment. I guess I wanted to know if my past years were spent in vain. I just had to see what would happen if I turned it on. With my right hand extended stiffly, I switched the lever into what I believed was the start-up position.

A ball of static electricity crackled and leaped across the room. The hairs stood up on my arms and legs. The room grew brighter, almost blinding, as the ball rather than dissipate, grew in size. The machine started to hum, and the floor beneath my feet began to swell, and I felt it rupturing.

I fell across the table, almost upsetting the machine which was glowing as if red hot. As I touched it, I expected to be burned and was surprised to find it was cool. I pulled the lever from the device which activated it and fell to the floor. Immediately the room was plunged into darkness. The candle went out from a gust of wind that came out of nowhere, and the ball of electricity disappeared as suddenly as it had come.

Fear overcame me. I was in total blackness and could not tell if I had acted in time to stop the machine from doing any further damage.

I remained there on the floor for a long time and listened. There was no sound but my violent breathing. Presently I stood up and groped in the dark until I found the box of matches.

As the light flared out, I quickly looked around the chamber and found everything to be as it was before, with one exception. On the floor, beneath my feet, was a long, thin crack that extended over three-quarters of the way across the room.

The incident was sobering. Regaining my composure, I became conscious of the sound of breathing in the vault other than my own. It was across the room, small and huddled in a dark corner. It was terrified. The little thing must have come up when the cellar floor cracked. The floor had rolled and swelled beneath my feet just as the candle went out. Then the crack, possibly much larger than it was then, could have closed when the violence subsided along with that gust of wind. Or maybe he just passed through the atmosphere. The poor thing was probably a sentinel perched on the edge of our dimensional plane waiting for the proper time to lead its master when I accidentally pulled him over to our side with my meddling.

He was small, hairless and ugly, and although he had arms and a head, he was not human. For that matter, I don't know if "it" was male or female. It was small, very small like a newborn infant, but without any legs. It propelled itself with its two muscular limbs. If human in origin, which I doubt, it was another species of human being.

The "Other," as I came to call it, looked vicious but that evening it was more afraid of me than I of it. I felt sorry for the little creature and responsible. The "Other" eventually became comfortable with my appearance as I did with it and after a short span of time, I was able to cradle it in my arms. It seemed to take great comfort in this and although it was very alert and, I think if there had been more time for us together, I would have discovered the creature to be intelligent. Its needs were childlike depending on a lot of comforting and play. It would romp through the old schloss with amazing alacrity walking and running on its two hands. It would disappear for hours on end only to be discovered peering over my shoulder while I worked or read. I never found out what the Other ate. It refused the offer of any food nor did I witness any of its eating habits. But it always seemed healthy, and as the summer solstice approached, the Other became more comfortable with its surroundings.

I stopped feeling guilty about it being with me after a while. To the best of my knowledge, the Other appeared to be happy, and it would only be a few more months when I would be able to reunite it with its kind.

The months that followed were the happiest I had known since childhood. Peter would drop in for short durations, and we would exchange notes, while at the same time I felt that in no way my beloved solitude was being violated. I kept the Other hidden in the tower on these occasions. Although Peter moved to neighboring Valsbach, his business would keep him away at Stuttgart for weeks at a time. He was not candid in discussing his business matters, nor did I care to delve into his professional life.

I did not tell him of my blunder in the laboratory beneath the schloss, nor did I say anything about my certainty that the time was at hand. If I had been able to harbor enough energy to almost set free the minions at that time, then after the weeks that passed to June there should be enough power generating from the cosmos to complete the task.

I can hear the hollow, mocking laughter that is outside the thin shell of our world. It fires me with rage. It gives me insight, not of God or some rational scheme of things but of Cthulhu and a new world yet to come.

In the seventy-plus years that I have dwelled on this planet, I have witnessed the growth of grotesque art forms. As well as a horrible global war, countless bloodbaths all over Asia, the death of God, the disintegration of culture, the cremation of Hiroshima and an international drug culture. Now there is a type of music which causes measurable damage to the hearing, Hells Angles, and terrorist bombings, is it no wonder that I seek a change.

I did not want to tell Peter of my intentions until the gateway opened. I wanted no one to try to stop me, and there was just something about his manner which I did not trust. Forgive me, my friend, but when the gateway is open, and the confusion passes, I know that you will find your way to my home and knowing the truth, you may join me on the throne I will possess. We will make this world right, together and none will be as powerful. The Old Ones will rejoice and leave us to rule our planet while they regain their command over the vast universe. The human race will be ours to shape and to rise out of the ashes of disillusionment; we will create the New Reichstag.

It was during the span of one of those weeks that I made the third discovery. The strange hieroglyphics that decorated the wooden box housing the two antique components to my machine had taken on a curious appeal to me. It was not the type of pictorial writing I was familiar. They were in no way similar to any of the writings I encountered in Abdul Alhazred's Necronomicon or the Dr. Dee

English version; nothing like that which appeared on my diagram acquired from the Innsmouth sailor, nor did they resemble in any way the style of writing occasionally referred to in the Pnatonic Manuscripts. Although their likeness was unfamiliar to me, I had a gnawing feeling in my bones that their meaning would open new vistas for me in my research.

It was quite by accident that I finally discovered their meaning. There were few books left in my uncle's library after the war and one in particular that never held any appeal to me. It was Espenshade's Ancient History of Britton. The volume was written in English, which probably explains why none of the German soldiers during the occupation saw fit to steal it. I am, of course, well versed in the language but I had no desire to acquaint myself with the subject until one afternoon when I knocked the book from its shelf while searching for another item. When I reached down to pick the book from the floor, I was shocked to find the same hieroglyphics that I had been researching adorning the open page.

After a quick examination, I found the symbols to be Runic in origin, and I further learned that they had been carved ages ago on one of the monoliths at Stonehenge.

With the aid of the Espenshade's book and my gifted talents, I was able to translate the symbols after only three days of work.

The first part of the translation was familiar to me which made it easy for me to unravel the rest of the cipher. The second section, although following similar lines on the poetic scale as the first, was new and lifted a dark veil from my eyes.

The translation read:

IN HIS HOUSE IN R'LYEH DEAD
CTHULHU WAITS DREAMING

The second verse read:

BENEATH THE EARTH IN N'KAI

YATH-NOTEP LIES SLEEPING.

After this translation, things began to take on a clear meaning. After nearly forty years of collecting threads of information on the Commorium Cycle, N'Kai and Cthulhu, the fabric of the studies were finally, and for the first time, beginning to weave itself into a neat, concise pattern.

Cthulhu waits dreaming. Yath-Notep sleeps. They both remain eternal.

But who was Yath-Notep, a name unfamiliar to me? It had to be one of the lost Old Gods of Hyperborea, banished with Tsathoggua and the others by the Elders before the Great Cataclysm. Yath-Notep could only be the missing link, but the intent of such a deity clouded my imagination. Through decades of research and ceremonial incantations, could the cults dedicated to the Ancient Ones have been appealing to the wrong sources when attempting to find the link between the dimensions? When the third and last line of hieroglyphics were translated, the total of their parts and their transparent simplicity was a shock to me.

With this translation, I hold the secrets to unlock the gateway and the time of the return is at hand. The others have been fools to profess that they know the time, the place and the secret. I know that it is here and now, and I shall stand next to the Masters when they again take reign, as they conquer by fear this world which is rightfully theirs. I will be the most powerful of men, and even the Order of Dagon will kneel at my feet. They will worship me as their savior and king, the new time of the Great Old One will begin soon. I shall be the one to lead him forth from the dimensional prison he has been forced to dwell in for eons, imprisoned by the Elder Beings who took heed to the pitiful cries of the ancient races. The world will be ours, and the way littered with the rejects, pitiful human rejects!

The entire fabric of the conflict between the Great Race of the Elder Beings and the Old Ones became clear to me along with the incredible fact that a single Old One had escaped the terrible wrath of the Elder Beings. When they banished the Old Ones from our universe long before the first timid mammal was born; One who yet lived to haunt the Elder Beings, and that was Yath-Notep, the fierce demon god of Hyperborea!

The ancient lands of Atlantis, Lemuria, and Hyperborea worshipped Cthulhu until the Elders who watched our world took action against these races. To punish them, the Elder Beings caused the Great Cataclysm and sunk Atlantis and Lemuria beneath the oceans and ice. Hyperborea was destroyed by earthquakes and great bursts of fire which erupted from the bowels of the earth itself. It was at this time that Yath-Notep was sent to the inner dimension of black N'Kai to dwell there for eternity.

The Elder Race used the machine, the wonder which I now possess, to imprison the Old One. And, as they captured the thing, so shall I release it. I, Heinrich Todesfall, will open the gateway and set forth the great dark thing, Yath-Notep to cry forth into the multidimensional planes to the Ancient Ones. First, the minions shall come; Dagon and the Deep Ones, Yibb-Tsill and the Gaunts of Dark Night, Yig and its serpent children of Valusia, and all the others. Then shall follow the six Old Ones: Cthulhu, foremost of the Old Gods on Earth; Azathoth, most powerful Ancient One who blasphemes at the core of infinity, Yog-Sothoth, the all-in-one and conqueror of space and time; Shub-Niggurth, the black goat of the woods with a thousand young; Hastur, the unspeakable; and Ithaqua, the wind walker. They shall all come again to regain their thrones!

It is a great risk that I take that they will favor me to stand beside them in their new domain and not send me into a black murk of screaming slavery with the rest of the human race. But, without my aid, they would remain prisoners of their fate for eons more and perhaps for eternity. And what if, after some undetermined length of time, they were to find themselves thrust back once again behind those dimensional barriers, would they not need my assistance to battle the Elder Beings and release them again from their prisons?

Yes, I feel that I will be a very valuable Tanist for them and that they will make me a new Lord among their timeless deity. I shall be immortal with the Old Ones, and they will let me rule over this planet. Nothing will stand in my way! I hold the secrets! I have interpreted that which the Elder Beings have written! I know the powers behind the machine. I know the scientific secrets which come from the time of the Elder Race on Earth when they eventually lived here in Kadath, a metropolis which once covered the entire planet.

The Elder Beings came to our world from beyond the stars. They found that the universe was beautiful and promising, but it was ruled by their adversaries, the Old Ones. The Elder Beings knew that if this universe was ever to be inhabited by new life, first the Old Ones had to be banished.

The Great War followed wherein the Old Ones were defeated, and the Elder Beings could enjoy the beauty and wonders of our time and space. Eventually, they came to dwell on Earth, a particularly rich planet with incredible potential. They brought with them many races from other worlds and times and among these prehistoric creatures, man evolved.

The Elders left the world to Man and the others, and only one Elder Being remained behind. It was written that this Being became a Sentinel and using the machine it kept guard over the prison of Yath-Notep and his minions.

Through placid ignorance, man remained earthbound. It is my opinion that the early men of this region were meant to be gods, while the others will once again wallow in slime and squirm in slavery as subjects when I am master and take charge, releasing the Great Old Ones from their bonds. No longer will I be forced to view the inferior races of men as they abuse this world!

The time of revelations is at hand. The Great Ones will again take reign, and I hold the key to vague and secret visions of dim gulfs beyond this world. I now have in my possession the book that holds the solution to the puzzle and all the runic symbols have been translated revealing the hidden way across the void through time and space to the multi-dimensional worlds.

The hour draws near, and I must be concise in my account. It is unfortunate that most of humanity is too restricted in mental vision to consider with patience and intelligence those phenomena felt by only a few psychologically sensitive individuals.

Quite possibly it is merciful to keep the human beings that occupy this planet ignorant to their surroundings, but I feel that some men were meant to voyage far! Men of special intellect know that there is little distinction between the real and the unreal and that all things appear as they do through our conscious and subconscious mental images of them.

All these thoughts rushed in on me in what was the most lucid moment of my life. My brain reeled in giddy elation at the third deciphered line that was before me. The words that must have been carved into the lid of that box thousands of years ago caused those series of thoughts to come crashing in on me, and the pattern came together. There, impossible as it may seem, was my destiny laid bare before me. My translation was unmistakable, and after checking it against Espenshade's book a third time, my hands trembled so that I could scarcely hold the paper. I set it on the table before me and sat down to ponder my fate.

How in the world could this be possible? Could those past eons that held the imprisonment of the ancient gods also included me in what now seemed an age-old plan. There could be no other answer. I had no choice but to discount coincidence and embrace the words before me.

The last line read:

YATH-NOTEP WAITS FOR THE SIGN FROM TOD-FAL

***

To people lacking the clear and distinct vision I possess it would seem that these writings were the ravings of a madman, but, is it not so that there are legends which are older than man? How then did we come by them if an intelligent force apart from man didn't convey them to this world? Of course, man has transformed them and molded them to conform to his pre-conceived notions of the universe. The ancient writings still exist and the age-old legends of mankind's early history, vague and unconnected as they may seem, remain everlasting through the generations.

For all the ages of man, there have been few who knew the truth, the ones who dedicated their entire being to the discovery of the power and the secrets of demonology and Satan, as it was foolishly labeled. If the people of our world knew or even had the slightest conception of the different dimensions and worlds beyond ours, they would welcome their imaginary devil with open arms.

Fantastic I know it must sound in the face of the scientific world we live in, but what is magic and what is science, except the preconceived notions of men. After all, is not black magic a science unto itself? Those dark brotherhoods consisting of alchemists, sorcerers, and magicians who worked and fought through the decades for the power and truth are all pitiful failures compared to me. The knowledge of Yath-Notep's existence is mine alone, and with this knowledge, my power will build, and when the time is at hand, I will open the gateway.

***

I received a letter from the Order of Dagon pertaining to a recent intercourse about my studies. They take delight in disagreeing with me at my every turn. Now they choose to argue about the time of the cosmic elations. They say the revelation time will be in the Fall, on the night of Satan and his hosts. I proclaim that it will be a midsummer's eve and the fools will soon know that they were wrong. Even Peter has sided with his old order on this matter, and I feel that it has affected our friendship because he has not been around in a while.

But my theories will soon be fact. I will call Yath-Notep to come forth from his chamber and he, in turn, will set his master Cthulhu free. The hour has finally come. The last forty years have culminated to this point. I will try to be concise with my notes.

The Other is in the tower. I have made everything ready in the vault. I have closed the magic shape on the floor with the name of Yath-Notep, and the powders burn orange in the clay urn. The machine gleams yellow in the light. It rests on top of the old wood table. I have not dared to activate the device since that one night, nor have I even attempted to place the two artifacts in their matching receptacles again, until now. The two pieces are in place. I have pulled the serpentine lever which was used so many centuries ago by the Elder One to put this machine to its devastating use.

There is a sudden humming and vibrating, and the mirrors are spinning at odd angles. The device needs no fuel or electrical power to run, and even though I was its builder, I doubt that I will ever know what powers feed it. The mirrors spin faster and faster, and the vibrations are not unlike the drone of many bees. The glass is beginning to reflect the light from the burning powders in the urn, causing orange fingers of light to streak about the room and to make geometric patterns on the rafters.

I am wearing the traditional robes of the alchemists. I feel the power building. I can hear the calling from the cosmos. My heart is pounding fast with anticipation. It is only minutes from the time. I am in awe, I have begun the incantations I acquired from the compilation of the two Necronomicons and the arithmetical hand signs that were on the scroll. First, the traditional words from the Book of Eibon as spoken by the countless sorcerers throughout the ages, then the ritual from Britton, as practiced by the magicians of old England. I have listed the Great Old Ones and voiced salutations to each in turn. You will find all of this in my notes. My voice booms loudly in the vault, and at times it would seem a tempest rages forth from my lips to shake the supporting timbers above. Dust is cascading down around me. Something is coming over me, a sensation, as if I am observing this from afar, and not participating. I see myself raising my hands over my head and hear the succession of words I knew so well echo back at me; "Kiah . . . Kiah . . . Rignum Azathoth! Kiah . . . Kiah . . . Rignum Hastur," and the rest.

I have formed the nine angles with my hands. "Kraken . . . Poseidon . . . Sabazios . . . Typon . . . Dagon . . . Setheh . . . Xicarph . . . Yath-NoTep . . . Cthulhu!"

I am taking this and myself to the limit and soon will be rewarded with the powers I will command. A brilliant light fills the cellar, and the mirrors glow with the approaching power. My mind is exceptionally clear; I can see a green mist begin to form on the floor of the vault. The very earth shakes, and a form is molding into various shapes. The mists are glowing, and I feel the ground beneath my feet swelling again. The form is taking a different shape. I am about to set free one of the servants of the Old Ones. The shape is filtering up past the rafters and actually through the ceiling. It and the beams of light from the machine are both fed off the stars in the cosmos above. I can see past the house and into the night sky as the power grows from the starlight.

There is a cry of fury from the creature that is taking form. The sound is so immense that I just screamed in mental pain along with the thing. I feel faint. The cellar is filling with other shapes and mists are oozing from the floor. The minions are gathering; shoggoths, night gaunts, serpent men, ready to come forth and make way for their master. I can feel it!

(Note: at this point, the legibility of Heinrich Todesfall's journal became very poor.)

The green mass is still growing upward. It is amazing. I can see its ascent by way of the ceiling. I can follow it through the many levels of the schloss into the night sky...I can see the stars above plainly as if I was standing outdoors . . . It is standing before me making squealing, slopping noises, it is changing shape again. It is rearing itself up to a tremendous height above the schloss.

It is done, I have completed the ritual.

The machine is working. The shape is familiar, I know it.

There is a hole . . . Oh Lord, that hol . . . Those things will come up from . . .

I could not have been mis . . .

I see it now; it is a hand . . . a giant hand . . . And it is pointing down at me!

PART III

A SOLDIER FELL HERE

The continuation of Janet's Story

I didn't finish reading until the last blush of sunset was masked from view by the distant hills. Nervous and shaken I downed one of my few remaining valium and sat motionless staring at the larger high back chair in the parlor. The sound of the word I had phonetically spelled "Thoo-Loo" kept echoing in my head. The last word uttered by the Doctor before leaving that evening, and now the name of Cthulhu as set down by the old man in his notebook, undoubtedly is the same.

Old man hell, sorcerer or lunatic is more like it, and here I sit looking at his chair. The Alchemist's throne. The carvings on that piece of furniture were so vaguely familiar at one time, but now it's all clear. They were the same as on the grave marker in the field and identical to the carvings on the old knife, most likely the image of Todesfall's god Cthulhu. If what he wrote of had some basis in fact, then were these creatures omnipotent, or were they a form of super beings shackled in an invisible prison and only seeming god-like to us because of their sheer power and longevity.

There were, I knew, certain strange and horrible survivals of religions or cults far more ancient than Christianity. Possibly Faren's great uncle practiced one of these surviving religions and his madness warped and deluded by time, and the Nazis forced him over the edge into unholy and unspeakable rites.

Good heavens, could he have made sacrifices to Cthulhu? Could they have been human sacrifices? I recalled the newspaper of that afternoon and the killings mentioned in it occurring less than a year before. Todesfall was still alive then. Could he have been the child killer? And what about that young girl? Did some maniacal religious cult snuff out a life not yet on the verge of blossoming or even worse, did she fall prey to some horror that was conjured up?

There may be another type of survival involved, something known as psychic residue, the lingering of evil in places where evil had once flourished. I have read that many paranormal investigators attribute it to a haunting. A traumatic death occurs, and a psychic memory of it resides in an inanimate object. This surviving residue could be a vast secret of primal knowledge that has extended for ages into the past and threatened to impend for ages into the future; an evil that has dwelt for ages in the shadows biding its time waiting to come forth and overwhelm all life. Is the gateway, as Todesfall called it, between the two worlds already open? Maybe it always was, and we are now just beginning to experience its effects?

Night came, and the fog rolled in steadily from the Black Forest. Faren was late, and I was afraid, but nowhere near as I was angry. I wanted a showdown. I wanted an answer to all his secrecy, and I wanted him home. I called the base, but they said he was in a meeting and could not be disturbed. I didn't care to be alone that particular evening. Many of my evenings were spent alone; all the same, I was unable to dispel the feelings of impending disaster.

I kept thinking of the child that I carried within me and the child that was so ruthlessly slain in the woods last night. I was terribly alone. There was no one inside of ten miles from the schloss. I am not sure why I did what followed. It must have been out of utter desperation for someone to talk to that drove me to so irrational of an act that now ranks high in my moments of insanity. I named my unborn child that evening and talked to the five-month fetus calling over and over to him, "Michael, Michael, everything will be all right." I wanted to reach out to someone, but there was no one there.

I caressed my abdomen gently. The outline was beginning to show the signs of my pregnancy. I imagined our pink smiling son cradled in my arms.

It was growing darker in the parlor, and I turned on our only lamp in the room. It was a bright lamp, and it illuminated the area. I was running a gamut of emotions. Within the next instant, I decided that inactivity was the devil's plaything and began to look for something to keep me busy. I pulled out the vacuum, turned on the radio to an English speaking broadcast and busied myself with cleaning the rug.

The radio commentator was joking about a celestial phenomenon known as the "Jupiter effect, a rare time" he said, "when the planets of our solar system in their orbits about the sun come into perfect alignment between Mercury and Jupiter." The noise of the radio drowned out when I switched on the vacuum. The radio and sweeper gave me a sense of security blanketed by the infusion of sounds.

I kept myself occupied for some time until I heard a rattling. I couldn't be sure if it were my imagination or a new form of punk rock coming across the airwaves penetrating the racket of the vacuum. Switching off the machine and turning down the radio I stood very still listening. All was silent. Some time passed, then the racket resumed suddenly and then ceased as abruptly as it had started. It came from the kitchen. I stepped lightly across the threshold between the kitchen and the parlor and looked around.

I found nothing out of place. The door and windows were secure, and all the cooking utensils appeared to be where I had left them last. I was about to leave the kitchen for the well-lit parlor when I noticed the drawer beneath the sink board slightly ajar, about an inch or so out past the opening. When I tried to close the drawer, it became jammed. Upon examining the interior, I found what had dislodged it. The writhing figures were only half visible in the shadows. It was unmistakably the knife. The evil looking dagger Faren had found. It was where he had last left it, but not quite in the same spot.

I remembered closing the cutlery drawer when I did the breakfast dishes that morning. It was in the back section where I keep the carving knives, and it closed without difficulty at the time. Now it had, by some means, been moved to the front with the hilt of the handle wedged between the drawer face and the underside of the sink board.

The appearance of the dagger, by then, upset me. It conjured up thoughts of Heinrich Todesfall, of weird little fish men and grave robbing. Not wanting to look at it anymore I returned it to the rear compartment where it belonged and quickly slid the drawer shut.

I couldn't have been back to my vacuuming for more than a few minutes when the noise of rattling cutlery started up again. I heard the drawer being yanked open and then there was a clatter as something dropped to the floor.

In the time it took to switch off the vacuum cleaner and let the hose drop to the carpet I was in the kitchen. The cutlery drawer was open wide, on the brink of becoming detached from the framework that held it beneath the counter. A fraction of an inch more and it would have fallen spilling my dinnerware. In the middle of the floor, a good five feet from the kitchen counter lay the old knife. My nerves were already pushed to their limit. So you can imagine the horror and dread I felt when I heard something skitter across the linoleum. My skin crawled in folds up the back of my neck, and I froze.

With a sideward glance, I saw by the light coming from the parlor a small and furry dark thing scurry across the room towards the cellar door. Whatever the little creature was (about the size of a small dog) it suddenly disappeared when, after overcoming my paralysis, I was able to move my head and look directly at it. It vanished. One moment it was there and the next it was gone. I know I saw and heard it, not clearly, but I know it was there.

An invisible spirit that can only be seen out of the corner of the eye, and then I remembered the "other" from the journal . . . Todesfall's mysterious little creature.

Unsteadiness overcame me. The memory of those passages combined with what I saw, or thought I saw, gave way to anxiety. An indefinite number of minutes elapse before I recovered enough to move. Forcing myself to take a deep breath I propelled myself to the cellar door and without so much as a glance below, closed and bolted it shut.

The exact order of the events that followed has become a free-for-all of ghostly phantoms. I believe I scooped the knife up from the floor holding tightly onto it feeling a bit comforted by having a weapon in hand. I was no longer afraid of the dagger, instead, rather the thing that was so intent on having it.

It was then that Faren called. I jumped at the sound of the phone ringing. I must have sounded very upset. I was ecstatic when I heard him on the line. I became hysterical. I begged him to come home. I kept yammering and screaming about the old knife moving around. I was crying and carrying on. I am sure I didn't make much sense. I probably scared the hell out of Faren. After struggling to get a word in he shouted and said that Jim hadn't been back with Vesta yet, but he wouldn't wait for him. Instead, he would take a taxi right away and leave word for Jim to follow.

He hung up, and I took another Valium. By then I had lost count of the quantity I'd consumed in the last hour. My hands shook so much I could scarcely open the bottle. I knew I was overdoing it with the drug. VonTassell had warned me against excess in my condition, but my imagination was in high gear. It was no longer conjecture as to the vocation of Faren's great uncle. I knew by then he must have been in some way a sorcerer of the black arts. How else could these turn of events have occurred? The dreams that have invaded my sanity or the eerie quality of this old house, not to mention the wooded glade and the stories whispered about it in the village. Then there is still that horrid garden, concealment or a crude joke to shield a cemetery for so many. In retrospect, I shudder at the image of all those holes dug at the head of each grave and the deranged mind that had made them.

Why had my legs been bruised and my stockings torn after waking from a dream wherein I was attacked about the ankles from below by a dark thing? Good, God! Could that have been real? Could my dream have been a reflection of real events, but what about that picture, the photograph taken by Jim Ruttick; wasn't that real? Could the fuzzy image have been Todesfall's "other" or one of those spirits of the hills? Maybe they are one and the same. Perhaps the camera saw what the naked eye could not.

The old alchemist Todesfall and his god Cthulhu; was this his reality and now it has become ours. Is there some unknown force out there that waits dreaming, fettered in a tomb although gigantic in proportions is at the same time so very minute that we are blind to its existence or rather its coexistence. How could any one person endure madness long enough to bring such a pestilence to earth? Have all the events which have lead up to this evening, and God knows how far beyond been the results of a foul deed only left half done.

I staggered across the parlor to the staircase. I felt giddy, partly from the valium and in part from the images I imagined. I hurried upstairs as quickly as I could. I wanted a place to lie down and wait out Faren's return. Before propping myself up in bed, I inspected the linen cases on each pillow. They were clean. I eased myself into a comfortable position.

Trying to sway my mind to more pleasant thoughts I concentrated for a while on the wallpaper, and the sun faded patterns of smiling children carrying baskets of flowers. I tried to imagine a childhood fairyland of sugar and spice. But I could not help from thinking about those poor souls buried beneath the tall oaks and pines only a short distance from our backyard. It sickened me that our home should lay so near to a burial ground, while at the same time my heart ached with pity, because of the violent way they had died and the mutilation their bodies must have suffered at the hands of Heinrich Todesfall.

The window was open and the thick mist that had blanketed the grounds every night rolled in at its usual time as if on cue. The glare of the bed lamp impaired my view outdoors. I turned it off and went to the window. The fog was much heavier than in the past. It crawled across the earth at a much higher rate of speed than I had ever seen. Lifelike, almost inspired in appearance, it fingered its way around every rock, hummock and tree stump that lay in its path and then resembling a swirling eddy of liquid the fog surrounded and surmounted each obstacle, enveloping them in a milky white tide pool.

For a while, I sat there transfixed by the ethereal movements of the fog until I noticed that it wasn't coming from within the Black Forest as it usually did. Instead, the mist came from the South end of the field! A lump swelled in my throat when I noticed the mist pouring upward from a small hole in the earth located directly in the center of the hill . . . the same hill that had appeared just days before.

At that moment a clap of thunder shook the house giving me a terrible start. It was followed by several more, like rapid gunfire. I moved to the edge of the bed and switched the lamp back on. The thunder was louder than I had ever heard in the region. I froze momentarily when between the peals of thunder I detected the low murmur of voices. I couldn't make out what was said but a light whispering filtered up from the courtyard at the rear of our property.

Even though it was still too early for his return, I hoped it was Faren. Going to the window again I looked out, but there was no one in sight. The fog had taken on the eerie green quality as it did when I first noticed the clearing that night from the tower, and as on that evening, I again detected movement in the glade amongst the wisps of vapor.

There wasn't time to think about it because the bedroom began to tremble and shake. The old chandelier wavered so that I was afraid it was going to rip loose from its ceiling mounts and violently crash to the floor. My perfume and cologne bottles on top of the dresser rattled, and a deep far-off rumbling vibrated me to the bone.

The bed table lamp flickered and grew dim casting intermittent strobe-like shadows across the wall. The images of the children imprinted on the wall covering began to change. Their smiles took on an evil quality. There were dark areas beneath the eyes, and the flowers they carried were no longer colorful but wilted brown, dead.

Before I ran screaming from the sight pushing my way through the bedroom and downstairs at breakneck speed, I managed one last look out the window. The yawning aperture located within the center of the hill had doubled in size, and in that brief instant, I observed a heavy thick cloud of vapor belch forth spewing a dark silhouetted thing upward. Less than a second had elapsed during the entire nightmarish spectacle, but it was long enough for me to make out a human outline, size, and shape, sporting wings of enormous size. It traveled through space straight up and out of plain view.

When I reached the kitchen, I stood there racked with fear and indecision. I suppressed any screaming long enough to notice the cutlery drawer hanging open and my entire dinner service for eight strewn across the linoleum. It had come back again, only to be disappointed. I hadn't realized until that moment that I still clutched the ancient dagger in my right hand since I first picked it up off the floor.

All that remained as sane and logical for me to do was to get away and somehow find help. Still clutching the dagger, I grabbed the car keys off the nail in the back door casing and fled outdoors.

The car was in the garage since my return from the village. I wasted no time in reaching it. There was no electricity within the old shed, and an inky blackness almost impenetrable had me fumbling my way to the car door.

Our German compact was old, and not all of its mechanical functions were in order. The courtesy lights would not operate when the door was open. The total darkness made me even more anxious. While nervously attempting to locate the ignition key on the ring, a noxious odor diverted my attention. It was the smell of decaying animal flesh. Following the strong stench was the drip, drip, dripping of rain showering the front fenders except it wasn't raining outside. There was thunder, of course, but no rain had fallen yet. And besides, the car was under cover.

Panic-stricken, I fumbled with the keys and dropped them to the car floor. Quickly I scrambled on all fours like an animal in search of them. There was nothing to see. The quiet night was interrupted by occasional claps of thunder and the continual dripping. I felt lost; without sight or a friendly sound, I could only rely on my sense of touch. Within a short time, I heard the puffing of heavy breathing. I swear my heart skipped a beat because I had the dreaded sensation that I wasn't alone. I darted frantically back and forth across the car seat on my hands and knees slipping on the slick upholstery and slid headlong into the steering wheel raising a small welt on my forehead. I felt like a fool. The breathing I heard was my own. My heart felt as if it was in my stomach and through all the excitement I had failed to realize the simple source of light that lay at my fingertips. Feeling incredibly stupid, I sat up and turned on the headlights. The beams lit the garage interior.

Briefly, I sat there disgusted with myself for behaving so childishly and in the next second I was clutched in stark terror. An unbelievable and grotesque sight stood over the front fender leering down at me with rotted sockets for eyes. It was a man. He was in the tattered remains of some uniform. The unblemished portions of his flesh were a sickly hue while most of the exposed tissue was cankered and rotted with large cancerous boils. The right side of the man's skull had been ripped away revealing a dark, pulpy mass the surface of which was tainted with a heavy layer of white maggots. Small segments of the cranium kept breaking away from the decaying matter lightly showering the sheet metal skin of the sedan with the limbless larva resembling the sound of falling rain.

The corpse creature staggered forward several steps and then flopped over the front fender. A chunk of dislodged brain matter rolled across the engine hood, leaving a fine trail of particles and came to rest against the windshield. The thing pulled itself up. I screamed.

There is blackness, a void in my memory. I recall running. I ran harder than I ever had in my life. For some insane reason, I went in the direction of the field. Towards that tumbleweed and root infested glade that terrified me.

Why did I choose that of all directions? In retrospect, I don't believe I can say that I ran in blind terror, because now, when I look back, I cannot for the life of me imagine why, no matter what state of mind I was in, I would have wandered into the woods. The road or even the house would seem like the logical place to flee for safety, all the same; I still don't remember.

No matter how many times I call to mind the thing I saw while seated in the car, it is like trying to redeem from oblivion those sequences of events that must have taken place afterward causing me to run into the woods. Unless, I did start out for the road, but I was stopped . . . stopped by something possibly even more horrifying than that rotting thing in my garage. Yes, maybe that was the answer. Whenever I think back on it for some reason, I'm struck with nervous anticipation at even the thought of that long dark driveway, the only access to the road.

It's like a vague memory of a certain feeling or a vague notion of dread. Maybe it was something so terrible that my mind blotted it out. If it was that awful, then I shudder to imagine what it must have been for the path I chose led me toward other terrors. The darkness was impenetrable, like the garage. The mist had risen so high that it blotted out the stars. I ran in abandonment of anything that lay in my path. Thorns and brambles tore at my skin and clothing. The cold ripping fingers of the overgrowth across my flesh was made painless by my dazed state of mind. I collided with a large unseen object. Driven by the force of the contact I toppled over backward. It was the gravestone of Heinrich Todesfall. The black piece of masonry had become invisible under the starless and moonless night sky.

My eyes gradually grew accustomed to the dark. I could make out the clock at the base of the monolith. The hour hand looked to be a little closer to twelve than I last recalled. I heard ticking. Something had started the clockworks. Possibly the earth tremors had been responsible for the audible tick, tick, ticking of its mechanism. A strong vibration could have set some part to moving within the clock. The clock's ticking, mingled with the gentle breeze that played amongst the trees, was a terrifying effect.

My run-in with the dark tombstone had brought me back to my senses. Withdrawing from it and the incessant ticking, I backed into a stout oak. I felt closed in, a profound sensation of choking claustrophobia overcame me. I scanned the dense thicket for a way home.

My eyes darted back and forth across the bordering brushwood. All about me lay the impression of impending doom. The dark, twisted trees and tall grass that circled the glade gradually accorded an alien life force. The soft breeze made the movement of the scrub wood appear animated. The thick and powerfully shaped branches gave the impression of grotesque caricatures of human limbs that became mystically imbued with a spirit that was tenacious of life.

Glowing orbs, spherical masses of eyes emerged between the gaps in the thicket and became fixed on me.

I could make out vague shadowy forms moving amongst the dark patches of the evening gloom. Pairs of staring eyes moved excitedly back and forth while some moved singularly in unison with silhouetted shapes. There were labored movements followed by a shuffling and dragging.

I wanted to leave but froze in my tracks upon seeing several hideous corpse creatures emerge from the thicket into the clearing and stagger towards me. They converged upon me from all directions. I was in the center of a circle formed by their inward plodding.

One of the figures was the partially headless thing I had seen in the garage. This time I recognized its clothing. It was a German army uniform. Through the heavy mist and darkness, I could make out a badly soiled swastika below the right shoulder.

The others were almost naked or wore the meager tatters of different uniforms. They were void of most of their flesh while several of them had limbs reduced to mere stubs. One of the walking corpses was the body of a woman. She was entirely unclothed, and her sex had been rendered repulsive by mutilation and decay. Her left side had been torn away leaving her with a worm-eaten and rotted cavity where the other breast should have been.

The walking dead were clothed in the remnants of the American army, some German, while others I was unable to identify, all, except for the female, had the appearance of military leavings. All of them showed visual signs of mutilation about the mouth and jaw, and they were caked with damp soil as well as the clotted residue of blood and mangled flesh.

I didn't cry out, not even so much as a whimper. Numbed by a sickening feeling in the pit of my stomach, I became paralyzed. I observed one of the undead rise from an earthen grave and join the swelling multitude. Many small mounds and hummocks that disrupted the otherwise flat ground erupted from the inside out!

The group swelled to six or seven. They had completely encircled me. I wanted to cover my eyes and scream but was terrified of what I might see when I uncovered them again if given a chance. Too frightened to close my eyes, in fear of what they might do to me if I took my eyes off them. I dropped my hands to my side ready to succumb to my fate and wept hysterically.

Their lumbering advance stopped about six feet from me. One of them spoke! It was a weak drawn out voice muffled as if being spoken through several layers of cloth. Still, I was able to make out the words.

"Help us," it said. Simply, "Help us."

It caught me totally off guard, and I broke into a tirade of unrestrained laughter. They seemed dumbfounded. They each looked like someone who had failed to understand the punch line of a joke. I couldn't help myself. Here I was amongst the greatest horrors imaginable frantically searching for a means of escape and one of them asks me for help!

A second figure hesitated as if employing extreme caution then approached slowly taking a few steps forward voicing the same words.

Soon a third joined in. Another took up the words, then another until they were a chorus chanting, "Help us."

Over and over they uttered the pitiful words. One especially misshapen thing that had been rendered mute by the absence of a lower jaw opened and closed its left hand in a clutching rhythm miming the others repetitive chant.

My back was still to the tree, but they kept their distance. They uttered their prattle as if afraid to come any closer. A corpse creature somewhat less decomposed than the rest, the body of an American I believe, broke ranks and we came face to face. He rested the putrefied remains of his mummified hand on my bare arm. I shrank away from his touch, and he moved closer, looked at me with his dead eyes and mouthed the same words. The flesh on his face no longer resilient with the essence of life cracked and flaked into pieces from the jaw movements. His mouth was toothless and maggot riddled with a cold breath that reeked with the foul stench of decay.

Sickened I averted my attention in a downward glance to fight off nausea. I looked down and saw another mound of dirt next to my feet. At one end of the unopened grave, a face was pushing up from out of the soil. With great effort, it too was mouthing the two words.

I pushed hard against the trunk of the tree and propelled myself at a good speed from the center of the encircling nightmares. I collided into one of them with a hollow sounding thud. The force of the collision drove the thing backward. It was the woman. I turned as I fled to see her body, a great pulpy mass, break apart and scatter amongst the brushwood. The sight was grotesque. It triggered a flash of childhood memory. I was no more than six or seven playing in the woods near my parent's home when I had come across a large toadstool at least a foot in diameter. I playfully kicked the umbrella-shaped fungi and watched it burst into bits and pieces. The woman's body broke apart in the same manner. Her breast lay amid the briar. Her arms and legs still writhing with their supernatural life force were strewn about the tall grass. And her head, Oh God, her head! It was resting on its side in the dirt, the lips still moving, still laboriously forming those same two words, "Help us."

I wasted no time in putting a great deal of distance between myself and the walking dead. The pace in which I ran compared to their heavy plodding movements must have put them a good way behind.

I paused at the edge of the wood next to a cluster of slash pines and drew the night air deep into my lungs swallowing several times. The taste of nausea was still lingering in my throat, and I felt dizzy from the long sprint. I could make out the rear of our home through the fog. The persistent mist stirred like an eddy and between its ebb and flow, I caught short but clear glimpses of the schloss. A light had shown brightly from the kitchen and parlor windows. It didn't look as menacing as it did just a short while ago and by then I felt it was my best sanctuary until Faren's return.

I contemplated the eerie mist, the wallpaper that assumed its evil visage, the knife that had remained in my hand all that time and the spirit that was after it.

In all the time that I was plagued by those undead creatures of the night I never once thought of using the dagger for protection. As grotesque as they were I found it in my heart to pity them. Besides their appearance, they did nothing to harm me. I was sympathetic towards them. The terrible fate that God for some unknown reason saw fit to bestow upon them was unthinkable. They were human at one time. All they did was fight in a war a generation ago. They were doing what they were told to do. Doing what they believed was right. Sometime, almost forty years ago a soldier fell here, many soldiers fell. Some from a bullet, some by mortar fire and many by God know's what other machines manufactured to inflict wholesale death. The evening air was tranquil once again. The wind had died down. There was not even a faint rumbling in the hills, and the brushwood was still and quiet. My pursuers must have given up. I could no longer hear their lumbering movements.

I made for the house. I was a bit more courageous by then, and the warm glow of the windows seemed to encourage my return.

I could lock the old schloss uptight and bide my time keeping a lookout until Faren came home. Moreover, I wasn't quite up to another trip to the garage, and the thought of marching down that dark, lonely private drive to the open road was still terrifying. It likewise was still an unrecognizable fear, but a fear none-the-less, even if I could not put it into words or understand its source.

I ventured towards more open ground in the direction of the schloss. In what seemed like only a few seconds I heard a flapping coming from above. At first, it was a good distance off, yet in only seconds it grew in volume sounding like the beating of large leathery wings. A loud thud resounded followed by rustling among the bushes. Something massive had landed nearby. From somewhere within the brushwood came a low growl. It was a forced throaty gurgle resembling a vicious animal snarl.

I made for the house in a wild frenzy. The growl, the leather flapping of wings, sent an unearthly chill up my spine. They were frightfully familiar to me. As a child who is afraid of a vague nightmare, I ran from the sounds in a blind panic.

I sprinted up the back steps and pulled frantically on the doorknob. The old door rattled and shook in its antique frame, but it didn't budge. The latch remained fast. The sounds of the growling thing grew louder, I tugged and pulled at the latch, but to no avail. Then briefly overcoming the panic long enough to come to my senses, I remembered locking it on my way to the garage, and the keys were still lying there, somewhere in the car where I had dropped them.

I imagined the hot breath of my unknown pursuer on the nape of my neck. Hoping and praying that the front door was unlocked I made a mad dash around to the front entrance. I bounded the porch steps in two strides, and to my delight after momentarily fumbling with the latch, the door opened, and I spun around into the peaceful security of the parlor.

I hastily bolted the door and wasted no time in securing all the windows. I even tested the bolt on the cellar door. When completed, I went about lighting every candle and lamp I could find. There were only three sources of electrical illumination within the old chateau, and they were the kitchen light, the one in the parlor and the third upon our bed table.

Despite having only a couple working electrical outlets in the house, I was still able to illuminate most of the rooms brightly.

You can imagine my fear and apprehension when the telephone went dead. I had made one call before the line went blank, thank goodness. I got through to Fort Blish once again only to learn that Faren had left sometime before in a taxi. Next, I attempted to make another call to the local police for help, the line suddenly became silent, and I was unable to raise the operator.

About a quarter of an hour had passed when the phone rang. I was sitting in the parlor when it happened and jumped out of my seat. I snatched the receiver from its cradle. Nervous, hopeful, I wished it to be my husband. It was silent as a tomb on the other end. I raised my voice and hollered into the receiver but got no answer. I was about to hang-up when I detected a queer noise on the line. At first, it sounded like a slight gurgle or the bubbling of liquid, a deep resonate, watery reply. The voice was foreign, but the accent did not resemble any tongue that I knew. It sounded as if the person on the other end of the line was having great difficulty with human speech. The pattern of speech was abbreviated, and the continual gurgling made it extremely difficult to understand. I asked whoever it was to speak up. There was a long pause and then in the same voice, and with audible signs of great effort it said, "Is this the woman of Todesfall?" I slammed the receiver down and trembled.

Downing another of the small yellow pills the Doctor had given me, I noticed that I had only one remaining. I was numbed more by the events of the evening than the drug itself. Calmly I obtained my diary from the lower drawer of the writing desk and leafed through its blank pages. It was a Christmas gift that I had tucked away with all good intentions but never got around to using. I was confident that my obituary would be as valueless as this unattended record.

Starting at the first page and ignoring the printed dates, I proceeded to tell my story in episodic detail.

***

Several hours must have elapsed since my telephone conversation with Faren, and he has not yet shown. Even if he had some difficulty finding a cab he should have been home over an hour ago.

The valium is beginning to sap my strength. I'm emotionally and physically drained. I have written everything that I dare and most of what I recall. I have left very little to conjecture, and I sense that my time has run out.

As I wrote in the beginning, I didn't believe that the terrors that lingered outdoors would venture across my threshold until the evening mist could hide their advance. Not so much from my eyes but from any passing motorist that may be using the old road late at night. If ever the time were right, it is now. The fog has completely engulfed the house and the surrounding grounds. The white vapor has visibly blocked every window, and the leaded panes run heavy with the moisture of dew. It is conceivable that Faren found the road impassable and he is waiting for the weather to lift.

In the past minute or two, I am certain I heard a rustling in the bushes outside my window, followed by a brief succession of heavy footsteps. For one fleeting second, I think I saw a face, the crude outline of something peering in through the parlor window. It happened so quickly that when I turned my head around it was gone, barely leaving enough time for a mental after image to register. I questioned my sanity, as I was becoming accustomed to by then, but my suspicions quickly vanished when I noticed the moist impression of a face on the pane of glass.

My exhaustion was so complete that I was hardly affected by it. If anything, it registered nothing more than a mild shiver.

My time is up, and I haven't the heart to cry out anymore. They can do what they want with me. My desire for life was outweighed by my complete and utter frustration.

I can hear the bushes at the north end of the house moving now. I know it is not the wind.

Something is thudding and grunting on the front porch. It's

scratching, scratching on the casing.

The main entrance is old but the door is strong, and the latch bolt is of heavy iron.

What is happening to me? Everything about me, no matter how dull and commonplace the day to day routine is, eventually becomes my personal horror. Everything from the bedroom wallpaper to a simple walk in the woods has taken on nightmarish proportions.

Oh God, it speaks! It's those words again, similar to those uttered by VonTassell in my dream. This time the voice isn't human, it's like it was on the telephone just hours before. A deformed mouthing as of some bestial creature with only half a tongue uttered syllables of meaningless horror.

Oh, God! The door is bending inward!

***

I am alive! Good God in heaven, I am safe! My arms are bandaged from the elbows to the wrists, but I am all right. I am at home, in bed, Faren is here, and so is VonTassell. I believe Jim is downstairs as well.

VonTassell gave me something to make me sleep, but the injection is slow at taking effect. I have been fighting the drowsiness ever since he saw the old alchemist's notebook curled up on the bedside table. The moment he laid eyes on it I snatched up the yellowed pages and tucked them behind the pillow. He acted suspiciously.

I know who Peter is . . . the one and only friend of my husband's late uncle . . . the old alchemist's friend and confidant and I am certain that VonTassell senses it. We stared long and hard at one another without exchanging any words. It was then that he gave me the sedative.

"Something to make you sleep, my dear," he said.

I asked to see Faren, but he countered with, "You must rest now."

I have to warn Faren; I am too weak to call out loud enough to be heard. The bedroom door is closed, and they are downstairs in the kitchen.

My strength is ebbing fast. I must fight this drug. It is a great effort for me to write.

Faren had come, in the nick of time. I was very lucky. He probably frightened them away. When the front door was about to give way, I rose to my feet and grabbed the old knife. This time I was prepared to use it as a weapon. My fear was put temporarily in check by the sudden and unexpected anger that raged within me. I was terrified by the unknown intruder but backed into a corner; I anticipated a fight to the death.

The old door cracked and splintered followed by a ferocious grunting upon the other side. The thing on my doorstep was only moments from entry.

I reached down within myself, summoned up the strength to slide our oak writing desk across the room and up against the hardwood door frame. I heavily secured the latch bolt by wedging the fire poker between it and the bolt carriage thus doubling the strength of the lock.

The thing on the opposite side of the passage must have recognized the change in the barrier because in less than a minute it broke into a bellowing tirade. It beat furiously on the door and moments later it hurled one of the large stone urns that rested on the porch outside through the bay window. The concrete urn was a good four feet in length and must have weighed well over two hundred pounds. It burst through the locked casement like a cannon shot. The triple sash panes inwardly exploded from the force spraying the room with splinters of glass. The urn impacted against the fireplace cracking the marble hearth.

I made for the stairs in a mad frenzy. If this creature was going to come for me, I had one more surprise in store for it. At the top of the stairs before the hall to the bedrooms stood another urn similar to the one that had just crashed through the window. If the thing came upstairs, I would roll the urn down the staircase and crush it, whatever it may be.

I don't know what possessed me; I was an animal. I was just as much an animal as that thing outside. I backed slowly up the stairs. Fear pulsated in my veins. Bloodlust and vengeance consumed my heart; I had to survive at all costs. I held the knife ready to pounce on any living thing that might cross my path. My lips curled downward twisting and contorting my features to what I imagine must have been a deranged look. Perspiration matted my hair, and it hung over the right side of my face. I reached the landing. The large pot was within my grasp, yet nothing came. There was only silence and not a thing stirred by the open bay. From the rear of the house disrupting the calm came a loud banging. Someone or something pounded on the back door. I was sure it was a trick . . . a ruse to get me back down into the parlor and catch me off guard. It must have second guessed my scheme. I wasn't going to move. Oh no, I wasn't going to fall prey to its strategy. My pursuer was going to have to come for me. I got behind the urn and made ready to push.

I stood fearlessly in the shadows. My eyes were wide and my breathing frantic. My eyes darted back and forth nervously scanning the parlor below and the darkened hallway to my left. Overcome by the feeling that there was someone behind me and there was only a wall to my back. Behind me was a blank partition with a mirror at the top of the stairs. There could be nothing else. The sensation became unbearable. The skin crawled in bumps and folds on the back of my neck. I turned slowly and peered over my right shoulder. It shouldn't have been. It was impossible. Nevertheless, it was there, in the mirror. The glass didn't reflect my image; instead, it was the form of a short hideous looking dwarf. It was a creature both legless and, except for a small bit of fur around the knuckles, hairless, so close was I that I imagined its hot breath on me. The nails on its hands were long, pointed and dirty gray. Its complexion was a sickly pale hue, and there rose to my nostrils the odor of filth and decay. It grinned at me with a mouthful of yellowed fangs.

The elfin creature reached outside the confines of the looking glass and grabbed me by the wrist. It tried to wrestle the knife from my grasp. The sharp nails on its furry hand dug deep into my skin and burned like acid. With a twisting motion of my right hand, I slashed its boney forearm. It screamed and let go. It was a horrible cry. It was an animal noise that sounded strangely human. The ear-splitting mewl echoed and reverberated deep within the recesses of the mirror; re-emerging as a chorus of a thousand wailing infants.

Instinctively, I lashed out with the dagger and repeatedly stabbed the glass. My left hand curled into a fist clubbing the mirror until it cracked and splintered and broke into hundreds of little glittering shards. Both of my hands worked furiously on the looking glass and the image it held. I shrieked and howled, bellowing like the thing that had been on my doorstep. Tears streamed down my face and blood poured down the walls. Weeping and sobbing, I yelled at the small creature behind the crystal. Over and over again I shouted, "Die! Die!"

The walls became red. The very air I breathed turned crimson. I became wrapped in a scarlet flame. A tremendous buzzing clamored in my ears. The house rocked on its foundations. I felt giddy. Then the floor rose up to meet my face.

***

I was sick, very sick. Faren held me with one arm as I emptied my insides into a wastebasket. I sat perched on the edge of the settee in the parlor, my arms bandaged, and I was an awful sight. My head throbbed, and I felt like someone had tied my stomach into knots. The house looked like the Russian army had marched through while a cool March breeze blew in where the east bay used to be. Wherever Faren walked, you couldn't help from hearing the crunch of broken glass underfoot. It was throughout the room, and it covered most of the furniture. The sofa was the only piece that wasn't showered with glass.

When I looked at the mirror all that remained was an empty

wooden frame. No signs of the silvered glass or its hideous occupant survived.

My body shook and convulsed as I told Faren what happened. He dried my tears and held me in his arms. He said that he believed me. He told me he would have been home sooner, but as I guessed, the roads were difficult to travel because of the fog. He had a hard time finding a cab driver that would come the entire distance no matter how much he offered to pay.

He held me tightly, the one thing I needed most. He cried and said that he was sorry for ever leaving me alone. We were to be with one another from now on, and we would see this thing through together.

Jim was on his way back with Vesta and Faren had sent for the Doctor. Even though I didn't like the Doctor, I welcomed the company. He also said that we were going to leave this cursed house tonight and return to New York. If the weather didn't permit then, Faren would ask the Doctor and Jim to stay the night, and we would leave first thing in the morning, safety in numbers. I was sure that help had arrived and more was on its way. I was grateful that the madness had ended, more so, I was grateful for Faren's presence, grateful that he was aware, alert and armed with the knowledge of our peril.

I was calmer by then, satisfied that things were becoming normal once more. Faren told me to relax while he cleaned up the glass and made us some coffee. While the coffee brewed, he swept the broken fragments into two heaps in the middle of the parlor floor. So that he wouldn't have to leave me alone, Faren promised to board up the bay window later, after Jim and the Doctor came.

The serpentine dagger remained at the head of the stairs where I had dropped it. Faren picked it up and stuffed it in the belt of his trousers. He carefully examined the carved hilt as if reassuring himself of the weapon at hand. There was a faint faraway look in his eyes for a moment. I recognized it from where I sat. He seemed to be looking not at me or anything else in the room. As if for a second or two he was glimpsing some other world, one entrenched far off in thought. I was about to call him out of it when he regained his composure only to stare momentarily at the broken mirror and then he proceeded to sweep the particles of glass down the steps and into the parlor along with the rest of the debris.

In no time he had the parlor, except for the smashed bay, looking orderly again and within the next minute he was preparing sandwiches and pouring coffee in the kitchen. The overall atmosphere had changed from stark terror to peaceful, almost homey. Faren even tried to make me laugh although his attempts were as poor as his jokes. My condition bordered on total exhaustion, but he did manage to get me to crack a smile or two.

I didn't realize how long it had been since I ate last but when he appeared with his back to the kitchen window proudly displaying a serving tray heaped with sandwiches and steaming cups of coffee, I was overcome with the ravages of hunger.

Faren smiled and bowed, I playfully applauded and within that next instant our peaceful sphere exploded. The bottom sash of the kitchen window discharged itself of its lower pane in a shower of splintering fragments. A massive pair of arms followed snatching Faren from behind and hoisting him into the air.

The tray of food crashed to the floor, Faren squirmed helplessly in the giant grasp and within the time that elapsed between the utterance of a scream and its audibility I was besieged by a collection of shadows.

Time slowed down. My mind was deluged by concepts so numerous and widespread that a second intervened and became a minute.

I could see part of the thing plainly. Half of it was shielded from the inside by the upper sash untouched by the violent intrusion while the lower half of its body reached inward through the shattered bottom pane. It was large, at least eight feet tall and its scale-coated flesh was of the same pale hue as the spectral imp in the looking glass. Although it appeared to have a massive muscular structure, the fabric of its framework was counter developed to anything that could be considered human in form. Disproportionate body features, organs out of place and looming up from behind the titan was a colossal pair of wings.

It was the face that triggered my memory forcing what I had suppressed earlier that evening to the surface.

Its face bore no resemblance to anything remotely human. Its eyes, pupil-less and deathly white, glared at me.

It wasn't so much the alien quality of the thing that made me faint. It wasn't its abnormal outlines or profile, not even the pair of mandibles set where a jaw should have been or the encirclement of snake-like cilia that surrounded the opening and hung like a beard from just below the eyes. It wasn't seeing my husband helplessly dangling a few feet above the floor in its grasp. It was more.

I remained conscious until the aspect of the creature caused me to remember what had happened, hurtling me into a gulf of blackness.

I am sure that Doctor VonTassell would write it off to stress, however in that brief interlude of a second, I saw myself from hours before as if observed from afar, running in a mad frenzy towards the woods. The one place that at the time I could not recall why I chose above all other directions to take!

As if time had flipped back the pages of a great book, I saw myself again, but this was before I had run into the woods. I left the garage and the rotting corpse thing behind and headed at a fast pace straight for the road by way of the long dark driveway. I had taken to the road! I did select that route first as I had guessed. I remembered! I saw what stopped me from going any further. I saw what sent me fleeing in such total terror towards the woods that I had blotted it from my memory.

It was the monstrous titan...that thing in the sky, the creature that held Faren in its grasp. The one I had observed being spewed from the bowels of the earth by a phosphorescent geyser and probably the same thing that intruded upon our front door. It was a horrible thing with wings. It had soared down from the stars and stood across my path.

***

Somehow Faren escaped from that hideous creature, but I don't know how. It must have happened after I blacked out.

All I can do now is bide my time and wait for the drug to take its toll. I am restrained by a numbness in my legs and the distance between Faren and myself; the parlor at one end of the house and the bedroom at the other. I tried calling for him, but my voice is so weak. Right now, I feel as restrained as when I was in the clutches of that tentacled thing in my dream.

All I can do now is rest and regret the day that we ever came to this godforsaken place. I wonder if God has forgotten this little corner of the world. If I should die here, will I find refuge in the kingdom of heaven or will I end up like one of those grotesque things stalking the black forest at night until my flesh rots into nothingness and my bones turn to dust?

Maybe God, that is the God of all things that are good, will intervene and the walking dead will have their salvation. Perhaps they are not evil at all. Perhaps these creatures emerging from graveyard settings are not based on the fear of death, rather on a fear of certain forms of life. Maybe death is not the end; maybe some things continue to exist in an ageless half-alive state, things that can be summoned forth again.

Didn't old Todesfall call up something that night? Some pages were missing from the old man's notebook, but I know that something did come up. It was the evening when the hand from that dark universe he wrote of pointed him out.

What was it then? There is that small, elusive creature of the night, had it squeezed through? Did it have some dimensional powers beyond our realm of understanding that would enable it to pop in and out of this world like a phantom? Or was it trapped and lost in our world? After the death of the old wizard, had it locked itself in the tower and taken the key with it?

Was Todesfall caring for it in the bedroom? The crib, oh my God, the handprints on the pillow. Was it lonely? Did it desire to come back to the place it had considered its new home? Was Faren's uncle sleeping with it like one who comforts a child frightened of the dark?

I am reminded of the child in the woods that was viciously murdered by an unknown assailant. Could Faren have, oh Jesus, he did know her address? It was inside the school books, and he could have been walking out there that night. The mud on his feet could be proof. But that is nonsense. No injury of the mind, no matter how severe, could force him to do anything like that. My mind wanders.

I am so tired; I must stay awake . . . must concentrate . . .

Different people worship and pray to different gods. I am afraid that we have stumbled upon some ancient sentinel that has slumbered for eons and is just now ready to emerge and lay waste to an unsuspecting world. Are we in store for a rebirth of horror on earth with Faren's great uncle acting as the willing midwife? Are we destined to return to a dark age of earth's past? In the end, will we be offered despair or hope for a new beginning, for then Cthulhu's return has only been delayed and the ever revolving cycle of time will schedule his coming again!

I . . . I hear footsteps on the stairs. Someone is coming. I wonder if it's . . .

PART IV

THE CRY OF CTHULHU

Transcribed from tape recordings made by Faren Church

It began for me the night I had the dream. It was an ordinary evening in our new home in Germany. I was exceptionally tired with the last two weeks spent getting the house in shape. My arms and legs ached with the memory of the completed chores, and my eyes were heavy.

After a while, my wife rolled over and fell asleep. She was sleeping soundly, snoring slightly. I was eager to fall asleep myself. My body shuddered slightly, and I settled down to welcome the rest. Still I found it difficult to relax. I had spent the entire day running around finishing the last of our repair jobs on the old house.

The next day I would be starting my new assignment with the company, and I had pushed myself to get everything done. I was physically exhausted, but my mind was still racing. I lay on my back for a while staring at the ceiling. I traced the cracks in the old plaster and started counting the many swells and bulges caused by years of patching until I was on the edge of sleep. Then, something jarred me awake. I sat up in bed with a lurch, my nerves shaking from the sudden start. I had heard something outside. We had spent several nights in the house by this time, and up until then, it had been relatively quiet.

I waited in the silence that followed for it to repeat. After a long stretch, I leaned back on my pillow only to hear the sound once more...or as near to the sound of something moving amongst the brush under our window.

Now alive only in my eardrum, not moving, not breathing, I waited. The ghost of the sound passed through gradual increases of rarity and volume. I first thought it was the sound of rain falling; then it sounded like the fluttering of wings, quickly becoming the confused words of water gurgling and then it became a ruffle succeeded by the noise of chewing...as if a large animal was eating the shrubbery!

Quickly, but quietly so I would not disturb Janet, I got out of bed and went to investigate.

Because of Janet's fear of guns, I have never had one in the house, so upon arriving at the front door, I opened it cautiously and slipped outside without a thought given to acquiring a makeshift club or a knife from the kitchen. It is definite proof that I was dreaming. I can't imagine being in my right mind going out alone in the middle of the night to look for an intruder without some means of protection. It is all so vivid though. Different fragments of the dream from time to time have the aspect of memories in a solid perceptible sense, but why then during this particular moment of clarity did I slip outdoors wearing only my shorts, yet the chilly evening did not have any effect on me, nor did I consider putting on any clothes.

The noises I had heard came from the opposite side of the house. In the semi-conscious daze of a dreamer, I walked alongside of the schloss in search of the source. A rustling in the tall grass at the corner of the house attracted my attention, and I stole cautiously up to the motion. There was no mystery about the sound by then; it was similar to a cow grazing. I slowly moved to the edge of the building and peered around the corner.

Then I saw the thing that made my blood run cold. Long and green and scaly, it was a tail! Like a giant reptile's tail, it slithered slowly, almost contentedly, over the lawn.

My mind was in turmoil as to what could belong to that tail. Even though my common sense told me to run, a drive, almost a calling made me proceed. I made my way further from the corner of the house to get a better look at the creature.

The tail lurched suddenly and began to curl and uncurl spasmodically. I jumped behind the wall again in sudden fright, waiting until the tail slowed down and its movement stopped. After a moment I moved away from the corner again for a better view.

Standing in front of me, munching lazily on the decorative bushes was a sleepy-eyed, green-faced, red-backed, gold winged dinosaur.

I was amazed, and for some unknown reason, my fears started to lessen. Curiosity overpowered me, looking back now it makes me think of the fables and tales that were born and told countless times in and around these forests. This creature must have come right out of one of those bedtime stories.

It was dark green and had large scales about the size of silver dollars covering its muscular body. Huge, golden membranous wings unfolded from its back, and a long flexible crimson spinal column ran its entire length to the very tip of its tail.

The most incredible thing of all was its face. Its expression reminded me of a Basset Hound. It was lazily munching on a hedge; eyes drooped, almost sleepy, its long pink tongue darting between dulled, yellow teeth.

Slowly it turned its huge head and saw me for the first time. It gave a start and took a sudden step sideways. Then it gazed steadily at me, and I stared back. My mind was a blank.

The dragon wearily tilted his head regarding me with hypnotically compelling eyes that glowed brightly drawing me closer.

The thing lowered its head. The muscular neck curved and appeared to form a dip, like a saddle. It kept looking at me, and I knew it meant for me to mount it like a horse.

The next thing I recall was laying my hand on its cold, scaly head. The scales warmed to my touch. I remember briefly speculating that the creature must have had a natural ability to adjust to its environment. Without knowing why I felt comfortable and safe being near the beast. There was no fear, and I did what seemed as natural as getting in our car to drive to town. After all, I was still in bed, I knew I was asleep, but a level of my consciousness felt playful. I lifted one leg over the head of the beast and easily mounted it.

I held onto the creature, and it lifted its head and flexed its wings with a huge arcing motion. The wings started flapping and caused a wind that raised dirt and loose grass all around us. The creature turned and lumbered out across the lawn. It began to pick up speed and started an awkward run into the wind. My dinner of sausage and beer must have fueled my dream because, after a couple of leaps that caused the beast to stagger, we lifted off the ground and glided smoothly for about a hundred yards across the earth. It then lifted, and I felt its muscles contract beneath me, and as if flexing some invisible power, we quickly soared upward at a steep angle into the night sky.

We flew over forests and mountains. I looked down and watched the scenery glide by below us. The familiar countryside was replaced by a wild land I had never seen before. Jagged, needle pointed mountains raised thousands of feet into the air, literally towering above the clouds. The surface of the country looked alien. The mountain peaks were black and menacing.

As I stared at the dreamscape unfolding below us, the creature abruptly made a sharp turn, headed straight up and the earth fell quickly away.

The land became smaller and smaller, and ahead the cosmos grew. I felt no discomfort. I had no trouble breathing. It was as if I were still sleeping with the blankets tucked under my chin. I knew without really knowing why that the beast was taking me back to the place from which it had come.

Some time must have passed, but I am not sure. I remember straining my eyes against the darkness. One star, in particular, burned brighter than all the rest. It loomed ahead of us.

Without warning the creature's wings folded back, and we gained tremendous momentum. Faster and faster we went until I am sure we would have appeared as a blur of motion to some alien astronomer on one of the planets we passed. I looked forward again and saw myself riding the creature up ahead. I turned and gazed behind and again I saw myself there . . . as if in two mirrors reflecting an infinity of images. The creature still gathered speed.

The night world around us contained a bridge of stars. Wild streams of violet and midnight glittered with dust of silver and gold. Spiraling masses of dust and fire swirled out from black spaces and became heavy with lights from worlds beyond. Oceans of gas poured past lit by a million suns.

In the very center of this whirlpool was one blood red star beckoning me and my mount to our destination.

The burning orb grew larger as the creature's speed increased. The flaming sun filled my field of vision, and my bearer continued forward straight at the core of it.

In the very center of the turbulence was a speck, a tiny blemish, like a black spot on a bright red plane. It was to this darkness we flew.

It grew around us, and we were engulfed by the black, sucked inside the hole and pulled at a tremendous rate through a tunnel. Further and deeper we sped through the tunnel. Total silence and darkness enveloped us as if in a vacuum that is void of sound and light. It built around us like inside the eye of a hurricane. Then there was a pinpoint of light at the center of my vision. No sooner than had, I spotted the point of illumination that the end of the tunnel was upon us. A misty white swelled until it encompassed us and we were expelled from the dark with a tremendous explosion.

I know it was a dream, but the effect was severe. I was frightened. When I think back on it even now my muscles will ache with the memory of the physical stress. I wanted to wake up. I didn't like the feeling in my stomach. I fought for consciousness, but it was a heavy sleep. Although my eyes were seeing this planetary vision, I tried with no success to open the eyes of the sleeper within me.

A smoky white world embraced us. I gave up and relaxed letting the dream run its course. The beast slowed down to only a fraction of its previous speed, a slow-motion pace compared to our journey there.

The mist soon lifted. The sky filled with incredible wonders of a strange new universe. Behind, the cosmos still raged, but I saw it from a different perspective, and I saw something that filled my soul with a cold, freezing horror.

At the center of a raging sun was a creature, a misshapen tentacled thing, burning at the core, its cries noisily enveloped by the continual exploding surface.

I looked away.

Planets revolved around the exploding sun. Each held a captive, more gigantic and gruesome in appearance than the other. There were a dozen terrors held in bondage on asteroids and small planets, retained by huge shackles and chains; molten mud and quicksand; giant blocks of ice.

Nearest the sun was a molten planet that held a burning serpent man in its fiery muck. At the rim of the solar system, a captive evil lay in the frozen wastes of an ice planet. Between these two prison worlds were terrible, rocky planets, each another prison for some hideous creature. Some of the fugitives were imprisoned on sundry minute planetoids which were scattered here and there along the outer reaches of the system.

One creature, chained to a burning planet, in a fit of rage, threw a molten fireball that narrowly missed us if it hadn't been for a deliberate, although languorous maneuver of the winged beast.

Except for the slight mishap that went practically unnoticed by the creature, it calmly passed this incredible spectacle of horror. The planets revolved their captive terrors about us as we rocketed on our way. As we passed the last body, the ice world, the cosmic fog again began to envelop us. It spread around us, thick and bright, denser than before. I lost touch with my senses. I felt numb, I couldn't feel my mount beneath me, and all sensation of movement and direction disappeared. I believe we passed through another barrier.

I began to gain my feelings once again and felt the creature slowing down. Its large wings began to move in slow, graceful sweeps. We were landing. We moved slowly through the glowing fog. As I peered ahead, I began to see a shape, a large looming form ahead of us. As we came closer, I made the shape out to be another huge, crouching creature, possibly another captive planet monster? As the living vehicle I rode neared the form, I saw that the large thing was a stone figure, a giant statue rising in the fog.

We approached the statue and rose above it and the fog. We circled the head of the idol, and I saw that it was the corner piece of a vast wall adorned with hieroglyphics and stone carvings. The colossal wall extended far down becoming lost in the bottomless fog.

The mist thinned at the higher altitude above, and as we crossed the top of the structure, there remained only wisps of it.

Rising out of the gloom was a circular tower. On the top of it was a flat landing plane where several ramps spiraled down into the fog. It was here that the creature finally landed.

Out over the top of the mist, I saw that the tower we had landed upon was only one of many. Other flying beasts were landing and taking off from similar towers. The discharged passengers descended on similar ramps that wrapped down and around the structures.

The vehicle creature lowered its head, and I easily slid off its back onto the platform. Two openings faced me. A glass gate blocked the one on the right. The opened one faced a slanted floor that moved, escalating downward. I descended on the ramp into the mist. As I slowly rode it down, I noticed on the ascending ramp on my right, alongside the one I was on, a two-legged being that was half man and half bird. I took this to be the beast's next passenger. We stared at one another in passing and not until each of us was out of view of the other did I realize that he regarded me with an equal air of surprise as I did him.

Although the fog was always present, it became thicker and surprisingly phosphorescent upon decent. While my eyes began to adjust, I started to make out structures. Buildings began to form in the mist, and it was obvious that I was descending into a city of incredible alien architecture.

In certain places, I beheld dark cylindrical towers which rose far above many of the other structures. These appeared to be unique, in nature and displayed signs of age and dilapidation. Nowhere in any of them could I find the traces of windows or other openings except for doorways at their bases.

Huge narrow pyramids towered around me joined by ramps and catwalks on which robed figures moved. The spiraling towers reached upwards disappearing into the mist-filled sky, and black monoliths loomed below them as far as my eyes could see.

I came to the end of the ramp and found myself in front of an immense five-sided arch that led onto some city streets beyond. I passed through the arch and entered the wide passages between massive domes and flattened pyramids. As I looked around noting the windowless structures, the lack of street lamps or lights of any sort also became apparent. The entire landscape was lit by the glowing mist that enveloped everything.

One minute detail I remember surprisingly well was that most of the buildings were of a dark granite masonry with lines of convex topped blocks fitting the concave bottomed courses which rested upon them.

I was far from the only inhabitant of the city. All around me the metropolis was teaming with a collection of strange beings. The city's populace crowded the streets and passageways. To my amazement, the gargoyles that adorned the surrounding buildings upon nearing them suddenly came to life and flew from their stone perches between the buildings. They reminded me of a flock of startled pigeons. Reptilian lizard and birdmen walked by me on the streets, passing with credulous stares in my direction. A centipede-like being slithered up a pole to disappear into the thick fog above; a group of huge insects stood in my path talking in sign language with their pincers, and I was forced to veer around them.

I knew where I was going or at least my subconscious did. All around me the lanes led in one major direction. I suspected that the city streets had been laid out similar to the spokes of a wheel, with the heart of the metropolis being at the hub.

I cut across an adjacent alleyway and heard a clamor in the street ahead. Some armored lizardmen riding bulky six-legged steeds bore down upon me. As the riders hurried by, I quickly moved out of their way. Behind them came a procession of reptilian soldiers clad only in leather breastplates and skull caps carrying a long wooden pole between them. Bound to the pole was a beast, a small but extremely muscular demon-troll looking thing, which growled and snapped at its captors.

Toward the rear of the procession, two more lizard men appeared carrying a large transparent orb wherein squatted a small creature that resembled a mud puppy. The creature swam in a green fluid, and it was trying unsuccessfully to break out of the prison globe.

At one point I had to stop to allow a caterpillar creature, the size of a large dog, to slither from a side street and cross my path into a darkened doorway.

Everywhere the streets and buildings crawled with alien creatures.

While much more probably remained unseen. I could only guess at their numbers when passing dark alleyways or the blackness of an opened passage. I sometimes could make out faint whispers and twittering cries. And always, above it all, loomed the catwalks joining the pyramids and on those catwalks moved robed figures. I never saw a robed being in the streets below, where I walked; they didn't come down and mix with the other city dwellers.

At the end of the street, I came upon another wall, similar to the one that surrounded the city but not as large. In front of me stood a pair of massive doors with some of the same hieroglyphics and carvings. Chained in front of the passage stood a dozen or so armored lizard men. As I approached them, they all moved forward and pulled on the great latches. The two doors of heroic size swung slowly open.

When the doors parted, I saw a courtyard within the surrounding walls. The floor was made up of giant blocks of masonry machined so evenly and laid so tightly together that they required no mortar to fill the joints. Over the polished stones moved the robed shapes I had seen on the walkways above. They came from many doorways like the one in which I stood and joined together to form a single line moving with a peculiar gliding gate into the center of the courtyard.

I took a few more steps and crossed the threshold. The courtyard only had one other structure in it. It was a narrow stone spire that towered up higher than the temple construction. At its top was a wide crow's nest platform overlooking the city. I could just make out a lone figure in the gloom. Robed and hooded like the ones in the silent earthbound procession, it was watching the sky.

Below, their gowns billowing about them, the cloaked beings glided with a fluid motion up a long inclined surface through a pentagonal opening in the temple. The robes hung to the ground and dragged on the cobblestones making it impossible to detect the existence of any legs. I couldn't help noticing the moist trail left in their passing. Each apparently secreted a thin layer of liquid, the results of an alien method of locomotion.

Mentally retracing my steps, I recalled that upon entering the city, not once did I see anything that resembled a staircase or a set of steps. Come to think of it, the curbs that joined the sidewalks and streets were all gradually sloped, and the sills of doorways that I had seen had been installed flush with ground level instead of being raised as is usual in conventional construction. I instinctively joined the procession, walked across the courtyard, and entered the building.

***

I passed through a long empty hall and came out into a sizable chamber with lofty archways leading in from the halls and rooms. Through these, the robed figures came and went. Lamps faintly illuminated the room through recessed panels bordering the high ceiling. The ceiling itself bore no resemblance to the exterior outline of the building's flattened roof. Instead, it rose from the walls in four triangular stone planes which slanted sharply to meet at a common apex above.

I was standing in what appeared to be the interior of a hollowed out pyramid. The ceiling of which was a perfect flawless white, the floor an equally perfect black. On the far side was an altar, large in itself but dwarfed by the mammoth proportions of the room. The large flagstones that comprised the floor were interrupted at one point in the very center of the chamber by a massive piece of granite. It was hinged to the masonry, a good thirty feet across, and sealed down with thick metal bands. It was a trap door. I sensed dim suggestions of a special peril beneath.

As if on signal the figures began to discard their robes. As the garments dropped to the stone, I saw them for the first time. I can still trace their monstrous outlines with uncomfortable ease. They were bizarre looking, iridescent upside-down cones, about nine or ten feet high and equally wide at the base and their flesh was made up of a leathery green, almost elastic material.

The base of each cone was fringed with a flexible substance that propelled them in a slithering lubricated motion across the floor through a series of expansions and contractions. Their heads were mounted on narrow stalks, and they peered through the gloom of the chamber at me with three eyes that glowed red. Surmounting the creatures' heads were four slender stems bearing flowered appendages, while on either side dangled eight antenna or tentacles.

This great race of beings had four cylindrical arm members each a foot thick; sometimes contracted to almost nothing while at other times, extending to any distance up to about ten feet. Terminating two of them was a series of trumpet-shaped suction appendages used, I guessed, for grasping tools and objects. The other two ended with lobster-like claws or nippers, and it was by means of clicking them that they communicated.

I was terrified. When they first disrobed, I backed quickly away without paying attention as to what was behind me. Almost at once the floor came up to meet me from behind. My head thumped a hard surface. A quick glance around told me of my predicament. Some of the tiles, in front of the altar, parted with noiseless ease and from the chamber floor rose a stainless steel table. My body was forced to it by an invisible power. I felt the cold metal against my bare skin. I couldn't move a muscle.

The shiny metal slab was covered with an assortment of shackles and restraining straps of all sizes and configurations. The table must have been constructed to hold and examine a variety of living beings.

The same unseen power that held me against the slab rearranged each strap and manacle adjusting them to my form. Once secured, the pressing force ceased.

What I mistook for an altar erupted in lights of every color. Objects which still puzzle me now quickly projected from the flat surface. Elusively colored and textured objects like nothing I have ever seen. They were lightly colored crystalline things. Some curves and shapes answered to no conceivable purpose and followed no conceivable geometry.

One of the creatures went behind the altar which by then looked more like an abstract art form, an alien control console. The console came to life with odd musical notes and softened light hues when the creature touched it. It reached out and grasped a crystal with one of its head tentacles, and a narrow beam of light shot upward at a slight angle meeting the common apex in the ceiling. It hung just below the geometric shape rolling and churning in its light source until a white ball of energy formed and grew in size. As if too massive to sustain itself anymore the glowing orb slowly floated down and descended to my eye level. It held my gaze steadily, hypnotically.

I felt the table tilt to afford me a direct view. My captives towered above me. All around me the creatures were clicking their claws in an excited frenzy while gliding around the table. In this position, it was very comfortable, almost natural to peer into the glowing orb.

My head was aching. I had a singular feeling that something was trying to get possession of my thoughts. At first, brief glimmering visions took shape. Chaotic visions which in the beginning disturbed me greatly. They were fragmentary dream glimpses which appeared, I sensed, in a chronological pattern.

My conception of time, my ability to distinguish any ordered continuity was disordered; so that I formed notions about living in the present while casting my mind over eternity, the past and future ages.

The pain in my head subsided followed by a relaxed numbing sensation. The part I began to play in these dream images was that of a disembodied consciousness with a range of vision wider than normal, floating freely about, but in one reality, confined to a metal slab and yet in another at home in bed.

I had witnessed several horrors. Any of which should have shocked me back into consciousness. I tried to call out to Janet who I knew lay beside me in the real world but my lips were numb, and I could only manage a low murmur.

The cone-shaped being behind the controls pulled at a cluster of glass tubes. I gathered that these creatures were incapable of physically reproducing human speech because the alien mechanism was employed on which frighteningly familiar sounds resembling the English language played as on an instrument.

The machine droned in musically piping tones with soothing clarity. The mechanical voice began to have a calming effect speaking directly to me, telling me not to be afraid that to watch and listen. It immediately formed a narrative, the contents of which unfolded as an account of the unusual race that had made me their prisoner. A succession of wild visions began to unfold all in such visual quality that I soon lost all sense of the massive chamber.

I was taken back through immeasurable distances of time and space. An incredible wave of inferiority swept over me, and I saw how minutely tiny each is in comparison with the total reality. I was taken back to the beginning, through many dimensions to the very creation of the universe.

Before the creation of our universe, this alien race dwelt on a black, almost dead orb. Not the physical semblances I was in the company of, rather their mental heritage . . . for the mind of the Great Race, I was told, was older than its bodily form.

The beings of the dying elder world, wise with the ultimate secrets of the universe, had looked ahead for a new world and species wherein they might have a long life and sent their minds into that future race best adapted to house them, the cone-shaped beings that peopled this alien metropolis.

They were probably the greatest race of all because it alone had conquered the secret of time. These Elder Beings had learned all that had been known or ever would be known in the universe through the power of its keener minds to project themselves into the past and future to study the lore of every age.

The images that continued within the globe revealed them to be industrialized, highly mechanized to the point that their machines demanded very little time from each citizen although from what I was permitted to view, I noticed a growing tendency towards the usage of mind control. One result I witnessed was when the invisible force overpowered me. The musical voice boasted that their abundant leisure time coupled with an individual lifespan of over ten thousand years was filled with intellectual and aesthetic activities of various sorts. Some of these pursuits included the creation of life forms from a plastic matter reared in laboratories used as a synthetic labor force.

They were dedicated to the art of learning and the improvement of the mind. After a great passage of time the Great Race, left unchecked, eventually developed into a civilization without instrumentalities; living and acting on the force of their minds alone.

The story of their universal migration and the eventual evolvement of a high civilization that spanned entire solar systems was spared me in great detail but was made clear by a rapid string of visual documentation highlighting the growth of their empire. The images slowed, and there was the flutter of fear. I sensed it as well as saw it. It was in the globe, in the room.

The mechanical voice fell silent, and a gloom spread across the chamber. The sensation of fear . . . an unnamable fear seemed to grip my jailers in frozen terror. I was stunned by the aspect. How could that be? I couldn't fathom it. They had to be the most evolved and advanced race of intelligent creatures since the beginning of creation. In all their greatness could they have even one fear?

I wasn't mistaken. The alien lifeforms stood transfixed around me, their many eyes nervously twitching. Two of their members skittered across the tiles and fled the room. I felt somehow that if they could have given to voice that they would have fled like screaming children. I was uneasy but as absurd as it sounds, I remained the calmest. They just stood there staring at the orb which, by this time, had replaced the pictures of their magnificent history with dark shadowy images.

It was a minute or two before I realized that this was the basis of their alarm. They were shadows, shadows out of a time of a horrible and utterly alien presence. I was not able to gain a clear hint of their appearance. They were only partly material, as we understand matter, the rest gave them their shadowy appearance. Despite the absence of wings or any visible means of flight, they had the power of aerial motion. They came through space (from where I never learned) settling at both polar regions of a planet and preyed horribly upon the beings they found there.

The Great Race waged an awesome war against the dark forces. Enormous armies utilizing the knowledge and fantastic devices that their researchers had drawn together. They employed unknown principles of energy, using weapons that produced tremendous electrical effects.

The dark armies battled across the brooding landscapes for many years. I don't know how long the war lasted but by the lapses in the images, the gradual changes in landscapes and the shifting of star patterns it must have lasted hundreds, perhaps thousands of years. At times they left the planet surface to fight amongst the stars where countless worlds were engaged in the combat. The war destroyed whole planetary systems. Many races and civilizations, even galactic empires were shattered or annihilated.

The dark ones appeared to be virtually indestructible. Just at the point in the fighting when I thought the conical people would give in and fall prey before the black science of the dark ones, a new weapon was produced.

The mechanism was small, probably less than a meter in height and appeared to be brass and highly polished steel. I believe that this device called upon the very power of the universe itself, for in one sequence of images in the heat of a great battle, a gap appeared in the fabric of space swallowing the dark ones . . . imprisoning them.

A war that lasted centuries was over in almost the bat of an eye. One moment whole planets were devoured in a hellish struggle, and the next second the heavens were at peace. The dark ones in full battle rage disappeared into a hole blacker than space itself appeared; they were sucked inside. Only a few immune to the power of the machine escaped. The largest was a formless mass, an amoebic shape that somehow sprouted arms and legs. The rest, few in number, were mostly small hairy creatures that clung like parasites to the great slimy thing for protection. Horrible they all were if there had been cause for the Great Race to comprehend horror and loathsome if they had any feelings of loathing.

Quickly and methodically they surrounded the predators and in a blinding flash of electrical fire drove them into the inner depth of a planet. The only exit from the cavern was sealed off by a mighty star quarried stone. Gigantic bolts were driven miles into the surface of the planet securing the huge piece of granite. As if this wasn't enough, the stone door was then hinged to the planet's surface and further secured by metal straps a couple feet thick and welded into place by the alien weapon.

Later, the trap door was surrounded by octagonal flagstones, and a temple constructed around it so that a constant vigil remained over the spot. At different times mixtures of chemicals were brought to the site and brewed in large caldron tanks. The resulting brew was poured into the cavity of the planet through a small port in the great slab. Always the shadow of a nameless fear hung about the sealed trap door.

I realized that I was in that very temple and the huge hatch in the middle of the chamber that I noticed when first arriving was the same as I saw reflected in the orb. I felt the gnawing fear that must have been harbored by my keepers. I struggled at my bonds, but it was futile. I wanted to get away more than ever. I could see the trap door from my position, and the very thought of the nameless black thing incarcerated below made my skin crawl.

Just then, a dreadful thought struck me. What if I was to be a sacrifice to that thing? Before I could continue on that line of thinking I became distracted when the room grew brighter. The orb, which hung directly above me, glided down with a white-hot radiance.

I couldn't see the rest of the chamber or the aliens in it, only the fiery light; I was certain the blaze would burn the flesh off my bones, as it came closer. I closed my eyes. I felt the heat from the orb. Then the most frightening thought I had since the nightmare began raced through my mind. "MY GOD THIS IS REAL!"

***

I stared at the ceiling for a full minute tracing and retracing the familiar cracks and swells in the old plaster. On my left, Janet still slept soundly. A storm had built up in the hills, and the bedroom would light up from the infrequent intervals of lightning. I felt a tremendous relief coming out of that nightmare and back into the real world.

I turned on my right side and waited to catch a glimpse of the time on the alarm clock. I wish now that the lightning had stopped and the darkness would have remained undisturbed keeping me ignorant of what lurked in the room. I was fully on my right side, towards the edge of the bed with the pillow tucked alongside my head when the room awoke again with the white brilliance of a double lightning bolt.

I was face to face with a small deformed dwarf. There was the smell of rotten flesh. The gnome gripped the edge of the bed suspending itself just below the chin and peered over the sheets. Its foul breath slapped my face. It was unflinching, staring and the head was hairless, almost embryonic, while the backs of its tiny hands were bushy with coarse hair. Its hands looked like the paws of an animal. The skin was leathery, and under the white radiance, it was difficult to ascertain its color. I believe it was brown or possibly even green. One color was prominent under the prevailing light, red. Its red eyes looked directly into mine.

All this I remember seeing before the room fell dark again and I cried out at the top of my lungs. The lamp on Janet's bed table came to life, and I felt the warmth of her body next to mine and her voice telling me to wake up and all would be well.

My little man disappeared. After a short search that began under the bed and terminated down the hall, I returned reassuring Janet as well as me that all was well and it had been nothing but a bad dream.

***

I couldn't sleep the rest of the evening and laid there until just before sunrise when I rose and went downstairs to make some coffee.

I sat in our little makeshift breakfast nook, a small Formica, and steel table surrounded on three sides by molded plastic chairs with an old mahogany dressing screen shoved up against the other end and wondered if the majority of people ever pause to reflect upon the significance of their dreams. I spent the rest of the early hours waiting for the coming of dawn while my thoughts were devoted to my dream.

I am not an extravagant dreamer, but there was one other time, in the past, when a dream had been as frightening and vivid. It was a similar nightmare as well. One steeped half, in reality, the other the product of a drug-induced state. It was quite a while ago, several years, but it became fixed in my mind that morning.

It was a time when the consequences became an eternity. It was a time of olive drab clothing and gunmetal gray, a time and lifestyle so overpowering that my life became one without individuality. We were alike as our clothing had dictated and the individual characteristics of complexion, eyes and hair color were subdued and blurred by the O.D. green and gray, blending us into a faceless unit of men systematically trained for killing.

Like many young Americans in my situation, I was there against my will. I found myself in a country, unlike any place I had ever experienced with a climate almost unbearable to human life.

Your local tour guide does not recommend Vietnam, but on the other hand, my excursion was not of my choosing, rather it was chosen for me by the U.S. Government. I thought the flying time I had under my belt as an amateur pilot would have placed me in an airbase somewhere, but the Classification Board discovered that I had slight inner ear problems and shipped me off to the infantry. A grunt no less.

The tour of duty was termed short, a brief two years in one's life as my Draft Board so kindly put it, one year stateside and one year fighting the VC. Nevertheless, it was a hell of a long time to a boy with a young bride waiting back home. I had decided to make the best of it though and attempted to remain as light-hearted as possible in my daily letters home.

The letters became fewer and more difficult to write after arriving in Southeast Asia trying to keep up the pretensions of a safe and secure atmosphere. The years have slowly elapsed, and most of my stay in Nam has mercifully blended into a vague blur of images, making it impossible for me to reclaim from memory any one particular day, week, or at times whole months from one another. I put in my time. That is all that was required of me. Fill out your 365 days and stay alive. Thank God it was labeled a "Police Action, " and not a war or I would have been there for the duration.

I went through the motions of battle like most. When a firefight broke out, I'd discharge my M-16 into the open air then took cover until it was over. Seizing upon the first opportunity to fall back, I would retreat to my platoon. It was not a conventional war like many thought. It was not the class of "45". It was guerrilla warfare. One moment everything was peaceful and the next some bush or rubber tree would erupt, raining death and destruction.

There is no benefit in lying, especially to myself. If these tapes are ever heard, I want them to know the whole truth. So I better make a clean breast of it. I have always been afraid of any physical confrontations. I guess every one of us experiences different forms of anxiety in these situations, but I would run from the first sign of trouble. As a child, growing up in an inner-city, I avoided the common grade school tussles. Even when I knew that I was physically the superior, I could not summon the inner strength needed to make a fist and strike a blow. Subsequently, I was always the one who got beat up, making me an easy target for any bully that came along; leaving me disgraced in front of my friends. It was almost as if I preferred the humiliation rather than a victory.

I've been faint of heart most of my life, but when I grew older, I developed other defenses; psychological intimidation always worked well for me. Looking someone straight in the eye with a few carefully chosen words normally has the right effect. It's been successful heading off conflicts and can be very useful in business negotiations. In most cases, it has left me free of victimization, but somehow deep inside I felt less a man for it.

The reason I bring this up is that just two weeks before my discharge, a cowardly act on my part marked my unexpected but early release from Nam. It is the only memory during that period of my life that has stayed completely in tack. I guess it will always be with me like a scar from a third-degree burn. Just too much for the old subconscious to handle.

Like most short-timers, I was counting off the minutes to my discharge, and with the thoughts of going home so near I became extremely cautious of my safety, more than I had in the past. I had known of other short-timers who had become careless on the verge of returning to the states, with thoughts of seeing their loved ones fresh in their minds or daydreaming about the first thing they were going to do the moment of their homecoming. These all but tangible sugar plums would dance in their heads concealing the dangers that surrounded them. In the thin veil of fantasy, these poor souls would walk haphazardly through a minefield, or lost in the minds internal heaven, fail to take cover when the order was issued.

I became paranoid of my surroundings more than was usual. Determined to return home in one piece, I called upon the things I knew best. The gift of sight has always been very precious to me going back as far as I can remember. My grandmother lived with us until I was twelve. She was blind and partially crippled and had to be looked after, until the day they came and took her away. I was her favorite, and she would often tell me I was special, referring to me as her "eyes." Probably the reason I chose photography as a career; as an extension of our visual sense. I can freeze the special moments on film. At any rate, I mentally charted every move I made carefully as if frame by frame on a strip of film, envisioning that hell hole and myself through an imaginary viewfinder of a camera.

I calculated everything I did with "my" safety in mind. I put entire thoughts of returning home out of my head, became reclusive within my thoughts, seeking an inner asylum, alienating myself from the other men and all conversations entertaining any considerations of a homecoming. I had to be cautious. I didn't want to end up like so many I had known. I was determined to live out my last two weeks in Nam as safely as possible.

It was while being occupied with this self-control that I became conscious of an unusual turn of events. Not quite as strange or fantastic as it has currently been, but in retrospect, I relate it only with those moments in Vietnam and not the terrifying implications which have recently taken place and which some of you, no doubt, have read about in My Uncle Todesfall's notebook and Janet's diary.

My last few months in Vietnam were spent bordering the nearby village of Dai Sut. Upon returning from patrols, the platoons occupying that region were in the habit of marching along a half-mile-long trail through thick stalks of towering bamboo and eventually through Dai Sut. The villagers were Montagnards, a nomadic tribe numbering about ninety, considered savages by the lowland Vietnamese.

Bloch, our platoon sergeant, said that they had claimed the highlands of Indochina for themselves several centuries ago but had always been peaceful. The only violence he had ever witnessed was the occasional sacrifice of a buffalo or the hunting of tiger with crossbows and spears.

When Americans first came to Dai Sut, the locals would line the mud caked paths on both sides and silently watch the procession. By the time our platoon moved in to relieve the fifth detachment of battle-worn troops, the fascination for the American soldiers had grown old, and we would usually pass through unnoticed. A few of the older tribesmen would occasionally monitor our passing. Faab, the medicine man from the village, was among them.

Like all the men in the village, he wore a woven loincloth. His teeth were black and filed to points. Faab's earlobes were perforated and filled with silver discs. Around his wrists, he wore several silver bracelets. He was very ancient looking. He was a skeleton of a man who limped when he walked with elbows that looked knobby and a very visible rib cage. By way of some unknown appointment, the old man would carefully scrutinize every one of us that marched by, as if he was searching our faces for some mysterious element.

At first, I took no particular notice of him but later learned that this was an honor bestowed upon us that none of the recent detachments of soldiers had witnessed. It was about that same period, just a few weeks before my discharge, that I became conscious of the old witch Doctor's special interest toward me. In the beginning, I chalked it up to my imagination that he took more than a casual notice of me. His stare was long, piercing, and each day I went by, his gaze stayed with me longer than before.

I was a little uneasy about it and started to become nervous at the sight of him. I would try to avoid his eyes but the urge to look at him eventually overcame me before I left on the path to the camp and I'd stare back into his wrinkled features.

One afternoon returning from a firefight completely caught up in thoughts of caution, I had forgotten about him. Lost in thought, he was the farthest thing from my mind. Then for a peculiar reason, I don't know why I broke concentration and looked up. I saw him, not at the side of the path where he usually was but at the end where the road made a sharp bend to the left away from the village toward the Ban Hai river in the direction of our camp.

He stood with his scrawny arms folded about his chest peering directly at me. I couldn't have been more than ten feet from him. He reached out with a wrinkled hand and motioned me toward him with the bending movement of a long bony finger. I felt compelled to follow, but took charge of myself, turned abruptly to the left and stayed in procession.

That night the stoic face of the old medicine man occupied my dreams, beckoning, calling to me from the village.

The incident repeated on the following three days.

On the fourth day, we returned after a skirmish with the NVA.

Our casualties were low, and my spirits were high. I had made it through another day and nearing my last, which would be heralded by a flight home on a C-130.

I slipped mentally, for only a minute or so buried in the excitement of that afternoon's victory and wasn't prepared for a meeting with the old Montagnards. When I realized his presence and compelling stare it was too late. Caught off guard, some of the guys noticed my surprise and made light of it remarking that maybe he had a daughter or better still, a granddaughter, he wanted me to meet.

Embarrassed, I didn't want to look like a fool in front of the guys, so I approached the old man. "What the hell do you want?" I said. I was standing less than an arm's length in front of him.

He was holding a small clay jar in both hands with a short length of bamboo sticking out of its top. He didn't say anything. Instead, he raised the jar and held it in front of my face. My platoon moved along without me, trailed by a succession of jeering catcalls and obscene gestures.

The harassment heightened my embarrassment. Faab still did not speak. I felt like an idiot. I looked back and saw the last of our troopers rounding the bend towards camp. A stabbing fear shot through me. I did not want to be left behind. I ran after them pulling up the rear just as they were going out of sight of the village. The old medicine man stayed at the foot of the path clutching the clay jar in his hands.

On the fifth and sixth days, our platoon wasn't sent out on detail, and there wasn't any reason for us to leave camp. When our complement of grunts was in base camp, we were allowed a certain degree of slack. We burned shitters and filled sandbags when it was necessary, but we were normally excused from any tedious work so we could rest up and hopefully recover some of the sanity we lost during our weeks in the jungle.

Just twenty yards south of our hooch was an old VC bunker which had become a makeshift enlisted men's club. I had gone there on our second day of rest out of boredom. I had been withdrawn for quite a while and needed some conversation. We were on R-and-R, and I didn't see any harm in breaking my self-imposed discipline on my day off. Who the hell was going to know besides me? Tomorrow I would go back to my regular routine.

The ceiling of the bunker was low, and most of us sat on the dirt floor or stretched out on woven mats. On one of the concrete walls hung three tattered Playboy Magazine foldouts; Miss April, May, and July. I have no idea what became of Miss June. In a corner, stacked up were the latest editions of the "Stars and Stripes," an old ammo box overflowing with DC and Marvel Comics. A dog-eared copy of "Electric Kool-Aid Acid Test" rested on the pile of magazines. The room was dark and filled with cigarette and hashish smoke. Weed was very prevalent in Nam. The Montagnards would trade a large bag of the dope for a couple of Marlboros.

There were only seven of us in the dimly lit room. "The original seven" we had started calling ourselves by then. There were 40 of us, in the beginning. Except for Sgt. Bloch, we had all shared a Saigon-bound flight a year ago with over 100 other men. Of that original group, ten were killed in action, 19 had been wounded severely enough to be medevac'd home early, three were MIAs, and Purdy, our corporal, had been stabbed to death by a roving gang of Danang orphans. One-by-one they had all been effortlessly replaced by new recruits. Young men just like me who stood shivering on the hot tarmac of an airstrip knowing that they were about to start day one in the combat zone.

Bloch, the only lifer amongst us, sat in the corner next to the door and watched Stash, an ex-biker from the Toledo branch of the Outlaws, rolling joints on the top of his mess kit. Stash's fingers moved with meticulous skill. He was wrapping his third Zig Zag around a small mound of cleaned marijuana when I came in.

"Your joints always look tailored made," I said sitting down.

"Comes from years of practice, man," he answered, never looking up.

Ike Washington, a large black man, sat cross-legged to Stash's right. A lit candle rested on the dirt in front of him. He wore a beaded stitched headband and no shirt. His eyes were closed, and he was humming something to himself. At that moment, Ike did not look like the streetwise black from Chicago. Instead, he resembled a Native American.

Reese Combs sat with his back to the wall gazing at the ceiling occasionally sipping on a warm can of San Miguel. Reese was lost in thought, probably daydreaming about the hills of Tennessee, the backwoods and his folk's farm back home.

Over in the corner, his head resting on the pile of comics slept Rinaldi. Rinaldi (his first name escapes me now) was promoted to Corporal after Purdy was killed. Besides being amongst the three that made it back home alive, the only other thing I remember about his background was that he was from Philadelphia.

Stretched out on a mat between the sleeping Rinaldi and Reese Combs was Bill Gibson. Bill had been my closest friend in Vietnam. We shared a hooch together along with Stash and Reese and had done most of our serious drinking together. Bill had pulled my ass out of trouble more than once in the past year. I owed him my life on at least three separate occasions. Even though there was only a few months difference in our ages, I looked up to him as a big brother. He always looked after me. I guess he knew that left alone long enough I could really foul things up. He was from Jackson, Michigan and he had a wife and little girl that he talked about often. We had the recognition of being the only two married men in our platoon and the only two with a college education. We were also scheduled to receive our discharge papers on the same day.

Bill had been adjusting the tuner on his transistor radio when I came in. Richard Nixon was giving a speech in which he said he would get us out of Vietnam. Bill leaned over and yelled at the radio, "Where were you when we needed you!"

"In the frigging Oval Office man," Stash added. "No gooks are gonna shoot at you there."

"They'd shoot your ass if you were there."

We all turned around surprised to hear Rinaldi. His position was unchanged; his eyes still closed. "I thought you were asleep," I laughed.

"What the hell you mean they'd shoot me if I was there?" asked Stash.

Rinaldi, position still unchanged, "Stash, if you were in the big guy's office, they'd probably import fifty of the little gook bastards to assassinate you."

"No. Not me man. You wouldn't catch me in there." He wet the Zig Zag with his tongue and smoothed out the wrinkles in the paper. His eyes were bloodshot. "I don't like round rooms. No corners to hide in." He giggled softly.

It was right then that I remembered one of the reasons why I was starving for conversation. I got up and started to leave.

"Sit your ass down, Church," ordered Bill. I sat back down. "Where were you off to?"

"No place," I replied.

"You've been all wound up lately. You need to relax, unwind that mainspring of yours. Here!" He tossed an alligator clip to me with the butt end of the joint stuck between the metal jaws. "We haven't gotten high together in a while."

The roach was less than an inch long. It was black with resin. Vietnam dope was heavy with THC unlike the poorer grades of Mexican or Columbian we had smoked in college. I lit the end with my military issue Zippo tilting my head sideways away from the flame so I wouldn't burn my nose. A thick blue smoke curled upwards. A seed popped spewing sparks onto the dirt floor. I drew the smoke deep into my lungs. It had a strong musty taste. I fought against the urge to cough.

"That's right," Bill said slowly. "Just what the Doctor ordered."

"Heap big medicine," Ike muttered coming out of his trance. He turned, looked at me and smiled.

Bill tuned to another station and the radio played "I am the Walrus." "Hey, Church-Boy, you know what today is don't ya?"

slurred Stash.

"No," I said, coughing out the smoke.

"It's the day before Tet...the lunar New Year."

"Oh?" still coughing.

"Yeah, that's heap big shit in these parts," Ike added in a poor imitation of an American Indian.

"You're all heaps of shit," growled Bloch from his corner.

Everyone turned and stared at him. Reese stopped gazing at the ceiling. Even Rinaldi opened his eyes and propped himself up on one elbow to see what was happening. I had not noticed the eight or nine crushed empties of beer littered across the ground in front of Bloch until then. Sergeant Bloch was not a man to cross when sober, and if he had been drinking, he was like the song says, ". . . meaner than a junkyard dog."

The atmosphere became tense. Everyone was aware that the Sergeant's short fuse could ignite with little provocation. Everyone except Stash who was probably too stoned to notice or care.

Bloch shifted his position on the empty C-ration carton he sat on and leaned forward. "Give me a reefer, shit-for-brains."

Stash didn't reply. I grabbed one of the joints off the mess tin and held it out to him hoping to avoid a confrontation. Bloch slapped it out of my hand with a quick movement.

"Not you asshole," he shouted, "I want the Hell's Angel here to give me one."

"I ain't no Angel, Sarge," he answered in a stupor. "I'm an Outlaw!"

"Was, shit-for-brains. You're mine now and will be until you're dead or medevac out of here." Stash defiantly picked up one of his "tailor mades," bent over and lit the end of it with the candle. He straightened up and stared back eye-to-eye with Sergeant Bloch, no emotion on his face.

Ike visibly worried piped in, "give him the damn joint Stash!" Stash smiled, with deliberate slow movement removed the marijuana cigarette from between his lips and offered it to the glaring Bloch.

"Smart move, shit-for-brains," said the Sergeant taking the offered joint. He tilted his head back like someone belting down a shot of booze and drew long and hard on the cigarette. The sucking noise he made sounded like air escaping from a punctured tire. At least half of that joint was drawn in on that one breath leaving a gray ash about three fingers in length hanging limply from the end.

The interior of the bunker came into sharp focus. The curling puffs of cigarette smoke began to look like blue-white strands of fabric, and the painted lettering on Sergeant Bloch's corrugated C-ration carton looked embossed. I felt a little lightheaded. I was feeling the effects of that one toke.

"Why you pissed off at me Sarge?" asked Stash, looking down at the floor.

"You know Stash," he replied looking down from his seat. Even though the box he sat on couldn't have been more than a foot and a half higher than floor level I was certain he towered above us by several feet. "The only time you listen is when the order to take cover is issued. I said you were all heaps of shit. That means all of you girls here." He made a sweeping motion with his left hand, and the ash from the joint fell on his lap, rolled across his thigh and disappeared into his crotch.

Rinaldi acting like someone who had heard it all before planted a phony smile on his face and yelled "Hey Sarge! How about you and me finding ourselves some old Vietnamese whore and bang the hell out of her all night?"

"Drop dead," the Sergeant grumbled. "All of you make me sick. Most Americans supported the war, until around sixty-eight or so. Now they're saying it's a worthless cause. Before then the men that were here believed in what they were doing. Now, all I get are terminal cases of acne that think they're John Wayne or short-timers like you. Hippies and Hell's Angels."

Stash started to say "Outlaw" but was stopped short by an elbow in the ribs from Ike.

"I got this Wop over here that made Corporal by accident and thinks me and him are in some kind of noncom brotherhood and an Oaky," pointing to Reese, "from God knows where that just learned how to wear shoes."

Bloch was on a roll, and I knew he wasn't going to stop with Reese. His eyes glassed over and he stared down at me. For a moment I thought he was going to kill me. "College boy, it's a wonder you are still around. You should have been dog food by now." The muscles tightened around his neck. He leaned towards me. "Tell me Church, have you ever shot anything besides a rubber tree with that M-16 of yours?"

I was terrified of Bloch. I didn't answer. If I had, I probably wouldn't have been able to utter anything more than a squeak.

"Come on Sarge, leave him alone," pleaded Bill.

Bloch Ignored Bill and leaned even closer. His breath smelled of stale beer and cigarettes. "If it weren't for your hooch mate here you would have been dead meat a long time ago. For a college boy, you don't know jack shit. You don't even know enough to come in out of the rain unless someone tells you to or your buddy Bill here drags your ass inside." He leaned back and put his head against the wall of the bunker and stared at the ceiling. "Hell," he said, "You didn't even know enough to accept the rnoom."

"What's rnoom?" I managed in a voice a bit too high.

He rolled his eyes at the ceiling. "Fermented rice wine college boy. It is kept in an earthen jar and sipped through a bamboo straw. Faab was honoring you with his offer. To refuse is an insult. He is probably pissed off at us now and will stop the women in the village from whoring to us. You screwed up, college boy."

"Yeah, you screwed up," Stash added with a chuckle glad to have the heat off of himself.

Bloch fell silent and kept staring at the ceiling. I looked over to Bill, and he shrugged his shoulders. The volume rose on the radio, and the Jefferson Airplane sang "We should be together." I quietly moved along the dirt floor and crawled out the low doorway. Bloch didn't move. He didn't seem to notice me. Crawling out of doors the hot afternoon sun singed my face, and I heard Stash from the cool dark recess behind me giggle, "Tet eve."

I could still hear the Jefferson Airplane singing inside when Bill came out slapping loose dirt off his fatigues. "Are you all right," he said.

"Yeah, I'm okay," I said with a voice that cracked.

"Look, don't take all that shit seriously. The Sarge has been a little crazy ever since Purdy bought it a couple of months ago."

"I am just trying to stay alive, Bill."

"I know you are. We all are."

For a moment I thought I was going to lose it. Then I got a hold of what had been eating at me all those weeks and spat it out like a bad taste. "It has been hard," I stammered. "It has always been rough, but now it's worse. I've only got two weeks to go here, and I am more scared than when I first came. It has been a prison, a nightmare and now when I am so close to getting out I feel like something is going to happen."

"Like what, Faren?"

"I don't know. I guess some cruel joke played by some cruel god that lets things like that happen. Just string him along. Let him think he's going home then napalm him the day before his discharge."

Bill laughed, "Hey, partner, you're not alone in this. Everyone in the whole platoon feels the same way."

"Somehow," I said, "I don't find that comforting."

"Stick with me partner, and we'll laugh about this in the transport home."

"Thanks, Bill, I appreciate the help."

"Hey, I'll tell ya what," he said in a too cheery voice, "let's blow this pop stand and go over to our hooch. I've still got a few belts left in that bottle of Ouzo, and we'll play gin rummy."

"No thanks partner," I said forcing a smile. "You go inside; I need to work this one out myself."

"Are you sure? Are you going to be okay?"

"Yeah. Fine." He turned, and I watched him hunker down on all fours and crawl in through the small opening. The music on the radio was suddenly disrupted by the scratch of static as someone attempted to change channels. "Hey Reese," yelled Bill. "Get your paws off of my radio. How many times do I have to tell you that they don't play country western in these parts."

I laughed a little and then walked away from the bunker. I was going to go back to my hooch and lay down, but for some reason, I never headed in that direction. I am not completely sure why. Maybe it was what Sergeant Bloch said about the rnoom. Maybe I wasn't meant to; I set out on the path that led to the village.

Dai Sut was not off limits to military personnel and visits to the village were fairly common. After passing the river and rounding the bend in the road I had expected to witness the usual sight of bare-breasted women, clad in brightly colored skirts moving about the village and naked children playing outside their huts. That was not the case. The village was still. The only thing that remained unchanged since my last time there was Faab. He was still standing at the end of the path where I had left him two days before only this time with no rnoom in hand. Behind him were four other elderly Montagnards sitting cross-legged on the ground. They stood up the moment I approached.

Faab smiled displaying his pointed black teeth and gestured with his left hand for me to follow. Not a word was uttered. They all turned at the same time as if on cue, reminding me of Monks on a silent vigil, and walked towards the village.

"You were waiting for me!" I said out loud, but it fell on deaf ears or at least they pretended not to hear. I should have been scared, but I wasn't. Maybe that one hit on the joint back in the bunker had relieved more of my tension then I had realized. I think I was so amazed at discovering my reception party waiting for me that I had little time to think of anything else. I had taken about a dozen steps before I realized what I was doing. I was following them into Dai Sut.

We walked through the village, I behind not understanding why I chose to come along. Twice I felt like turning to run back to camp but as if my thoughts were read the moment the urge to flee overtook me, the old medicine man would stop, turn and gaze at me with eyes wide and all considerations would leave me.

We walked a good fifteen minutes and, while I imagined each thatched longhouse and hut we came upon to be our destination, we passed them all by without me having to alter our pace. Each time I anticipated the next hut and then the next to be our stop. Most of the villagers had taken refuge from either our passing or the tropical heat, although I occasionally spotted a few solitary figures by their huts or on the cliff oasis that surrounded the village. We appeared to be the only ones who braved the afternoon sun.

As we went on, I became more and more aware of a power other than my own will guiding my steps. When I'd attempted to halt the ridiculous hike, an attraction to go on swept over me as inexorably as the desire for a narcotic.

To my surprise, we had walked through the entire village and terminated our journey at the southeast base of the Dalat Mountains. In front of me was the mouth of a cave. It was their Kroong. I was expected to enter the forbidden domain.

I had seen it before through field glasses at a good distance. The Kroong was a place of worship used by the elders of the village. A small handful selected by sheer age and custom were permitted to enter its revered walls. All who lived the good life and saw ripe old age eventually found solace within the Kroong. Our company commander saw fit to respect their religious customs. Even with the wild rumors that circulated about it being a Chinese storehouse for weapons; our CO believed that repercussions could result from defiling their religious customs. Besides, the Montagnards were notorious enemies of the North Vietnamese. So a decision was made to make the Kroong off-limits to servicemen, for the time being, while at the same time keeping it under careful surveillance.

I froze at the entrance to the cave, held there by the orders set down by my superiors, coupled with a gnawing fear of the unknown.

What was in store for me by the hands of these people? Did they plan to use me in a religious sacrifice? Had I insulted them by not drinking the offered rice wine?

I resisted all temptation and prompting to enter. The compelling stare of the old medicine man could not budge me. He recognized this after only one failed attempt and approached me, gently laying his hands on my shoulders. My anxiety melted away with his touch. I felt emotionally drained. I looked at the old man, and if I had had anything left within my empty shell, I would have felt awe. Instead, I allowed him to lead me to the cave.

The blazing heat of the sun was halted by the dampness and darkness of the stone walls. The sweat on my brow turned icy cool, and my head swam momentarily from the sudden drop in temperature. During the time it took to regain my senses we were well within the heart of the cavern.

It was very large inside. Bare rock walls occasionally encrusted in spots with quartz crystals and rising from the floor in several areas were stalagmites, some fusing into columns with stalactites from above, giving the impression of pillars supporting the cavern ceiling.

I was escorted to the deepest portion of the cave, so far in that the light from outside didn't reach us. Sitting on stone, with their backs against a wall of smooth rock were four more old men from the village, all just as ancient as the rest, bringing the total to nine. At their feet, a small fire was burning, and amongst the glowing embers, a clay pot rested. An acrid chemical odor lingered in the steam that rose from a boiling liquid inside and exited through a perfectly round hole chiseled through the stone ceiling. The hole was a little larger than a man is wide and the blue of the afternoon sky appeared rich and distant through it.

Acknowledging a gesture, I sat down in front of the clay pot with the others facing me across the fire. There was a moment of silence, possibly in prayer or meditation, then the eldest mumbled a low, barely audible chant in his native tongue and tossed some fragments of tree bark into the boiling mixture. The same man scooped some of the liquid from the kettle with a large wooden spoon and after drinking from it passed it in turn to the others.

The ladle was then filled again and passed to me. I refused to drink at first, Faab gestured that it was harmless and I gave in once again to those compelling eyes.

I had noticed that the others only drank a very little amount of the mixture and I made sure to do the same. It wasn't until later that I learned that the concoction consisted mainly of rnoom, a variety of large pinkish colored mushrooms that grow in the shadowy caves and crevices of the Dalat peaks and bark from the Belphegor tree.

I forced a small mouthful of the awful tasting brew down and returned the spoon to the pot. There was an instant numbing sensation as the liquid slid down my throat immediately anesthetizing my insides.

Faab drew a crude pentagon in the sand with a stick. He then pressed a small charm into my hand. It was the size of a quarter and made of a green stone. It had five points on it like the star he drew in the sand, and the surface felt slick, soapy. The old man who had handled the passing of the spoon threw some green crystals on the coals and the flames shot up.

With the cave brightly illuminated I could make out the wall behind the village elders in every detail. It had been painted into a mural of brightly colored hues and shades, spanning a good twelve feet in width, depicting a weird alien battle. I use the words "alien" and "battle" here because they seem the most appropriate to describe the curiously odd art form.

The painting did not utilize much of the spectrum, but the colors that were employed were strikingly clear and vivid. There were brilliant mixtures of deep blues and purples. The color green was the most predominant but red was not altogether lacking, as it was occasionally used to highlight small areas of conflict. The most striking oil from the unknown artist's pallet was the vigorous use of black. Rich and hauntingly deep in its shade the ebony background struck out at the eye creating a three-dimensional illusion. Another color was apparent also, but I don't know what to call it; I am not sure if it was ever there or a trick played upon my eyes by the unusual brew.

The color was either alien or unknown to me or continually at change because I was never able to identify it. Sometimes green, while at others yellow, then gray, then orange would be exorcised into an array of angry shades setting into motion the illusion of writhing movements.

I was caught up in the perfect blend of artistry and color and decided that this Raphael of the underworld must have applied quartz minerals to his oils before they dried to achieve these effects.

The shiny element at the center of the work appeared as a great tentacled thing surrounded by a siege of lights and queerly shaped flying orbs that appeared to press the monstrous form into the ground. While in the background outlined in the night sky was a large five-sided stone perched on edge next to a dark, yawning aperture.

I dragged my attention from the scene to my nine companions. They weren't looking at the mural. They were sitting in line side by side, with their backs to the magnificent work, parted at the middle, situating themselves on either side of the fire as if to afford me a clear view. They became a part of the pictorial setting adding to the three-dimensional quality. The floating orbs against the sea of black hovered over their heads. The tentacled thing in the painting with its oddly shaped head looked up towards the heavens, and so did the Montagnards.

I followed their gaze upward until my eyes came to rest upon the hole in the ceiling. The afternoon sun to my amazement had vanished and in its place was an evening sky filled with stars. I felt light, weightless, all sensations of legs and limbs had left me. I had the impression that I was caught up in a whirlpool, drawn in spirit, funneling into the void beyond the cavern ceiling. Outside a point of light grew steadily brighter until it became a rotating green sphere. The surface came into view just as quickly; ranges of mountains, emerald green oceans, and flatlands, now and then broken up by lakes, valleys and rivers swelled up into my field of vision. What first appeared as mountains, upon getting closer, revealed them to be the buildings of a city so colossal in its proportions that it spanned the entire globe terracing the tallest mountains, invisibly suspended across lakes and rivers, and bridging the gulfs of great oceans.

The architecture was captivating, I was caught up in the marvel, and I didn't give a second thought to my existence, let alone "any whys or wherefores" to my trip through space. There was a numbing sensation, like when I drank that soupy mixture, but external. I was a disembodied bubble floating above the clouds of this alien world. I became dumbfounded by the pure creation of engineering genius that must have constructed so great a wonder.

Then from out of the void came a blackness, so black that it eclipsed itself, a terrible dark clawing thing that slowly ate away at my fascination with searing blasts of fear. I believe it was behind me if there is such a thing as behind or front or even up or down in outer space. There was no front or behind to me. There was no more me in any solid perceptible sense that there is in a puff of smoke or a slight breeze. None that I could be sure of at least. It came in a general direction, as I perceived it, from the rear, and invisible like myself I never saw it, just sensed the iciness of its existence and the blackness darker than the rest of the surrounding void. I also sensed that it had been watching me all the time. Rather than creeping up on me from out of the expanse, it just appeared as if it had opened a window in the ether directly behind me.

Chaos and fear, followed by disorientation of the emerald planet, flooded in on me. The inkiness was beginning to envelop me strangling my senses. The giant city with its architectural marvels was no longer visible. Although still without a body, I had the impression of suffocating. I was no longer in control of my faculties.

There was a flash of white. From out of the void came a hand, human, which grabbed hold of my spirit dragging me from the blackness and yanking me back through a vortex at a tremendous rate.

My head swam, and the old Montagnards tribesman sat once again before me within the cave. Faab's hand was clutching my shoulder.

I remember trying to recall if it had been real or the results of the drug. Maybe I had left, and the old medicine man with his mysterious perception had reached out through the void at the proper time and brought me back. Possibly he had never left me at all but was guiding me, directing me on the current course holding on to me all the way only I thought I had made the journey alone.

Of course, I didn't consider the most obvious explanation until the effects of the drug wore off, and that explanation was the hallucinatory drug itself.

The next morning I woke up on my cot still clutching the tiny star stone in my fist. I had no idea how I got back to my hooch or what time of day it was. I am not sure how long I laid there in a semi-conscious state before realizing that I was shaken from my slumber. My head weighed a ton, but eventually, through the grogginess, I was able to recognize Bill. It took some moments before I came around and even though he and I had been buddies for close to a year, his face appeared unfamiliar and distant until I cleared the cobwebs from my brain. I was beginning to concentrate. He was shaking me by the shoulders and shouting something about "bugging out."

It wasn't clear, but I knew what the words "bugging out" meant. We had to pull out, back and in a hurry. It meant that the whole camp was in danger. If there is one thing that I've learned about the military is that when given the order to retreat, things must really be hot!

I staggered to my feet trying to recall the correct evac procedure drilled into our heads during basic training, but I lost my powers of reason amongst the scrambled eggs I had for brains. I grabbed my helmet and weapon and staggered into the hot morning sun. Tent stakes were ripped from the earth and all the camps canvas structures that had been our home for almost a year sagged inward and collapsed like slowly deflating balloons.

Soldiers scurried about, and orders shouted. The sky funneled inward before my eyes. I reeled like a drunk maintaining my balance and leaned up against the communications post that stuck out of the ground in the middle of the compound; loudspeakers radiated from the top.

Someone shoved me aside, and I tumbled to the ground. Another yelled, "Soldier, get to your platoon!" It was like a bad dream. Everything had a surreal distorted quality to it. Then all hell broke loose. The air shrieked painfully, and shells fell exploding in every direction. I started to run for cover, but shells were coming down everywhere. To the south, they fell where reconnaissance last reported the enemy encampment. The hit the road and even the village.

Bloch appeared out of nowhere calmly standing in front of me; he acted as if he didn't notice the bombardment. "Let's go" he shouted above the shriek of an incoming eighty-two millimeter. "We're hitting the jungle south of the perimeter. Church, you've got the point."

I hesitated aimlessly for a second or two trying to recall which way was south when Bill came up from behind and slapped me on the shoulder. "It's okay partner," he screamed in my ear. "You pull up the rear. I'll take the point."

"But it's my turn to take the ..." I started to say, but my voice trailed off never completing the sentence because Bill had already run ahead. He slowed down his pace for only a second when catching up with Sergeant Bloch, yelled something close to his ear than ran on. Before following, Bloch shot me a glaring hard look over his shoulder, motioned for everyone to follow then headed for the edge of the perimeter.

Everything moved in slow motion. I remember Stash and Rinaldi jogging past me. There was a blur of O.D. green. Two helicopter gunships hovered low over the perimeter like huge dragonflies. My legs were lead. It was the sensation of time being out of sink you can have in a nightmare. You try to run from some danger, but your feet become glued to the pavement. Our entire platoon must have trotted past me because I was the last to hit the jungle.

A ground fog or a fog of my imagination hung over the jungle floor. Smoke and the smell of cordite filled the air above giving the morning sun the appearance of artificial lightning. I was a character on stage in a play. The scenery was in place, the background and lighting were all set.

In front of me was the barrier that surrounded our camp on the side of the jungle. Constructed of three rings of concertina wire with the spaces between the rings and filled with trip flares and low tangles of barbed wire. It appeared impassible except to the trained eye. There was a low spot in the earth just below the first ring of concertina wire covered by a small outcropping of pepper hedge. The pepper, planted by the first infantry division who originally set up the camp and carefully trimmed so that it wouldn't grow too large and overshadow the wire barrier but trimmed in such a way as to still maintain the appearance of wild growth.

The low bush marked the easy entrance and exit to and from the perimeter for any knowing grunt. All you had to do was to plop your butt down on the pepper and slide under the wire. Once inside the first and second rings, you could scurry on all fours to your right about a hundred feet, and you would come across another clump of bush allowing you to slip under number two ring. The third and last ring could be crossed at another bush approximately fifty meters in the opposite direction. Carefully navigating the trip wires and barbed wire between the three rings of concertina you would find yourself outside the main barrier to our camp.

I had crawled safely under the first and second rings and was making it around my third trip wire when the sounds of a firefight made me freeze. First, it was the cracking of AK fire, then after a moment or two, it was followed by the reports of several M-16's. A full half minute later the sound of two M-60's roared from the bamboo. I knew it was our guys. They probably came smack up against some VC or worse the North Vietnamese regular army. I knew this had to be a major offensive on the part of the North Vietnamese. Why else would we have been ordered to pull out?

I also knew I wasn't functioning on all cylinders, but I pressed on anyway. The thought "I've got to help" was the only thing on my mind. The banks of the Ben-Hai were within view, and I saw a herd of barking deer, no larger than dogs, nervously skitter along the river's edge.

Seconds later I saw a salvo of eighty-two-millimeter mortars descended to the south flattening several acres mowing down the bamboo. The whumping sounds of the exploding shells were deafening.

I laid face down in the dirt for a minute then lifted my head to the sounds of men screaming. They were death screams. The chilling sounds made by the severely wounded. Visions of maimed bodies and torn limbs swam before me. I tried to force the thoughts out of my head and moved on. I only had to pass the third ring, and I would be out.

The third clump of pepper lay just ahead. I scrambled on my belly toward the concealed opening in the concertina wire.

To my right caught up in one of the low tangles of barbed wire was an arm. I first saw it out of the corner of my eye. I knew how it got there. I didn't want to look at it. I was afraid. I knew it was from one of our guys. The shirt sleeve was the right color. It had to have been ripped off at the shoulder from the concussion of one of those mortar shells.

I only gave it a passing glance. You learned to do things like that in Nam to maintain your sanity. Just move along and try not to take in too much of the scenery. Then my eyes caught a glint of yellow. Bright yellow reflecting the suns rays. It was gold. There was a bracelet around the wrist. Bill wore a gold bracelet on the wrist of his right hand. Was that a right arm or a left arm? I couldn't keep going. His wife gave it to him the day he was shipped out.

I crawled toward the severed arm. Bill and his wife had only been married a year when he got drafted. Their daughter was two months old when he left. The elbow turned away from me and the thumb on the hand pointed down. Oh God, it was a right arm. Their love was strong, and she had the two words engraved on the face plate where he could easily see them. "Forever Always." I crawled closer, red veins and an artery hung from the shoulder socket. A demon within me dragged me toward the ugly thing. I didn't want to look at it. It could have been another infantryman's arm. A similar bracelet.

The arm, turned in such a way, that seeing the gold plate was impossible. I shook uncontrollably and took hold of the wrist but jerked back the moment I touched it. The flesh was still warm. Momentarily dislodged from the wire the arm slid sideways turning the faceplate upward. "Forever Always" it read. "Forever Always . . . Forever Always" screamed in my thoughts. Just then another salvo hit the jungle. One shell after another exploded as if mocking the words that screamed inside my head.

I ran on my hands and knees leaving my weapon behind and dropping my helmet to the ground. I moved recklessly along the perimeter occasionally snagging my shirt and trousers on the barbed wire but never stopping. In that crazed state, I somehow navigated my way back through the perimeter barrier toward camp. I got to my feet and staggered to the edge of camp in time to witness two 122-millimeter rockets slam into the motor pool. The roof lifted several feet into the air, then collapsed. Fragments of metal, glass, and wood showered the compound. The concussion from the explosion knocked me down. Mortar shells kept falling all over the area.

I managed to crawl to the garbage dump for cover and lay there quivering between the concussions of each volley, squeezing the stone trinket in my palm. My brain swam feverishly from the confusion of the attack and the still clear memory of my dream from the day before. Dust and shrapnel choked the atmosphere, and through the raging tumult, I imagined the old medicine man's face looking down at me. His arm was stretched out, a finger beckoned. I jumped up and followed the outstretched hand of my imagination to the other side of the camp, explosions screaming in my ears.

Halfway across the compound, the garbage dump erupted behind me with the force of an eighty-two millimeter. I turned from the explosion and looked beyond the Ben Hai river in time to see a large bombardment strike north of the village. My vision of the old Montagnard disappeared when portions of the rock-faced Dalat Mountains gave way under the violent detonation.

I was face down in the dirt after that, sandwiched between a half-track and the mess tent. I heard someone screaming close by, and after several seconds elapsed, I realized that it was my voice.

I came to one hundred seventy-five miles southeast of camp and found myself in a bed of the 93rd Evacuation Hospital. Bed space was at a premium and wounded were pouring in every minute. My head was clear of the drug and except for a slight pounding in my skull I was fine.

I watched for a familiar face amongst the men that hobbled in on crutches and rolled in on stretchers. Then I noticed Corporal Rinaldi. He was in the bed next to mine. I thought I was hallucinating again, but the thought passed when I heard him laugh. Evidently, the look on my face told all. I babbled on briefly about how good it was to see him alive then fell silent. His right arm had been bandaged from the shoulder down. Tubes ran from his side, and his arm was supported from above by a sling. I felt stupid. I remembered what happened to Bill.

The next day I learned from Rinaldi that the bug-out was a fake. A ruse trumped up by H.Q. and known only by a handful with the direct purpose to flush out the guerrillas hiding in the south causing them to tip their hand and reveal their location.

A company of four platoons was immediately taken off evac procedure sending half to sweep from the east and the others from the west with the enemy caught in the middle leaving no retreat available as artillery was supposed to keep them pinned down hammering at the south and our divisional headquarters' field guns to the north.

Artillery, unfortunately, made an error dropping shells around camp and the village until after few costly miscalculations they located the southern target. The camp had suffered heavy damage by the time our C.O. got on the horn and convinced the one hundred and fifty-first that their shells were a little too close for comfort. The people of Dai Sut weren't so lucky; it was one of these volleys of fire that I witnessed falling far north of the target destroying the village. Rinaldi had a better view than I. While being pinned down amidst a crossfire he saw the base of the Dalat Range reduced to rubble. The shelling sealed the entrance to the cave of the elders with tons of rock.

The campaign, however, was a successful counteroffensive. There were reports of how the American victory had set the NVA back several months. The aftermath of the battle had only Rinaldi and a handful of others making it back. Collateral damage killed at least half of them, and although the guerrillas were cut down in large numbers, only a few of our guys remained to tell about it. Those that were lucky enough to make it through the barrage met with a fierce battle that lasted almost a full half hour.

There I was, a cowardly survivor of the battle that had killed most of my friends. The only injury I had sustained was to the mind, while the few that did come out of it considered themselves fortunate to be only wounded.

Rinaldi never made it to the firefight. Unlike me, he'd been stopped by a chunk of shrapnel in the right arm.

It was, I know, fortunate that I didn't go into that battle and the artillery barrage as well. Nor am I fool enough not to realize how lucky I was to return home in one piece. But I did panic. Whether it was the drug or the shock of battle or both, I don't think I'll ever be certain of the answer.

On the last day that I saw Rinaldi, he sensed the guilt I was harboring; the loss of our friends that we grew to know during our period of internment. Their tragic deaths will forever mar the joys and hardships we shared just trying to stay alive.

When the morphine wore off Rinaldi's shoulder would give him a lot of trouble. Even though I felt cowardly and ashamed of the outcome, somehow I sensed that he envied my situation.

Before being shipped stateside, they sent me to Heidelberg, Germany, and the doctors put me in a nut ward feeding me Thorazine for a month. After thirty days I was declared "cured" and sent home.

I left Vietnam without ever knowing if Faab had survived. I made an inquiry with H.Q. but nothing ever turned up. Even though his presence at the garbage dump that afternoon had to have been a hallucination, I still today cannot get over the coincidence of his disappearance that was timed so precisely with the bombardment of the Dalat Mountains.

***

Before I go any further and possibly wander off, I better tell you how I acquired the position of head photo technician for the NATO West German Missile Deployment. The job title is important sounding enough, and the pay was great, everything else was disappointing. I have never told this to anyone, not even to Janet in its entirety and though the situation was odd, circumstances made it imperative that I take the job.

The fighting in Vietnam ended shortly after I returned home. Afterwards, jobs were scarce. They had been before, but the costly stalemate of the war just made things even worse. I spent the first couple of weeks in New York City re-acquainting myself with Janet and civilian life. I met my wife's friends, Emma and Harry, and the four of us had some great moments together. The adjustment was tough, and Janet's job and my discharge pay got us by for awhile, but rising inflation and a desire on both our parts to raise a family sent me out amongst the job force to look for work.

A dream of mine has always been to become independent, self-employed with my own business. The desire was stronger than ever. Two years in the military taking orders has that effect on a lot of people. Commercial photography was the field of course, and I needed money to make it a reality. A business needs capital and contacts to get started, so I had to find employment. I was determined to find work in a related field. Almost an impossible task. It became a real hardship. In fact, any job at all was difficult to find.

I busied myself for a while taking odd jobs in the neighborhood, running deliveries, washing windows and painting vacated apartments for our landlord instead of rent. I filled the remaining gaps by frequenting the different employment services and combing the want ads. I put together a portfolio of some of the better pictures I had taken during my college days and a very short resume. The war had left me little time to further my talents. I was rusty and updated the portfolio the best I could within our budget. I spent evenings brushing up on new techniques published in the current photo journals and magazines.

Life turned stagnant, and any hope of starting a career looked grim. I had virtually no job experience, and unemployment was at an all-time high. I was very confident at first of my abilities, but the employment situation was such that it was almost impossible to get even an interview, and the few that would condescend to talk to me held my work record against me.

Everyone wanted "experienced help only, " and with the jobless rate, as it was, they had the pick of the crop. There were moments when I resisted the urge to beg for an opportunity to prove myself. One interviewer refused to look at my portfolio unless I had a minimum of five years experience. I wanted to hit him. I became depressed and took to sleeping in late and watching television, seldom leaving the apartment. If it hadn't been for Janet, I probably wouldn't have eaten regularly. I began to think of myself as a failure in life . . . a loser.

Janet had described those times pretty good in her diary except she left out one very important word, and that word was "bum." That was me. I stopped believing in myself by then. I chucked my portfolio into a closet and went about making a career of boozing it up and getting myself fired from as many transient jobs as humanly possible. I took one uninteresting job after another. A couple paid pretty well too, but I normally got canned in a few weeks or a month. Those months turned into years, and I found myself playing this loser game for quite a while until one day when Harry got the loan of a cabin in Connecticut from one of his customers, and the four of us took time off from the city for a week of hunting and fishing. We returned on the following Sunday, and I picked up our mail from a neighbor down the hall.

As usual that morning, I scanned the want ads. I came across the following:

LOOK NO MORE!

If you are seeking entry into an expanding nationally recognized corporation. Need key person with knowledge of photography for a supervisory position with rapidly growing firm. Good pay, excellent benefits, with many opportunities for advancement. No previous job experience necessary. Veterans preferred.

Apply in person at . . .

The address given belonged to a temporary office that had been hastily set up behind a vacated storefront off of forty-second street, much like those that spring up at tax time, boasting cheap assistance, auditing individual returns.

I figured that I didn't have one chance in hell to get the job and knew how swamped they would have been with applicants. It had run in the previous Friday's paper, and by the time I read it, the ad was a week old. The position had to be filled. If it hadn't been for the blurb about photography, I naturally would have assumed it to be another come on to sell vacuum cleaners door to door. My curiosity was up, I had nothing to lose and it at least deserved investigation.

When I arrived at the address, I was pleased to see that they were still accepting applications. It wasn't difficult to notice because a string of hungry applicants were lined up outside the front entrance for a block and a half, and taking into account the size of a city block in New York, that made for a helluva long line.

The wait cost me over three hours, and when my turn came around, I was certain that I wasn't going to get the job. If anything made up my mind for me that afternoon, it was the conversation I struck up with a fellow from Pittsburg in line in front of me. He was ten years older than me, well polished and packing a very impressive portfolio with fifteen years experience to his credit. He was out there looking to relocate. He was willing to pack up the wife, kids and worldly goods, lock, stock and barrel and move to the big apple the moment he found something in his field. I convinced myself that if anyone got the job, it would be him.

When my turn finally came, they directed me to a small desk. There were only two other people in the room. One sat behind the desk shuffling papers and the other stood at the door ushering applicants in and out.

The interviewer, if he can be called that, was very brief. He was a nervous, thin-lipped man with the disgusting habit of salivating excessively so that the corners of his mouth welled up with little beads of moisture. He was about my age, but an unusual skin defect made him appear older. The skin on his neck heavily wrinkled into folds and a kind of greasiness about the fellow added to my dislike. He was evidently given to hanging about the fish docks because he carried with him much of the characteristic smell.

The man never looked up at me for more than a second at a time and refused to examine my portfolio. He was more preoccupied with starring at my hands while he kept his folded. He had little more than a worthless regard for my resume and asked few questions regarding my experience. Instead, he was more interested in my personal life rather than if I knew one end of a camera from another. He asked where I was born, questions about my family background and military service. I questioned what it had to do with the job requirements, and the interviewer replied that the owner of the company was a devoted family man and it was his policy to take great interest in the backgrounds of all his employees. He said "family" in a peculiar almost cooing voice and smiled when he said it.

I found him even less cooperative when inquiring after the type of position and the company that offered it. The only explanation the interviewer would give was that it had to do with running a photo lab.

I left there that afternoon knowing less than when I went in. I saw the gentleman from Pittsburg by the curb trying to hail a cab. We both smiled at one another and shrugged our shoulders. I guessed he had received the same run around as I did.

***

"Fat chance" is what I said when Janet asked if I got the job. My conviction did not remain steadfast through breakfast the next day. Our morning meal was interrupted by a telephone call. A woman's voice on the other end of the line said the job was mine. She didn't ask if I still wanted the position just that I was to report to work the next day.

I am not going to dwell on what happened next but will try to briefly outline some of the more unusual events while under the stateside employ of Emmerson and Pryne. By the way, that is the firm's name. They are a public relations company, a very classy firm, as their uptown address indicated. A tall chrome and glass structure overlooking the Hudson.

They made me a good offer. Truthfully, I would have accepted any offer. I couldn't understand why they chose me over all the other applicants. I hadn't even finished college. I didn't openly question their reasons because I was certain it had been a mistake. They probably had me mixed up with another applicant, and I wasn't about to say anything for fear they would recognize their error and I would be back on the street again.

Emmerson-Pryne, public relations, had a wealthy client base

comprised of large corporations and government service contracts. They would take ground floor products, concepts, up and coming politicians and even new ideas in law enforcement and legislature and promote them favorably into the public eye. Most of the work was done on a consulting basis outlining new programs and supplying data, but the firm commercially handled some of it. Primarily in the line of new products and politicians. That was where I came in. It sounded to me like a field that would be in need of my photography skills. Unfortunately, as it turned out, the part I eventually played wasn't all that glamorous.

After completing a very thorough medical examination, another of the company's policies, I was shut away in a darkroom with the tedious task of developing someone else's work.

My involvement with other employees in the firm was seldom, most of my dealings were with Falbridge, the nervous little man with the continuous drool, and he kept me so busy that I hardly had a chance to meet anyone. At times, the work would pile up, and I would have to take my lunch in the lab. I hadn't the opportunity to meet the owner, but Falbridge was continually full of praise and said on many occasions that Mr. Pryne was very pleased with my work. It was a bit of a surprise because most of the work was mundane. What was given me was handed over with little or no instructions as to what was to be done. Sometimes I was given exposed film never really knowing if I was just to develop the negatives, make prints or blow ups. I spent a good deal of time once making enlargements. A lot of it was commercial work. New products, mostly in the electronics field, and children's toys.

I did work for a whole week touching up a series of publicity photos for a governor and ex-real estate magnate that had entered the presidential primaries.

Their political track record was astounding. Out of thirty-three Senatorial candidates across the country that they had helped promote, twenty-seven of them had attained office. Most of this work was done by someone else, and I was left with the lonely and tiring tasks of simple printing and developing. When I first started work, Falbridge told me that I would be running a photo lab. I thought I would be working with other people.

A straight diet of this soon developed into a lack of enthusiasm. I began to play around with the material given me. On one occasion, I printed every other frame on a roll of negatives, just to see what the reaction would be. Once I did some enlargements that I purposely overexposed the entire batch. In all cases, the work was accepted with the highest praise from Falbridge and never returned.

I had grown bored after two long, tedious months of this and would sneak in books, a radio and a thermos of coffee to kill time. It wasn't difficult to bring in comforts from home. I was instructed to use a rear entrance by Falbridge. He said that Mr. Pryne forbade his employees to use the front entrance, although I never met any of the employees when I arrived daily because the entrance was right across the hall from my lab. I even had my own private restroom in the lab. So I had no idea if Mr. Pryne's rule was strictly enforced, besides in my case.

After a while, my work fell behind, and I would only turn out a bare minimum to have something to give Falbridge at the end of each day. My skin grew pale from continual darkness, and I soon gave way to listening to footsteps at the keyhole.

Instructed that if I were ever to leave the building, I was to take my lunch at one, whereas my keen listening had perceived that everyone else broke for their's at twelve. I felt like a freak, left out of everything, a crazy relative shut away in a closet.

Determined to mingle with the other employees, one day at noon when I heard them coming from the other end of the building, I threw open the door to my lab and leaned against the jamb maintaining a casual manner. At least a dozen people were coming down the hall in my direction.

Several of them were limping, and one had so much difficulty that he needed the aid of a metal walker. All wore dark glasses. Some were clad in white lab coats and the rest in dark suits. I only saw their features briefly, because when they noticed me, they turned away, covering their faces. The ones I saw their skin was shiny, oily and their noses flattened.

I remember thinking that they looked disfigured, as if by fire or disease. Two appeared to have physical deformities. One, a woman attempted to conceal her hand within the lab coat she wore. It looked flattened and narrow. I could not discern any separation of the fingers, and the impression I got was that of a flipper rather than a hand. The man in the walker moved along with a peculiar shambling gait, and his feet were abnormally large. The more I studied them, the more I wondered how he could find shoes to fit them.

A grotesque thought struck me while watching the unusual procession. I remembered reading once about the physical defects caused by thalidomide. It was a sedative used in the late 1950's to treat morning sickness. Thalidomide was withdrawn from the market after being found to cause severe birth defects. I had heard tales of small societies of the commonly afflicted people. I wondered if this was one of those groups.

My demeanor changed, but I kept up a pretty good front so I wouldn't offend any of them. Before I could open my mouth, Falbridge appeared from behind pressing me into the lab, inquiring if there was anything I needed.

"Who are those people?" I demanded once inside.

"They are employees of Mr. Pryne. They are of a special nature, and I must ask you not to interfere." He hesitated briefly, then patted me on the shoulder. "They are very sensitive, and Mr. Pryne doesn't want them upset."

He left, closing the door behind him. His manner, although firm, was sincere and I felt like a fool. I was beginning to get the picture of this Mr. Pryne. He must have had a particular interest in the severely handicapped, so much so that he had dedicated an entire department just to themselves and my presence would only make them feel uncomfortable. I gave up any further attempts at making social contacts with anyone in the building beside Falbridge and went back to listening at keyholes only to pass the time.

There were others that I heard coming and going besides at lunch. One, in particular, would travel from one end of the hall at two-thirty every afternoon, then fifteen minutes later I would hear him walking in the other direction. I am sure it was the same person both times because of the unique sound of the shuffling strides. The person must have been badly crippled and probably used a cane or crutches to help propel themselves along. The noise of his walk through the keyhole resembled a short hop followed by the dragging of feet.

It was at these times between the coming and going of the footsteps that I detected an odor. It was a fishy smell. Like the odor, I detected on Falbridge during the interview. At times I couldn't detect the odor on him while, at others, the faint scent was apparent. On the occasions of the shuffling feet, the odor was much stronger.

Remembering my embarrassing encounter with the other people in the building, I set upon an idea to get a view of my two-thirty traveler. Pieces of weather stripping shielded the cracks around my darkroom door preventing any light leaks, that might spoil the undeveloped film and consequently didn't afford me a view of anything on the other side. I removed the screws securing the metal and rubber strips one afternoon and shortly after two placed my chair next to the door and sat there waiting. When the half-hour struck, the shuffling and hopping began. Whoever was in the hall crossed in front of the door, and a shadow blocked out the light. The smell was stronger than ever, and the shadow lingered. I became upset, unglued. Whoever it was, was just standing outside my door, possibly listening or trying to peak in through the keyhole. Then it dawned on me. It was happening every afternoon. What I mistook for the common comings and goings of one lone person down the hall as two separate jaunts were in reality just one with a rest stop at my door for a fifteen-minute interval.

The full quarter of an hour elapsed with me sitting there facing the closed door trying to summon up the courage needed to fling it open and see who was on the other side. The smell, as I said, was stronger than before, probably because of the removal of the strip from around the jamb. It also enabled me to detect breathing. Twice I reached out for the doorknob, but my hand on both occasions dropped to my side after losing the nerve. At 2:45 my visitor departed, and I just sat there staring at the closed door.

I never related these events to Janet. Oh, she knew that I wasn't too happy with the job, but the money was good and when I returned home at the end of a day all nonsense of the afternoon was dispelled by our happy home life. That evening was different though. I started to take my job home with me, mostly in the privacy of my thoughts, but I am sure Janet detected the change.

I decided that I had to get out of that darkroom either by means of a promotion, a transfer or as a last resort by way of a resignation.

An idea had come to me while developing a batch of photos given to me by Falbridge. He had requested a series of large blowups made from specific frames. The request itself wasn't unusual, but as I came to learn after working there for a while, that any request, no matter how small, from Falbridge in regards to my work, was abnormal. I didn't question him at all but rather attacked the job with a new found zeal for I felt that I was given my first assignment since I joined the nuthouse.

The photographs were unlike anything I had developed for them. I couldn't see where they had any commercial or political value at all.

They were aerial photos, the kind used for geological map making. Most of it was of the countryside, but there was a small town pictured in a few of the shots. I had no idea of the town's location. I found myself staring at them for a long time. I wished myself into the small town, wondered how many people lived there and what was their lifestyle?

That was when this idea struck me. The photo of the town reminded me of a time years ago when stuck in a little burg in Indiana, and the sale of a portrait of the town hall to the mayor awarded me with enough money to escape. Falbridge had mentioned to me in passing one day that they were going to do the cover for a special issue of "Life Magazine." The cover story was to depict the anniversary of the World Trade Center. The company had never seen any of my work as a photographer, and if awarded the cover photo, my life with Emmerson-Pryne could change radically.

I wasted little time in putting my plan into effect. I had to wait until the following Tuesday for an overcast day to get the right light. It had rained the night before, and the effect was tremendous. I used up two rolls of thirty-six exposure on the Twin Towers to ensure the proper angle and about the same on the Empire State Building.

I know you're probably wondering what the Empire State Building had to do with my project. I won't bother with the details, but I did what is called a paste-up in the lab. I found a remarkable old photograph at the library of a dirigible in flight. I copied and reduced its size and had it hovering over the top of the old skyscraper. Over the World Trade Center, I airbrushed in a jet stream. The results had the skyscrapers side by side in a wide-angle perspective, leaning away from one another, contrasting the old with the new.

I blew the whole thing up to cover size and waited for Falbridge. He came around at his usual time, but on this occasion, I had two parcels for him. One parcel was the aerial photo assignment and the other with my work inside. I had taken the liberty to mark the outside "Attention Ephraim Pryne." When I handed him mine, I said that they were for Mr. Pryne personally. I received a raised eyebrow for my boldness, but Falbridge was condescending as usual. When he took the package, I noticed for the first time a webbing of flesh between the forefinger and middle finger of his left hand.

After it was all over, I felt a bit nervous wondering if I might have been out of line. I went home that evening, still wondering.

My usual solitary arrival was disturbed the next morning when I discovered Falbridge waiting for me in my lab. He came to deliver a message. Mr. Pryne wanted to see me. Falbridge seemed irritated at having to fetch me, but he did confess that Pryne had liked the work

I turned in. "Life" didn't use my photo that month, nor any month after that. My work had been knocked down in favor of an article about the Trade Center's excessive expenditures during construction and the loss of profitability from its original projections. A monument to New York's dying economy. A real epitaph for an anniversary.

What the boss did like was my enlargements of the aerial work. It came as an ego-deflating compliment, if you can imagine such a thing, and would have spoiled my whole day except for the nature of our first encounter.

I stepped out of the elevator onto the top floor and couldn't help but notice that the halls were adorned with fire protection equipment. There were twice as many extinguishers than on the ground floor, with manually operated alarm boxes at every ten or twelve feet and an abundance of heat sensing alarms and sprinkler heads cluttering the ceiling tiles.

Falbridge noticed my curiosity and chuckled in a voice that had almost a maniacal ring saying that "water is the enemy of fire."

He led me through a set of double doors into a large study.

Mr. Pryne's office was a penthouse. A large office was at the center with adjoining rooms running in all directions. Many of them probably housed his living quarters, but I never saw them. I suspected that he lived there all year around. The room smelled from the excessive use of air freshener. The atmosphere felt heavy and moist. There was a set of glass doors off to the right of a large desk that overlooked a patio. The area beyond the doors generously landscaped with bushes and shrubs had been allowed to become overgrown and wild. In the center was a swimming pool that showed the signs of being ill-kept. The water had turned green with algae, reeds were growing up from the bottom, and lily pads covered a portion of the watery surface.

There were small puddles the size of footprints leading out of the stagnant pool and with an icy chill I observed that they terminated indoors leaving wet blotches on the carpet. I guess the whole thing if

I would have had time to dwell on it, might have become eerie, but as it happened, my meeting became rushed, and the overall appearance of Ephraim Pryne diverted my attention.

When we first came face to face, I knew then the reason why he had such an overwhelming concern for the disabled. Mr. Pryne was confined to a wheelchair. Supplied with a little electric motor, he had full access to the room which had been constructed at a level about him so that he could reach everything.

What was even more unexpected was his physical appearance. Covering his lower torso was a thick green wool blanket that had been tucked tightly around the waist and legs. His hands surprisingly enough were concealed behind a pair of bright yellow mittens, while a full beard, mustache and a bushy head of hair, all the shocking color of red, masked most of his features. I could make out a flattened almost non-existent nose and eyes that were anything but deep-set. His appearance was similar to those poor unfortunate souls that afternoon outside my lab.

All in all, with red hair, yellow mittens, and green blanket, he would have been comical if it hadn't been for his intense and congenial manner. He had forgone the handshake explaining that he had been disabled in an accident and any such contact was painful to him. His actions towards me were kind, soft-spoken and almost fatherly referring to me occasionally as, "my son." Not at all the personality, I expected from an entrepreneur.

I learned that Emmerson had passed away several years ago leaving Pryne, the sole owner of the corporation. Ephraim had decided to dedicate his remaining years of business, whenever possible, toward the execution of social and political change, "for the good of the masses." He repeated that at least three times in our short conversation. For who's good and what changes, I wasn't quite sure nor did I get a chance to ask. If it hadn't been for his massive enterprise, I would have sworn, by the way, he talked, that he was a Marxist.

Pryne did all of the talking while Falbridge just stood and nodded.

I had a tough time getting a word in edgewise and after a while gave up and became a disciplined listener like Falbridge. I did manage to ask if he had seen my piece on the Twin Towers but the question was ignored and substituted with praise of my simple blow-ups. I figured that he saw something in them that I failed to notice.

The meeting went along this way for a while then they laid the transfer on me, to all places can you imagine, West Germany, for no more than one year. The purpose was to head up a special photographic team and crew of lab technicians. The reason; a photo-geographic study of a selected area in Germany backed by the United States Air Force and the Army Corp of Engineers to map out in detail a mountainous wooded region in the southwestern corner of that country, the Black Forest.

On the surface, the assignment seemed authentic enough, even though I didn't understand why I had been chosen as one of the principal players in the deal. There was, of course, a precise aim to this project. The military believed that the densely wooded areas would be an excellent place to conceal missile sites from Soviet surveillance satellites. The last of our military bases slated for withdrawal because of the old Yalta agreement was Fort Blish, a U.S. airfield 60 miles southwest of Stuttgart could be saved from extinction by the arrival of one hundred-eight Peacekeeper ICBM's, and the influx of forty-three hundred Americans needed to maintain them. The military creatively called their missile deployment schedule "Project Firefly."

Valsbach, a placid town of two thousand, faced a cultural revolution if the Americans decided to take up residence at the old World War II airbase down the road.

The locals split in a dispute over living alongside NATO's new nuclear missile silos. The shopkeepers and people in business wanted the Americans to stay and looked forward to economic gains when the basing started late that year. While some rural residents planned to expand local stores and hoped to grab a share of building contracts, others feared for the future of their small community. The fear is that U.S. support crews will crowd the small town causing an increase in crime, prostitution, and drugs and the threat of violent demonstrations to a one-room general store village was a greater threat than the missiles.

The European press was having a field day with public appeal and the Emmerson-Pryne public relations department was hard at work letting the American and German public know what a fine job we were doing with our deployment to offset the Soviet arsenal of SS-20's aimed at Europe. "After all," said Mr. Pryne, "it is better to have Peacekeepers in your backyard than an SS-20 on your roof."

I guess I could have said no to the transfer, but the thought hadn't occurred to either Pryne or Falbridge because they had already made plans for my departure. I wasn't too keen on working for the military again, but the money was too good to turn down. My salary would be double, and there would be a fifty thousand dollar bonus upon my return to the states. I knew I was taking the easy way out, but in a years time I could kiss the job good-bye and be back home with enough capital to start my own business.

***

My job with the military was as disappointing as the one I held at home. At first sight of the airbase, I was gripped by the sudden fear that I might be forced into re-enlisting.

I was given the ten-cent tour by a young nervous pimple faced lieutenant from security that spoke in such a halting, agitating voice that he would stop in the middle of every other sentence and clear his throat. He pointed out different installations as if rehearsed and managed to squeak out the areas of the base that were off limits to civilian personnel, which was most of the surrounding eleven hundred acres, and which areas I was permitted to frequent. It was one gray melancholy concrete building situated in the middle of a gravel parking lot.

The building was a narrow, single-story construction, flat-roofed and stretched about ninety feet in length. The only windows were at the front entrance where my guide hastily deposited me inside. Here everything was painted with gloss enamel in the same lack of color as the exterior. Grateful to part company, the lieutenant left me in the charge of an SF, a United States Air Force Security Forces Military Policeman.

I was greeted by a large grinning face that appeared uneasy not knowing if he should maintain a military attitude in my presence or give in to something more informal. Taking the first steps and with an outstretched hand, I introduced myself. I am sure my arrival at that moment caught him off guard because he had just gotten through shoving a wad of Skoal in his mouth. The can of chewing tobacco remained open on his desk blotter. He behaved like the cat that swallowed the canary and suppressing my amusement I hoped he didn't swallow it. He swept the can of Skoal into the center desk drawer and rose hesitating briefly between saluting and being at ease.

Finally coming forward, he took my extended hand with one the size of a ball mitt and said, "Sergeant Ruttick, James Fennimore Ruttick. Friends call me Jim." He shifted the chew from the left cheek to the right and glanced around for a place to spit.

Jim Ruttick was the only color within that drab building. His story only added to the comedy. The sergeant didn't know a thing about photography or map making. By virtue of his great size and an overflow of personnel at the motor pool he was assigned the day watch at the lab, I figured that the young lieutenant was probably responsible for the assignment. He was to guard the front entrance against any possible intrusion of unauthorized personnel.

Jim became more my shadow than a policeman. He went with me wherever I went on the base and would report at regular intervals to security, an unnecessary precaution I thought, because as time progressed I didn't see where any of the work that came out of my lab would have been of any international interest. All discussions as to what work was relevant were made elsewhere, out of my hands by powers unseen. I didn't mind it though, his character, on the surface, though tough and brash, was harmless and unassuming and we soon became friends. He tagged along, always asking questions about the lab work, and me pretending to tolerate the simple inquiries all along secretly welcoming the company.

We didn't see much of each other while working, mainly during breaks and lunch. I spent most of the day in the darkroom and Jim at his desk doing God knows what.

We took lunch together frequently, locking the building up at noon and retiring to the enlisted men's mess. We weren't sure if it was permitted, but so long as no one said we couldn't, we went right on doing it. It was one of the rare times I would get out into the sun, and it felt good.

My contract required me to put in long hours. Coupled with a healthy drive to and from work, if it weren't for our lunch breaks, I was almost under a continual cloak of darkness. Arriving every day at sun up and always coming home after dark. I started wearing sunglasses whenever going out. Spending the majority of the day in my darkroom made my eyes painfully sensitive to light yet acutely more perceptive in the dark.

At lunch, I would attempt to manipulate the conversation. Jim, if left unchecked, would wander on about the latest in automobile parts or the recent advancement in weaponry. He had a good knowledge of antique weapons and boasted of a large personal collection which he tried to relate to my field occasionally mentioning that he hoped to catalog them on film someday.

He was obsessed with talking about World War II, and I found him several times wishing himself back in those days. He said he was a soldier without a war to fight, referring to the historical conflict as "the real war." I didn't tell him about my two years in the service. The area around the schloss where I lived didn't present many opportunities to meet English speaking people, nor did the isolation of a darkroom, so the conversation was appreciated.

I believe the sergeant had a drinking problem. Even though some mornings his eyes were a bit bloodshot I didn't become aware of the problem until I began to notice his irregular eating habits. Hamburgers and tomato soup in the morning, while only picking at his lunch in the afternoon and a compulsion for sweets.

Perhaps he drank out of loneliness. His desire to make friends was strong. I felt sorry for him and invited him to dinner one weekend. One thing I came to learn when in the service, living in close quarters with other men is not to be critical of someone's behavior and accept them for what they are. As I said earlier, I welcomed the company.

Jim was the only one I got to know well on the base. The rest were just acquaintances in the form of messengers dropping off the exposed film, delivery men and the Cutters, as Jim called them, of others, there were none. I worked alone.

The Cutters were a group of young geologists assigned the task of cutting up and trimming the aerial blowups our labs produced and piecing them together like a large jigsaw puzzle. Thus they were dubbed "The Cutters." They were a cliquish group and impossible to get to know. Most of them refused to acknowledge our presence. Any friendly inquiries on my part were answered with as few words as possible normally followed by indifferent stares. One time I had a door slammed in my face. I gave up any further attempts to make friends and returned to my lab feeling like the new kid on the block who was not allowed to play.

Early in one of these encounters, I noticed that at least two displayed the same physical deformity, the webbing of skin between the fingers. One wasn't that noticeable, but another and probably the most tight-lipped among them had fingers and thumbs completely joined by thick expanses of tissue. I hadn't encountered this rare affliction since Falbridge in New York and the connection, if one existed, between them gave me an uneasy feeling.

Jim decided to avoid the Christmas rush and hate them early. After noticing their slight bow legged and arched back characteristics he started calling the two of them "frogs" behind their backs. Then after watching a couple of afternoons of them crawling along the floor moving the large puzzle pieces, he was reminded, he said, "of monkeys in the zoo" and for a while couldn't decide on a proper handle. His labeling process soon fell upon "Monkey Frogs, " and there it stuck. "Monkey Frogs and Cutters" or "The damn Cutters are frigging Monkey Frogs." Followed by crazy monkey shenanigans of his own.

I know it was cruel, abusive as well as discriminatory but I couldn't help from laughing. Jim tickled a mischievous child in me. On occasions, while suppressing laughter, I would beg him to be quiet when they were in the building, fearing they would hear him. Jim's manner was anything but quiet. He would save up his comments until in the hallway just outside their room and across from mine. Because of Jim's size, I figured that he was not the type to mess with if angered. I guess the geologists were of the same opinion. If they heard him, they carried on as if nothing was said and whatever grudge I might have harbored against them because of my suffered indignation was cheerfully avenged several times over by James Fennimore Ruttick.

Two shifts ran the lab. Mine, the day shift, of course, and the other at night. Our check in and check out times must not have coincided, because I never met any of my evening counterparts. Jim was on the same shift as me and never met any of these people. I think that in time I would have found out more about the other people that worked in the building but as it happened my employment, there was short-lived. I often wondered if there was more than one to the night shift or if there was another like me, lonely and isolated from the outside.

I began to fantasize that there was something diabolical afoot. Without an exact knowledge of geology or topography, I had come to my new appointment a bit apprehensive, but my duties were even less than in New York. I thought I was to head up a lab and work with photographers and geologists in the field. As it turned out I was more disappointed than when I first started with Emmerson-Pryne. I only processed film.

Now, to someone not familiar with a modern processing lab, you may not realize the menial task I had. I didn't handle any printmaking or blowups while there. The night crew did that work. Very little of what I did was color work, mostly black and white. A task today handled by a processing machine that requires little skill to operate. A messenger relayed my orders and delivered hundreds of shots daily for developing or by way of a work order that was left in the overnight box. There were so many to develop in a day that I very seldom had the time to examine them closely.

Twice I was shaken from the tedium by a long distance phone call from Falbridge, but these were as uneventful as my duties. He was only concerned that I was on the job, not with the quality or quantity of the work and would always cut our conversations short. I was ready for him the second time he called though. I threatened to leave if there weren't some improvements and received a raise in pay mixed with shallow praise.

Forced to work under these conditions, and overpaid as well, I was achieving results any high school student could do. I kept thinking of that character in Arthur Conan Doyle's, The Red-Headed League that was kept from his shop being handsomely paid to copy by hand the Encyclopedia Britannica, while his new employers tunneled beneath his store to a neighboring bank, and into the vault.

I was becoming a creature of the night, hardly ever seeing the light of day during the week and gradually shunning daylight on the weekends. I would become restless after coming home and spent a lot of time wandering in the woods. Those subsequent walks at night as a search; only I had no idea what I was hunting.

My appetite for music dwindled as well. I have been a great fan of classical music for years, and my favorite is an obscure German composer and violin player by the name of Erich Zann. Zann died over fifty years ago, and I have a collection of his old recordings. His world of beauty laid far in his imagination, and I am usually in the custom of devoting one hour in the evening listening to his fugues of captivating quality. But since I started working at the Fort Blish Lab,

I have had an aversion towards the old recordings, shunning them as if with an unconscious dread and I haven't touched them since.

While puzzling over my nocturnal wanderings and my lack of appreciation for Zann's recordings I came in contact with a strange set of events.

When the Cutters were not in, we had free run of the building, except for one room. The door had been marked "authorized personnel only." Jim didn't have a key to it. There were two labs in the building. Mine was used only for processing, the other contained enlarging equipment and was manned exclusively by the unseen night crew. Across the hall from the two labs on the west side of the building was the place occupied by the young geologists. Requiring adequate floor space to lay out the aerial maps it ran nearly the length of the building on that side minus the area taken up by the lobby.

When first arriving at Fort Blish I was surprised to find that the work area assigned to me was a carbon copy of the one I had in New York. Exact in almost every detail save for the spacious area to the right side of the room where my enlarger would have stood was empty and in its place was a door. It opened into that restricted room. It had always remained locked, and the knob on my side had been removed. I suspected that it was probably larger than the two labs combined because both of them occupied less than half of the east side of the building and the rest seemed to be taken up by the locked room.

The room was visited by the geologists always drawing the lock behind them when inside. The Cutters would gather selected photos from the map room and take them to the authorized area.

On my fifth day at Fort Blish, I was distracted by what I interpreted as joyous commotion. Leaving my processor, I went down the hall and witnessed two of the young men with armloads of photographs at the door to the barred room carrying on a conversation. They were excited, caught up in the emotional zeal of some new find. One of them was pointing to several large blow-ups pasted together while the other said, "There has been a definite uplift in the terrain since last week." I had no idea what he meant so I approached the two of them and said, "what's up?" That was when I had the door slammed in my face.

Under this environment, I would have fallen into my old habit of letting my work slide if it hadn't been for the circumstances of the next week. I am not even sure if it can be called circumstances, a feeling, a sense of disorientation rather than any physical set of events that I can describe.

It was the lack of circumstances that troubled me. I became aware of a lapse or loss of time, after the period of our coffee breaks. At ten every morning Jim would have individual decanters of coffee brought in on trays, and we would break for fifteen minutes. He was always looking for an excuse to interrupt me. I was afraid that he might blunder in some day and spoil a batch of film, so I got into the habit of locking the door behind me. I normally take my coffee black, with no sugar, but the coffee from the base mess tasted bitter, and I would have to sweeten it down a bit. It was after these interludes when I was back at my processor that the rest of the morning would slip by me and it was time to break again, this time for lunch.

Initially, I let it pass with little concern. We have all experienced that timelessness caused by an intense concentration on an immediate task. All distractions are shut out, and in this "zero state" the mind focuses only on what is at hand. I believe the Japanese call it "muga." I was content and even comfortable at the onset of these lapses. I became less rattled about my job and even entertained the notion that I was learning to cope with the situation and may eventually like it.

I did say that I originally felt that way because last Thursday I wasn't in the mood for conversation and took my coffee in the lab avoiding Jim. I was cutting negatives and pouring my second cup when I became aware for the first time of the incessant ticking of the clock in the room. It was as if it had been stopped earlier then continued without further interruption. The hour was noon. Two hours had mysteriously disappeared, and the balance of the coffee in my carafe was cold.

***

That same week was when I detected a change in Janet. A change that concerned me in the days that followed, yet not enough, I am ashamed to admit, to recognize the warning signs in time to flee that shunned house and return stateside.

Even with all the unusual occurrences at work, I somehow became increasingly comfortable with my job, regarding the extraordinary as rare amusement, and as odd as it sounds, I felt at home with my surroundings and indulgent of the old house with its unnatural setting. Meanwhile, these periods still occupied me with strong urges to walk the woods at night and roam the countryside.

These feelings comprised the better part of what normally should have been my common sense so that when faced with Janet's plight, in the beginning, I laughed it off almost as cruelly as the horrors that assaulted her. I was, I must confess a mass of conflicting emotions, usually easing away from the confusion and lapsing into a luxurious solace of the mind.

I left work that day with the incident of the clock and the cold coffee fresh in my mind. I stopped on my way home to pick up a list of things in Valsbach for Janet. She was always giving me little lists of items to fetch in town. I parked in front of one of the local merchants and saw Falbridge through the car's windshield leaving the telegraph office and walk down the street.

I got out and called to him but did not receive a reply. He stepped up his pace and rounded the corner of the block. I was reasonably sure it was Falbridge. I had only caught a glimpse of his face, but the resemblance would have been too uncanny if it wasn't. I jogged to the adjoining side street but found no sign of him when stepping past the corner. I hung around for a few minutes inspecting the windows of several shops hoping to catch sight of him again.

Later, my shopping list filled, I made a point to navigate the business area in my car going around the block several times and gave up when it grew dark.

The encounter would have probably lived in my thoughts for the remainder of the evening, but Janet had other ideas in store for me. She was asleep on the sofa when I came home and awoke with a start. She reacted in that child-like way of hers that I love so much, pouting and complaining that she had slept the day away feeling useless in the outcome. It took a moment or two for her to wake up completely. She followed me in a few minutes to the kitchen, and while I put away the groceries, I saw that she was distant, preoccupied with something and became edgy when I asked her if anything was wrong.

We made dinner together and afterward settled into the project of breaking into the tower. Janet gave a full account of our entry into that old dusty room in her journal, although I wasn't to read it until a few nights later. I feel no need to repeat the story here except for a few details.

What had come before my eyes by then was my great Uncle Heinrich's notebook. It came into my possession one morning shortly after moving in. It was when I was cleaning out the basement. Covering the cellar floor were pieces of broken and oddly cut mirror glass, fragments of silver solder and bits of wire. I swept the mess into a pile and was looking for something to scoop it up with when what I took for an old magazine caught my eye, wedged between the blocks of masonry in a narrow slit that once contained mortar. Intending to use the stiff cover as a dustpan I withdrew it and knew right off that what I was holding was not a magazine but a notebook . . . a personal journal. I had been in the cellar many times before then, and it had remained unnoticed, written on yellowed bound paper, it blended nicely with the beige colored mortar joints.

It was in an unfamiliar hand, marked in a crabbed script which was scarcely legible and yet had about it a singular directness.

I wrestled with the first few pages realizing by then that it was my great Uncle's writing, then Janet came downstairs surprising me. My immediate reaction was of concealment. I wanted to keep the thing from her and presented it as the fragments of an old diary which we would set aside and read when we weren't so busy.

I know it has the ring of conspiracy to it, but truthfully I meant only the best for her. Contained in those first few leafs that I read were the obvious ravings of an insane man. When alone I finished my Uncle's record and was certain that in his deranged mind he thought he had come close to unraveling a nightmarish riddle, the knowledge of which drove him to madness and subsequently was the cause of his death.

My concern was for Janet's peace of mind. Not that I believed any of my uncle's insane ravings, instead I was afraid that she might begin to have doubts about the mental health of our child she was carrying. For a woman in her condition, a notion like that could become an obsession. And so I faked the loss of the manuscript saying that I must have accidentally tossed it out with some other papers.

Insanity does not run rampant in my family, in fact, this is the only case that I am aware. There have been stories in the past of course, what family is without them, but all of which except in my great uncle's case are unconfirmed.

My uncle was mad though, as mad as they come. Who else but a madman would wish such terrors on an unsuspecting world let alone his involvement in the Nazi party? It is difficult now to say whether he was ever a sane man. Nevertheless, I am certain he must have spent his last remaining years a raving lunatic. He had been a recluse from the rest of the family, separating himself from all of us by thousands of miles of ocean and several continents. His hermitage was so radical that I had no knowledge of his existence until the notification of his death just a few months before.

My chief point in bringing this up is that my ancestry and background, on the whole, are altogether normal.

I feel obliged to say this even more than a defense of my actions in suppressing certain facts from my wife, but for the statements, which will follow and when you are done listening to this recording, I am certain you will understand why I am taking the time to rationalize my sanity.

Even though Heinrich Todesfall was mentally unhinged, many of his delusions must be based on portions of reality, and I was afraid that one of those bases, in fact, was the actual existence of the cemetery. So when I entered the tower that night, I took with me the knowledge of my uncle's mania. The clearing amidst a patch of the thicket that delighted my wife left me with a sickening feeling. I had searched for it on previous evenings when wandering the woods alone, but the brush and scrub trees had concealed it well.

I tried to dissuade Janet from going there the next day, but I was unsuccessful. I didn't say much actually to discourage her since infatuation thrives on opposition and if I did, I would have had to confess to my Uncle's insanity and the lie about the lost notebooks. We did, I thought, compromise and agree to go together but as it turned out, she went on her own the next day.

I perpetuated the lie further, discounting the unusual handprint on the window seat and as if outside myself, heard my voice rationalize away its origin.

I couldn't help wondering, though, about the experiment conducted by my Uncle before he died resulting in his reference to the "other." Whatever it was he saw fit to include little description or explanation about it. In spite of the obvious fabrication of an over-imaginative mind, I had difficulty shaking an uneasy feeling about the tiny handprint. Could it have been left by the "other?"

***

There were other parallels to my great uncle's story. One was the sailor from Innsmouth that he wrote of meeting and his journey to that town on the coast of Massachusetts years ago. Those people he met, if there were such people, they really must have been revolting in appearance, and I gradually began to have misgivings about that meeting, the journey, its outcome and the webbed hands. Once again a parallel. I had come across some people having either all or part of the fingers joined by flesh. First Falbridge, then the two cutters, and now the men in my uncle's chronicle. There had to be more to it than mere coincidence. I am not superstitious, but the chance occurrences seemed like an omen.

The star stone supported these irrational feelings. My great Uncle Heinrich degenerated severely after parting with it. I still had the charm that Faab had given me in Vietnam. Todesfall called it the starstone of Mnar and its description was similar to the one I own. I developed an attachment for the charm, and after rummaging through my old gear, I kept it with me for good luck. I started to believe that it had protective powers, protecting me once before in Nam and it became comforting having it with me.

***

The charm was on me the evening I visited Doctor VonTassell and whether it had any influence on my world is probably dumb to speculate, although I did intrude upon his apartment with a remarkable amount of courage.

Some people do not come to full flower until they are well over fifty. Among these are all males named VonTassell. Dr. VonTassell would have been nothing without his gray whiskers and scholarly background. Since bachelorhood is another essential attribute of the Doctor, I wonder how his breed is continued.

Except for our brief first meeting the day Janet and I arrived at Schloss Todesfall, Doctor VonTassell has been good-natured towards me. On that first encounter, we caught him off guard making introductions awkward. Ever since then he has always beamed and twinkled benevolently.

So it wasn't too surprising that the Doctor treated my unannounced call with the courtesy and manners of a good host. I came there demanding an explanation. He was the only one that I had contact with that knew my Uncle. He was probably the last to have any communication with him.

The Doctor was of little help even when I presented him with my uncle's notebook. His look and color changed perceptibly, and his left hand quivered when turning the pages. He remained silent the half an hour it took for him to read it. At one point in his reading, he became motionless and stared at one of the pages for a full five minutes before continuing. When finished he never commented on its content and tried to persuade me to leave it with him.

When I refused, he got up, left the room, returning shortly with two snifters of brandy appearing a bit paler than before, while making nervous attempts to maneuver the conversation to other topics.

It was obvious that he didn't want to speak about his association with my great uncle. I was not in the mood for small talk, nor could I induce him to talk about it no matter how hard I pressed. Besides him admitting that Todesfall had not been a well man, which I already knew, and some general speculation about his physical health, he failed to produce any new information. I asked him about my uncle's war record and his friend Peter he referred to in the journal but received only a well-raised eyebrow and evasive replies.

I did eventually evoke a response from the Doctor. He had been very polite the whole time, and I am sure that I was an unwelcome guest. Especially at that late hour. I realized by then that I had barged in on him demanding answers without giving an account of myself, putting him on the defensive. I was confused, angry and needed to talk to someone. I owned up to my feelings disclosing my fears for Janet's health. In particular the health of our unborn child. He hadn't been aware that Janet was pregnant and when hearing of it his face flinched then jerked back to its former expression. He did something peculiar after that. He gazed at me with a blank stare then without warning broke into joyful congratulatory remarks about my impending fatherhood and while reaching out to take my hand in his, he overturned my glass spilling the brandy. The move appeared forced, almost deliberate.

He mopped up the brandy with a handkerchief then hurried to the kitchen and refilled the glass. His cheeks had regained most of their color when he returned. VonTassell rushed the rest of our conversation, encouraging me to drink up and go home to my wife. Pressing me to leave, he voiced some assurances that in most cases insanity was not hereditary but thought it wise not to mention any of it to Janet for her peace of mind. Before I left, he offered his medical assistance, urged me to have my wife make an appointment with him so he could prescribe the proper vitamins and then gave me several telephone numbers to contact him.

As it happened, our next meeting was sooner than I had expected. That Friday I returned home from work after dark, as was usual, and found Janet upstairs in bed. She was asleep still wearing all her clothes. Her hair was in tangles, and her mascara had run leaving muddy tear stained streaks across her face that circled down and around her high cheekbones, welling up in the corners of her mouth where it overflowed then settled under the chin creating an outline of a skull mask.

A pillow was laying on the rug, and when I picked it up, I noticed a small set of prints tracked across the linen. They were the same size and shape as the one we discovered in the tower. I sat on the edge of the bed for several minutes staring at the tracks, worried that Janet might have seen what had caused them.

VonTassell arrived within only fifteen minutes after telephoning but not before I had removed the pillowcase from the bedroom and woke Janet. When he arrived, she was sitting up in bed sipping tea. The cup and saucer trembled in her hands. Janet had told me about her walk in the woods, the little girl she had met there and the discovery of my great Uncle's grave. Repeating the story for the Doctor, to my surprise, he listened with only partial interest and treated it like a flight of fantasy. He followed it with a tasteless remark about the effects of nervous tension brought on by overwork and an active imagination.

I was madder than hell. Some men in the medical profession lack the talent of a good bedside manner. I did not think that VonTassell would be that unfeeling. I felt Janet needed comforting above all else, not ridicule.

I left VonTassell to perform the mechanics of his trade suppressing the desire to tell him off and went downstairs.

In the living room, I snatched up the flashlight and started outdoors to see the grave for myself. Unlike my previous evening jaunts when my search for the clearing came up empty-handed, I had little difficulty locating it. The tall grass was brittle, and the areas trampled by Janet created an easy path to follow. It ran in several directions, apparently when she changed her direction and after carefully exploring each route she took, one path opened onto the clearing. The moon was high, and it provided adequate light to see by night. To the north, in the area behind the summer house, I could make out a slight rise in the earth creating a knoll about forty or fifty feet in width but barely a few feet higher than the surrounding ground area. It was insignificant, although I wasn't sure that the earth had sloped like that before.

I experienced some of the same uneasiness Janet spoke of and almost became sick to my stomach at the sight of those narrow mounds disinterred at one end while remembering my uncle's reference in his notebook to his theft of the gold fillings.

I walked around the glade keeping close to the edge of the thicket not wanting to venture into the cemetery. A tall grouping of brush and grass loomed up on my right, and beneath the beam of my light, I discovered my great uncle's grave just as Janet had described it. The headstone shielded from view by the outcropping of shrubbery. The charcoal-colored stone wore a wig of snakes and serpents carved from the same material with a similar design engraved on its face. Embedded in the belly was a clock and below, sprawled upon the earth, were the books. Everything as Janet had said.

I was taken by a sudden urge to return as quickly as possible to the house. I had the feeling I was being watched and felt the woods and earth about me breathing. Gathering up the school books my flashlight briefly illuminated the name of Heinrich Todesfall on the stone and below the dates of birth and death.

I left quickly, walking faster than when I came, harboring a childish fear of the dark. Halfway out of the thicket I picked up the pace and ran. I didn't stop until the lights of the house were in plain view. I didn't see or hear anything beyond what I have described. The overall aspect of that glade wasn't for one person to experience alone, at night, even under a full moon. I didn't feel ashamed of my actions until well within the comfort of my living room.

I practically threw the books at VonTassell when he came downstairs. The point was taken. He stared long and hard at the stack of elementary school books. He relaxed into a nearby chair. His expression was apologetic, and the fingers of his left hand tapped nervously upon the table.

"The stories are true then," I said but received no reply. I pressed him further saying that he must have known that my great Uncle was buried in the glade.

"I never examined the body, and I never saw a death certificate," he spoke hurriedly, and I imagined that he even looked frightened. "The funeral arrangements were made by a private organization unknown to me at the time."

"The Order of Dagon," I declared. He nodded yes and sensing that I had the upper hand I leaned closer and with voice raised I said: "One thing Doctor that has troubled me since we met, you have remarked that you and my uncle were friends, although he never made any mention of you in his journal. How do you explain that?"

As if reverting to my original unanswered question he replied, after a long pause, "there is some basis in truth in what Heinrich Todesfall wrote about but only in the physical sense. His military career, the last battle close to his ancestral home and his reclusive activities afterward are all I can vouch for, the rest with the possible exception of a few intervening occurrences were the fabric of a deranged mind. My involvement with your uncle was a little more than clinical. I tried being a friend in hopes of convincing him to commit himself. As to the lack of any reference to my part in Heinrich's journal I can only speculate. Not wanting to admit to his insanity I am sure that he was probably embarrassed to acknowledge our relationship. I, of course, realized my failure when his body was discovered in the cellar."

"The cellar!" I almost shouted. "We were led to believe that he had died while tending his garden." I realized the absurdity of the statement the moment after I had said it. What garden? I knew well by then that there was none and what my uncle had tended was a cemetery.

Maybe Janet had sensed there was something wrong all along with the cellar. She was more intuitive than me. Possibly something lingered there, a psychic residue perhaps that kept her from going downstairs.

The Doctor, relieved to get a great weight off his conscious continued. He told me of a workshop and study that Todesfall had down there, and of a secret room. The workshop was no surprise to me. I had cleaned up the mess left by my uncle's tinkering weeks before but a secret study chamber, my curiosity ran high.

"It was where he carried on his studies and dark worships," said the Doctor with a solemn face.

I led the conversation and the Doctor to the cellar steps eager for the hunt, and as we descended the wooden stairs, he gave a rational account of my uncle's behavior. "Heinrich Todesfall believed that although most wars are the gristmill of government propaganda and the media, two of the bloodiest conflicts of the 20th century were born from this country. Not due to the disillusionment of man but rather the cause of it. An influence dark in nature and as old as the very earth itself. A force normally at rest is able at certain times to manipulate the darker side of man. He acquired his ideas from an ancient almost forgotten religion. The head deity of known in most cultures as Cthulhu."

Some minor similarities in the legend and my dream struck me. It brought to mind the vision I was presented in that dream and was about to tell the Doctor about it but decided not to mention it fearing I would be next to have my sanity questioned.

We went over the area where the body was reported to be found next to the walled-up archway. It didn't take me long to fit the pieces together. Heinrich Todesfall in his last few minutes on earth must have concealed his notes within a crack in the stones where it stayed until I discovered it. And almost at the same moment with the chill of discovery clamoring up my spine I realized that what we had taken as a fortification of the old masonry could have been used to conceal another room. There were signs to that effect. The walls of the old cellar were of irregularly cut black granite that had the appearance of being chiseled from larger blocks and large stones probably quarried from the surrounding area. While the rocks used to brick up the arch were of sandstone colored to match the rest of the wall. They had been squared off to precision and if tied together properly could be light enough to swing freely admitting passage.

Doctor VonTassell confirmed that he had come to the same conclusion several months before but was unable to budge the stones and soon decided that the notion of a secret room was just another one of my Uncle's delusions. Even a combined effort on both our parts had no effect. About five feet up the sandstone, a little below eye level were a set of handprints. Human palms and finger impressions that were spaced about three feet apart, each fanning over areas where two blocks had been eliminated and filled in with cement. The signature of the mason must have been impressed into the fresh cement before it had a chance to dry.

Before giving up, I was struck by the idea that the two marks could also signify the position of a fulcrum. The area on which a lever rests, or which it turns when moving weight. I applied all my strength to the two spots fitting my hands into the impressions repeatedly throwing the weight of my body against the wall. Nothing happened at first, not until I relaxed momentarily leaving my hands still in position while gathering the strength sufficient for another try.

I remember quite clearly what I did next. I was staring just above my hands, catching my breath and the word "open" formed in my thoughts. As if by my mental command and to both our surprise the sandstone wall blocking the arch slid inward a few feet.

The section of wall was a good foot thick leaving us an opening of only a couple of feet to squeeze through. I went in first but stopped when VonTassell took hold of my shoulder and in a guarded tone spoke of spells cast by my uncle to ward off intruders. Whether they are to be believed or not, great Uncle Heinrich felt that it could be broken only by him or one of his bloodline.

Shrugging off the nonsense I entered the partially opened door, and VonTassell followed. Inside, cloaked in gloom, a narrow corridor stretched out before us. The floor littered with rubble and fallen masonry had thousands of cobwebs interlacing the ceiling. At the end of the corridor, a second door barred our passage; this one was wood though. I pushed it open, and by the light of the open door and my flashlight, we stood swaying on the sill staring inward. Beyond was a small room, barely ten feet square, with a low raftered ceiling. I knew the floor plan of the house above quite well by then and immediately realized that the room served as a foundation for the tower above.

The chamber masked in shadow, which until several candles were found and lighted, exaggerated the harsh edges cut by the beam of my flashlight. The walls were covered with a thick layer of mildew and fungus while beads of moisture slowly trickled between the remaining exposed joints. The few blocks still left uncovered by the encroachment of algae were larger than those used in the rest of the cellar. They were the same dark granite that the smaller stones had been chiseled from and fitted together with convex and concave joints. It led me to believe that the room and possibly the tower were part of the oldest construction of the schloss.

We saw in the center of the floor a design, not the conventional magic circle drawn in chalk of the horror films, but a geometric shape. A shape of five angular lines converging at regular points and closing in an area. Again, everything in fives. I reminded me, once again of the five-sided drawing made by the old medicine man and of the many times it had appeared in my dream in the form of archways, doors, and architectural structures. Even my good luck piece was of the same design. My left hand was in my pocket, and I had been unconsciously rubbing the stone charm between my thumb and forefinger for several seconds before I realized what I was doing.

With the candles, we were able to get a clearer view of the room and the pentagon inscribed in black upon the cobblestones. At first, we assumed that it was drawn with coal as the medium, but after rummaging through some of the implements of alchemy on a back shelf produced a large segment of animal bone, the femur I believe, charred on one end, the artist's pencil.

The design was about six feet across leaving only a two-foot walkway around it. Below four of the lines within the pentagon shape, contained letters or symbols. If they were letters, they were of a language I had never seen before. I have reproduced them on paper and will enclose them along with the recordings and other papers.

Editor's Note:

According to Mr. Church here is what had been set down. The first and nearest to the east:

The next, south going clockwise:

The third:

And, on the west side:

Beneath the fifth and the northernmost line of the crude magic shape drawn on the stone, Todesfall had scrawled two words: YATH NOTEP.

There was no room for any furnishing, except for a small reading stand at the center of the drawing and on top of that rested a book. If I had known the events that were to follow, if I could only have looked into the future that evening, I swear I would have avoided that book like the plague, would have shunned that house and the very ground it stood on. Many times since then I have wished my eyes had never rested on that black cover. The writhing figures it contained would have been kept from me, along with the unrest, the terrors, and the madness!

But, never dreaming of the secrets that were unleashed from those pages, I fondled it casually and remarked: "An unusual book. What is it?"

The Doctor came around and peered over my shoulder. Across the cover were engraved the words "OLAUS WORMUS."

When I opened the yellowed pages, I pulled back with involuntary revulsion at the odor which arose. An odor that was suggestive of physical decay, as if the book had lain among corpses in a tomb and had taken on the smell of death.

"It is the Necronomicon" the Doctor whispered. "A Latin version printed in Spain during the seventeenth century."

His manner was so exacting that I was startled by his knowledge, noticing my amazement, he continued in a more subdued tone. "It was believed to be only a fable. Your uncle spoke of it often. Its original author was an Arab around the 8th century by the name of Abdul Alhazred who supposedly transcribed it from stone tablets from an unknown age. It's possibly the rarest book in the world, and only handwritten translations were ever made, much like the legend of ..."

"What is it about?" I interrupted.

"It's a ledger of spells, alchemic potions and geometric formulas the main theme of which is a plan for the extermination of all human and animal life on earth." Then casually he turned and looked closer at the open pages. I was unable to read the dead language, and even though the Doctor appeared to read some of the handwritten pages quietly to himself, I hesitated to ask him to translate after noting two lines written in different hand upon the cover leaf of the book. It was in English and read:

"When age falls upon the world and wonder goes out of the minds of men."

The handwriting was unknown to me but the second line although printed, was that of my great Uncle Heinrich's.

"THE DEATH OF CREATIVITY = NOW!"

I didn't care to learn anymore and wanted to leave the room with the design on the floor. I began to feel certain vibrations within that black magic shape. My toes and fingers tingled, and my thoughts careened through black gulfs of time, and I envisioned huge mucous flowing masses reaching out towards me with thought commands. My mind filled with hideous whisperings, I was becoming abnormally sensitive to the vibrations, dangerously sensitive! I jerked back from the book catching the heel of my shoe on an unseen object and fell backward landing against the damp algae-covered stone wall.

I was unharmed, and VonTassell was by my side within a second. White splinters of refracted light glittered and danced across the Doctor's face and hands. We both turned at the same moment and saw the origin of the reflected light. Beneath the reading stand in a hollow recess was a luminous object comprised mostly of brass or highly polished gold and glass. The source of illumination was my flashlight. It had rolled across the floor settling in a crack between the cobblestones where it rocked to and fro shining brightly against the object. It wasn't very large, not more than a couple of feet tall. We dragged it from the recess and sat on the cold stones examining the mechanism. Once out, and in plain view, I recognized it instantly. A weird arrangement of rods, wheels, and mirrors constructed with clock-work precision. The rods were smooth and round as anything you can imagine, and it was gold, solid gold, girdled with wide bands of silver. The central mirror was circular and convex while the rods, silver at their base, connected with long gold wands gradually tapering into needle-like spires pointing straight up. It was the same device used by that alien race in my dream, and I was certain then it was the one my great uncle boasted of constructing.

Up until this time I had rationalized the similarities of my nightmare. There were some resemblances between my drug-induced hallucination in Vietnam and the dream a few weeks ago. Most, of which, can be rationalized. Hallucinogens can have renewed effects even years later, such as the re-occurrence of the five-sided shape. At first seen by me in the cave as a sand drawing and later the Indian charm. The design most likely was recreated by my subconscious in a dream state. Probably a common cabalistic symbol, the reason I witnessed its use here thousands of miles from that southeast Asian cave. The remainder was mere coincidence.

But now the device had no basis in this reasoning. I had never witnessed anything like this in my life. The mechanism was alien, as alien as when it first appeared to me in my sleep. I couldn't question the actuality of the fantasy; I would have to start questioning reality itself. The Memory of its construction made me shiver, made from the gold dental fillings of my great uncle's Nazi comrades.

We sat there in silence fingering the delicate parts of the device. It wasn't until much later that I realized that neither the Doctor nor I voiced any speculation as to its possible use. The only conclusion drawn from the device that evening was that some parts were missing. Two small holes close together in the top of the central mirror and a narrow slit a little more than an inch long was visible on the base. If it were a machine, there were no apparent means to activate it. Maybe, I thought, the missing pieces held the answer.

Before leaving the damp chamber, we took another look at the old book. Feeling squeamish about remaining within the pentagon symbol I moved it to the wall shelf. There was a marker in the center of the book. Many of the pages were worm-eaten and rotted by centuries of decay, so I had to take great care when turning them. The pages opened before us did not display any of the ancient Latin. Instead, they contained hieroglyphics much like the ones scrawled on the floor. Although some of the characters looked evil in design, they meant nothing to me. The piece of paper was a letter folded in half lengthwise and used as a bookmarker.

The letter, written in English, in a hand identical to the one that wrote the first line on the cover leaf of the Necronomicon. The correspondent was unknown. He had only signed with his initials. It read:

> To H.T.;
>
> If you are right and an error does exist in previous translations, then Cthulhu and Yog-Sothoth know the gate, but they are not the gate! Yath-Notep is the gate. Yath-Notep is the key and the guardian. Past, present, future, what has been, what is, what will be, all are one in Yog-Sothoth and Cthulhu.
>
> But if Yath-Notep is the earth elemental, the reigning servant of his master left behind, then Yath-Notep knows where the Old Ones, his masters, broke through of old, and where they shall break through in time to come when the cycle is completed.
>
> If you have found the key, the missing link in the age-old quest to the other dimension, you have found it where others have failed. Glory and be praised to Yath-Notep. He will deliver us.
>
> The Old Ones were, the Old Ones are, and the Old Ones shall be. Not in spaces known to us, but between them.
>
> Forever
>
> H.P.L.

If there would have been some authority that I could have carried our discovery to, I am sure the evidence would have been overwhelming, but there is none in such cases. I had to let the matter drop for the rest of the evening. I thought for awhile that I would have to restrain Dr. VonTassell physically from removing the old book, but he soon gave in and agreed to leave it be. He became very excited almost to the point of agitation when, after many repeated attempts to reseal the opening, failed. We discovered the secret to unlocking the masonry passage, but no matter how hard I tried, or what we did, we could not move it back to its former position.

It irritated the Doctor even more. Assuring him that Janet never went down into the cellar and that I would bolt the door at the top of the stairs as soon as we left, appeared to have a settling effect on him.

The knife came into my possession at that time. Making one more attempt at closing the sandstone door and hopefully waylay any of the Doctor's anxieties, I searched amongst the stones of the wall for a lever or switch that might activate the stone door. A glint of steel caught by my light revealed what I thought was the answer. Wedging my fingers between the blocks I tugged at it. It slid out easily. A second later I stood there dumbfounded holding a very beautifully crafted dagger. The blade shined like new steel, but the intricate artwork on the handle spoke of extreme age. It was badly pitted although a bulbous-eyed head was still visible. It had a slit for a mouth and worms for hair that coiled past the neck of the carving and around the remainder of the handle forming complex twists and spirals. The shapes flared out in an intertwined pattern where the handle met the blade creating a fierce looking hilt. Halfway up the blade was notched like the cuttings on the edge of a key. The serrated edge made the weapon appear all the more gruesome as if made for tearing than slashing.

My thread of trust for the Doctor was stretched thin. The man, who the evening before couldn't wait to get rid of me, was now becoming a pest at that late hour. Janet was very healthy, he had assured me earlier, and was soundly sleeping after he gave her a sedative. I hadn't had my dinner yet. My head was pounding, and my patience wore thin. I finally had to usher him outdoors and to his car refusing him another visit until the first of the week. More than his new found enthusiasm disturbed me. I knew that he was keeping something from me and his reluctance to divulge the truth heightened my suspicions.

***

Morning and I found all was not well. My head was still aching, my hands trembled, and I felt nauseous. I went to bed without supper the night before, and I suffered from it by rising before dawn. I had scarcely slept. The rest of the night had passed without incident, but I had tossed and turned most of the evening with thoughts of dark faces and unlocked doors.

Janet was still asleep when I crept downstairs and put on a pot of coffee. Watching the sunrise over the glade I remembered the school books, and after fetching them to the kitchen, I looked at the inside covers for the owner's name.

It wasn't difficult to locate the little girl's parents. Her name and address appeared on the cover of each book, and a quick look through the local directory produced their number. When the sun was high enough, I telephoned and made arrangements to return them that morning.

The Kritchners lived in a small off the road scattering of cabins about three miles from the schloss. I maneuvered the car slowly along the rough road. Though few lifestyles are shabbier in the other regions, I couldn't help feeling sorry for the inhabitants. If the two governments decided on the area for their Peacekeeping Missiles, these people would probably be uprooted and moved somewhere else.

The houses were small wood frames and most in need of repair and painting. The population was not large, and I occasionally saw solitary figures on crumbling doorsteps or on the sloping rock-strewn meadows.

After a few inquiries, I located the Kritchner's home. Our meeting was short, and I never saw the child. Able Kritchner, the little girl's father, was a tall, lanky man aged beyond his years. It was probably from years of hard physical labor and improper diet. His face was boney, unshaved and his eyes deep in their sockets. His head supported thin wisps of sandy colored hair mixed with gray.

My German is limited, and so was Kritchner's English but we managed to communicate.

"I am Able Kritchner. You telephoned me?" With several pauses of concentrated effort in his speech.

"Oh, yes," I said. "I have your daughter's school books here."

He stepped out from behind the screen door and came over the wood porch peering cautiously down both ends of the dirt road before taking the books from me.

"It's a good thing, Herr Kritchner, that she put her name and address in them or she'd have lost them for good."

The girl's father looked confused and just stared at the armload of books.

"What was your daughter doing out there anyway?" I spoke slower. "Was she coming home from school?"

"Yes, I will not let her do it again."

"Oh, no!" I said, "It doesn't bother me if she walks there."

"She will not do it again!" This time more emphasized.

Confused I asked if his daughter was sick.

"She is not sick," almost echoing me.

"But she was ...," I said.

"No," he snapped, and before I had a chance to tell my wife's story, he looked at me defiantly and stomped towards the front door stopping with his hand on the knob. He glanced again at both directions of the road then in a harsh, but lowered voice and as quickly as his limit of the language would allow said, "Herr Kirch...I have heard things, some people believe them. Since the war, people that walk there." He nodded in the direction of my estate. "Feel wrong."

I stood there watching the screen door slam behind him, dazed by his comment and his lack of appreciation for the return of the books. Some of the neighbors had come out and stood along the gravel paths in front of their homes looking at me. The sound of my car's engine running in the drive called to me.

The course of events took less than thirty minutes, and within ten I was back in the kitchen brooding over a cup of coffee, Janet still asleep upstairs.

***

Chemicals wash across the surface of the paper, slowly bringing the details to life. The only source of illumination during the process is a colored light turning the white of the paper crimson and all blacks even richer. Everything else in the room is stained with graduations of red while the master of this operation, as quietly as he chose his art, selects the proper moment to halt the formation.

A developing bath can contain both pleasant and gratifying results. I eagerly waited while the eight by ten developed in the tray. The negative had been too small to see any detail, but there was a spot on the film in the same area where it had affected Jim's Polaroid photo. I snuck into the enlarging lab next to mine after hours but didn't encounter any of the night crew. I was probably still between shifts. I was afraid to attempt it during the day when the Cutters might be around. If caught, I wasn't sure what might happen.

Jim had come by for the first time on the afternoon following the return of the school books and stayed most of the day.

I was a little self-conscious about our friendship in front of Janet. No sooner had he set foot in our house than he burst into a nervous horse laugh for no apparent reason. He was his usual self. Janet surprisingly enough found him a barrel of laughs and welcomed the company much in the same way as I did.

Later I got him aside and filled him in on some of the strange goings-on, leaving out the dream related parts. I am not sure what I thought I'd accomplish by bringing him into it. Probably felt comfortable with reinforcements. I held back very little and even produced the dagger hoping his knowledge of antique weaponry might help.

Jim Ruttick, however, was the type of person that was sure that almost everything was done by mirrors. Consequently, he was unable to shed any light on the mystery. In fact, he did very little to disguise his disbelief, although he did offer his services, out of friendship, reassuring me that there can be safety in numbers.

It was about then that he took the picture. He flashed a photo of Janet and me together in the parlor. The results were disappointing, and as you know if you have read my wife's account of the whole thing, a ghostly shape appeared just to the right side of the snapshot. The shape was familiar to me.

I set my Nikon up on the tripod and shot a series of time exposures of the area bracketing each exposure while at the same time trying to remain nonchalant about the entire business. Jim was concerned that there was something wrong with his Polaroid, but my concerns were on a different line of thought.

Now, looking into the developing tray waiting for the images to rise to the surface of the paper I secretly wished that I had taken up smoking as a vice or that there was a good stiff drink handy.

Jim had taken Vesta with him that evening. It was a nice gesture and a way to get a return invite to dinner on Monday. Vesta didn't mind. She would have if she knew the trip was going to end up at the veterinarian. She and Jim had become pals during his visit, and the big black lab liked the idea of a ride in the car.

The living room window slowly took form on the Kodak paper. First, the wood muntin bars crisscrossed the glass then the afternoon sky came into view.

I had the remainder of the weekend to think over the events of the last few days before returning to work on Monday. More and more I realized as I went on that there were other forces at work leading me along. I didn't know where I was heading but wondered if it had anything to do with my ancestral bloodline. Encountering increasing clues and increasing bafflement I found it difficult to draw any conclusions. There had been too much that I accepted as coincidence, and I felt sure that it involved a conspiracy. A conspiracy I was certain that had its roots in the Emmerson-Pryne Corporation and a good chance it could be uncovered in my lab.

Gripped with the enthusiasm of a plan I burst into the lab Monday morning tossing the work order left in the overnight box aside and set about developing the negatives from my Nikon.

It was a black and white enlargement, but the textures in the fabric of the living room sofa gradually stood out just the same along with the furnishings, wallpaper, and floor coverings.

At ten, as was usual, coffee was brought in setting everything in motion. I watched unobserved from down the hall. A young private brought the tray in and left. Not once until Jim summoned me did anyone touch my thermos. The coffee always had a bitter quality about it, and if someone was tampering with it, it was done outside of the building. I felt a little relieved; I hoped that Jim wasn't involved. Maybe, just maybe, I thought Ephraim Pryne had not been able to successfully infiltrate all of the air force's security and Jim Ruttick, as a result, was not one of them.

I talked with Jim a few minutes pretending to take occasional sips from the cup. Then when I was sure that no one was looking, and no Cutters were about, I dumped it down the drinking fountain.

I went back to the lab and fiddled with the processor waiting to see what would happen next. Minutes crept by like hours.

The quiet was broken by a click. The sound of the latch drawn back. I turned and looked at the door to the hall. It remained undisturbed. Then I remembered the other door. The one behind me that barred entrance to the room on the other side. It was at my back, and I twirled around with an invisible intruder creeping up behind me. The intruder was indeed invisible, only in my mind.

Even though there was no knob on my side, I checked to see if it was secure and saw that the deadbolt was drawn by peering through the crack between the jam and the door. I returned to my stool and removed several aluminum canisters of undeveloped film from the morning's work pouch. I was checking the sequence numbers on the rolls when I detected a movement. One of the wall tiles over my bench slid to one side revealing a hollow recess and the glint of glass. I froze. All movement left me.

Before I could react in any way, the strings of a violin filled the room. They were strains of music I had never heard before, but the style of the composition was familiar. It was some of the wildest playing I ever heard yet unquestionably that of the composer Erich Zann. Haunted by the weird, familiar quality of the music, the sounds filled me with the dread of vague wonders and mystery. The vibrations held suggestions of nothing from this earth, and at certain intervals, they assumed a symphonic quality which could have hardly been produced by one player. I wanted to cup my hands over my ears and block out the sounds, but for some reason, the music of Erich Zann held me paralyzed...almost hypnotic.

The music subsided, and the light in the room slowly dimmed. The light gradually diminished leaving me in the dark. I could have jumped up and turned on the darkroom bulb, but my muscles had involuntarily relaxed, and I found myself staring at the recess in the wall . . . it had taken on an irresistible quality. The glint of glass or crystal spun out a flicker of white light. It twinkled gradually picking up speed and brilliance until it created a strobe effect. My eyes became accustomed to the brightness, and my lids grew heavy. I remember mixed thoughts racing through my head. One was just to give in, succumb to the dazzling effect and sleep. The other was a feeling of déjà vu, I had been through this before. It felt perfectly natural. Then out of a corner of my consciousness sprang the terrifying answer. "My God!" I cried within the privacy of my thoughts, "I'm being hypnotized!"

This snap back to reality kept me awake and later alive. My composure remained outwardly tranquil and even lacking the effect of the drugged coffee I am sure that I was partially mesmerized. Then there was my plan that demanded an answer . . . an answer to a question I wasn't even sure was a question. I had to stay there and assume a relaxed position to find the solution.

If it had not been for the voice, I might have eventually succumbed to sleep and tremble even now at what the outcome would have been if I had.

It was a low voice, almost guttural. It plainly said, "Sleep . . . sleep." Over and over again. I closed my eyes, but I remained in control. Thank God because I was able to shut out the light and remain awake. Shades of flickering light endured as an after image. The retinal image quickly faded leaving me alert and aware.

The voice discontinued its "sleep" chant and began calling my name. I wasn't sure what to do but felt it deserved an answer. "Yes," I said.

"Are you asleep?" inquired the deep voice.

The question was almost comical, under the circumstances. I didn't laugh but replied "yes."

He began slowly, in conciliatory tones to lay down a set of instructions. He stopped calling me by name and referred to me as, "my son."

"Now listen carefully, my son," said the voice. "This is the last time we shall talk. The time has come. The words that have been carefully taught to you must be spoken this evening. The windlass will be in place and the time is one minute past midnight." He paused, and I heard the rustling of papers.

"At fifteen minutes before the hour, you will forget everything. Forget what you are doing, stop whatever you are in the middle of and go to your great Uncle's grave. Wait there and precisely at twelve the windlass will be made available to you."

The command caught me momentarily off guard, and I almost slid off the stool. I gripped the edge of the work counter tightly. Had my eyes been opened, I am sure I would have seen the knuckles on my hands turn white. I had no idea what the windlass was but was well acquainted with the eerie grave site. He paused again, and I waited in the intervening silence for him to resume. Had my actions been observed, I hoped that my slip had gone unnoticed. My fears subsided when I heard the rustling of papers signaling his return.

"Take the knife of Alhazred with you. The dagger you found three nights ago in the cellar is the one. When the clock in Heinrich Todesfall headstone begins to strike, insert the knife blade into the base of the windlass and say the words:

Ya-R'lyeh . . . g'wah Cthulhu

Fhgthagn . . . N'ggah

Ggll . . . Ia! Ia! Yath-Notep"

I was told to repeat the instructions, and what seemed like gibberish and I surprised myself by reciting them word for word.

He echoed the set of words three times then followed again with the instructions. Over and over again the hidden voice spoke my intended lesson each time pausing at the end of those meaningless phrases I was expected to recite and each time I recited them from within a deep hidden memory. The voice became steady, a uniform succession of words almost unvaried in inflections, no doubt he was reading the commands and his sameness or lack of variety of expression was the results of repeated readings.

I kept my seat and played the frustrating game until a few minutes before noon the whole thing stopped, and I was instructed to forget everything and follow the given instructions before midnight.

I decided when the ordeal was completed to go about my daily chores as if nothing had happened. It gave the appearance of success to my controllers and me, time to think. My nerves were on edge, and it required a tremendous amount of self-control not to become high strung and do something foolish that would give me away. The episode was enough to unhinge anyone, but it was that voice that shook me. The tone and quality were familiar, and I recognized it right off. It was unmistakably the voice of Ephraim Pryne.

The living room in the photo became very clear. On the end table next to the sofa, the last thing to come into plain view was a little translucent blob that resembled an embryonic head and torso vaguely. The thing solidified some cutting in darker lines of resolution revealing a legless gnome supporting itself on pipe-thin arms above the table. It was the same little creature I saw that night clinging to my bed sheets. It wasn't a trick played upon the eyes anymore. I was wide awake with tangible proof in hand. Could there be such a being? One that could take ghostly or invisible shape while at other times become solid. A growing horror swelled in my throat. I found it difficult to swallow. Not wanting to look at the photograph anymore I inserted it in the dryer and stood in the hall trying to clear my thoughts and piece together what had happened.

If I were to make any sense out of this, I would have to begin by believing in the supernatural and accept what my uncle had set down in his journal as fact. Uncle Heinrich had mentioned several times the Esoteric Order of Dagon and its leaders, the council of the unknown nine. Even VonTassell verified their existence. If there was such an order, as this Dagon, then they must be people equally deranged as my great uncle and possibly equally as dangerous.

I was certain that Pryne, and probably the entire corporation, were behind this. Could they all be a group of lunatics bent on a demented plot for world domination? And this job I held, a Red Herring to lure my family and me here to further their plans. I wasn't about to wait around for the outcome. I had ended up in the corner of a lunatic asylum. I wanted out. Get the hell out of there, away from that house, Fort Blish, and VonTassell. I wanted to go where there were people, lots of people . . . where I could surround myself with the crowd from a large city.

I had to wait though. Janet had the car, and Jim had gone to pick up Vesta. He said he would swing by the base after stopping at the vet's and it was at least an hour before he would arrive.

I called Janet on the lobby phone to tell her to throw a few things in a couple of bags so we could leave immediately. She was hysterical when answering, mostly incoherent. I pleaded with her to relax, slow down and explain but she stammered and went on so I could barely understand her. Janet screamed something about the old knife moving around the house. I couldn't make any sense out of it. It was all I could do to keep from bursting into tears. Her hysteria tore into me. I struggled to get a few words in trying to console her, but it was useless not knowing what troubled her. I hung up after telling her I would get a taxi cab home right away. "I love you," I said before putting down the receiver.

After phoning for a cab, I tried reaching VonTassell, but he didn't answer. We were supposed to have dinner that evening at his home. I left a note for Jim taped to the front door, asking him to pick up the Doctor and follow. Then I went back to the lab for my coat and the photograph.

It had been quiet all along, and there was still no sign of the night crew. I had my coat in hand and was removing the eight by ten from the dryer in the other lab when I heard muffled voices. Down the hall I could see the closed door to my lab and further down on the same side, the door to the restricted room stood open. I crept cautiously across the polished floor conscious of the sounds my rubber soles made on the tiles. The door stood halfway ajar. The room was empty, the light had been left on and it hung by a cord from the ceiling. The ceiling was much higher than in the rest of the building and as I had suspected the room was a great deal longer than the other rooms on that side combined. Besides a large flat work table in the center, it lacked any other furnishings.

There was no one in the room as I said, a fact that lent an additional haunting quality to the setting. The walls, plastered with black and white blowups pasted together by the geology crew stretching a good thirty feet, covered the concrete blocks and reached nine or ten feet high. The effect was breathtaking, almost panoramic, like being suddenly thrust in front of a super widescreen movie without warning. Except these were all aerial photographs taken from the belly of an aircraft shooting straight down. Gripped by a sensation of falling I stumbled forward across the threshold into the room. I regained my balance clutching the edge of the work table. I had to look away from the map for a bit to shake free of the trick that played on my equilibrium.

Getting close to the photo mural, stealing short glances at first then longer stares, I was taken back by the lack of any markings that might designate future missile sites. The region was the Black Forest, an area according to Pryne and Falbridge just begging to conceal the silos.

I presently became attracted by something singular in the arrangement of a certain topographical element. It was a conic projection or upheaval of earth that had been charted by the cutting crew and circled in red grease pencil. It was a characteristic common to maps of the most varied kinds. The plotted section of terrain was based on observations made by hundreds of individual photographers. It appeared almost dead center in the thirty-foot mural, and it took six blowups stuck together to encompass the area. Blanketing the surface of the work table were three other sets of six all displaying the same area spanning four weeks. The photos were inscribed with the date and time in the bottom left corner with the same red grease pencil.

There isn't a way of representing curved surfaces of the ground on a flat plane without some distortion of its useful features desired on maps. On large scale maps, such as this one, covering areas of only a few square miles, the distortion is negligible. The map projections were an orderly system of parallels and meridians on which new maps are drawn. Thus the detail needed by NATO required the use of a larger scale. There was, however, still a distortion covering the relatively small area, not caused by global curves, but an uplift in terrain.

Each set of photographs across the table were arranged in chronological order from left to right with the most recent taped to the center of the wall. Each one in succession revealed increased distortion of the spatial relationships. I remembered the excited words of the one cutter that afternoon when he said, "there has been a definite uplift in the terrain since last week." I didn't know what he meant then, but now I had a good idea.

I grew accustomed to the widescreen effect of the map and was able to back up taking in the full view of it once again.

The raised terrain was a mountainous wooded region. To the left, only inches away on the map was a heavy thicket surrounding a small glade. No sooner had I interpreted it as such than the realization of it fell in on me.

I scanned the bottom of the huge mural where it met the floor. There were a regular outcropping of rocks, two-foot paths, a large shed, and a small house. If there were any other structures, below the mural, they were cut off where the photos, attached to the wall, met the floor.

I grabbed a magnifying glass off the table and examined the clearing in the center of the thicket. Several small mounds and hills swelled up into the glass. Some fifty or sixty blemished the earth. At the edge of the glade, alone in its placement, was a larger mound and at one end a black speck. I knew what that speck was. It was the headstone of my great uncle's grave. The rocks to the bottom of the mural were the remains of an old patio wall, the shed, the garage and the small house, the summer house bordering the edge of our property!

Somehow I wasn't too surprised to find this out. What puzzled me then was if there ever was any intention on the part of the military to install NATO controlled nuclear missiles in the hills. Was the air force involved in this conspiracy or were Pryne and God knows who else, just playing them along in order to use their facilities?

The urgency to leave was stronger than ever. I knew that the taxi would be at the front gate any minute. I remembered the rear exit that led out of that room, opening it, I stepped out onto the gravel parking lot. The evening sky was partially visible through the clouds. The moon was full, and it lit the area well.

From this point, unobstructed by any other buildings, I had plain view of the main gate and the road. The cab hadn't arrived yet. Turning to go back inside I saw a black limousine parked alongside the building. It was empty. I remembered the muffled voices again and that both doors which earlier had been latched now stood unlocked. I quickly retraced my steps in my head and realized that I had been through every room except my lab. Someone could have easily come in through the rear entrance without me knowing it and entered my processing lab through the adjoining door.

Off in the corner, concealed before by the opened door was a broad open-topped metal vessel with handles on the side. About the size of a bathtub and constructed in the same way as an old fashion laundry basin. The broad, clumsy container was filled with water about a foot from the rim. The floor around it was wet and slippery while the edge of the tub was encrusted with a white powder. Wetting a finger, I tasted it; it was salty. Some of it had been spilled over the edge and puddled up in the cracks of the tiles. Smaller puddles had been tracked across the room in the direction of the processing lab and stopped in front of the adjoining doorway, the door that would have opened into my lab if it wasn't barred shut and minus a knob on my side.

I found it unlocked as well. The latch had been drawn back and secured to permit re-entry to the cutter's room. I turned off the light in the map room. The door swung in noiselessly.

The sole illumination in my lab was the small red work light over my bench. It took a moment or two for my eyes to get accustomed to the red gloom. I gradually became aware of the presence of two other forms. The first and foremost in the light was Falbridge. With back turned toward me, I quietly observed him cementing a loose wall tile in place. To his right, strewn across the white Formica counter were a few hand tools and a small light projector. A simple device comprised of a mirrored cube with alternating sides blacked out. Mounted on a thin shaft, connected to a small electric motor then supported in front of a cheap bulb housing and lens, it would, when activated, produce very brief flashes of light. Controlled I thought from probably the cutter's map room using a rheostat to increase the strobe light effect gradually.

My presence wasn't detected, and though I was determined to confront him, I felt it wise to wait, letting Falbridge continue the concealment, not to let him know I was on to their hypnosis trick. Instead, my eyes traced the wet tracks, which under the prevailing darkroom light, resembled pools of blood. They continued into the room veering off from where Falbridge stood and made for a darkened corner where a second form crouched.

It was too dark to make out anything clearly. A concrete block pilaster constructed in the wall to increase structural strength jutted out casting a greater blackness into the corner making it difficult to see. Whoever it was, was stoop-shouldered and must have worn dark clothing because no characteristics stood out amongst the shadows.

I should have gotten out of there, but I was caught up in the intrigue of confronting Falbridge, eager to see him surprised, caught off guard, and I was curious about the stranger. Besides, I didn't see that any danger was imminent. He was a frail man by comparison and didn't pose any real threat to me. I shouldn't have been that foolish. It would have been much better for me if I had just receded quietly back into the map room then run like hell. Because, while I was straining against the dark, trying to make out the other man in the corner, I was struck by the odor of fish. It was the same fishy odor I smelled in New York while the intruder was at my keyhole.

I was certain that it came from the corner where the dark man stood.

Then he spoke. It was not at all what he said, it was simple and innocent enough by itself, but it was the sound that the voice made when he said, "hurry up" to Falbridge. The deep guttural sounds had a watery quality to them this time. I recognized the voice all the same and its laboriously formed words only too well!

I gasped. Falbridge turned with a start. I never got to witness the look of surprise that must have crossed his features because I was still staring into the corner. I heard Falbridge with a start yell at me. His voice seemed far away. "Faren," he shouted.

I didn't look at him. I couldn't keep my eyes off the corner. "What is this? Who are you?"

The man in the corner answered. "We are the remnants of what was left behind."

The sound of that voice again gave me chills. Falbridge took a step toward me but came no closer when I turned and met his gaze head-on. He was nervous, excited, and he said, "We are driven from our home, your population keeps growing, and our habitat grows smaller. We were content to live as we were, but your kind made that impossible."

"So you resort to drugs and cheap tricks to persuade me to help you with your crackpot cause."

He was lost for a reply and looked for support from the man in the shadows. The voice whispered in the darkness. "Right now my son, there is an imminent dissolution of your civilization. The fabric of mankind's existence is already irreparably torn to the point that shortly this earth, depleted of its resources, torn by civil disorder and dense with population to the verge of madness, will be laid to waste anyway. It is only a matter of time."

"And you two lunatics are only trying to rush it along," I said.

"Oh, no," Falbridge said. "The process is already underway."

"You're crazy!" I yelled.

The Emmerson-Pryne executive assistant swallowed hard. He tried to remain convincing as he spoke, his voice almost cracking. "Cthulhu is the destiny of the world. His history is the poetry of our destiny. He can be your destiny too. We would rather have you voluntarily than as a puppet. There are some of your kind that thinks the same as we do! Your great uncle was one of them."

"Go to Hell," I roared.

I don't know why I did it. I guess I didn't believe my senses and had to see for myself. In the confusion, I leaped to the other side of the room and turned on the overhead lights. Falbridge threw his body in front of me but was too late. When the lights burst on, he pressed close to me. He was thoroughly agitated. The drool that normally welled disgustingly in the corners of his mouth ran down both sides of his chin. He blocked my view of the corner, and with an outstretched arm, I shoved his frail body against the processor.

A crouched form stood blinded by the bright light. It was a green slimy thing. The skin was smooth and blotchy in color. A narrow dorsal fin ran the length of its curved spine. Its back and shoulders connected to the head with no neck apparent. A low hairless brow slanted back and away from a pair of bulging eyes. Two small holes in the face where a nose should be dribbled moisture and a wide lipless mouth hung open. Narrow gill slits just below the drooping chin flexed open and closed rhythmically. My eyes ran down the length of the thing. Its unclothed body dripped water on the floor. Arms and legs that although massive at the shoulders and hips trailed out thinly and, attached to where normally hands and feet ought to have been, were webbed flippers.

Bear in mind closely now that it wasn't the actual sight of the thing that caused me to run. To say that a mental shock was the cause alone of what I deduced . . . the last straw which sent me racing out of that gray concrete building, through the parking lot to the main gate and the waiting cab, is to ignore the last few plain facts of my experience.

The ride that followed was spent in partial delirium, leaving the base, out through the surrounding countryside, through Valsbach and only after frantically coaxing the driver, finally reaching Todesfall's house.

I ignored the drive and scenery. My mind was consumed by what I saw resting on the vacant wheelchair. I have no physical proof even now whether I am right or wrong in my crazy deductions. At any rate, before I ran from the room, while my eyes were still running down the length of that frog-like thing, I became attracted to some things in the chair. It was to the right of the creature and propped alongside the wall. The wheelchair had been folded up and collapsed on itself. I noticed then for the first time the presence of certain objects draped across the loose folds in the seat. The objects were four in number and although there was nothing of actual visual horror about them; they did lead me to conclude other things.

For the things in the wheelchair were a green wool blanket, a pair of yellow mittens, and a large red wig and beard, the disguise that I had come to know as Ephraim Pryne.

***

It is amazing to me, when I look back, that everyone else in the world spent that evening as if it was any other. Everything seemed safe and tranquil.

The daily routine of life that surrounded all working, eating, sleeping; continued peacefully. While beneath the thick glade in my backyard festered an evil so great and powerful as to interrupt that serenity and change the face of our planet as we know it.

From this point forward my statements will be found to include incidents entirely out of the range of probability. Up until this point all that has happened can be logically explained away and some incidents by way of coincidence, others interpreting it as the misreporting of information and some diagnosing an inability on my part to distinguish between reality and dreams.

I know it's hopeless to obtain any credibility for the rest of my story, but I'll go on trusting in time and the progress of scientific curiosity to verify some of the most important and more improbable facts of my statements.

When I reached home, a storm front had rolled in, and the temperature had dropped considerably. There was fog everywhere. Around the schloss it was more than a fog, a thick green moldy smelling mist had swelled up.

The cab driver was nervous and in a hurry to leave almost drove off without being paid.

Through the fog, I could see the windows ablaze with light from the inside. It was reassuring, and I was comforted by the peaceful, homey atmosphere it projected.

Off to the east, a dense blanket of clouds glowed with the soft radiance where the moon was trying to break through, and the lack of any southerly breeze gave no promise of clearing skies.

As I approached the drive I could see that the square-paned windows alongside the house were thick with dewy moisture; the air had become heavy and unbelievably cold.

A blue-green cold swam across the tiles of the roof running down the walls to where the mist churned below the window sills. I couldn't help wondering if centuries of dark brooding had given the crumbling structure a peculiar vulnerability to such a phenomenon.

We had always been in the habit of using the rear entrance and making no exception then I headed around the back. For an instant, I thought I detected a movement on the front porch but shrugged it off as an action of the fog.

The rear door was locked, and after trying my key, it still would not open. The bolt must have been drawn from the inside. A loud crashing of glass followed by a heavy thud broke the evening quiet. I pounded on the door yelling for Janet and a few seconds later heard the breaking of glass again. It wasn't as loud, sounding further away, upstairs perhaps. It was as if someone was hammering plate glass with a soft blunt instrument. Then I heard Janet scream. It didn't sound like her at first. Not until I heard it repeated did I recognize her voice.

The door broke in on the third kick. The living room was a shambles. The fog had reached there too. The mist was so thick that it leaked in through every crack around the front door and billowed in through a gaping hole in the wall where the east bay used to be. The large cement urn that used to sit on the front porch lodged against the fireplace, and the marble hearth was cracked in several places. My strides brought sounds of crunching glass underfoot and caused small tight swirls and eddies to churn in the mist that clung about a foot off the floor.

I called for Janet several times, but there was no answer. I stopped calling when looking, up I saw her body at the top of the stairs.

I was in tears when I reached her, and you can imagine my relief when I found her breathing steadily.

The mirror at the top of the stairs was shattered, and all that remained was the frame and the thin wooden backing. Blood splatters were on the wall and carpet. There were cuts on the sides of her hands leading up to the elbow and clutched in her right hand, beneath her crumpled form, was the old knife.

I carried her to the sofa. After cleaning her wounds, I found them only to be superficial, thankful that none of the glass had severed a vein. I applied a dressing to the arms with some bandages out of our first aid kit and brought her around with some smelling salts.

She reacted like she was coming out of a bad dream. I held her in my arms until she was fully conscious. It was several moments before she could talk, but when she did, the words poured out of her. I listened to her story never doubting a word, trying to reassure her that it was safe. I hoped I sounded convincing.

I don't have to tell you what happened as I am sure you already know. Whatever was after Janet wasn't the same thing that appeared in the mirror, it was larger, and from the size and weight of that stone urn, it must have been very strong. The front door was two inches thick and constructed of oak planking and the bolt of heavy wrought iron. Even with this testament to its strength the door showed signs of cracking down the center and the bolt bent slightly inward. If Janet hadn't reinforced it with the desk and fire poker, she might not be alive today.

The little creature in the mirror even though its appearance was supernatural by design, was less baffling to me. If a being who on one occasion could appear solid and real, while at another be invisible to the naked eye, but not the lens of my camera, could just as easily cross the boundary of a looking glass into a mirrored world.

The cab driver had refused to stay no matter how much I had offered to pay. I knew that the fog would delay Jim and the Doctor just as it had me and we would have to wait for the two of them before leaving.

Everything was quiet by then. I hoped that my presence had scared the intruder off and we would be spared another visit . . . at least until reinforcements showed up. I pretended to be calm, at ease and in control of the situation for Janet's sake, all the while keeping my ears open and an eye peeled for anything that may have been lurking.

I tried to restore some order to the living room and at the same time cheer up Janet. I started a fire in the hearth after rolling the urn aside. The heat from the fire dissipated most of the mist, driving it to the ceiling where it condensed to precipitation dripping from the plaster.

I put on a pot of coffee and while letting it brew; I swept the glass into two piles. The window would have to wait until the others arrived. I didn't want to let Janet out of my sight even if only for a minute to go down to the cellar for some lumber to board up the opening. Without saying so, I knew that she felt the same.

The back door was also in need of repair. The jam broke when I kicked it open. The screen door was unharmed, so I bolted it shut.

Janet's spirits were gradually lifting, and she required less and less comforting. She was still nervous about me being out of her sight for more than a few seconds so when I started making the sandwiches to accompany our coffee, I kept jabbering across the room in light-hearted tones about any silly thing that came to mind.

I would pop my head in and out of the parlor every minute or two so she could see me and carefully shifted our conversation to thoughts of returning home and seeing New York once again.

I had picked up the knife while cleaning and slipped it between my belt and trousers at the hip, so it hung there in case I would need it. It was probably the best weapon if not the only one in the house. All the time that I swept up the glass and tried to bolster Janet's spirits I remained alert. I was careful to always keep a smile on my face or an assemblage of good cheer. Janet had been through a lot, and she was just starting to believe that it was safe again.

It was while I was caught up in those thoughts of our homecoming that I became careless. The taste of our return was sweet. I imagined us back home in our little apartment surrounded by our friends. Janet was caught up in the charm of the idea and almost beamed. Some color had returned to her cheeks.

I stacked the cold meat sandwiches on a serving tray along with two steaming cups of coffee and headed toward the living room. "I'll bet Harry and Emma will be surprised to see us," I hollered across the room.

The bottom sash of the kitchen window exploded behind me, and

I was lifted off my feet by a powerful force. The tray of coffee and sandwiches I was holding scattered across the linoleum. A huge scaly powerful arm had me about the chest and was lifting me up. My feet kicked and dangled in mid-air. Its grip was crushing, suffocating me. My back was to the thing, so I had no idea what it looked like except for the arm. It was gigantic. The size of a man's leg. It rippled and curled with muscles all in the wrong places. The scaly flesh of the thing continually fanned open and closed, back and forth, it was breathing through the pores of its skin. The hand or claw-shaped paw was as big as a bear's, and I noticed the lack of any outward signs of joints at the elbow and wrist. The thing's structure must have consisted of an interlacing of cartilage that flexed and bent like rubber.

Its grip was tight constricting my windpipe. I fought against blacking out. My head swam, and the room spun.

It could have easily crushed me to death with its one arm, but instead, with the other free hand, it grabbed the knife from my belt. I thought it intended to slit my throat when the blade whizzed by my shoulder. I realized that it wasn't after me. It wanted the damn knife.

I heard Janet scream. If I had been facing the window, I would have also seen the car coming up the drive because while the thing still had me in its clutches, Dr. VonTassell appeared. He was standing outside on the back porch behind the locked screen door calling my name. He took a step backward, then with a violent lunge he kicked the door open and looked about. His jaw slacked, and his eyes bulged, thinking fast the Doctor grabbed an empty Coca-Cola bottle off the kitchen counter and sent it hurling over my head with surprising force and through the upper sash.

The bursting glass must have shattered into the face of the thing because it released me from its grip and I fell to my knees. It bellowed with a blood-curdling roar that trailed off into a woman's scream. The knife dropped to the floor beside me. VonTassell was at my side and grabbed my shoulder before I could fall into the broken glass. From outside I heard gunfire; several rapid shots as if fired by an automatic weapon. The noises followed with the familiar barking of Vesta. I tried to stand up and had difficulty breathing. The Doctor gave me a hand up with orders to breathe deeply.

"Where did it go?" I said.

"Around the front towards the road," he said while helping me to my feet.

"The road! Why the hell did it go that way?"

I turned in time to see the car door slam and Jim at the wheel cutting doughnuts in our lawn with his back tires while quickly turning around. The bright beams of the headlights burned into the fog as he raced down the drive in hot pursuit. A hunched shadowy figure retreated into the distance.

Jim and Vesta must have scared the thing out onto the open road. I heard his car at the end of the drive skid into a turn then roar northward down the road in the direction of Valsbach.

I bent over and picked up the knife. My left side ached, bruised ribs, other than that, I was more rattled than hurt. It was the Doctor that found Janet. In the excitement, I had forgotten about her. I slipped the knife behind my belt and dashed to the parlor sofa where she laid. The shock had been too much for her. She was unconscious. Her body quivered with small jerky movements of the hands and feet.

VonTassell tried to call for an ambulance, but the phone was out of order. We carried her upstairs instead, making her as comfortable as possible, bundling her up to keep her warm. The Doctor remained at her bedside monitoring her condition when Jim came back.

He and Vesta were on foot looking a bit lost and confused. Jim wore a Mets ball cap on his head, and a vintage World War II M1 slung over his shoulder. Vesta looked chipper as if she had just come back from chasing rabbits bouncing back and forth on her front and hind legs trying to get Jim's attention. It looked as though the dog was attempting to cheer up the Sergeant.

He was evasive, stopping at the kitchen window when coming in to look at the broken glass. "Whatta mess! What happened anyway?"

"It grabbed me through the glass," I said.

He leaned over and examined the broken window feeling the serrated edges. "Oh, yeah . . . whatever that thing was, it must've been pretty anemic."

His comment puzzled me. He kept stroking the smooth flat sides of the shattered pane between the thumb and forefinger. Then briefly startling me he thrust a finger in my face. "There isn't a drop of blood on this glass!"

I had to admit it was more than strange that any living thing could mangle a window so badly without sustaining even a slight cut. Maybe it was tough skinned, or it had a different kind of blood. I didn't know, but one thing was obvious, Jim was trying to find something else to talk about other than the chase. I knew that what had happened had gone against his simple logic, but I was anxious to hear about it.

He probably thought I would think he was crazy but after getting him to sit down and pouring him a glass of cooking sherry, the only liquor we had in the house, I managed to get him to open up.

It seems that when he and the Doctor drove up, they saw a large dark form at the kitchen window. It was several seconds before they understood what was happening. The Doctor, of course, ran around to the back door, and Jim got the M1 out of the trunk. He had brought it along to show me part of his collection, hoping to do a little target practice in the woods. Little did he know that it would be live targets.

Before he had a chance to use the weapon VonTassell made his move driving the creature screaming past him. He squeezed off a couple of rounds at the thing but wasn't sure if he had hit it. Vesta, out of the car by then, chased after the thing yapping at its heels. It ran into the tall grass alongside the drive with the dog behind. Jim jumped into his car and tore after it. Halfway down the drive the thing came out of the grass and headed towards the road with huge bounding strides. Jim stopped long enough to allow Vesta to jump in. He said the dog kept snorting and blowing air through her nostrils rubbing her snout against the seat cushions as if she was trying to rid herself of a bad scent.

The story ended less than a quarter of a mile down the road. With the creature still in sight, Jim raced across the gravel; the accelerator pressed to the floor.

"I slung the M1 across the fender holding it in place with my left hand while steering with the right. I was going to charge it like a friggin Panzer and empty the full clip into it."

But Jim hadn't gotten a clear view of the thing before. He took a big gulp of the sherry.

"Damn it, Faren, it just stopped. Stopped running in the middle of the road with its back turned toward me. It turned as if it was casually strollen' down the street and looked over its shoulder. I guess it was a shoulder. It was big. It had these big dead white eyes. It scared the crap right out of me! I must have been doin' sixty by then, and there was no way I could stop in time. That's when it happened."

"What happened?," I said.

He took another pull on his drink then stared at me not sure if he wanted to continue. I nodded for him to go on.

"It . . . It sprouted wings and took off. Straight up."

I think he expected me to laugh but I didn't. I could tell that Jim had been drinking earlier that evening, but I knew that this was no hallucination. What Jim saw was real. It was probably a good thing that he had a few drinks before he came otherwise the overall effect it might have had on an otherwise sober mind could have been too much for him.

"Where's your car?" I said.

"In a ditch. I couldn't believe my own eyes. I stuck my head out of the open window as we sailed by and watched it until it was over the top of the car and in a second out of sight. I didn't watch where

I was goin' and plowed straight into a drainage ditch. I think the axle is broke."

It presented a new problem. Jim's car was out of commission, and I recalled uneasily something that Janet had told me.

Without explaining, I asked Jim to follow, and we ran out to the garage. We were outside and across the yard in less than a minute, and before we entered the old shed, I could see the faint amber glow from the headlights of our car. Janet had left the lights on when she fled from that corpse thing earlier, and there wasn't enough current left in the battery to turn over the engine.

There was no auto club out there. The phone didn't work, and we were fifteen miles from town. There were neighbors, of course, just a couple miles away and even if I could find my way there in the dark and the fog, I doubted that any of them would be willing to help. They were a strange and isolated group of people. My one visit there to return the schoolbooks told me that.

It was very dark outside but darker in the garage with no electricity. The garage was also small presenting a cramped workspace. Shifting the car into neutral Jim and I pushed it out into the open. There was a slimy residue crawling with maggots smeared across the hood. I shuddered, remembering what Janet had told me. With a handful of rags, I swept the wet lump to the lawn.

We tried to jump start the car. The both of us pushing and when picking up speed, I would quickly slip into the driver's seat, throw the shift lever into first with the ignition on, and engage the clutch. After four or five unsuccessful attempts we gave up. The battery had been run down too low even to start the car that way.

Jim suggested that we leave the car sit for a couple of hours and the battery may recharge itself. I wasn't about to wait. His car may have had a broken axle, but the battery would be good. We settled on Jim walking up the road to his car after we got the spare flashlight from the kitchen and some tools from the cellar.

VonTassell was coming downstairs when I unlocked the cellar door.

"She will be all right now," he said. "She's awake and feeling much better. I gave her a sedative to relax her and make her sleep."

He asked what we were doing, and I explained. His expression exhibited objection even before he spoke. He thought it unwise to move Janet and offered to stay the night to look after her.

"There may not be another night in this house after this one if we don't leave. The minute the car is fixed we are getting the hell out of here!" I had raised my voice and was shouting. Baffled, Jim just stared. VonTassell, on the other hand, appeared surprised as if I had revealed a hidden truth.

His demeanor was shaken. The large frame that normally towered diminished slightly and his shoulders sagged as if a great weight laid upon them. His voice cracked. "It's tonight?"

The two words shot through me. The old fossil had known everything all along. He knew exactly what I was talking about and from the look on his face I guessed that VonTassell knew more than me. If there had been the time I would have forced him into an explanation but getting the car running with the four of us in it was foremost in my mind.

As if in answer to the rage that was building up inside of me he began to tremble and shake. I couldn't bear to look at him anymore. Jim was shaking too, a bottle on a shelf fell and broke in the kitchen. The room, the entire house was shaking. Jim shouted "earthquake" and toppled onto the sofa. I had to grab hold of the doorjamb to keep from falling over. A rumbling sound vibrated beneath my feet followed by a grating noise like the tearing and splitting of masonry. The ceiling in the parlor opened up raining small chunks of plaster and dust from the cracks. The unseen force halted abandoning the tremors to a deafening silence.

My ears still rang in the quiet. I noticed a hole had opened in the ceiling spilling plaster dust onto the sofa where Jim Ruttick sprawled. Chalky dust covered his head and shoulders. Vesta barked and yelped frantically. The barking came from the cellar. The three of us clamored downstairs. Her barking had faded into the distance, echoing as if coming from a vast empty chamber.

Jim had the flashlight, and I grabbed the other one off the workbench the moment we hit the bottom of the stairs. We searched the great stone walls and floors for a sign of the dog. Jim at one end of the cellar and me at the other sweeping the area with beams of light. Centuries of dust that had adhered to the overhead floor joists were in the act of settling. Clouds of the falling matter were as thick as the evening fog outside when struck by the lights.

I called to Vesta and was answered by a faint receding whimper. I thought that it came from the small hidden chamber. I ran to the west end of the cellar. The stone door was open, left as it had been the other evening when we were unsuccessful in closing it. I groped my way along the short corridor, blindly stepping into an open hole in the floor, falling forward and striking my head on the wooden reading stand. My surprised cries brought answering calls from the others. I had skinned my ankle on the rough concrete surface and my head seared with pain. My nerves had been on edge all evening and this only made my blood boil. I stood up cursing the oak stand and my stupidity. There was a large crack in the floor; a crevice had split the magic symbol in two.

I knelt down next to the opening and saw that it ran the length of the room and down the narrow corridor. It must have been dumb luck that kept me from stepping into it sooner because it crossed the same path that I took in getting there.

Calling to Jim and the Doctor and urging them to be careful of the crack, I summoned them to the chamber. By my flashlight and the advancing beam of Jim's, I could make out the extent of the damage to the floor. The crack that had once been small, hairline in some spots and had traveled from the east end of the foundation disappearing behind the stone door to the alchemist's chamber, had now opened severely. As wide as three feet at the center of the small room and no narrower than one foot at the other points, it was dangerously deep. The effect of the settling dust wasn't as heavy there although the combined illumination of our lights was unable to penetrate the blackness of the hole. The flashlight beams picked up an occasional dust swirl in the air, but they didn't strike anything solid. A cool, musty breeze filtered up from the crevice, and for a brief moment, I thought I detected a rustling movement and the faint smell of decaying flesh.

I wasn't alone in my feelings. As if in answer to my thoughts, Jim crouched closer to the gaping crevice. We heard the last receding cry of Vesta then. It sounded like she was just below us. Jim, excited, hollered that something moved. "Its got Vesta." Before I could stop him, he had raised and aimed the rifle. Two reports burst from the barrel. Thunder echoed in the darkness. The noise was extremely painful on the eardrums. I ripped the gun loose from his grasp and tossed it across the room in a fit of rage. I was taking my anger out on poor Jim. I realized then that he was as frightened as the rest of us. Somehow I had thought him void of the emotion. Jim's large size and boastful ways made him seem fearless. I called him trigger happy and after settling down eyed him coldly. He was worried, pleading that in the excitement he could not have shot Vesta. He was certain that something else moved down there. In a few minutes, I cooled down and allowed him the security of his M1.

Vesta never answered our calls after that, nor could we find any traces of her. Lying at full length at the edge of the brink, Jim holding onto my belt and I holding both flashlights downward at arm's length to see what lie below produced nothing. I cringe now when I think of what was down there and how close I probably was to it.

VonTassell lit the candles in the room, and while I was still hanging below the level of the floor, I heard him announce that the machine was missing. The reading stand had narrowly missed falling into the crevice. Perched on the edge of the crack; the Necronomicon endured as well, pages unruffled by the quake. But the machine was gone. We had placed it in the recess at the base of the reading stand the other night. It was empty. The chamber was beginning to clear, and there were no visible signs that it had toppled into the hole. If it had, some of its delicate glass parts would be littered around the opening.

I understood then what Ephraim Pryne meant when he said the windlass would be in their possession. The device, constructed by my great uncle was the windlass, and now somehow they had it. I suspected as well with a sinking feeling what it was that moved within the depths of that fissure.

***

We laid some planks from the cellar workshop across the broader expanses of the crevice and took the rest upstairs to board up the east bay window.

I felt a need to fortify the house even if it was only for a short while. I nailed the lumber in place while Jim hiked up the road to get the battery. The minute the car was ready we would abandon the old schloss and head for Stuttgart.

VonTassell had brought the old book up with him. I didn't like the vile smelling thing, but I didn't protest. My temper was short, and my nerves were on edge. I was a short fuse primed by suspicion and keeping myself busy and away from any confrontation with the Doctor was good therapy. I knew that if we did confront one another that I might lose control and I didn't want to succumb to the rages of anger when a level head and an alert mind was needed most. There would be plenty of time for questions later in the car. If it hadn't been for the repair tasks that I occupied myself with while waiting for Jim, I probably would have ended up pacing the carpet.

VonTassell never offered to lend a hand. Instead, he sat in the kitchen leafing through the rotting pages of the Necronomicon, mumbling something about finding a key.

I repaired the back door, nailing the jamb back together after the windows were secured. When the last nail was hammered into place, I returned to Janet's bedside and started to pack. I tried to temper my discontent with pictures of an early return home, with health intact, and Janet, and of a homecoming which would be almost a triumphal ceremony.

Janet stirred restlessly against the sedative. She muttered my name in her sleep sobbing that the baby was wet and, "he would catch a cold." The words were agonizingly sad. I held her in my arms and gently caressed her until she settled quietly. I talked to her, although I doubt she heard any of my words. I told her that all was fine and we would soon be home. I prayed to God that I was right.

Strewn across the bedspread were Janet's diary and some loose sheets of stationery. Knowing that it had never been used, I was surprised when looked inside and found the pages crammed tight with a hastily scrawled hand. All of the pages on both sides had been written on in my wife's feverish but recognizable handwriting. She must have been writing for many hours throughout the entire evening and even later, upstairs, until the moment the drug took effect. The last few pages, written on separate stationery, after running out of pages in the diary, bore a large swirling scribble that trailed off illegibly at the end.

I scooped the papers together along with the diary and started reading the last few loose pages. Even under the drug, her remaining words were hurried and frantic. She wrote that she had discovered who Peter was. My great uncle's closest friend. It was almost as if she was leaving a warning, perhaps for me, but never had the chance to finish the message.

The name Peter had no sooner formed in my thoughts when the answer to Janet's discovery unfolded in my mind. I never realized until that evening that I hadn't known Von Tassell's first name, always calling him "Doctor." When we carried Janet upstairs earlier, I noticed the engraving on the clasp of his medical bag. It read "P. VonTassell, M.D." At the time I didn't give it a second thought. There were too many other things on my mind. Janet must have seen it too when she came around. I wasn't in the room, and the realization of it must have frightened her.

Then I realized something else. If Janet knew about Peter, then she somehow had read Heinrich Todesfall's notes.

Jim was at the foot of the stairs calling my name in a loud whisper before I had a chance to read further.

"What is it?" I said, a bit irritated after coming to the head of the stairs.

"Somebody's on the grounds. I saw him on the way back."

VonTassell was looking out the rear kitchen window when I came up from behind, followed by Jim. I squinted my eyes and stared out into the fog. Jim pointed over the Doctor's shoulder and whispered, "There."

A figure scurried by in the distance and headed into the small summer house, apparently unhindered by its padlocked door. There was only one way in and no other out. I couldn't make out who the intruder was, but from the outline, it was plain that it was a man or at least a human shape. And, if I acted first, he was trapped. The idea overcame me. I felt a wild rage. Without giving a second thought to the possible consequences, I spun around, unlatched the back door and ran across the lawn. VonTassell shouted for me to wait but I didn't pay him any mind nor did I pay any particular attention to the van backed up alongside the summer house.

A shape moved in the darkness. I slammed my shoulder against the partially opened door sending it crashing into the wall. A silhouetted figure struggled feebly in my grasp, falling to the floor amid the shattering of pottery and glass. I had my hands around a throat. A match was struck, and a kerosene lantern lit the room. Doctor VonTassell lowered the glass chimney of an oil lamp on a nearby table. Jim stood military style, rifle in hand, blocking the entrance. The apparition was not a visitor from the shadows. I had Rudolph Hausmann pinned to the floor with my knee planted squarely in his chest. I released my grip from the old caretaker's neck and grabbed him by the collar shaking him violently. I was in an insane rage, screaming accusations, blaming him for the harassment of my wife.

The Doctor shouted at me to let him go. "He is harmless,

Hausmann is not behind these odd events."

I relaxed my grip on the old man and turned my attention to VonTassell, looking up I saw murals and paintings covering the four walls. They were ghostly looking oils heavily framed about four to five feet in length. The framing was in two shapes, all of equal length, half of them rectangular and the rest oval in configuration. The individual canvases pictured different settings of a strange city of massive domes, gigantic pyramids flattened at the top connected by a network of bridges to towers and other structures all made of a night-black masonry. The works of art created a visual vista of chill; that feeling of déjà vu again . . . "my dream," I said in a half whisper.

The surroundings hypnotized me. Slowly no longer regarding Hausmann, I slid off of him and sat dumbfounded on the floor.

The old caretaker scrambled to his feet and headed toward the door. Jim stepped in front, cutting him off, menacingly tapping the stock of the M1. He was, at last, having something earthly to handle.

Hausmann shot a pleading look to the Doctor who announced, "He is here by my instructions." I rose to my feet fascinated by the trappings of the room. There were two windows blocked out with cardboard from the inside. A small one at the front, near the door, and a larger casement at the back with a cushioned window seat below. The summer house was piled high with unusual furnishings. The paintings covered most of the wall area, and the remaining surfaces, covered by red and black velvet drapes that hung over tables and benches that overflowed with a tremendous array of books and pottery. In the center was a small wood burning stove, a library table, and chair. Fragments of stone tablets, old melted candles and a wide assortment of books, manuscripts, and papers, many of which exhibited extreme age, littered the surface of the table.

Among some of the books were titles that I couldn't begin to pronounce and have noted some of them here. Some of them were familiar while others, although unforgettable, were completely unknown to me. There was THE EGYPTIAN BOOK OF THE DEAD, something called COMTE D'ERLETTE'S CULTES DES

GOULES, a paperback edition of Van Daniken's, CHARIOTS OF THE GODS, and Koestler's ROOTS OF COINCIDENCE and a worn copy of MEIN KAMPH and even an Arkham House edition of H.P. Lovecraft's AT THE MOUNTAINS OF MADNESS. One baffling work by a Ludvig Prinn called DEVERMIS MYSTERIIS and another equally as mysterious THE UNAUSSPRECHLICHEN KULTEN OF VON JUNTZ. There were fragments of a puzzling work entitled THE BOOK OF EIBON and a great odorous thing that seemed to reek of nameless terror with a heading that read; THE PNAKOTIC MANUSCRIPTS.

And one other. I was surprised to see it. It was another copy of the Necronomicon and in English. It wasn't as thick as the one discovered in the cellar, about a third of the pages missing and it appeared to be much newer. Besides the size and age, it had a similar cover as the other except that it bore no title.

"What is all this?," I asked. Hausmann speaking for the first time approached me fearfully. "These are Professor Todesfall's . . . I was coming to take them away tonight."

"You were not supposed to be here when he came," added the Doctor. "If our dinner arrangements would have come off as planned, Rudolph would have emptied the contents here into his truck substituting some old tools which he would have retrieved on another day when you and your wife were at home." It, I guessed would have left the impression that he had finally come to get his things.

"But why all the secrecy?"

VonTassell fingered the pages of the English copy of Olaus Wormus. "This is a very good reason." He looked almost grief-stricken then continued. "This book is an imperfect copy of Dr. Dee's English version of the Necronomicon. Originally part of the Whately estate, an old family that resided at one time in Dunwich, Massachusetts. They had a sordid past. In 1955 it was stolen from the Library of Miskatonic University in Arkham, Massachusetts.

I followed his line of thought but didn't have to say so. The look on my face gave me away.

"Your great-uncle could not be trusted. He was a dangerous man with a dangerous vision. He was an outsider with a passion that, even a world war could not quench. Todesfall probed into the deepest roots of man's origin in search of an ancient evil. He wanted to know who or what Satan was and tried to locate the very gates of hell. He found them," he mused. "I suspect somewhere in our darkest slumbers. He theorized the memory of times and hells and secrets long gone. Of course, a few wakeful eyes remain, in our archetypes and visions." He broke off and stared at me for a moment then went on. "Like those few depraved cults scattered around the world that have striven for thousands of years to release the Old Ones but failed because they could not discover the secret of the key."

"That is why Todesfall required two copies of the Necronomicon. He began to collate the two texts with the aim of discovering a certain passage, a formula containing the frightful names of Yog-Sothoth and Yath Notep. Listen to this," he said to me. "Some of the words should be familiar to you."

He flipped a page of the English copy and read:

> "Nor is to be thought that man is either the oldest or the last of earth's masters, or that the common bulk of life and substance walks alone. The old ones were, the old ones are, and the old ones shall be. Not in spaces we know, but between them. They walk serene and primal, un-dimensioned and unseen. Yog-Sothoth knows the gate.
>
> Yog-Sothoth is the gate. Yog-Sothoth is the key and guardian of the gate. Past, present, future, all are one in Yog-Sothoth. He knows where the old ones broke through of old and where they shall break through again. He knows where they have trod earth's fields, and where they still tread them, and why no one can behold them as they tread. By their smell can men sometimes know them near, but of their semblance can no man know, saving only in the

> features of those they begotten on mankind; and of those are there many sorts, differing in likeness from man's truest eidolon to that shape without sight or substance which is them. They walk unseen and foul in lonely places where the words have been spoken and the rites howled through at their seasons. The wind gibbers with their voices and the earth mutters with their consciousness. They bend the forest and crush the city, yet may not forest or city behold the hand that smites."

Sliding a finger down the page, he ignored one passage then read further,

> "Man rules now where they ruled once; they shall soon rule where man rules now. After summer is winter, and after winter summer. They wait patient and potent, for here shall they reign again."

The words were familiar in spots but slightly different from what I had remembered. The passage the Doctor read was similar to the letter we found in the cellar, but with one definite change. "There was no mention of the mysterious Yath-Notep."

"Exactly" the Doctor proclaimed after I made my thoughts known. "Your late uncle realized that certain discrepancies and ambiguities existed with the "Dee" version of the text but the Latin copy of Olaus Wormus was an excellent one and supplied the necessary information by comparison. The answer lay in the many duplications of the god Yog-Sothoth's name although inscribed in haste in both copies; the older, Latin version produced after careful translation a different name. It was the discovery of a lesser deity, an earth elemental, Yath Notep. Possibly, it was something that had been slurred in the earlier Greek and Arabic translations. There is a definite similarity in the two names, an obvious reason why scholars in the past, encumbered as well by the illegibility of the texts, had read it wrong."

"This is insane," I said, disgusted with the whole business by then, "He was crazy to believe in all this. He was weak with age and in poor physical condition. More than likely weak of mind and spirit. Even if he did truly believe why would he prefer that world to this one?"

"It requires more courage and intelligence to be a sorcerer than the folk who take experience at hearsay think," the Doctor snapped back. "Heinrich Todesfall was a brilliant, but vengeful man, embittered by a world that treated him cruelly, giving him nothing but pain. Perhaps he envisioned himself immortal, standing side-by-side with the great Old Ones as mankind crumbled before their power, or perhaps he did it out of sheer madness. In any case, it seems I underestimated his level of vindictiveness."

"You mean the translation and the machine?"

"And the time," the Doctor answered gravely. "I've journeyed through much of this world, seen a great deal, travels which cultivated an interest in anthropology until it became my major preoccupation. The legends and folklore abounding in the Black Forest drew me to this region, from my New England practice, and so I met Heinrich Todesfall.

"From Todesfall I learned of the lore and legends little known by the rest of the world. I began to suspect his intentions early in our acquaintance, but he was guarded of his secrets and never let me totally into his confidence. I never found out the time of the coming, only that it would occur somewhere between the Lammas and Vernal Equinox, a span of nearly eight months.

"Until this evening I didn't know that the time was so close. I hired Rudolph here to help me move your Uncle's effects. We had tried unsuccessfully once before, the day you first arrived at the schloss."

"So you weren't the Welcome Wagon after all. We happened to arrive at a bad time for you."

"I am not a thief." He replied with some indignation. "And neither is Rudolph. I hoped that a close private study of Todesfall's things would provide me with the answer to undo what had already been done."

"Please, for God sake, tell me what he has done?"

"Apparently Todesfall used the machine and in doing so altered time and space slightly and released some of Yath Notep's menial servants."

"Like that thing that attacked me through the window?"

"Yes. Either the energy released or possibly certain words spoken also reanimated the bodies of the soldiers from the old battlefield into the living dead your wife claims she saw."

"This is crazy . . . I don't know what is going on around here or who's behind it all but I'm leaving here tonight with Janet to get help."

Suddenly alarmed, he cried out, "you can't!"

"And why not?" I answered in a challenging tone.

"I know all this sounds insane to you, but you must realize that there is danger . . . great danger . . . in allowing others to meddle with this. Because of my hesitations, we may be witnessing the beginning of something horrible; it could be Armageddon."

Jim shifted his position, and I advanced a little closer to the Doctor fearing he was about to crack. He covered his face with his hands, relaxed a bit then continued slowly with his arms stretched out.

"I shall always be sorry for not acting sooner but now I must! There is still time. We're armed and alert . . . remember, these beings are not ghosts or poltergeists, but real physical creatures that can be killed. Stay and comfort your wife; she is in no condition to be moved anyway."

Real physical things or not, I knew that even though they could be killed so could we. VonTassell read the hesitation in my expression and pleaded, "give me until a half an hour before midnight; I must find out to what extent Todesfall succeeded . . . please, you must trust me!"

After some consideration, I agreed to give him the time. Jim was about to protest, and I started to wave his objections down when the sound of the van starting up stopped me. Hausmann when our backs were turned, had slipped out.

He had already started down the drive when I ran out. I called for him to stop, running after, but my shouting only made him go faster. I had hoped to use the van for our escape. Jim threw his arms in the air in despair, walked over to the car and started in on switching the batteries.

Back in the summer house VonTassell had removed the cardboard from the windows and had some of the candle stubs lit. For the first time, I could see the view from the rear window. It overlooked the glade. The swell in the earth was directly in sight and from where I stood the ground appeared elevated slightly more than it had the day before. I don't know if it was a trick played upon the fog by the moon but the large expanse of ground that had risen several feet seemed to be offset from the rest of the surrounding glade by a faint shimmer of light.

The night air had become very cold, and the Doctor started some kindling in the pot belly stove with scraps of the cardboard and candle wax. VonTassell was his old self again busying himself with his study. I fetched the other copy of the Necronomicon for him from the house then set about helping Jim.

Ruttick was angry as hell until I explained that I had no intentions of honoring my agreement with VonTassell. I had only said as much to quiet him down so the rest of us could get away quickly.

Jim was having difficulty adapting the battery from his car to fit the other mount. The cables were corroded badly making the removal difficult, and he was going to have to tie the battery casing with rope to the fender to secure it.

When I was sure that Jim didn't need my help, and before I went back up to Janet, I crept over to the summer house and peeked through the front window at the Doctor. Seated next to the library table he was hunched over a pile of papers. The lantern was turned up high, brightly illuminating the room. He was engrossed in his work. The Doctor got up from his chair, and I thought my presence was detected. I relaxed when, after he walked over to the pot-bellied stove, he took up the fire poker to sir the glowing embers. Replacing the poker next to the side of the stove, he returned to the table. I breathed easily, then before leaving I quietly bolted the door from the outside locking him in.

***

Peter VonTassell M.D. was not to be trusted either. My great Uncle's manuscript was proof enough for me. I hated to lock him away in the old shack but thought it best for all of us. Although the Doctor was a man in his early sixties he was still strong in stature with broad shoulders and thick arms and I was afraid that he might give us trouble when the three of us attempted to leave.

I planned to abandon him, and when well out of reach I'd call the local authorities letting them know where he could be found. The summer house wasn't built to securely, and if the Doctor tried, I am sure he could find a way out. The windows would provide a quick means of escape, and by the time he could break one and get out, we would be long gone. In the meanwhile he was unaware of his imprisonment, being caught up in his studies.

I did a thorough job of packing, leaving little to want. I managed to get all our clothes, toilet articles, money and passports into three bags. Everything else would have to stay behind until I was able to send for them.

It was 10:15 p.m. and I was relieved to be well ahead of the dreaded hour of midnight. I could see Jim from the bedroom window, and we exchanged progress reports shouting through the open sash. The fog was getting thicker, and I could barely make out the car and his outline. He waved the flashlight overhead when answering and my eyes gradually adjusted to the gloom. Even his voice sounded muffled in the mist, but I made out the words well enough. Jim said that he'd be ready in about twenty minutes. The night air hadn't changed, and I closed the casement to keep the draft off Janet. I had bundled her up in a robe and blanket barely disturbing her slumber. She mumbled lightly to herself when I wrapped her in the blankets, but beyond that, the sedative kept her quiet. Jim and I would have to carry her downstairs when the car was ready.

You can imagine how guilty I felt when I found my great uncle's notebook between the mattress and her pillow. It had been rolled up and hidden there by Janet. During all that time what she must have been thinking of me? Weeks before I lied to her about it being lost. She must have found it under the front seat of the car, and I was certain she had read it.

I pulled up a chair next to her bedside keeping the window and Jim in view and set about reading Janet's diary. It was a work against time, written under pressure. The delicately poetic and sometimes delirious style of Janet's narrative was set down at a feverish pace. The contents of it added to my depression. The words were like daggers to me. I had never realized the full extent of my wife's dilemma. It had been a nightmare for her, which let me say here, was shared equally by both of us. I wish now that I would have confessed all that I knew to her. She was much stronger than I had ever imagined. Together we may have had the combined strength to have licked this thing.

I was right. Janet had read the alchemist's notebook. She had also become suspicious of me. Her convictions had been clouded by my deception, not knowing if I was reliable.

I had become drowsy going over the diary and dozed off after I skimmed over it and the rereading of the last few pages falling into a brief light sleep. I was only out for a short period. A dream of quiet flapping like the beating of leathery wings invaded the silence. Some time passed, then I awoke with a start. My ears rang echoing the after-effects of an unknown sound. I wasn't positive, but I thought I heard a scream. I jumped up, cursing my stupidity for dozing off.

I turned to Janet to see if she was all right. She was sleeping soundly. A look out the window revealed a thicker, heavier fog than before, blanketing almost everything from sight. I could no longer make out the car but could see the faint lights of the summer house dimly through the mist. It was a while before I realized what I saw. From the vantage point of our bedroom, it was impossible to see the window at the rear of the old shack. And as I said, there were lights, more than one, two that glimmered back in the fog. One source of light was the small front casement and the other, much bigger, could only have been made by the opened door to the summer house.

I called for Jim but did not receive an answer. A quiet hush clung like claws in the night air. There wasn't the rustle of a single leaf or branch from the wood. Not an insect chirped nor did I hear the familiar clanking and rattling of Jim's labor. The dense stillness of the mist had muted all sounds into a dead silence.

The clock on the bed table read ten minutes after eleven. The evening was almost over. A wave of anxiety swept over me. My misgivings about the approaching hour of midnight left me with a nagging fear.

I paced back and forth from the window to the bedroom door unable to decide on my next move. On one of my trips to the window I hollered for Jim at the top of my lungs, over and over again, but still, there was no reply.

I nervously slipped my hand into my pocket out of habit, and the tips of my fingers struck the soapstone charm. I started rubbing it.

Touching the small five-sided stone had a soothing effect and Janet's silent form, peacefully asleep in bed renewed some of my courage. I felt by degrees relief from the stress. Bewildered, I knew just as well that if we were ever to leave that house, I would eventually have to go downstairs.

From the kitchen window, I would be able to make out the summer house clearer than from the second story window. Down the stairs, I went.

The fog was not as heavy at ground level, and the outline of the summer house and part of the roof were visible. The grass was wet, slippery underfoot and in the brief span, it took me to run across the yard the moisture had penetrated my shoelaces and dampened my socks. The door stood open, swung inward; the clasp and padlock had been ripped loose from the jam. My attention was drawn to the back of the single-roomed house. Standing in the doorway looking past the large casement I saw once again the slope in the earth and the eerie green mist. The ground had advanced at an angle towards the curtainless window and had risen a couple of feet in the past hour and a half. It took only a second to take in the scene. My eyes quickly ran down the square panes to the body of Doctor VonTassell. He was lying motionless across the window seat; his left hand clutched at his side. His clothes were covered with blood, and his eyes were wide and fixed blankly staring in my direction.

Giving him up for dead, I jumped when VonTassell moved and motioned for me to come closer. Half kneeling by the Doctor's side and surprised to see some life in him I asked what happened. "Who did this to you?" I asked.

VonTassell's pain-stricken eyes looked past me to the corner of the room. "I . . . knew too much, the Old Ones ordered their minion to take care of me." A wry smile crossed his lips as he gestured to where the cast iron stove rested. "But I got the upper hand."

Some instinct warned me that what had taken place was not a thing meant for the eyes to see. The room was full of a frightful stench. An odor that I knew too well. For a second I didn't dare to turn and look. Summoning up the courage I slowly turned and peered over my shoulder; it was sprawled across the library table like a sacrificial beast on an altar. Too large for the table the thing lay half bent on its back in a pool of green tarry liquid. Amid bloodied books and papers, impaled by the fire poker, was the serpent creature that earlier had attacked me and eluded Jim on the open road. A segment of its massive shoulder was torn away. Jim's aim had been accurate after all. It wasn't quite dead hanging on for only a moment twitching silently and spasmodically while its chest heaved for one last time then became still. Scattered about the room were bits of paper and fragments of books. The green sticky fluid poured from the open wound where the pointed end of the fire poker rammed through its chest. It ran out and across the table in great pools dribbling to the floor. The Necronomicon lay open under the table stained with blood not entirely from the Doctor.

I mentioned something about trying to go for help, but VonTassell insisted that there was no time and in a voice that became stronger ordered me to get the book. In picking it up, some of the green sticky liquid dripped on my hand. Repulsed at the thought of coming in contact with it I shook my wrist causing the drops to fall on the open pages where they mixed with the Doctor's blood.

"I've got to talk," he said elevating himself on an elbow.

I cradled the old book in my arms. The ancient binding had snapped loose when it fell off the table, probably during the struggle. I had some difficulty at first keeping the large quantity of paper together, holding them firmly so they wouldn't fan out from between the front and back covers and spill onto the floor.

"The primal myths . . ." he coughed with a sudden harsh expulsion of breath. I noticed a deep gash in his left side and by the light of the lantern that I had brought closer. I could see that he was bleeding heavily. I started to make a move to comfort him, but he waved the action down as a futile attempt.

" . . . and Todesfall's modern delusion joined in their assumption that mankind is only one . . . perhaps the least of the highly evolved and dominant races of this planet's long and largely unknown history. One of these races has already lived, in the past, over fifty million years past. It was the world of the Permian or Triassic age."

He was lecturing. He bordered on delirium. I tried again unsuccessfully to interrupt, but he kept talking, raising his voice whenever I tried to intervene. There was an urgency in his voice. An alarming urgency, that continued unchecked, as if he knew that he only had minutes left to finish his story.

He told me that my great uncle had managed to recapture from years of extensive research, a vivid and connected picture of this earth millions of years ago.

He declared that Heinrich Todesfall was a student of magic in his later years and that local legend reported that at times when the moon was right and harvest season was about he could raise great rumblings beneath the hills.

"Your uncle told us, in his notebook, that before our universe was created an elder race dwelt in the dimension known as Yith," said the Doctor. "This alien race existed there for countless centuries until a fleet of exploring and adventuring elder beings set forth on a great excursion. They took with them members of countless races. Their quest was to cover time and space and set up the seeds of civilizations to blossom into beauty and wonder for their people to enjoy.

"The Elder Beings came upon the makings of a fine new dimension, and they shaped it to fit the wants of their own wonder.

"These beings eventually left our universe in its infancy to travel and enjoy other worlds. The Elder Race intended to return in time to see how their work had progressed.

"Left in this unprotected state the star system was threatened by others; they were monstrous intrusions, a malign cosmic force.

"When these Ancient Ones came upon our universe they saw that it could be a place to dwell and rule. It was the goal of these creatures to conquer and dominate everything they came upon."

VonTassell glared at me with a piercing stare.

"The evil, in their new dimension, grew to tremendous proportions. Their spawn took reign, and the Elder Beings lost control over this portion of their environment."

I gathered by then that Dr. VonTassell was quoting from memory. His voice filled with dread and feverishly he continued, "The most powerful spawn to dominate and exist over the world was Cthulhu. Along with its brothers, they became known as the Old Ones."

The Doctor once again broke from his recitation and stared long and hard at the low-raftered ceiling. He grimaced then flinched. I wasn't sure if he was reacting to the pain he must have been suffering from or if he was trying to regain something from memory. I moved to say something, but he cut me off and continued.

"The Elder Beings became aware of the Old Ones growing hold and knew that they would have to stop the spawn from enveloping the entire universe. Ultimately, the Elder Race returned and had to do battle . . . to take back the heavens they had created. The Elder Beings intervened . . . thus was the Great War."

The Doctor shifted his position slightly and his face distorted into a twisted expression of pain. I adjusted the window seat cushion behind him, and he relaxed some. "Please," I said, "don't talk anymore. I'll go for help."

"Many of the evil hordes fled the battle, but Cthulhu and his kin remained. Led by their fearsome liege, the Old Ones waged an awesome war against the Elder Beings. The Old Ones could not be killed by any conventional means, and the Elder Beings had been rendered invincible by the advancement of their sciences. The conflict waged fruitlessly and spanned a full millennium. How do two indestructible forces defeat one another in battle? The question plagued both sides. The outcome of this was that the Elder Beings selected a number of their best minds to research and experiment on the matter of the Old Ones, and their weaknesses.

"Cthulhu, by then, adopted another brother. It chose a small planet close to a bright star to mold its creation. In the gray beginnings of this planet, there existed a formless mass that reposed amid the slime and vapors. Cthulhu touched it and gave it form and purpose. He gave the earth elemental arms, legs, and a mouth. Cleansing it with the blood of the bodies of the mortal creatures that inhabited the planet he christened his new brother Yath Notep."

It dawned on me then that the Doctor was quoting translations of the Necronomicon like someone quoting the scriptures.

"Cthulhu instructed Yath Notep in the secrets of the spatial dimension until finally, the end came.

Utilizing the fantastic devices the Elder Race had invented, employing advanced principals of energy, they were able to expel dreaded Cthulhu and its brothers into bordering dimensional prisons.

"A penal colony encompassing an entire solar system was employed, with one planet cool and green with fertility as the home of its wardens.

"In this prison dimension, the Old Ones would remain exiled forever unless the astral bonds in which their fantastic jailers chained them were shattered.

"But one brother remained. Yath Notep still roamed unchecked across his small home planet. It was the new dwelling place of the interstellar jailers. The wardens, living on the green sphere were surprised to discover that the Earth Elemental had somehow been unaffected by the dimensional forces.

"The Elders rounded up Yath Notep and his small band of minions, mostly subhuman races such as the serpent children of Yig, the Night Gaunts, and Yath Notep's Pilot Demons and drove them into a subterranean cavern . . . N'Kai, the Black Realm. The Elder Beings chose the prison well. It was a deep chasm that leads to the center of the planet. There was only one way of entry and exit, and this was sealed by a massive star stone quarried in one piece from solid granite and lashed to the surface of the planet. The opening was sealed shut by the very same device that imprisoned Yath Notep's creator.

"It is here that the hybrid of earthly life and its horrible minions yet remain, imprisoned.

"The Elder Beings feared that Cthulhu had an escape plan. It had imbued his creation with one vital element of time travel. Cthulhu had left behind a key that it hoped would elude its jailers. That key was Yath Notep and when the time was right, and the planets were in their proper position and Yath Notep unfettered, the creature had the power to lead his creator earthward once again.

"Cthulhu was immured behind a thin veil of expanse known as R'Lyeh, the only escape from which was through a narrow passage. This wormhole in the fabric of things was invisible and only large enough to permit passage during a certain alignment of the planets.

When the time of the "coming" was at hand, Yath Notep by the sheer cry of his great voice could shatter the last remaining hold over his master's prison, summoning and leading him blindly through the gateway simply by calling after him with its alien imbued tongue.

"As a measure against Yath Notep ever escaping, the Elder Race built a temple over the prison tomb, and a constant vigil was kept over the spot. Around the temple, other buildings sprang, and the City of Kadath grew. Years past and it became a teeming metropolis that spanned the entire globe.

"Approximately sixty-five million years ago there was a great cataclysm. The planet was shaken by tremendous earthquakes and volcanic activity that engulfed over half the population. It was the flood, a product of upheavals, which shattered and submerged continents tumbling the architecture of the Elder Beings beneath the crushing weight of rolling oceans and toppling mountains.

"This once Great Race left the planet. It is not known just where they made their exodus to but only that the meager remains of their cities and a few of the pre-human races were left.

"One member of the Elder Race had remained on Earth. It was Tod-Fal, the Elder Being."

I was caught up in the myth and its remarkable similarities to my dreams and my Uncle's notebook. But when I heard the name of that Elder Being and saw it printed no less in the Necronomicon I dropped the book and scattered its pages across the floor.

He went on barely taking notice of the accident. He said that Tod-Fal was left as a sentinel at the Temple of Kadath. The temple had been constructed well and stood through the catastrophe.

"The Elder Being," he said with a voice that grew weaker "watched how the many races evolved and used their world. Tod-Fal marveled at the quick and powerful way man built civilization.

"It had been said that the Elder Race would return to look after their great secret, but as the centuries passed, it became apparent to Tod-Fal that it would not be during his time.

"Tod-Fal took a female human as a mate, his queen. The half-human child consummated from this mating became the first to a long line of Tanists. They were the custodial heirs to the gateway of N'Kai. For countless generations the descendants of that Elder Being have served as the custodians, keeping the secret of Yath-Notep safe and the gateway undisturbed.

"Over the ages, Yath-Notep became known by many names: Demon of Sorti, Beelzebub, Devil of the Black Shadow, Satan. Legends grew, fabricated from the lost history about the Devil being cast out and sent inside the earth to rule in hell."

His voice slowed down and became dreamlike, "Throughout this time and from beyond the universe dark forces schemed and plotted against our world. Evil cults rose in dark corners of the world. Druids sworn to the service of the ancients performed their terrible ceremonies to release the Old Ones from their prisons.

"Then came disaster," he gasped. "The weak link finally was born in the Tod-Fal chain, a moderate when it came to defining the forces of good and evil. The chain was broken, influenced, and directed by the minions; a pawn to the black forces. As you may have guessed, the gateway is partly open, and the time of the cosmic elations, when the planets will align, and the forces will be strong enough to finish the abominable task, is near.

"It is not certain where the weak link first began. Some of my colleagues speculated that it started with your great Uncle's father. He died in mysterious circumstances shortly after Heinrich was born, and some of us speculated that he was killed by his very own brother who recognized his insanity and destroyed him the moment the new Tanist was born in hopes of carrying on the great tradition. Others believed it started with Heinrich Todesfall. He was raised by his Uncle, his father's brother, a good man by all that we can gather, but his guardianship was taken from him, and the boy's mind perverted by the Nazi order. No matter, the harm is already done."

I began to wonder, VonTassell was using the words, "us" and "we" as if he was not alone in all of this. I didn't say anything. I guessed that if I listened long enough, I would have the answer.

"If Yath-Notep is freed, it will act as the catalyst to a chain reaction, liberating all the Old Ones to return to our world, and man will descend into a black murk of slavery."

He had been speeding up progressively with each sentence, but he paused for breath then and in a more normal tone and at a reduced rate he went on. "Heinrich Todesfall would have probably learned of his destiny sooner if he had been allowed to have been raised by his Uncle. Nevertheless, as fate would have it he learned at a slower, but highly dangerous pace."

A rumbling in the hills interrupted him. He looked over his shoulder and stared out the window. The earth tremor subsided, and he returned his gaze to me. "Todesfall, according to his manuscripts, had discovered the ancient lore then?" I said.

He shook his head, "An indisputable fact that he had in his possession that horrible book. I wasn't certain of the other copy, Dr. Dee's English version, I strongly suspected that he had it, but wasn't sure until that evening when you let me read his notebook."

He breathed deeply, and I heard a rattle in his chest. The eyes of the Doctor stared past me. "In 1955 your great Uncle journeyed to America. He broke into the Library of Miskatonic University and stole the rare English copy. Unfortunately, the old curator of the library was working late that night and got in his way. Todesfall murdered the man. His name was Henry Armitage; he was my father."

"Your father!" I was stunned. "But . . . but your name."

"Is Milton Armitage. I followed the same course of studies as my father and have resided at the University since 1957. A small select group of us at Miskatonic were able to read the signs left behind by the Elder Race and spent our lives searching out legends that were whispered about in certain corners of the world.

"We learned of your uncle by intercepting his correspondence to the Esoteric Order of Dagon and were struck by the similarity of the name to the Great Elder Sentinel as you were.

"The rest was easy. I adopted the identity of Peter VonTassell, physician, and head of the Council for the Order of Dagon and came to Germany. My extensive background in the Cthulhu cycle, not to mention the personal vendetta that motivated me, a small knowledge of medicine, and being the youngest of my colleagues made me the obvious choice.

"My mission was either to convince him to stop his horrible quest and if that failed, kill him. Murder was not beyond me," he confessed with a long sigh. "I killed the real VonTassell in Innsmouth before assuming his identity, and I came close to poisoning you the night you came to visit."

I thought that I was beyond surprise by then, but it is one thing to have someone calmly tell you that you were once the object of murder. It didn't take a college degree to figure out what he was talking about. The night he spilled the brandy, I sensed it was deliberate then, the damn thing must have been laced with poison. I swallowed hard before I asked the next question and tried to assume a calm attitude. "What made you stop?"

"You told me your wife was pregnant. The war had eliminated many a family tree, and we were not aware of any distant relatives. I thought the line of Tanists had ended with Todesfall. I had by that time been resolved to carry on the tradition myself. Even though I am not part of the bloodline, I have been successful with some of my meager magic. That afternoon in the glade, when I rescued your wife from a minion, was an adequate demonstration of my powers. I thought it possible to carry on with help from Miskatonic, and as long as the University would survive, we had a chance.

"Besides, I am not a heartless man. Although I wasn't willing to take a chance on your internal strengths and sanity and would have eliminated you without a second thought, but no matter how hideous the outcome may be I could not bring myself to kill a mother and her unborn child."

"Then why didn't you kill my uncle when you had the chance?" I challenged.

"I failed with him as well. He was reclusive and highly suspicious.

I had difficulty getting close to him. I finally worked my way into his confidence by presenting him with some artifacts he needed to complete his studies. They were kept under lock and key at the University but given to me to be used as a last resort if all else failed. I never believed that the implements would ever be useful and gambled that they would get me close to the old Tanist so that I could catch him off guard and complete my task.

"But his suspicious nature always kept him guarded. He was never without his automatic which he kept strapped to his side night and day. Whenever I was over, or if someone would come to his door, he would unsnap the flap on the holster and rest his palm on the butt.

"We even spent an evening drinking together, but he always did the pouring keeping one hand on the bottle while the other hand never left his gun.

"My visits were frequent; each one predicated on a new idea for assassination and each eventually thwarted. Then one day I hit upon a plan. Todesfall was obsessed by a dark vision, the location of the gateway. Some of my colleagues believed that Cthulhu laid supposedly dead, but dreaming' in an unknown sunken city known as R'Lyeh, which some have thought to be Atlantis, some Mu, others with multiple theories.

"Todesfall's belief, however, was much more radical, abstract and scientifically accurate I am afraid. He discounted all the previous theories and reasoned that the Old Ones could not be retained by any physical means and set out to prove their existence in those spaces between time known as the fourth dimension.

"His theory . . . the old gateway where whence they came was Germany. The region of the Black Forests a discovery through the irony of circumstances brought him back home.

"Todesfall had made an error when selecting the time. I believed that this was his destiny.

"I knew that Heinrich Todesfall's calculations weren't accurate. His mind had become twisted and his estimates too hasty. He had chosen a date too late in the year. Actions such as this normally occur during either the fall or spring equinox.

"An undertaking of this kind if not carefully planned and executed at the proper time, can backfire with devastating results.

"Todesfall was old, in his eighties and his health was poor. I figured that the error in his calling could cost him his life. So I stopped my visits giving him rein, the freedom he needed to play out his final hand. And with a manifest human weakness he ultimately failed . . . and so have I.

"Todesfall, in his meddling, has left things in limbo, an unnatural order exists. I fear that Yath-Notep now wakened from his slumber, all that remains is to unlock his cell door or wait for time or some other intervention to do it for him.

"According to the mythos, Cthulhu has been planning for this time, thousands of years before you and your uncle were born."

He laughed out loud. It was so unexpected that it scared the hell out of me. His voice became wild, excited and delirious talking faster and occasionally chuckling to himself.

"Do you suppose," he screamed, shaking his bloodstained fist under my face, "that for one minute our animals know that they are being used as food when they are taken off to the slaughter? Our planet is one large breeding ground waiting for the butcher to return."

The Doctor fell back against the casement, rattling the panes. He chuckled lightly then as if reciting verse stared at the ceiling and spoke softly.

"...that is not dead which can eternal lie, and with strange eons, even death may die."

His strength was ebbing fast. I made one last attempt to convince him to let me get help pleading that Jim probably had the car repaired by then and we could possibly make it to Stuttgart in time for him to receive medical attention. He regained his composure but looked deathly pale. "There is more." He said as he gasped for the air in which to speak.

I felt responsible, guilty for his condition. I confessed my suspicions to the dying Armitage and told him that I had locked him in the summer house out of my distrust.

He seemed amused, declaring the padlocked door a blessing in disguise. If it hadn't been for the racket, the creature made when breaking in it might have caught him off guard.

I relaxed a little then and related my dream to him. I told him of the fantastic ride and my visit to the alien city and how, until this evening, I had doubted the validity of my own experiences admitting that I might be hallucinating, or going insane.

He didn't act the least bit surprised and almost seemed to expect it. Propped against the casement sash and with his eyes closed he listened to my story with grave intent occasionally nodding at certain parts.

When I disclosed what I knew of Ephraim Pryne and his plot his eyes popped open and he stared at me with amazement.

"So the people of Innsmouth are involved, too. Probably from the Order of Dagon.

"There are certain inferior ones," he went on, "who are not quite as free as others and subject to many of the same laws which govern mankind. Their existence is normally well disguised to conceal the vast network of brotherhoods they operate."

I told him of the bulbous gnome in the photograph and wondered if this was one of them.

"Not quite," he said. "The little creature you speak of is probably a Pilot demon . . . I've never seen one. The Necronomicon describes them as 'ethereal puffs of smoke that, occasionally, solidify and take form.' Not unlike the pilot fish of the whale. I gather that they grope in the subterranean darkness, leading Cthulhu's half-brother to the upper world."

"But you said they're trapped in the earth along with Yath-Notep. How could it surface?"

"Through cracks in the earth. I am responsible for that I'm afraid. The artifacts I brought your uncle were to be used with the machine."

He had me fetch the Necronomicon again, and I crawled across the floor gathering the pages together. I held it up, and he feebly leafed through the pages.

"One of the pieces is that dagger you're carrying, and the other is here." He pointed to a drawing on a badly faded page, holding it close to the lamp I could make out the crude outlines of what appeared to be a medallion. The patterns drawn within its circle were remarkably similar to the carvings on the hilt of the knife.

"This amulet and the dagger are the two integral parts of the cosmic device . . . the windlass. The machine is useless without them. The knife when inserted in the base acts as a lever to activate it, and the amulet fastens to the top and serves as a forward and reverse switch.

"The Tanists wore the artifacts at all times. In case the windlass fell into the wrong hands, it would be ineffectual without the two pieces."

I had jumped when he said "windlass." I was familiar with the word, of course. Pryne had used it several times instructing me earlier that evening, and my great uncle wrote about it in his journal. I was certain that it was that gold and silver piece of machinery that had been in my cellar.

"Funny though," he mused, "there has to be another windlass. I never thought of it until now but the one Todesfall used was a copy and the artifacts I gave him had to be duplicates. The original was supposed to be handed down to each succeeding generation. It is hidden well, I bet Todesfall's Uncle and guardian must have been the last to possess it, and he probably concealed it in the schloss where no one will ever find it. To think Heinrich Todesfall spent a great portion of his life constructing the duplicate and the original was probably somewhere in his own house.

"The barriers are weakening. The only thing that remained was action, quick and decisive. Only I wasn't quick enough." He indicated the body of the creature draped across the library table. "I couldn't find the machine in time to undo my mistake, but I did manage to unscramble part of the puzzle.

"The ritual is short and simple. It utilizes a ceremonial chanting and the machine, but the amulet is the answer. I didn't find out what the words are but the amulet I believe will reverse the procedure. The words are needed to wake Yath-Notep from his slumber, and the machine can sever the bars that hold his jail door shut, but the amulet is the key to reverse it. The words won't be necessary then, and the device topped with the alien instrument can reseal the tomb, drive the beast back into his lair and even unmake Todesfall's interfering."

"But where is the amulet?" I put forward.

"Around the neck of your great uncle."

My heart skipped a beat. I knew what that meant and under no circumstances was I into grave robbing. His condition was worsening. I was sure that a great portion of his story was true, but I was just as certain the rest was the fantasy of his insanity.

"The machine is no good without the artifacts, and the artifacts are no good without the machine. All I know is someone of your bloodline must activate it. Your bloodline leans more toward the human side of the beast than did your great uncle's. Quite possibly the strain has lessened by degree.

"I apologize for the task that awaits you now, but I was kept from participating in your great uncle's funeral arrangements by that blasted Order of Dagon. The amulet was not with his things. It must be buried with him."

He was gasping for air, and his eyes had partially glazed over. "The Tanists of Kadath were guardians of the gateway, not despoilers of it. If the Old Ones are unable to control your actions, they may settle on another course and raise the dead. Abdul Alhazred wrote about such a possibility and, if it is true, they'll raise your great uncle to finish the ritual for them. If this happens, he must be stopped . . . Alhazred wrote that the gatekeepers voice must be stilled . . . exhume the body . . . get the amulet . . . "

"And having located the machine and the amulet," I cried, "What then? I'm not sure I'll want to use them."

"The choice may not be yours." He looked at me for a moment, smiled gently and died.

***

I am reluctant to tell you what occurred next. The events that followed will always be with me. I doubt that anything will be able to remove them from my memory no matter how minute the details. And those grim recollections will sour every moment in my future.

I stood up and backed away from the body of Milton Armitage. I ran from the place, not even taking time to blow out the lamp, slamming the door behind me. The latch was missing of course, and the door bounced away from the frame swinging inward again.

Outside, the fog was very thick. I stopped and shouted for Jim. I was unnerved to discover that he was still not answering. I Looked across the lawn and started toward the parked car. I rushed to what I took to be the middle of the yard. I didn't get very far, however. A rock that lined our drive sent me sprawling, and I slid across the wet grass.

My ears detected a sound; it added to my uneasiness it was a fleshy sound, like the licking of lips. It might have been water dripping, yet it seemed too irregular and muffled. When I picked myself up, I could make out the front fender of the car and Jim's outline through the rising swirls of mist. The moonlight struggled through the clouds, and I could see him leaning against the fender. His manner was relaxed, almost careless, after all, that had happened to stare at me so calmly over his shoulder.

I called to him as I approached saying that I hoped the car was fixed because I was ready to leave. Under the scant moonlight, he looked very pale staring back at me grinning with a ghostly expression on his face. He was facing me, though his shoulder was turned away. For a moment I thought that it was a contortionist trick he had practiced to disgust his friends. I realized that the sound was much louder . . . it was something dripping.

Up close I could see that Jim Ruttick was still at his place. He hadn't altered his position in quite a while. He was bent over the front fender of the car just as I had left him an hour before, except his head had been twisted around. His neck was half torn from his shoulders, and the spine, broken and protruding from the skin gushed with a mixture of blood and spinal fluid.

I let out a yell and backed away. The M1 lay on the ground, the barrel bent in half. I looked frantically around me for a hidden assailant until it dawned on me what the course of events must have been. The creature, that monster VonTassell fought must have stopped here before entering the summer house. It took revenge for the bullet wound it had suffered earlier, and poor Jim never saw it coming.

I touched his arm, and his body slid sideways along the car's fender, falling to the ground. The twisted corpse laid on its side staring up at me with a contorted grin.

I couldn't locate the flashlight in the dark. Striking several matches I saw that the battery was in place and one cable remained to be hooked up. I hammered the cable onto the post with my fist, slammed the hood shut and jumped behind the wheel. The engine started immediately; throwing the gear shift lever into reverse, I backed the car across the lawn up to the rear porch and ran inside to get Janet.

If there was an impending apocalypse, the world was going to have to face it without me.

Janet was impossible to wake up. No amount of prodding would revive her from the sedative. I had to struggle to get her to her feet wrapping her in a couple of blankets, then carried her downstairs. I sat her in the chair next to the fireplace so that I could run back up and get our bags.

I talked to her trying to make her understand that we were leaving. Realizing that she was beyond reach, I gave up and hurried to get the suitcases.

When I came back down, she was staring blankly into the fire mumbling. The flames illuminated her features, and for a brief moment, I felt as if I was seeing her for the very first time. She seemed distantly familiar, and for that short period I couldn't remember her name, I couldn't even recall that we were husband and wife. She was a stranger; something was tugging at my brain. My conception of time, my ability to distinguish between living in that old house and notions about being in another scene became distorted; chaotic visions disturbed me, there was a clawing, knocking . . . Uncle Heinrich . . . R'Lyeh . . . the gate . . . my head ached . . . Something was trying to get possession of my thoughts!

I grabbed the blade of the dagger that hung below my belt and squeezed its sharp edge into my palm. The knife drew blood, and the pain snapped me back to this world. I shook myself free of the feeling and rushed to the back door with the bags. I yelled over my shoulder to Janet that I was going to put them in the trunk and would be back. I was scared. I had never felt like that in my life. I tried not to think about it, afraid it would begin to make sense. If it did, I might start accepting everything the Doctor . . . I mean Armitage, said as true.

When I reached the kitchen, I stopped and dropped the suitcases. The walls reflected an orange glow coming from outside. I advanced slowly towards the door. Through the screen, I saw our car roaring in flames. The side window was open; flames shot out of it like an erupting volcano and the upholstery, the seats and the dashboard gradually melted out of view.

I stared at our car in a panic. A cold chill ran through me, and sweat poured down my forehead. I knew how the fire started. The cans of kerosene I kept on our back porch to fuel our kitchen cook stove were missing.

Just beyond the blaze, moving quickly down the driveway spewing gravel in its wake, was a long black limousine. Hypnotized, I watched the stretch drive away from the house and out the side drive. I followed its course dumbfounded. First watching it through the opened back door and then as it wound around the schloss and passed the kitchen window on my right. The black tinted glass that wrapped the upper half of the car in privacy flickered and glared orange back at me, reflecting the fire. It was impossible to see inside. Nevertheless, as it left, I knew that Falbridge was at the wheel and that slimy thing that called itself Ephraim Pryne was in the back.

I spun away from the door and went back into the parlor, forgetting that the phone was out of order, I attempted to call out. No number came to mind, so I tried reaching the operator. A high-pitched wail came over the receiver as I lifted it to my ear. At first, I thought it was an electrical malfunction, but the disturbance on the line was a lamenting, a half-human voice echoing from a great depth. I dropped the receiver, and it swung back and forth, emitting the wailing sound.

Then the television came to life. The picture tube lit up, and the sound of static filled the room. A blue, distorted image formed and reformed on the screen. In the flashes of clarity, I saw a mass of crawling, thrusting flesh and a cluster of eyes.

I rushed to the set and tried to turn it off, but the knob came loose in my hand. The image remained constant.

Janet was sitting in the chair between the fireplace and the television oblivious to what was happening. She had wrapped a portion of the blanket in front of her as if she had a child in it. The blue light of the television flickered across one side of her face while the flames from the hearth illuminated the other giving her an insane look. She muttered to herself. "It's all right . . . pretty baby . . . so cold, we'll sit by the fire."

Behind me, the telephone still screeched, and the voice on the receiver eerily coincided with the fluctuating movements on the screen. I snatched the phone off the table ripping the cord loose from the wall and forcefully threw it into the picture tube. The screen exploded in a white flash, and the image vanished hissing as the electronic parts of the set fused together.

Then the lights went out. A fuse blew when the wires in the television set shorted. The gloom only took a second to get used to; it didn't become completely dark. The fire in the hearth helped a bit and a few of the candles that were lit earlier that evening had remained as flickering stubs.

Outside, thunder crashed, and I heard deep hollow rumbling sounds. The house shook violently for a moment. I spoke reassuringly to Janet telling her everything was going to be all right, knowing deep inside that I was trying to convince myself as well. She hardly saw me. I couldn't worry about that now. I had to do something, anything, even if I didn't believe in it. I thought frantically, the last dying words of Armitage hummed in my head, "get the amulet . . . the gatekeeper's voice must be stilled . . ."

Maybe death was far better than facing a world of monster-gods and a dark brotherhood dedicated to bringing them back to life. Looking at Janet, I couldn't allow myself to believe that. I knew what grizzly job had to be done.

I was going to need a light. It was too dark out there to see more than a couple of feet. The other flashlight was in the cellar where I had left it.

The house rattled and shook on its antique foundation, and I almost fell down the rickety stairs. By the light of my last match, I groped my way in the dark through the vast cellar and made my way to the workbench and the flashlight. The instant I switched it on, and the beam cut through the darkness, a loud splintering and crushing jarred me. A handful of boards atop the crevice erupted and were scattered by a tremendous force. The crevice was exposed again.

A rank odor filled the cellar. The same smell I had detected before, coming from the cracks in the floor, only now stronger. I turned my flashlight on an exposed square yard of gaping blackness . . . the stench came from there.

I stepped forward then, back with a start when greeted by an uncanny noise. A moaning varied at brief intervals by a slippery thumping. As my light shown down, the moaning changed to a series of guttural tones. I crept cautiously forward once more, again came the sound of blind, futile scrambling and thumping. I trembled, unwilling even to imagine what things might be lurking in that hole, but in a moment mustered up the courage to peer over its rough edge.

A dark groping mass of eyes and ooze welled up, back and forth, too large to fit through the crack. It was like the thing I saw on the television set. A multitude of unblinking eyes glared back against the light. I squinted to get a better look at the moving thing. A huge snake lashed up from the depths and whizzed by me. In the beam of my light, I saw that it was a tentacle, like that belonging to a great sea creature. It uncoiled and slammed into the rafters. Blindly it banged around the floor joists to the upper level. Then the tentacle whipped around toward me. I backed away and tried to fend it off with the flashlight. It struck me knocking the light from my hand sending me backward. The flashlight fell undamaged to the floor. The slippery, tentacle coiled around it and dragged it below. For an instant I could see the tentacle and the light perched on the edge of the crevice, receding into the blackness, then nothing. I was in total darkness.

I rolled desperately away over the damp concrete. Crawling, on all fours, I tore my hands on rough, loose stones and many times bruised my head against several of the upturned boards. The utter blackness and stench overcame me. Then, at last, I slowly came to my senses. I staggered to my feet regretting the loss of my flashlight bitterly. It wasn't difficult to figure out what had happened to it. The sound of crunching teeth and breaking glass told me of its fate at the bottom of the pit.

I looked wildly about for any gleam of light in the damp cellar. My sense of direction was scrambled. The inky blackness made it impossible to tell my position within the cavernous basement. The black granite that was used originally to construct the old foundation just added to the darkness. I couldn't see the staircase. I had no means of producing light. All my matches had been used up, and I was afraid to blunder ahead fearing I might collide with some unseen object or stumble into the uncovered crevice . . . or worse meet up with that groping tentacle in the dark. I strained my eyes in every direction for some faint glint or reflection of light that might be left in the kitchen upstairs.

After a while, I thought I detected the hint of a glow above me and got back down on my hands and knees I crawled toward it in agonizing caution. Then my hands touched something I knew to be the steps and presently I was running blindly up the stairs. In a moment I reached the top and stood once more in the kitchen; trembling with relief, I watched the last sputtering of the candle I left on the table. The kitchen wall clock read fifteen minutes to twelve.

The thunder rose to a deafening clamor. Compelled by a madness that was only delayed while I caught my breath, dashed outdoors and ran back to the summer house.

The windows and the open door still radiated from the light of the lantern, and I felt reassured by its warm glow. Inside I once again came face to face with the crumpled form of Milton Armitage, the man I had known as Doctor Peter VonTassell. The green serpent man hadn't moved from its spot amongst the clutter.

A shovel leaned against the open studded wall. Grabbing it, and snatching up the kerosene lamp, I headed for the door. Seized by an idea I stopped. The only weapon I had with me was the dagger in my belt. About to leave, I found myself wishing that I had a better weapon.

It was then that I remembered Armitage's tale about the gun. The German Luger, my great uncle, had mentioned in his writings. In the weeks that I had lived there, I had been over the old house from top to bottom and never turned up the gun. Possibly it was stored here in the summer house.

I tore through the single room searching every box, crevice, and drawer all the while trying to avert my eyes from the human and inhuman corpses. I was about to give up when every place was searched, except one.

I summoned up the courage and slid the drawer out from under the library table where the putrid remains of the creature rested. The barrel of the automatic stuck out from between two sheets of paper. I checked the clip in the handle; it was loaded. Slipping it in my belt, along with the ancient dagger, I ran out into the night.

Lightning sliced continually at the night sky. For brief intervals the white of the lightning became black and the black of the night became light. I kept going in the direction of the field but slowed down the pace. I couldn't believe my own eyes. The lightning seemed dark, and the dark seemed light. It must have been a retinal after-impression left by the flashes. I thought of the cosmic alignment and wondered if this was an effect of it.

The wind steadily grew, and the flashes of lightning became even more frequent. I didn't stop to wonder or think of turning back but plodded on as if to some ancient rendezvous, assailed by grotesque compulsions and memories.

As the cemetery drew nearer, I heeded its wooded side, more than its sparsely marked graves. The trees loomed up so dark and foreboding that I wished they could keep their distance. An elder fate had manipulated my life and others to this very point. My great uncle, the Doctor, my wife and even Jim had all been masterfully controlled, the overall extent of which I had only then become fully aware. Noise in the brush caught my attention, but when I raised the lantern, nothing came to view only the gray aspect the light played upon the leaves and shrubbery.

I came to the grave marked by the unusual headstone. It seemed taller, towering and the black stone darker. It faced the north end of the glade and the cemetery. Previously I thought the position of my relative's resting place was situated to overlook the graves of his wartime comrades but to stand out like a marker against the burning fog of green phosphorescence I could see that it was in direct line with the knoll.

At that moment, millions of miles from earth, the giant planet Jupiter was slowly rotating into alignment with the other planets.

Not known to me at the time, the predicted effect was taking place.

I started to dig. The ground was soft, the burial had taken place less than six months before, and the earth was still loose.

Occasionally the shovel would strike a small stone and the sound it made in the surrounding woods bouncing off the headstone, had the effect of coming from other directions. When this would happen, I would stop and look around wildly searching for phantoms. I turned up the wick of the lamp, got a hold of myself and ignored my frustration, scooping the earth into huge piles alongside the family plot.

I was down a few feet digging furiously, no longer concentrating on the sound of the shovel strokes when I heard ticking. Not the glancing blows of the shovel. It was at consistent intervals. I was bent over, and my ear was next to the tombstone. I froze, staring into the blackness in front of me, and listened, trying to figure out the source of the sound. I didn't move, but the ticking kept on. I jumped back when I realized where it was coming from; it was the clock. The clock in the belly of the headstone had started up. It wasn't operating before. The single hand on its face to my knowledge had never moved, and now it was ticking!

I knew it could mean only one thing and hoping to halt time itself I smashed the crystal and clock works with one blow of the shovel.

Time was running out. It gnawed at my insides. My muscles worked heavily against the damp earth. I was like a machine, the end of the spade handle the extension of my arms and legs, casting heaping shovels full of dirt into the air. Suddenly my spade struck something harder than earth; I scraped away more dirt. The surface I uncovered was moldy and rough. I scraped further and saw that it had shape. The exposed area was long and planked with crude boards. It looked like a packing crate. I scraped more. I leaped out of the hole and got ready to throw back the lid on the roughly hewed pine box.

I tossed the shovel aside; the coffin was unearthed. I laid a shaky hand on the lid then quickly withdrew it. As unexpectedly as the ticking of that morbid timepiece I heard a click followed by a soft whir. I thought it was the clock at first. A gear or cog still caught up in the final movements of the mechanism. I narrowed the sound down to a slab of stone on the base of the grave marker.

It moved. I sat on the edge of the excavated grave and watched it turn and slide horizontally on a corner pivot. Beneath it lay a small circular hole. The whirring started up again, and the windlass, the gold machine, my great uncle's gateway device surfaced above the granite base. It glittered softly in the fog and stood out stark, gleaming bright yellow in the flashes of lightning. It was beautiful, a systematic blend of art and technology. It was hypnotically beautiful, compelling; I fought an urge to get closer to it.

I stood up, no longer in control of my movements. My brain buzzed with dark thoughts and the whispering of many tongues. I walked stiff-legged to the black monolith drawing the dagger from my belt as I moved, all the while fighting against the powerful control. With an involuntary movement, I made a stabbing, sweeping motion of my arm and sent the blade into the slit at the base of the windlass.

I could no longer see this world. Images of smoky skies obscured my vision. Wild streams of violet midnight glittered with the dust of gold; the giant red eye of Jupiter glowed luminously. A crimson pillar of light streaked out, skewering Mars reaching down to earth.

The handle of the dagger loomed up out of a vortex of dust and fire. A silent command compelled me to pull the blade switch. I staggered stiffly amongst the vortex raising my head above it to a sterile blue twilight where with a burst of will, I never dreamed that I possessed, I screamed, "I won't do it . . . I won't," over and over I screamed summoning an inner strength that seemed to come from somewhere else.

Tearing loose from the last grip of control and pulling the knife free I tossed it to the ground. I dove onto the pile of earth created by my digging and scrambled on all fours to the open grave. The coffin lay at my feet. The amulet was foremost in my thoughts. I had to get it.

I bent over and picked up the lantern and squatted down nervously trying to pick a focal point in which to stare. I was afraid to chance a look at the machine again for fear of what might happen and squeamish at the thought of viewing my uncle's corpse.

Before I threw back the lid, I imagined the grizzly job in progress and hoped that I could avert my eyes from his decayed remains while removing the amulet from around his neck.

The damp wooden cover hadn't been nailed down, and it slid off the moldy oblong box easily. I screamed idiotically and my madness dissolved into hysterical laughter because the shrieking corpse of Heinrich Todesfall swiftly rose to a sitting position . . . a nightmare caked and clotted with moldy shreds of flesh and hair. It was no longer a dead man passive and silent. It was a contorted face in diabolical fury, and its jaws were dripping a yellow ooze. I knelt frozen before it, the sight of those white nostrils and those black eyes burned into me.

The Tanist's corpse crawled out of the grave toward me. A white fleshy hand touched the serpentine dagger. The earth trembled again. Aroused from my state of shock enough to become aware of my dead uncle's intent I ducked to one side just as he lashed out with the sharp blade piercing my left shoulder. I felt a stabbing pain and scrambled from the edge of the open grave.

The ground pulsated and shook. I saw the mound in the glade visibly move. It rose higher and higher as a great pressure beneath it pushed upwards. The earth sighed from the hidden force passing puffs of pinkish smoke through newly formed cracks expelling the gas into the night air. The earth held, the pressure relaxed, and the mound receded some becoming quiet.

The shoulder wound throbbed keeping me alert. Behind me, I detected a movement. It was one of the living dead my wife informed me. It came out from behind a tree, dirt crumbling off its newly risen form; clad in the remains of an American army uniform. Trapped, I thought, between this creature and what used to be my great uncle. Instead, it ignored me keeping its distance, slowly turning as if harkening something's approach. Another of the living dead soldiers appeared at the edge of the wood listening, watching. Even Todesfall had lost interest in me and had turned away.

I crept, closing the gap between us. He was inserting the dagger in the base of the windlass. I flew across the remaining distance and tried to wrench the dagger free from his grasp, but I was too late. His strength was superhuman. He held me off with one hand as I watched him pull the ancient lever.

A beam of energy sliced through the atmosphere and was intercepted by the machine. The windlass burned with cosmic energy from the stars and channeled the beam through its interior until it flashed out through its many mirrors, cutting across the field into the glowing patch of fog. There was a terrific explosion, and a crater appeared over the spot where the mound used to be. In the confusion following the blinding flash, I lunged with a free hand to grab the knife and broke loose from Todesfall's grasp.

One step and I was upon the machine reaching out to switch it off. Then, something seized me by the throat from behind. Claws dug into my neck, their sharp edges burned into my skin. My hands went instinctively to my throat working at the powerful grip. Furry animal fingers came in contact with mine. I shifted and rocked from side to side trying to wrench it loose. I found I could turn around freely. No one or thing stood behind me. A heavy cold and clammy wetness sat on my shoulders. The fiery pain became unbearable; it tightened its hold and teeth gnawed at the back of my neck. I reached over my shoulder grabbing a handful of flesh and hair and with a downward bending motion tore the thing loose sending it flying headlong through the air.

The pilot demon struck the edge of the headstone. Its skull cracked, belching dirty white ooze.

I stood there gasping for breath. The oversized head foamed and frothed continuously. I watched its little body slide down the slick granite surface where it sank like a lifeless rag doll next to the windlass.

Todesfall turned toward me. He withdrew the knife from the machine and ceased his preparations. The action within the device stopped. He slowly stepped away from the headstone and began gliding toward me with a wolfish grin on his pale, black-lipped face.

I remembered the Luger, drew it out and at point-blank range squeezed the trigger. Nothing happened, it wouldn't fire. I kept at it cocking the breach several times ejecting live ammo into the air as I backed away, but the trigger was stuck fast. The safety was rusted shut out of neglect. The gun was useless. I gave up and looked around for something else to use as a weapon. My great uncle raised the dagger and came at me. I picked up a segment of dead tree limb lying on the ground and swung it at him. The branch connected squarely against his side. Again, I struck out, bringing it down upon his chest but the blows glanced off of the decaying body doing it no harm.

I swung one more time, taking a firm grip on the makeshift club, I took aim, pivoted hard and with a quick sweeping motion knocked the dagger to the ground. Another object caught my eye kicking up the dirt as it fell. It was his hand. It was torn loose at the wrist from the rotting carrion by my club.

My uncle's corpse lying in its coffin for six months must have lost the pliability of his flesh, deteriorating into a fragile puffy mucous, his bones becoming dry and brittle also lost their strength, the vitality of life gone only the reanimation of dead tissue remained. I made a quick double take and found my adversary equally surprised. He wasn't outwardly displaying any signs of pain, but his look told of astonishment. I rushed him. The amulet hung on a thin gold chain around his neck. I was upon him tearing it loose before he realized what had happened. The amulet came away freely in my hand. The chain, broken, still draped across his chest, parts of it disappearing into the folds of his neck where it had taken root in his flesh.

Before I could back away, he grabbed me with his one remaining hand and planted the stump of the other firmly in my belly. He lifted me over his head and threw me into the open grave. I glanced off an earthen side, my head narrowly missing the edge of the coffin. Laying there, amazed that I was still conscious, I heard him growling like a wild animal. My great uncle's corpse appeared over the edge, enraged, his dead face hissing down at me.

Taking hold of the shovel, he tried to spear me. I dove out of the grave dodging the shovel's end. I managed to get to my feet only to be knocked down again. He struck me with the flat of the shovel, and I went sprawling head over heels beneath an oak tree. The blow had caught me between the shoulder blades, and I laid there spattering and coughing for air.

Dazed, I saw Todesfall advance then toss the shovel aside. He looked at me with a kind of triumph that was terrifying. He stretched his arms out toward the sky, and his jaw began to work up and down. A fluttering of movement caught the corner of my eye, and the dagger skittered across the earth in front of me. Dumfounded, I looked in the direction it came from and saw the skeletal corpse of the American soldier retreat behind a tree.

In the moment that followed I heard my great uncle speak for the first time. His voice distracted my attention from the soldier. He was speaking the words that Ephraim Pryne had instructed to me. Never have I heard a voice like that before. It had a strange timbre and accent that was slurred and alien. He seemed to speak in syllables of burning ashes:

"Ya-r'Leh . . . g'wah Cthulhu

Fhgtha . . ."

He never finished the words. I scooped up the dagger and in one swift movement, propelled by the fear of the outcome if he finished the sentence, leaped up from the ground and lunged for his unprotected throat. I drove the knife into the jugular just below the jawline and with both hands brought my full weight to bear against the handle slicing deeply, diagonally through the larynx.

He froze briefly in his tracks, then, flailing his arms wildly in the air, began to stagger backward. I saw he was edging toward the open grave. In another instant, he had lurched backward falling into the hole and was lost to view.

I found it difficult to stand and fell to my knees, grateful that it was all over. I was about to give thanks to God, but the intermittent flashes of lightning kept on as if they hadn't realized that the advancing tirade had been stopped. The negative lightning effect kept on as well, and it hurt my eyes. The memory of my shoulder wound throbbed and between the claps of thunder I felt the earth move again.

It was a violent tremor, much stronger than anything I had felt before. The headstone slipped slightly on its foundation, and I had to brace myself with one hand on the ground to keep my balance.

Beyond where the knoll was, was now a pit. Another quake shook, and the earth shifted, splitting in two. A crack drove across the glade, intercepting the crater, stopping at the edge of the wood. There was a fluttering followed by dark shapes. Small black things raced out of the earth, resembling rats pouring out of a hole. More Pilot Demons, hordes of them, dozens, fifty; hundreds!

I stared in wonderment and curiosity as something moved in the pit, something big. A bulkhead of topsoil and a burnt brush angled upward, the dirt and dead plant life tobogganed off the slope. Gleaming, broken metal bands, as thick as a man and a slab of granite as big as a house, was revealed.

Oh God, that is what I saw. The door to the pit, the pit of N'Kai was opening. The five-sided granite door stood perched momentarily at a right angle in front of the crater, the bottom edge sinking slowly, the soil beneath giving way under the stress of tons, then it toppled from an upward shove and cascaded down the slope tumbling end over end. The collision it made with the earth felt like the aftershock of a quake. The sound was deafening. The wonderful fortification of the Elder Race lay defeated, its thickly fashioned securing straps of alien steel severed by the cosmic force, the barrier was shattered.

Dead silence elapsed. The brush crawled with dark things, and I knelt in trembling fear watching, waiting. It wouldn't be accurate to say that no human could describe what I saw, but it will be difficult to visualize by anyone whose ideas of contour and shape are too closely bound to common life. At the edge of the jagged chasm, a monstrous knobby shape reached up pulling and tugging and tearing at the earth. The shape reached further, a giant three-fingered hand groped. Many luminous disc-like eyes appeared above the crater. A huge rounded bulk larger than the opening squeezed up slowly. It glistened like wet leather. A lip-less mouth quivered, then slapped, and tentacles writhed as the clumsy body pulsated and heaved.

It was no doubt the giant being Yath-Notep that my great Uncle raved of in his notes. Armitage told the truth and, as he had guessed, Yath-Notep had awakened from his slumber by the previous meddling of Heinrich Todesfall. All that remained was to unlock his cell door. The words were spoken months before.

For a fleeting second, I wished that Jim's M1 was undamaged and lay in my hands, but I laughed out loud recognizing that the attempt would be like bows and arrows against lightning. The laughing became uncontrollable, my emotions were out of control, and my voice rang out with peals of hysterical laughter.

The bulk rose higher and higher towering until its slimy body protracted out of the hole with a sickening sucking sound. Another flock of Pilot Demons swarmed out of the depths, taking to the air on invisible wings, surrounding their master.

The eyes were unblinking; scaly skin stretched tautly over the hairless head. A wattled bulge hung below the creature's face, with slits on the sides that opened and closed continually. The mouth, if you could call it that, extended nearly the width of its face so that when opened the top half of its head appeared to lift off displaying rows of tiny, serrated teeth.

The knife lay in the dirt before me, and I dully recalled the medallion. I still clutched it tightly in my left hand. There were two short prongs on its bottom edge and during the struggle I had driven them into my palm. I relaxed my grip and opened my hand. It hung just below the thumb joint. I stared at it trying to recall why I wanted it before. Why had I risked life and limb for this thing? It was one thing to chase an unknown entity but quite another to face it. I had lost all sense of who I was in the outcome.

I looked back up at the thing that oozed up from a world of unknown nightmares. My eyes scanned what was left of the glade, the summer house door was still ajar, the main house stood unchanged with the smoldering remains of my car faintly flickering, and the grave open, but still ominous with its black evil headstone.

My movements were mechanical, not driven by an unseen force, but by the memory of Armitage's dying words.

My hand found the knife, and I crawled. On my belly, I crawled under imaginary barb wire, under an invisible crossfire slowly creeping up on the enemy.

The knife slipped easily into the base, and I heard the notches in the blade mate with its counterparts. I fumbled with the amulet in the dark for several seconds until I found the matching holes in the top of the windlass that corresponded to the two prongs. It clicked into place.

The mountainous bulk was by then outside of the pit wallowing triumphantly in the wet spring grass and began to spread its tentacles. It rose to its full height, stood boldly and stretched out its arms as if to pluck the stars from the heavens. Its mouth of razor sharp teeth yawned in twisted mockery at the moon.

"The amulet is the key, to reverse it," I whispered to myself only half believing. I closed my eyes and pulled on the knife blade switch. A great shaft of light striking the windlass preceded the first blast. When I opened my eyes this time, I was surprised to see an enormous luminous ball fired by electrical energy rolling across the glade in the direction of the crater. Close upon it came an awful thundering voice. It was deep and musical; powerful as a full orchestra, but as evil as the book of that Arab. It echoed out across the sky like doom, and the windows in the schloss rattled as it died away.

Yath-Notep, his hope of freedom in jeopardy screamed in agony, and raging frustration as tendrils of light shot up, entwining themselves around his titan form.

Seconds later a chill wind blew at my back. A sucking current of air was drawn into the pit creating a wailing howling torrent that pulled at the Pilot Demons who fled, attempting to escape their lord's fate. From the depths of the Black Forest, hundreds of dark forms were pulled, drawn into the sucking chasm.

It had the force of an atmosphere rushing in to fill a vacuum, though no trees appeared to move and no solid objects or even myself were affected other than Yath-Notep and his minions. The force was very powerful as one small demon demonstrated vainly trying to escape. It grasped the limb of a tree and was raked across the branches when the limb broke. Then Pilot Demon, limb and all hurtled through the night sky disappearing into the pit.

I had no idea how far reaching or exacting the power was until the next day after examining a hole in the lower panel of our screen door. The configuration of the opening made it easy to imagine. A pilot demon fleeing the disaster must have turned into its gaseous other self, slipped under the crack below the door, and confident of its escape solidified on my kitchen floor. The perfect outline the head and outstretched arms made ripping through the screen wire was proof that it had misjudged the fantastic power of the Elder Race.

In my weakened state, I observed Yath-Notep slowly sinking back into the earth, futilely trying to resist the all-consuming pull. It screamed, and its tentacles tore away towering pines like matchsticks in one last attempt to escape. Yath-Notep stretched out a colossal hand, leveling the summer house in its grasp, dragging it and the foundation down with it. The demon of Sorti was cast into hell, and only huge furrows from its plowing hands remained.

There is little left to tell before I passed out. The glade and the surrounding countryside lay quiet. Electronic fingers played across the crater healing the earth, sealing huge cracks and mending furrows. The energy programmed centuries ago lifted the granite slab slowly, carefully to a great height, then after precise alignment let it fall with the full force of its several tons, corking up the hole sealing the evil genie in its earthly bottle. I heard crackling like arc welding, then a light tremor and what was left of the knoll fell inward. I remember Janet running up...I smelled ozone, and everything became dark.

***

I recovered enough in a few days to send Janet ahead to be with her folks in the states, and through the recommendations of the bank, I engaged a property management firm to close the house and maintain its upkeep until its eventual sale.

The wound in my shoulder, after cleaned, wasn't as bad as it had appeared and I was able to tend to it myself. I didn't want to bring anyone in from the outside if I could help it, there would have been too many awkward questions to answer. I stayed behind to tie up loose ends putting the house in order trying to make things appear as normal as possible.

The windlass is safe, well hid. I concealed it in the schloss where no one will find it without the proper instructions. The dagger and amulet I have kept with me, they should be kept separate from the machine. When I reach Massachusetts, before going on to Essex I will stop in Arkham and give them to Miskatonic University along with the instructions to locate the windlass and the words that I have carefully taken the time to write down. I have written ahead to the colleagues of Armitage at the University informing them of his death and what had happened. When they receive my letter, I believe I will also find a buyer for the estate.

The summer house and foundation had been ripped clean from its spot, and very little rubble remained to show proof of its existence. The body of Milton Armitage, alias Peter Von Tassell M.D., had disappeared along with it. Besides a few loose stones and broken boards, I only found one page from that old book. It had a contrasting irony about it when I discovered it under the flattened library table, the only evidence that the Doctor was there. The single page bore a combination of Latin and Arabic transcripts rendered unreadable by the mixed splattering of human and alien blood.

I buried Jim Ruttick in the old battlefield. He didn't have any relatives, and few would miss him. I hope that he will find peace with the other soldiers buried there. Poor Jim died needlessly, never getting much into the fight, he would have been a great help if he could have and I am sure he would have enjoyed it. I'll miss him.

There was a horrible smell in the glade after it was all over, primarily in the area where the knoll was. The stench left quickly though, but I doubt the vegetation will ever come right again. I imagine that there will always be something strange and unwholesome about the growth around that region.

The papers the next day reported many strange occurrences around the globe. The west coast of the United States suffered a large earthquake, and a tidal wave struck the coast of Australia. The weather was unusually active all over the world causing storms at sea, floods and even one hurricane was reported building up in the southern Pacific.

The U.S. Naval Observatory and other astronomy institutions were busy quelling fears about a phenomenon popularly termed the "Jupiter Effect." While on an international level, the emergency wards of hospitals in major cities around the world had their hands full that night with an abnormally large amount of rapings, muggings and shooting casualties and several asylums and prisons reported incidents of violence and riots. There was no explanation offered by the press or authorities, but it is believed that one would probably be shortcoming after a joint investigation by all nations concerned.

There were a lot of disturbances that evening, but there will be scientific explanations for all of it because these Old Ones are not gods. They were evil, sentient beings that deserved to be locked up where they can't harm us. There is a higher God in the universe.

I am at the Heathrow Airport in London waiting for the fog to lift. There has been a fog every night since that evening, and it seems to have followed me even here. The airport is socked in, and all commercial flights are grounded. I have managed to book passage on a small private charter to the states that somehow got clearance, when all other flights, according to reports are not allowed in or out until probably sometime tomorrow morning.

I bought this tape recorder and several blank tapes a few hours ago when I saw the pilot and crew entering the terminal, making boarding preparations. That was when I discovered that I am the only passenger listed. I listened in on their conversation, but I don't think they noticed me. It was the pilot that shook me up. He was a thin, stooped shouldered man under six feet tall, dressed in a gray uniform, wearing a frayed pilot's cap. His age was perhaps thirty-five, but the odd deep creases on the sides of his neck made him appear older. His head was large; he had watery blue eyes that never seemed to blink, a flat nose, a receding forehead and chin, and small, underdeveloped ears. I jumped with a start when he reached for the flight plan, noticing something familiar about his hand.

I could leave here and come back and get a commercial flight when the weather clears, but I know I am being followed. They have been tailing me for quite a while. I have tried to shake them several times in the past week, but just when I thought I had lost them, one of their kind would always turn up keeping a watchful eye on me. I believe that even if I could slip onto a plane undetected that they will just find me some other way. If it isn't now, it will probably be later. Maybe they mean me no harm. Maybe they are only keeping tabs on me. Whatever the situation is, I am too tired to run anymore. Besides, I can take care of myself.

The dagger is in my tote bag along with the amulet, and if I have to, I can always fight if any trouble comes up. I am going to package up these tapes, Janet's diary, and the notebook and send them to Miskatonic University in America for safekeeping. There is a postal service here in the airport, and the mail will probably be the safest and less conspicuous route to use.

For the record, my name is Faren Church, and until a few days ago I resided with my wife at Schlactfield Strasse, rural post number twenty-seven, Valsbach Dorf, Schloss Todesfall. A fact now I don't mind if it is made public, because if I make it back, my wife and I will slip into hiding, change our names and move to where hopefully no one will find us. Maybe Miskatonic will be able to help.

There are a lot of these Innsmouth people. They are after me I am afraid, for who can say that the job is completed, and that other phenomenon do not exist in other parts of the world. It is an invasion. There is a war on, one that is not restricted by conventional borders and trenches but is only bounded by the universe itself. Surprisingly enough I find myself longing for the human conflict of conventional war rather than this. In those days at least you could tell who the enemy was. Not like now. They all walk, talk and pay their taxes like everyone else. Many of them appear as normal as you and me.

There are forces out there in the unknown, beings so powerful that man and all his achievements are dwarfed beyond human comprehension. I know it sounds like the ravings of my late Uncle and that the testimony I have given will not only be considered strange by whoever may hear it but will be judged in the end as the fabrication of an over-imaginative mind. I may not have another chance to tell my story, and that would be a dangerous conclusion, an ill omen. The handwriting is on the wall. I fear that even though the world was spared, this time, due to my intervention, or some master plan, man may not be free to walk the earth long, before an outside force enters and plucks us off.

I beg whoever hears these tapes to listen with great care and pay close attention to my wife's diary and the old alchemist's notebook. Caution the world to tread lightly when exploring the unknown or uncovering some newly discovered ancient secret. Arm yourself with knowledge of the Elders for there lies our only salvation from the impending apocalypse. Then maybe we will have a chance to fight this thing, keeping it at bay until its wardens return.

I was a good Tanist, and if what Armitage told me about the vigilant efforts of Miskatonic University are correct, then I can't fault them or believe that they'll do anything but their best.

A new problem has risen though, out there in the hills; the two NATO countries will be digging soon to conceal their missile silos. They must stop. The horror still exists, those unexplored recesses of the earth are still there, and the combined warheads of all the NATO countries won't be able to stop the Coming if it reaches the surface again.

It's a fantastic claim, I know, but it's true. I know now that every part of that legend is fact. If all that had to be dealt with was Yath-Notep, then the problem would be small by comparison. The giant creature I am sure could eventually be contained or possibly even killed, but that's not what worries me or has made me a believer. It was what I heard that night; after it was all over before the earth spun away that evening and I was driven mercifully into unconsciousness. It was after that hell hole was sealed and everything was quiet. I was looking to my left wondering what had happened to the walking dead soldier that had helped me. All that was left of the once animated corpse was his skeletal remains clothed in the tatters of an American

Army uniform. His skull face seemed to be smiling toward the heavens. Then I heard it.

It was coming from overhead after the alien activity around the knoll had stopped. The sound was so simple that almost a minute elapsed before I understood and passed out. I could have imagined it, you'll say, brought on by the shock of the struggle or from the loss of blood. I heard it all the same. I can recall it clearly, even now. I can't sleep at night thinking of it and have to take tranquilizers when it thunders. If God is merciful, then let him remove the memory of it so that I can live out the remainder of my life in peace . . . it was a voice, a sound produced by alien vocal cords, the ultimate piece to the ancient puzzle, the embodiment of all the fears of the Elder Race. It excited shadowy recollections of a snarling chaos that lurked behind all life, the origin of which was so terrifyingly real that it caused my mind to slam shut because filtering down from the sky, sounding as if it was calling through a long tunnel, was the faint answering cry of Cthulhu!

Editor's Note:

Examining the facts of these three narratives has produced little evidence to support their authenticity. My inquiries with Interpol, Federal authorities, and branches of the American armed forces came to a dead end as well. All reported having no information on Faren and Janet Church. They either were telling the truth, which supports the hoax theory, or they have chosen to remain tight-lipped about the case. Inquiries with Miskatonic University were just as disappointing.

Never knowing Mrs. Church's maiden name made it impossible to track down her parents (Faren Church never made any reference to the location of his family) and I gave up searching after running an ad for several months, with no results, in the Essex Examiner asking for any information leading to their whereabouts.

The disappearance of Ephraim Pryne has become public knowledge. The collapse of his corporate empire was widely covered by the media. I was well into the editing of the manuscripts when the news reached me. Allegedly Pryne and some of his associates had been slowly converting the company's liquid assets into gold, then disappeared abandoning their complex to their creditors. It is believed that he left the United States. He was last reported heading for the eastern seaboard of Massachusetts where it was assumed that he fled the country.

All my efforts to locate Faren Church have turned up practically empty-handed, and if his existence was indeed real, then his disappearance was truly complete.

The only clue to his whereabouts was in the form of an article, although released by U.P.I., was evidently so fantastic that only a few newspapers across the nation, including the Arkham Advertiser, saw fit to print it, albeit on the back pages:

> "Lost Plane" Lands in Arkham
> By Fredrik King
> United Press International
>
> ARKHAM, Mass. -- A twin-engine Cessna jet owned by the Emmerson-Pryne Corporation and reported missing shortly after takeoff from London Tuesday made an emergency landing today.
>
> During a frantic concerted search effort by the Coast Guard and the plane's owners, the jet unexpectedly appeared over the town of Arkham, Mass., where it made an emergency landing about 2:00 P.M., 13 miles south of the town at a small rural airport. The jet, with only a single unidentified passenger at the controls, was guided down by instructions radioed from Phillips Field Airport. According to the frantic passenger, no pilot was on board.
>
> The jet was guided down to a safe landing, just stopping short of the end of the runway, when an unidentified passenger was seen running from the plane and into an adjacent vacant lot, disappearing into the surrounding woods.
>
> Upon examining the plane, and finding no other passengers on

board, the local sheriff was called in to investigate. Airport officials who immediately boarded the jet found no other passengers but noticed streaks of what appeared to be blood inside the cabin.

One of the officials who observed the landing mentioned that the fleeing male passenger was carrying a duffel bag and suggested that the jet may have been used for smuggling purposes. "There's not enough evidence to substantiate any speculations at this time," said Arkham Sheriff Caleb Marsh.

A representative of Emmerson-Pryne, when informed of the recovery of the Cessna jet, and the circumstances surrounding its landing, declined to comment when after careful examination of the aircraft there was found clinging to the exterior handle of the door to the passenger section, an amputated hand or claw. Although at first what was thought to be a human hand, a closer inspection revealed certain odd characteristics that suggested otherwise.

"The hand . . . if that's what it was," said one observer, "was webbed. I frankly don't know if it's human or not."

ABOUT THE AUTHOR

Byron Craft started out writing screenplays, moved on to authoring articles for several magazines and finally evolved his writing style into exciting, sci-fi, fantasy, horror novels.

Craft has published two novels in a planned five-novel mythos series that reflects the influence of H.P Lovecraft. Byron Craft's first novel "The CRY of CTHULHU," initially released under the title "The Alchemist's Notebook," was the reincarnation and expansion of one of his most memorable screenplays. Craft demonstrates he is as capable a novelist as scriptwriter. Craft's second novel, "SHOGGOTH" continues with all the ingredients of a classic Lovecraft tale, with some imaginative additions.

The Arkham Detective series, which includes "Cthulhu's Minions," "The Innsmouth Look," "The Devil Came to Arkham," and finally, "The Dunwich Dungeon," are currently available individually and as a collection in both a Kindle format, and softcover.

Craft enjoys writing full-length stories and would love to get feedback from his readers. Please visit his website: www.ByronCraftBooks.com

If you would like to read more books by Byron Craft, please visit his website: www.ByronCraftBooks.com or *go to Amazon.com*

The Mythos Project Series

The CRY of CTHULHU

(Originally published under the title: The Alchemist's Notebook.) This novelization of The Cry of Cthulhu film project is about a shell-shocked Vietnam vet, and his wife. They inherit an old country estate in Germany around the time his company transfers him to the same area. The two soon discover that the coincidence is really too good to be true.

Their home rests near a timeworn door into the earth that is poised to open, exposing all to a horde of four-dimensional beings. Soon the line between our reality and that other space-time will be blurred forever, leaving mankind to be consumed by shrill, shrieking terror. Only one man has the slimmest chance to save our planet and, even though he has no place to hide, he prefers to run. [*Book One*]

SHOGGOTH

An accepted theory exists that millions of years ago a celestial catastrophic occurrence wiped out every living thing on the planet. This theory may be flawed. Fast-forward to the 21st century. A handful of scientists, allied with the military, discover a massive network of tunnels beneath the Mojave Desert. Below, lies an ancient survivor, waiting...and it's hungry! [*Book Two*]

The Arkham Detective Series

Cthulhu's Minions

A Novelette introducing the Arkham Detective. Cthulhu's Minions are Pilot Demons. Nasty pint-sized legless creatures that crawl on their hands with razor sharp claws and fangs. The diminutive beings must be stopped before they conduct one of Cthulhu's Old Ones to the back alleys and streets of Arkham, likewise the entire planet. The story takes place during the Great Depression, a spot in time where H. P. Lovecraft and Raymond Chandler could have collaborated. Henceforth the narrative begins, through the eyes of an Arkham Detective.

The Innsmouth Look

The second story in the series that brings the detective back, investigating a murder and the kidnapping of a small child, which leads to Innsmouth by the sea, the frightful creatures that lurk there, and what they plan to call up from the depths.

The Devil Came to Arkham

Follow the Arkham Detective as he attempts to discover the source of a deadly epidemic. Is it the devil? Is it a Night Gaunt? Or both? Find out when you read about a soul sucking creature that is bent on turning Arkham, Massachusetts into a ghost town.

The Dunwich Dungeon

In this final chapter, a seven-foot tall man in black has caused the Detective's good friend to go missing. A woman is brutally murdered in a museum, and mysterious artifacts lead us on a trail to inter-dimensional horrors. This time the Arkham Detective is armed to the teeth, and determined to avenge murder with mayhem.

Keep reading for an excerpt from Byron Craft's
SHOGGOTH

SHOGGOTH
©Eric Lofgren
Byron Craft

CHAPTER 1

CONSCRIPTION

Trihl's long green tendril inched along the shelf. The slender appendage wormed its way past stacks of bulky file drawers. After carefully selecting the correct bio-number in one stack, a stud moved, and a ready light winked. The lower lobe of Trihl's third brain projected the combination, and the fluid lock in one of the drawers gurgled briefly, raising and lowering the levels in its five chambers to their prescribed heights. Within the span of a few seconds a shiny metal box slid out of a narrow recess, unlatched, and noiselessly swung its top open.

Trihl would have smiled if Trihl had something to smile with, but the wooden expression on the big Kroog's face was indigenous to their race. While Kroogs had an advanced level of multiple brains, colossal size, and strength, unparalleled dexterity of tentacles, tendrils, and antennae, they lacked any facial muscles. Nevertheless, there was a warmth inside the huge conical body that radiated joy because Trihl was about to come full circle.

Trihl had completed the Kroog conscription that all of their species must commit to and now the journey of millenniums lies ahead.

Excitement shot through Trihl like a bolt of electricity. It was doubly exciting because not only was Trihl now free to travel through time visiting the lives of future ages, but Trihl's contribution to the Kroogian race had been equally as magnificent.

Trihl had spent three-fifths of a pentad developing the new life form, and Trihl knew that the outcome of this discovery would radically change the lives of all Kroogs in the galaxy, this was Trihl's conscription.

Trihl placed the fifteen sealed tubes of proto-cells in the box where they would be preserved, if need be, for centuries. If ever there was a need to call up any one of these original formulas they would be here, safe in stasis.

Enthusiastic about the adventure that lay ahead, Trihl quickly gave the locking command. The lid snapped shut from a heavy, invisible force and the stasis box slammed back into its recess. The noise echoed within the library chamber and down the granite hallway. That echo, Trihl thought, with a touch of cosmic irony, may reach farther than my travels; only time will tell.

CHAPTER 2

FEEDING TIME

Isaac looked around the damp room; it was almost time. Charlie Youngblood will be here soon. That Narraganset had an uncanny sense of time. Although he never carried a watch, he can tell you the time of day within a couple of minutes of accuracy.

Isaac was nervous. He allowed his mind to wander, anything rather than to think of feeding that thing behind the door. More and more its ingesting of its food became repulsive to him.

He recalled when he first came to the area. The desolation was unbearable. It still was. It took almost eleven months to travel the distance by wagon train, and he had almost died that first year of influenza. Another year followed in which the tunnels were located, and his house could be built over the site.

Isaac's eyes followed the hieroglyphics along the curved walls of the subterranean room. And here I have been these past seven years; he brooded, painfully deciphering the history of a lost age.

Isaac forced his attention to a ledger on the writing desk, dipping a feather-quill pen in an ink well he made an entry on page fifty-seven. Printed across the top of the page in bold letters was the word LIVESTOCK. Below, written in longhand, were the words: 6 cows, 2 sheep. Below this, Isaac wrote "the amount of food needed increases with each feeding."

It would not be so bad if it ate like any one of God's creatures, but it did not. It . . . absorbed its food, he decided. It drank its painfully mewling prey slowly, savoring each moment of the animal's agony.

Isaac was sure the thing savored its food. He had a sickening feeling in his stomach. He always felt that way when it neared feeding time. He remembered when they first started to feed it. It was small then.

Isaac used to observe the terrible process with a mixture of horror and scientific curiosity. Then it started to grow, it got bigger, and its needs grew along with it. It would only feed on living things; nothing else would satisfy its lust. Small game was enough at first; jackrabbits, squirrels, prairie dogs, even lizards, and mice. It did not discriminate as long as its dinner was alive.

Soon its needs outgrew prairie dogs and mice. It ate much larger animals now, mainly cattle and sheep, occasionally an old Mustang if one could be caught, and on one occasion, a pig. Isaac cursed God for that day. The agonized ululations emanating from that pig were blood curdling and unforgettable.

He had bought it that morning from a Yuma Indian on the outskirts of Darwin. He had paid an exorbitant price for the two-hundred-fifty-pound sow, but livestock was scarce that spring. An early and harsh winter the previous year had delayed the cattle drives from west Texas and New Mexico, and the surrounding desert offered very little. He could have purchased a dairy cow from one of the locals, but they were beginning to get suspicious.

Charlie Youngblood had told Isaac that he had heard talk in Darwin centering on the abnormal amounts of livestock they required for a household that consisted of only Isaac and two servants. The last thing Isaac needed was a group of superstitious and excitable townspeople bursting in on his studies.

He had done his best to keep a low profile, staying at home as much as possible, only venturing out when it was absolutely necessary. When he did go into town, he was always cordial to everyone he met, but never lingered. If asked, he said he was an archeologist studying the Indian artifacts and petroglyphs that could be found in and around the Coso Range.

He had also done his best to keep the noise down when it was hungry. At these times, they would blanket the door to the tunnel with bags filled with sand to muffle the sounds it made followed by a careful search above ground for any fissures or old volcanic vents that may have opened on the desert floor with the shifting of sand. A vent, if opened into one of the tunnels below, could allow the noise to be heard for miles.

He was afraid that they would be discovered when the pig started to squeal; that was, he recalled with a shudder, the worst day of his life. The poor animal uttered a sharp, shrill, prolonged cry when the thing latched on to it. The sow did not see the creature at first. It grabbed the pig from behind and pulled her squealing and screaming into its jelly-like mass. The creature made sucking, slurping sounds. It was quick, deadly quick. The sow was stuck fast, rooted to the flesh of the thing.

Inside the dark, gelatinous layers of flesh, Isaac noticed something glowing with a golden light and parts of the thing briefly became translucent. He had seen this before when it fed. It would happen to lesser or greater degrees depending on the size of the animal it was devouring. He wondered if it was the spark of life that ignited that golden light. Perhaps the spirit of the animal it absorbed?

The female pig was still conscious after several minutes. Her squealing rose in volume until it became an ear-splitting shriek. The creature held the tortured animal off the floor of the cave. The sow's legs kicked and her body wriggled and squirmed, only to be drawn deeper into the thing.

Isaac had never been more repulsed at feeding time than he was at that moment. For the first time, he questioned the morality of his studies. It was worse than being in a slaughterhouse. His stomach knotted, and his skin crawled in tight folds along the back of his neck.

Within the dark, cavernous vault, the torturous murder of this poor, dumb animal seemed to Isaac, the work of the devil. The deadliest of sins, a sacrifice made deep in the bowels of hell.

Isaac abruptly turned from the squealing horror and ordered Charlie and his brother, John, to stop it.

"Stop it," he shouted. "Kill it now!"

Charlie and his brother, mesmerized by the spectacle, jumped when Isaac issued the command. Charlie was the first to regain his composure.

Stepping forward, he dutifully cocked the hammer on his Springfield. John Youngblood was close behind, imitating his brother. The sound of the two muzzleloaders firing was deafening, but not as ear splitting, thought Isaac, as the cries of that sow. The small section of the tunnel filled with smoke and the smell of burnt sulfur.

Isaac saw the lead balls from the two Springfield rifles strike the gelatin side of the thing. It reminded him of stones striking the surface of water. The two projectiles penetrated the flesh of the thing causing a mild turbulence within, a rippling effect.

The creature, unaffected by the two bullet wounds, continued with its feeding. Isaac watched helplessly as the sow, already three-quarters enveloped in a gooey slime; strained her vocal cords to their limits. He saw the flesh on her back, and one side slowly blister, then melt.

The pig's prolonged cry faltered and broke into a shrill staccato echoing off the tunnel walls like maniacal laughter.

Isaac stepped forward and moved to draw his pistol. It kept screaming, he thought, it no longer sounded like the squeal of a tortured animal; it was more human. The sow looked past Isaac with eyes that gazed into another world.

He meant to put the poor creature out of its misery, but he stopped before he had his gun half drawn from his belt. He knew what the outcome would be. It would be simple to put a musket ball in the sow's head, silencing her forever, but then they would have to cope with "it." He was certain that if he had killed the sow, the creature would have nothing to do with her. It only fed on living things. Then, they would be plagued by its cries of hunger again.

Aching inside, Isaac realized that the cries of the tortured sow, no matter how heart-wrenching and murderous they were, were not as bad as the shrieks of hunger from this creature of the tunnels.

As if in answer to his decision to do nothing, the pig gagged suddenly followed by a rattling in her throat and the tunnel gave way to an eerie silence. The sow's eyes were glassy. Blood and white foam oozed from her snout. Her sides heaved in and out with the force of labored breathing. Respiration is still functioning, as always, he reminded himself. She was still alive, just unconscious. He was familiar with the entire, grotesque procedure by then. She'll stay that way for weeks while it draws on her, feeds on her, until there is nothing left but a dried out husk.

Isaac remembered the sickening details that followed with painful clarity. He had run from the tunnel's end to his house above, staggered through the parlor, out the front door, and into the desert. The sizzling heat of mid-day slapped his face. Isaac's knees gave out, and he fell, face forward, into the sand only a few steps from his front porch, raising himself to his knees, he began to vomit. He kept vomiting until his sides hurt and there was nothing left in him but air.

The memory of that afternoon always haunted him when it neared feeding time. He was glad that the creature only craved sustenance every three or four weeks. If he had to feed it daily, he would have gone mad a long time ago. Isaac leaned back in his chair and rubbed his eyes with closed fists. He was pale, and there were dark circles under his eyes. His black, scraggly beard and hair hadn't been washed in weeks. He had increased his study schedule constantly working during the day and through most of the night only breaking from the routine for a late supper. After eating he would crawl, exhausted, to a cot he kept alongside his writing desk where he would sleep until a little before dawn when Charlie Youngblood would come and wake him, and the process would begin all over again.

After years of research, he was beginning to decipher the hieroglyphics that adorned the walls of the circular room. They had also discovered what he had guessed to be a library of records consisting of over a thousand scrolls.

The scrolls were of a thin and surprisingly flexible metallic substance. They had discovered them in an adjoining tunnel only a month after they had uncovered the subterranean passage. The scrolls yielded the same strange writing.

Bit by bit he had unlocked pieces of the past, unfurling the history of a forgotten age. Isaac learned some things about a once great race, some things about their accomplishments, some things about their dreams, while the creature of the tunnels remained a mystery.

He was certain that he had discovered its origin. But, what it was and what purpose it served in the ecological scheme of that ancient civilization had yet to be answered.

The creature had grown considerably since that afternoon when they had fed it the sow and it started to change its shape. It was becoming elongated, and it looked as if it was growing a flattened head or face at one end. The results, although repulsive and alien, were somehow familiar to Isaac.

What it reminded him of he could not recall. However, as he witnessed its daily growth and change, something knocked and clawed at his subconscious with frightening familiarity.

That was why he had stepped up his research. His desire to leave was greater than ever. Although he had no idea what the result of the creature's change might be, he felt more comfortable in learning about it from his translations rather than witnessing the metamorphosis.

If he pushed himself, he would have the answers he needed to this age-old puzzle before the next feeding interval. A few weeks, he hoped. No more than a month. Just this one last time, just enough to quiet it so he would not have to listen to its constant wailing to be fed. Just long enough to keep his sanity intact and his will alive so he could gather up the evidence he had accumulated over the years and deliver it to those on the East Coast who once scoffed at his theory.

Isaac signed and dated the bottom page of the ledger. The feather-quill pen made a scratching noise across the paper. He heard footsteps approaching and looked up.

Charlie Youngblood stood quietly in front of the desk. His white cotton shirt looking yellow from the pale cast of his lantern. A long, thin scar down the left side of his face combined with the red bandanna wrapped tightly across the top of his skull gave him a menacing appearance.

"Is it time?" Isaac asked in a solemn tone.

Continue reading SHOGGOTH, by Byron Craft

Available at Amazon.com

Made in the USA
San Bernardino, CA
18 March 2019